D0366401

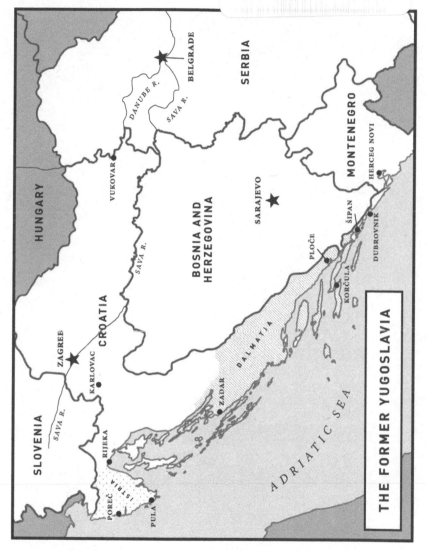

HUNGARY

SLOVENIA

CROATIA

ZAGREB

KARLOVAC

RIJEKA

POREČ

ISTRIA

PULA

VUKOVAR

SAVA R.

SAVA R.

DANUBE R.

SAVA R.

BELGRADE

SERBIA

BOSNIA AND
HERZEGOVINA

SARAJEVO

MONTENEGRO

HERCEG NOVI

ŠIPAN

DUBROVNIK

PLOČE

KORČULA

DALMATIA

ZADAR

ADRIATIC SEA

THE FORMER YUGOSLAVIA

PROLOGUE

I am Lazarus, come from the dead,
Come back to tell you all, I shall tell you all
—*The Love Song of J. Alfred Prufrock*,
T. S. Eliot

THE WATERS OF Croatia's Adriatic are crystalline blue and turquoise to a depth of ten metres and more, so that the coral fans and round black spiny sea urchins on distant bare rocks appear to be no more than an arm's length below the surface. The clarity engenders a sense of vertigo. Schools of fish are seemingly suspended in unaccountable space between the skin of the surface and the seabed, where they flow and flutter like leaves on the wind while their shadows undulate far below.

The waters are kept pristine by friendly currents that carry rubbish to Italian shores. Which was why the Italian state police in Bari, on the western Adriatic, where Italy's heel meets the rest of the boot, eventually turned their attention directly east by two hundred kilometres, to Dubrovnik, at Croatia's extreme south — a corpse had washed up on one of their beaches.

Yugoslavia was hurtling towards civil war after Croatia had declared independence only a couple of months earlier. In the past, Rome would have made formal requests to Belgrade for police cooperation; these would have then been passed on to the local authorities in Croatia's major coastal towns. But the Croatian leadership was no longer speaking to Belgrade, and the Italian government did not formally recognize the Croatian state. So the head of the police in Bari took it upon himself to make an informal call to the senior detective on the Dubrovnik force, with whom he'd worked before, and who he knew spoke good, if German-inflected, Italian.

This was how Detective Brg found himself taking the ferry from Dubrovnik to Bari. The crossing was slow, but there were no longer any direct flights, and to have gone by way of Zagreb and Rome would have taken as long and cost eight times as much.

Detective Brg's first instinct had been to send someone else or to regretfully refer the Bari police to Zagreb. He just didn't have the time to take a day off from his other duties to inspect a corpse in a foreign jurisdiction on the off chance that it might have floated over from his shores. He was handling an ever-growing number of responsibilities in the Dubrovnik police's increasingly depleted squad.

And that too was down to politics.

Dubrovnik is a distant appendix in Croatia's far south, at the end of a narrow strip of land along the Adriatic coast, separated by a chain of mountains from Bosnia and Montenegro, two republics that were still within the control of the Yugoslav federation. Though an ancient and massive fortress city, Dubrovnik would be all but impossible to defend against a modern military onslaught. Theoretically, that didn't matter — it had no military value. It was purely a site of historical and touristic interest, and the Croatian government assumed it would be left alone so long as nobody there provoked the Yugoslav army.

But the Dubrovnik authorities weren't so sure. Within their modest means, they set about quietly creating a defence force. Unfortunately, it was built around the police department, leaving regular policing duties to a small, very overworked team led by Brg.

What swayed him to make the trip was the description of the body. A red-headed woman, a little above average height and probably in her late twenties or mid-thirties. He'd been working on a case that involved the violent deaths of two American men found in a villa on an island less than twenty kilometres to the north of Dubrovnik, and that also involved a missing American woman. A redhead, aged thirty-two, 170 centimetres tall, and weighing around fifty-eight kilograms. Zagreb had official control of the investigation, but inept bureaucracy and a diplomatic impasse with the local American consulate had left Brg's team working on the case more or less unaided.

A detective from the Bari force was waiting for him at passport control. Because Brg was pressed for time — he was adamant that he had to be on the overnight ferry back to Dubrovnik — they skipped a courtesy visit to the station and instead drove them straight to the morgue.

The medical examiner was a locum, a retired professor named Dr. Angelo Albini. In Brg's experience, pathologists tended to be supercilious stuffed shirts, irritated at being questioned, intolerant of the smallest sign that a cop might not understand the jargon. Then again, he thought, with that sort of bedside manner it was just as well they were only inflicted on the dead.

But Dr. Albini was unlike any Yugoslav pathologist Brg had ever met.

The professor looked like a pink-cheeked elf, with white hair, bright eyes, and an ebullience that belied his age. He moved with obvious discomfort and a heavy limp, but his incessant chatter was that of a ten-year-old boy expounding, with endless digressions, on his latest enthusiasm.

"Detective Brg, Detective Brg, very interesting case this one. Very interesting," Dr. Albini said, leading Brg to a bloated and bleached body on a stainless steel table in a sterile, windowless room. "Brg? Sounds German somehow. German, is it? You speak Italian with a German accent."

"My father's family was from the north, near the Austrian border. They're all German-speaking. Brg is the Slavicized version of Berg," Brg said, trying to sound detached as his stomach turned at the smell and sight of the once-living flesh before him. He understood now why his local police liaison had another, suddenly urgent piece of business to attend to.

"Ah, of course, of course. Austro-Hungarians, the lot of you up there. Our own Tyroleans speak with a German accent. Very interesting, very interesting." Brg couldn't tell whether the professor was referring to his name or to the dissected corpse he now leaned over. "I must apologize for the aroma. I'm told the compressor on the air conditioner failed." He lifted an arm to expose the corpse more fully. "New parts. Take forever, eh."

New parts for the corpse or the compressor? The old man was beginning to overwhelm Brg as much as the gruesome yet somehow sanitized effigy in flesh.

"German, eh?" Albini said. "You should have been here three days ago. You could have talked to the German couple who found her. Camping. Not her — the German couple. She was bobbing around on the beach. Must have been a heck of a shock. Well, probably for her too. But the German couple, you should have heard them. You'd have thought they'd found a body on the beach." He tittered at his little joke. "Have to feel sorry for them. Well, for her too. But the German couple ran all the way back to town to raise the alarm, and what do our police do? Say thank you very much? Not likely. Fined them for camping illegally. Not just fined them, but didn't issue them a receipt. We all know what that means. You Yugoslav — my apologies, *Croatian* — police probably don't know much about corruption." He gave Brg a theatrical wink. "But we Italians can write whole encyclopedias about it. Shame nobody ever thinks to bribe medical examiners, eh? Never think of it. Poisoners might, I suppose, but never get round to it. Anyway, here she is, our inanimate guest."

Brg nodded. He pulled from his briefcase a thin, shiny sheet of fax paper showing a photograph of the missing American woman. It was hard to reconcile the image with what was in front of him.

Albini hobbled over to Brg's side of the table to have a look at the fax.

"Gout. Me, not her. Terrible. Look at my poor leg."

Albini pulled up his trouser leg to expose his limb, swollen to twice the normal size and as red and purple as a bottle of claret. It looked like it might have belonged on a corpse. Brg nodded with what he hoped looked like sympathy, but the old professor had already switched his attention back to the subject at hand.

"You wouldn't think a girl who looked like this could look like that, but that's what a couple of weeks in the water will do to you," Albini said.

"A couple of weeks?"

"Probably. I'd put it between ten and twenty days."

Brg nodded. The Americans had been killed a little more than two weeks before, and the woman had gone missing around the same time.

"The weather's been cold but the sea's still warm, and that usually speeds up decomposition. She's been nibbled at by some of the sea life, but she's in much better shape than you'd expect. Probably because the Adriatic has been all fished out. Nothing left to feed off corpses, eh? Just as well, wouldn't do to be served corpse-fed fillet of mullet."

Albini hobbled back around the table, nodding knowingly at the body, its whiteness made all the more stark by the cold fluorescence of the overhead lights.

"What can we say, what can we say? Haven't written my report yet, of course. That'll take another few days, and by the time it gets processed you might not see anything official for another month. This is just me and you talking informally, right?"

Brg nodded and began to say "Of course," but the old professor cut him off.

"Well, if you look at her musculature and fat content, she was very healthy. Very healthy indeed. Athletic, even. All the organs clear of disease. Officially, I'd put her age between twenty and forty, but unofficially I'd say early to mid-thirties. Don't ask why. I've been doing this sort of work for fifty years. Eventually you figure things out in ways that aren't worth explaining. Hair, red. Real red, no dye. No indication of poison or heavy metals or drug use in the hair samples. Teeth, very good. A bit of dental work. The quality suggests northern European or North American. When I say North American, that could mean Australia or New Zealand too. We found some coral embedded in the skull. That and the pattern of abrasions suggests she drowned at a rocky part of the coast. We're sand on this side, so it means more likely the eastern Adriatic. Head's heavier and tends to sink lower, gets dragged along that way until the gases associated with decomposition float the body again."

Brg had taken out his notebook. He was finding it hard to transcribe the professor's words while translating into Serbo-Croat at the same time, and instead ended up writing a pidgin Italian. He prayed he'd be able to decipher it later on.

"Drowned, you say?" Brg asked.

"Oh, yes. Quite a lot of water in the lungs and residuals of foaming that you get only with drowning. Though the foam doesn't tend to last this long. Saltwater drowning too. There's that movie, can't remember what it's called, where somebody was found drowned in a pool, except the water in the lungs was salt." Albini paused for a moment. "Or the other way around.

Something we always check. Too easy to drown somebody in a bath and then pop them in the sea. Except it's not very easy to drown somebody in a bath. People tend to struggle, and then you get all sorts of other indications the drowning wasn't accidental. Abrasions, odd bruises. And then they have to get the body into the sea. People tend to notice bodies being lugged around. What was I saying?"

"She drowned."

"Oh, yes, quite clearly. And not an accident or suicide either, in my professional opinion," he said.

"Why is that?" Brg asked, intrigued by the professor's methods.

"Tied up. She was tied up in such a way that she couldn't have tied herself up. Needed somebody else to do it. Suppose you could be suicidal and get somebody to tie you up and pop you overboard. But then it's not suicide, is it?"

"Somebody tied her up and threw her in the water?"

"Oh, yes. Proper fishermen's knots. Houdini couldn't get out of those. Maybe they drowned her because they failed to kill her some other way."

Brg looked puzzled. Albini pointed to an injury high on the fleshy part of the corpse's hip.

"Puncture wound. Probably from a projectile. Bullet would be my guess. Pattern of bruising suggests not too long before she died. But it didn't cause her death. Would have been painful, but not fatal. Well, it might have got infected and then it would have killed her a few days later. But it wasn't the cause of death."

Once again the old professor paused, shaking as if a small tremor was running through him. "Ay. Never get gout. Hurts like the devil but doesn't kill you. Maybe I'll get somebody to truss me up and toss me off a bridge. Sorry, that's a joke, by the way. Pathology, very funny business."

Brg nodded, struck speechless. By the corpse. And Albini.

"Right, what more can I tell you? Ropes were probably

Yugoslav-made, judging by the fibres, but we're running tests on that still. She wasn't. Yugoslav-made, that is. Or if she was, she didn't live there. Wasn't just the teeth telling us. Her clothes were all American-labelled. Everything down to the underwear. She'd also been fitted with an American intra-uterine device — that's birth control to you. No evidence she ever bore a child, but these things can be deceptive. What more can I tell you? Oh. She probably floated over from around the Dubrovnik coast."

"Let me guess," Brg said. "She had a postcard in her pocket."

"Oh, no. Nothing like that. Wouldn't have been very useful anyway. People carry around postcards from all sorts of places. No, it's the hydrological office that tells us. Normally the stuff that washes up on the beach here comes from farther north, north of Split, towards Fiume. What do you call it? Oh, yes, Rijeka."

Albini smiled slyly, watching to see whether Brg would take the bait. Fiume had been an Italian city with a majority Italian population, but it was nonetheless given over to the Yugoslavs after the First World War as part of the postwar redrawing of boundaries. The Yugoslavs renamed it Rijeka. Both words mean "river." The port town was briefly "liberated" by the Italian nationalist poet and adventurer Gabriele d'Annunzio and a handful of his followers. D'Annunzio then went on to declare war on anybody who did not support Fiume's return to Italy. Including Italy. D'Annunzio was eventually defeated and the postwar settlement was reimposed, though he emerged a hero. For many, that rebellion had marked the beginning of European fascism. For some, Croatia's nationalist rebellion against Yugoslavia was merely a continuation of something D'Annunzio had started.

Brg ignored the comment. Living under Communism had taught him that debating history or politics only ever led to an argument at best and jail at worst.

"Most times the body would have originated further north,"

Albini continued, "but a big bora was blowing last week. Surface currents would have taken her on a much more direct course across the sea."

The bora was a cold wind that blew from the north and the east. In the winter it could freeze sea spray onto lampposts and ships' masts, raging with near-hurricane strength. The one Albini referred to had been strong enough to keep yachts in harbour for days on end and had caused a number of the Dubrovnik-to-Bari ferries to be cancelled. Which was another reason Brg did not want to miss his boat back. The bora could rise again very quickly. He looked at his watch.

Albini smiled at Brg. "I think our officers would like very much that it's your corpse. Makes less work for them. But anyway, they're pretty sure she's not Italian. Doesn't fit anybody in our missing persons files. There was almost a match, but our lady here still has her appendix."

And then, with an exaggerated shrug and raised hands, Albini made it clear the interview was over.

"Thank you very much, Dr. Professor," Brg said. The identification wasn't conclusive, but it was good enough for him. He'd pass her on to Zagreb, and maybe with some luck the Ministry would give him a pat on the back and send somebody down to investigate the dead Americans. So far, all they'd done was take the corpses back north. Now they had a full set.

He looked at his watch again. Just as well he wasn't hungry. There wasn't enough time to stop for an early dinner before getting the ferry. He wasn't looking forward to the journey back.

DUBROVNIK, SEPTEMBER 1991

STRUMBIĆ'S TONGUE FELT its way uncertainly around his mouth, as though it was travelling an alien landscape. He was once again surprised by the jagged corner of the bicuspid two back from his left upper incisor. The gouge inside his left cheek was no longer hot and swollen but it itched and demanded to be prodded until the pain came back. The bitten flesh on the tongue itself had become a knot, lumpy and huge as it slowly healed.

A sharp, pungent odour hit him. It took him a few seconds to realize it was his own clothes he smelled, his own stench. They hadn't let him change his suit for . . . how long was it? Two weeks? No, more. At least he'd been allowed to shower in that time — a special privilege, as his jailers let him know. But Strumbić had a talent for getting things out of people.

He'd been waiting in the interview room on his own for a good ten minutes before the detective showed up, carrying a case file.

"So, Mr. Smirnoff, shall we try this again? Maybe a few days in the cells has cleared your head. Let some of those memories fall back into place."

Strumbić hadn't met this cop before, the third one to interrogate him since his arrest. He was a few years younger than

Strumbić, dark hair, medium height, and solid build. He wore a cheap suit, the tie hanging loose around his collar. A moustache followed the full length of his top lip. His stubbled cheeks, puffy eyes, and sagging expression spoke of very long nights. The detective didn't seem dissolute, so it must have been work keeping him up.

It was unconscionably early. Strumbić hadn't even been fed breakfast yet. He'd had to be roused from his bed, though he wasn't quite sure of the exact time. The clock on the wall was stuck on half past two. The first thing they'd done when they booked him was take his Rolex. He'd signed a receipt, but he was certain he'd never see it again. If he was lucky, they'd replace it with a cheap East German Timex knock-off. He knew how these things worked.

"Okay, so, for the record, could we have your name again?"

Strumbić hesitated, almost said "Julius," and then remembered Josip.

"Josip Smirnoff," he said.

"How is it that the only identification on you is a . . . what is this, a loyalty card for a British department store?" the detective asked, stifling a yawn. "What the hell's a loyalty card?"

"Well, Detective . . . I'm sorry, I seem to have forgotten your name."

"It's Brg. Mr. or Detective to you."

"Not from around here, then, Detective Brg?" Strumbić said.

"Perceptive," Brg replied. It wasn't a conversation he was interested in having right then. "So where's 'Smirnoff' from? Other than a bottle of vodka."

"Russian. I still have spiritual ties," Strumbić said.

Brg nodded, too tired to appreciate the wit. "You were explaining the . . . loyalty card."

"I'm loyal, it's a good shop. Marks & Spencer. They do nice suits," Strumbić said. "You should try them the next time you're in England."

The wallet Strumbić took on his jobs only ever had cash in it. Not all criminals appreciated doing business with a cop. Explaining a lack of ID, when it came to it, was easier. The card must have been an oversight from when he'd been in London earlier that summer. Stupid.

Brg rested his eyes on Strumbić. Yet another middle-tier crook. All Brg wanted to do was get home and go to bed, but he had to deal with this asshole first. He wished he hadn't gone back to the office to drop off the documents from his Italian trip. He wished he hadn't seen the prosecutor's note sitting face up on his desk: *You've run out of time on this guy. Charge him or let him go. This morning.*

They'd have done it two weeks earlier if he hadn't somehow fallen through the cracks. If the arresting officers had taken proper interview notes. If somebody had been paying attention. Well, it was down to him. Quick interview and then a quick charge. Leave the rest to the prosecutors.

"So maybe you can explain how it is you came to be in possession of two thousand compact discs and to be consorting with people who shoot at police officers?" Brg asked.

Two thousand? Strumbić's eyebrows climbed. It had been three thousand dockside. It seemed that a couple of Dubrovnik cops were richer not just to the tune of an expensive Swiss watch but also by a thousand pirated compact discs.

A wave of regret washed over Strumbić. The scam had had so much potential. A Turk copied American rock and heavy metal CDs in Istanbul, packaged them with photocopies of their proper labels, and packed them into boxes. His associate took them up the Adriatic, along with other goods for other clients. Some Montenegrin fishermen picked up the cargo in international waters and delivered it to Strumbić at night in the mainland village. All Strumbić had to do was load them in his car and drive them up to Zagreb. He'd lined up buyers, quoted competitive prices to whet demand. Restricted his initial investment in case they were duff, but he'd had a good feeling about this line of business. He had generated interest in five times as many CDs as he'd ordered from the Turk.

And then it went sour.

How was he to know the Dubrovnik cops were staking out the village dock? Bad timing. The stakeout had nothing to do with him or the Montenegrins. The village was opposite a pretty island called Šipan, where, unbeknownst to him or anyone other than the local cops, there'd been a double murder a couple of days before. A pure coincidence.

Though maybe not so coincidental. Strumbić had chosen this particular loading point because he knew the area well, and he knew the area well because he owned a villa on Šipan.

The Montenegrin smugglers had shot at the cops and got away in their very fast boat. And Strumbić had been left flat on his belly, licking the salt off the stone breakwater as he tried not to get in the way of any passing bullets.

Once things had calmed down, Strumbić's first reaction had been to do what any Communist apparatchik did as a matter of course. Because that's what he was. A senior detective on the Zagreb police force, recently seconded to Croatian military intelligence as a captain. High-intensity beams still on him, he jumped up and, as pissed off as a bear who'd lost his dinner, made ready to tear strips off the cops for ruining what he was going to tell them was an undercover sting operation.

Only he didn't get the chance.

The cops were still shaking with anger, fear, and adrenaline over being shot at. And the bigger one of the two hit Strumbić hard enough to chip a tooth and knock him down onto the stone breakwater before he'd managed to say more than two words.

By the time Strumbić got his jaw working well enough to string a comprehensible sentence together, he'd worked out that he was better off keeping his mouth shut. Better off praying the cops didn't figure out who he was.

"Two thousand?" Strumbić asked. He was surprised that only a third of the CDs had gone walkabout. Had the tables been turned, he'd have taken half. More, even. Leaving only enough to give the investigating prosecutor sufficient evidence for a smuggling conviction.

"That's how many my officers tell me were in the boxes," Brg said, his look challenging Strumbić to contradict him.

"Seems an awful lot," Strumbić said mildly. "Didn't think there was a big enough market for the things. On account of how nobody has any money these days."

"Couldn't say. I'm not much of one for economics."

"Nor accounting, it seems."

Brg started to say something, but thought better of it. He took on a chillier formality. "So what were you doing with those CDs, Mr. Smirnoff?"

"Me? Like I've been telling your colleagues, I had nothing to do with any CDs, Detective. I'd just been out for a bit of night fishing and these gentlemen landed the boat and started unloading the boxes."

"An innocent who just happened to be at the wrong place at the wrong time."

"Exactly."

"So what happened to your rod and reel?"

"Must have fallen off the dock in all the excitement."

The detective paused to riffle through the thin file in the blue folder.

"So you're from Herzegovina, are you, Mr. Smirnoff? The Yugoslav army's between here and there. How'd you get over?"

"Hitchhiked. A tank stopped for me, said they were heading in this direction anyway," Strumbić said.

Brg nodded, cursing himself for expecting anything other than obstruction. There was a long silence. Brg's eyes became slits. Sometimes cops did that because they thought it might catch the suspect off guard. Sometimes they did it because they were finding it hard to stay awake. Strumbić figured Brg was on his last legs.

"And you didn't tell us where you were staying in Dubrovnik, did you, Mr. Smirnoff."

"Hadn't gotten around to finding a place. Nice of you folks to help out, though I don't like abusing your hospitality. Shouldn't you have charged me for something by now? Or let me go?"

The police jail cells weren't bad. It had taken Strumbić a couple of days to sort himself out, but he knew how cops operated, he knew the rule books, and, more than anything, he had a roguish charm that made people warm to him, do things for him they might not otherwise. Besides, anyone who owned a Rolex and wore a British suit was given the benefit of the doubt.

It didn't take him long to organize a private cell and decent food and even clean underwear, though he hadn't managed to get his suit laundered yet.

Life wasn't bad. And it had been as good a place as any to stay safe, as long as he remained anonymous.

"Bags?"

"I travel light."

Brg stood up, walked around the desk, and perched on the corner. *He must have seen that in a movie*, Strumbić thought. Be friendly with the suspect. Coax a confession out of him. Or maybe it was the best way for him to keep from falling asleep.

It was the opening Strumbić had been looking for.

In a breach of interview protocol, Strumbić stood up too, catching Brg by surprise. Strumbić moved in a way that deliberately wasn't threatening, shifting his limbs as if they creaked from the hard bed of the past couple of nights. A supplicant approaching the great lord.

Strumbić knew that if he tried anything, the cop stationed just outside the interview room would finish the amateur dentistry his colleague had started the night he'd been arrested.

Brg wasn't alarmed, just taken aback slightly.

Strumbić knew he had to work quickly, that he had maybe a minute before the detective put him back in his place. He took the detective's hand, grasping it gently but refusing to let go. He used the pressure of two fingers on the inside of Brg's wrist so that Brg swivelled slightly, opening up his body. As he did, Strumbić stepped deeper into Brg's personal space, forcing the detective to rise up off the desk. All the while, Strumbić kept up an inane patter.

"Detective, I know you're a kind man, you're so gracious in seeing me. I mean, someone of your seniority taking time over such an irrelevant little person like me, I know it will be no time at all before a man of your capabilities will be able to resolve the matter . . ."

The fingers of Strumbić's free left hand brushed the detective lightly, like a tailor taking pride in a suit he'd just fitted. Even above his own jailhouse stench, Strumbić could smell that Brg was a smoker. A heavy one. He hadn't lit up yet, but it wouldn't be long.

What Strumbić was doing wasn't so unusual in ordinary life, though maybe it wasn't quite normal for the subject of a police interview. People in the Balkans often had a strange sense of propriety, needing to touch the person they were talking to, to get as close as lovers, especially when dealing in confidences.

Strumbić continued to work quickly. Brg might be tired, but he was still a professional and didn't seem stupid. Adrenaline sharpened Strumbić's wits. He had thirty seconds left maybe. He lifted his forearm so that it hovered at Brg's chest, not touching but close. Now he finally let go of the man's right hand.

Working, the whole while working, Strumbić's fingers remembering everything they'd learned two decades before, when he was a rookie cop. The things he'd learned watching the street criminals and gypsies, interviewing them, standing them drinks in bars to draw out their secrets. And if they were recalcitrant, he'd make them talk by arresting them and threatening to break their fingers.

Distract the mark's attention. Shake his hand and keep hold of it while drawing closer, into his space. Use a forearm as cover to keep him from seeing what was happening. Keep the friendly, subservient chat going. Apologize for not being more helpful, tell him it was a misunderstanding. All the while, the hands move fast, lightly touching the mark, feeling pockets, patting his back.

Not once during Strumbić's brief performance did Brg show any sign that he realized what was really happening. Strumbić returned to his seat after less than the full minute. Brg, ever so slightly perplexed but not entirely sure why, returned to his side of the desk.

"Detective, can I ask you a favour?" Strumbić said.

"What?" A wariness had crept into Brg's expression.

"Could you spare a cigarette?"

Brg gave Strumbić a look that said, *You're pushing your luck.* But he clearly needed one too. The detective patted his jacket pockets. One side, then the other. He patted the front pockets of his trousers and then his jacket again. A cloud of consternation passed over his brow and then he stood up, patting himself over again.

"I seem to have left them in my office. I'll be back in a couple of minutes. Try anything stupid and the officer outside will have something to say about it," Brg said, and left the room.

Strumbić counted twenty seconds after the door shut and then reached forward for the phone on the interview table. He picked up the handset. It was for the cops to make internal calls only. But internal calls could be switched through to other police stations — it was one of the country's few communication systems that actually worked properly.

Strumbić called the Zagreb police department's automated switchboard. Once he had a connection, he dialled the code to get an external line. And then, from memory, the private number he needed. Easy.

The phone rang. And rang. Della Torre didn't answer.

Strumbić figured he had five minutes. Maybe ten at most. He held the phone to his good cheek with his shoulder, reached into his pocket, and pulled out a packet of Lords and a transparent orange imitation Bic lighter.

Brg's Lords and Brg's cheap plastic lighter.

As the phone continued to ring, he checked the contents of Brg's wallet and took out a couple of thousand dinars, just in case he needed money to bribe the guards — he didn't know how long he'd be the guest of the Dubrovnik police — but he left enough that Brg wouldn't immediately suspect he'd been robbed, and then he flipped the wallet under the table, where it landed just under the detective's chair.

Strumbić had spent years perfecting his pickpocketing and lock-picking skills, which he had learned from the masters. Thieves as good as the Serb Borra, who'd become famous travelling around Europe in circuses, entertaining people with his magic: his ability to take watches off men's wrists; ties from around their necks; hell, even glasses from their faces, without their noticing. Strumbić's gypsies were just as good. Only for some reason they'd never managed to become as rich as Borra.

Where are you, Gringo?

He pressed down the receiver. He had to find somebody to get a message to della Torre. Anzulović? No, too risky.

He dialled another number. A squeaky voice answered.

"Hey, doll, it's Julius."

"Yes?"

"Listen, it's urgent. I need a favour from you."

"Julius? No one here by that name. I'm afraid you have the wrong number." She hung up.

"Bitch," Strumbić said aloud, grinding the cigarette butt onto the linoleum floor. This time, he'd really sort her out. Like he'd done for her cop boyfriend. Even now it galled Strumbić to think how one of his own men, one of his own police officers, had been sleeping with his mistress in the secret little apartment Strumbić had set up for her. He gave her money and she'd done the dirty on him. Cretinous cow. And now she refused to help him.

For some stupid, sentimental reason, he'd let her stay in the place after finding out her deceit. He was too soft. No, it was her tits that were too soft to give up. But Strumbić had made sure that the squaddie got busted down to traffic — and then, when cops were being transferred into the civil defence force, Croatia's proto-army, that he was sent to the front line in Vukovar.

He wouldn't forgive her again, though. He'd sort her out properly this time. He'd put her back on the street, where he'd found her.

His mental clock was ticking. Three minutes? Four, tops? There was one last chance. One last call. He had to make it count. He knew he had no other choice. He'd do it only as an act of desperation. Not just because he'd rather have his teeth knocked out with a chisel than talk to his wife, but because he knew they'd be monitoring his home phone.

"It's me."

"Where are you?" Her voice grated on him like steel on slate. "The light in the toilet has gone again, and all sorts of people have been trying to get in touch with you. Phoning non-stop. Constantly at the door."

"Listen. Take a message, will you." He tried not to raise his voice, tried not to yell.

"Minute you leave the apartment, that light stops working. What did you do to it? You rig it up to make me miserable, don't you? Have to use candles. A month you've been gone, without a word."

"Will you shut your trap and just listen for a minute, woman?" he hissed. He could see her pinched face, top lip pursed under her sharp nose as if she'd detected a bad smell. Her thin frame, desiccated by a lifetime of bitter complaint. How many times had he told himself that if it wasn't for her strudels he'd have left her long before?

"Don't you be swearing at me. If my father was still alive, you'd be watching your tongue."

"Well, the old thug isn't, is he?" he said, exasperated. "Will you just for once in your life stop yammering at me and listen?"

"So that's how it is, eh? What's next? You going to beat me? You going to break my arm like Franz down the way did to his old woman? Knocked her right into hospital and left her blacker than blue. Only last week . . ."

With a pulse of cold dread, Strumbić felt every second evaporating. For twenty years now he would have been happy to beat her. But not while the old man, Zagreb's ex-chief of police, was alive. No, not now either. If he ever laid a hand on her, he knew she'd cut his throat in the night. And no one would blame her.

He caught himself. Forced himself to be calm. Forced his voice to become even, neutral, pleasant.

"I'm sorry, darling. Really, I didn't mean to get off on the wrong foot. I will get a good electrician in to look at the light. A proper one, not like the monkey last time."

"And a new washing machine . . ."

"And a new washing machine. Could you please do me a favour? Please?"

"And all sorts have been looking for you."

"Who?" he asked.

"How do I know? Police," she said. "Detectives. People. Past couple of days."

The secret services wouldn't be able to trace the call beyond the Zagreb police exchange. But he'd have to be careful about what he said. "Can we get back to that favour?"

"What?" She didn't sound mollified, but it was an opening.

"Could you please write this down?"

"I'll remember it."

"Please could you write it down."

"I'll remember," she said. "My memory's as sharp as it was

when I was seventeen, and when I was seventeen I could recite, verbatim —"

"Okay, okay," he said, trying to hide the exasperation in his voice. "Use that seventeen-year-old memory. Can you get in touch with Marko della Torre? He's in military intelligence. My new office. Get in touch with him, get a message to him. Tell him I'm with our colleagues —" He paused, trying to think of something della Torre would understand that no one else would. "— near that Italian staircase he liked so much."

Della Torre had marvelled at the staircase in Strumbić's villa on Šipan. If he had any sense, he'd know the Italian staircase meant "down south" and the colleagues were the Dubrovnik cops.

"Why can't they get in touch with him if they're colleagues?"

He felt a hot, wet tear on his cheek. It was as much as he could do to control himself. "It's an undercover job. Top secret. Inside stuff."

He could almost hear her snap to attention. Why hadn't he thought of that before? A top cop's daughter knew her duty.

"Della Torre," she said.

"Tell him that I'm a guest of our colleagues but I'm using my pub name."

"Your name's a pub?"

"My pub name."

"Your pub name?"

"Yes. He'll know what I mean. That's as much as I can say." Smirnoff was the name he'd used in London. Della Torre knew all about that. And pubs were found in London.

"I'll make sure he gets the message," she said, all efficiency.

He heard the door open behind him and put his hand on the phone's kill switch without saying goodbye to his wife. For once, he knew she'd do as she was told.

"Calling someone, Mr. Smirnoff?" Brg asked.

"I was just about to ask them to page you. I was starting to feel lonely."

Brg nodded and went round to sit on his side of the table. As he pulled out the chair, he stopped for a second and stared down at his feet. He bent over, picking up his wallet. He slid it back into his pocket without looking at the contents and sat down, staring at Strumbić with a strained expression.

"Did you manage to find some cigarettes?" Strumbić asked, as sweet as candy floss.

"Why don't we get back to those questions, Mr. Smirnoff. I don't have a lot of time to waste on you. I've got three dead Americans to worry about."

Strumbić felt a chill. He didn't like how the detective had said "Smirnoff." Nor did he like that the number of dead Americans had risen to three.

In the back of the patrol car the night he was arrested, he'd listened to the cops talking about the two dead Americans on Šipan. They were keeping an eye out for anyone making the crossing from the island. The mention of dead Americans had quieted Strumbić, made him think twice about revealing who he was.

He'd been dealing with some Americans on an official job only days earlier, while he'd been setting up his distinctly unofficial CD-smuggling scheme. In fact, one of them had stayed at his villa on Šipan. She still had the keys to the place. Two dead Americans on Šipan. A third now.

He had nothing to do with their deaths. But it wasn't something he wanted to argue from a jail cell. He knew it would be hung on him, on Captain Julius Strumbić of military intelligence, unless they found out what had really happened. And as far as he could tell, they had no clue.

Strumbić hadn't a scintilla of doubt that della Torre was somehow tied in with the deaths. Della Torre would have to get him out of the mess. Just as well then that, however much trouble della Torre kept landing in Strumbić's lap, he was also the only man Strumbić trusted with his life.

"I don't really know how I can help, Detective," Strumbić said, helping himself to one of the cigarettes Brg held out, not allowing himself to show any of the unease he felt. "Like I said, I was fishing and suddenly found myself in the middle of the O.K. Corral."

The Dubrovnik detective riffled through a second file he'd brought into the room, pulled out a sheet, and contemplated it for a long, quiet moment. He raised his tired eyes, took a final drag on his cigarette, and trapped the other man in his gaze. Strumbić's amusement at having so thoroughly picked the other man's pockets faded a little. His certainty of having found a safe haven, a comfortable little hideaway, was evaporating. He found himself feeling increasingly unsettled. It wasn't an emotion he was used to. Brg ground out the cigarette in a cheap tin ashtray.

The Dubrovnik detective contemplated the man in front of him, more seriously than he had less than half an hour earlier.

Brg had gone back up to his office, pissed off at the petty smuggler he was having to deal with, when all he wanted was sleep and then to report back to Zagreb that the American redhead had been found.

Brg was sure that, in his tiredness, he'd left both his cigarettes and his lighter on the ferry. He got out another pack from the carton he kept in the bottom drawer of his desk. But the spare matches he had to hunt for on his desk.

It was while he was shifting the papers that the fax roll with the dead woman's photograph fell to the floor. He picked it up and it unspooled. As he looked down the pages, folding them so that they'd fit more neatly into the file, his eye lighted on a photograph of a man, middle-aged, receding hairline, flabby face and tired eyes. Captain Julius Strumbić of military intelligence, formerly detective lieutenant with the Zagreb police, missing, wanted in connection with the deaths of two men in a villa on the island of Šipan, and a suspect in the disappearance of the American woman Rebecca Vees, now in an Italian morgue. He must have seen Strumbić's photograph a dozen times before without noticing it. It was fuzzy, barely bigger than passport-sized. Unlike the woman's photo, it hadn't been posted anywhere in the station. No one else on the force had seen the picture. Why? Because the note next to the photograph said the suspect had probably fled the country, most likely destination Italy or the United Kingdom.

England. Marks & Spencer.

Seeing the picture was like a shot of slivovitz injected into a vein.

Detective Brg had brought the incriminating fax with him to the interview room. He sat for long minutes, comparing the photograph to the man in front of him. The other man didn't break the silence. Brg's eyes prickled from cigarette smoke and fatigue. At last he spoke, quietly, without aggression. "Why don't we stop playing games, Detective Lieutenant. Or is it Captain Julius Strumbić?"

Brg gave Strumbić credit for not betraying any emotion.

Strumbić merely smiled. "I'm sure you're mistaken, Detective. My name is Smirnoff."

Brg turned the fax towards Strumbić. "This says it isn't."

Strumbić leaned forward and pulled the thin thermal paper across the stained blond wood table, turned it with three fingers, and considered.

"It's a reasonable likeness, though it's a pretty small picture and not particularly clear. Could be me. Could be any one of a hundred men within a kilometre of here. What did you say you want the man for?"

"As a witness, probable accessory, and possible perpetrator of three murders."

"Three? The Americans? Sounds like a dangerous fellow. But like I said, it's not me."

"What do you say, Mr. Strumbić, would you like to have a friendly chat with me or do you want to wait for the Zagreb investigators? I hear they're a lot less nice. Plenty of former UDBA types."

Silence. UDBA was Yugoslavia's hated former secret police. Strumbić knew more than a few of them. Such as della Torre.

"What I don't get is if you killed those men, why, just a couple of days later, you'd want to be smuggling stuff onto a dock in a village on the opposite side of the channel," Brg continued. "I mean, you don't strike me as being stupid. They don't make stupid people detectives in the Zagreb force, do they?"

"Detective, those are all very good questions. But you're asking the wrong guy."

Brg was fading. Questions kept crowding his mind. Irritating tiny details overwhelmed his brain. It was as if Strumbić wasn't there and he was just asking himself.

"Says here you own that villa on Šipan where two of the Americans were killed. We had a look and it's not in any official records. All we could find was that it's registered to an Italian company. Your company, Mr. Strumbić?"

Strumbić was surprised at the turn of questioning, but played along.

"Thought Italians could only own up to forty-nine percent of a property in this country," Strumbić said.

"Oh, well, that's the clever thing. One Italian company owns forty-nine percent of the property and a Yugoslav firm owns the rest. Except forty-nine percent of that Yugoslav company is owned by an Italian company. Coincidentally, the same Italian company. The rest is owned by another Yugoslav company. You guessed it — forty-nine percent of that is owned by the very same Italian company. In the end, the only domestic ownership we could find was some lawyer in Varaždin who owns less than one percent. You won't be surprised to hear that he's only holding on behalf of a company based near Venice. Illegal, but what can you do? Lawyers. Anything to do with you, Mr. Strumbić?"

Strumbić shrugged sympathetically. "What our country's coming to." He shook his head sadly. "All the ills of capitalism have already filled in the cracks left by the noble but failed Communist experiment."

Brg felt his head nod forward. He needed sleep. He knew that dwelling on stupid details was a sign of how tired he was. The villa's ownership? Who cared about the complicated scheme designed to hide the owner? Strumbić owned it. And Strumbić was there, sitting in front of him.

Brg needed to be sharp to deal with Zagreb. And he needed to be even more on the ball to handle as wily a character as Strumbić.

Four hours of solid shut-eye. If he left for home now, he'd get that much rest and be awake again by lunch, have a bite to eat, and then get back to the station, refreshed. Call Zagreb, tell them he'd wrapped up the whole of the mystery, found the missing woman, had the lead suspect in a jail cell. Formally charge Strumbić with everything from smuggling to murder to fraudulent property ownership.

Hell, how could it hurt to delay calling them by a couple of hours? The woman wasn't going to get any more dead, and Strumbić, well, he'd already been sitting around in prison for more than two weeks. Another quiet morning wouldn't do any harm. Just in case, Brg would have a cop stand sentry outside Strumbić's cell. Keep an eye on him the whole time.

Four hours. Brg thought. *What could possibly go wrong in four hours?*

ZAGREB, LATE SEPTEMBER 1991

MARKO DELLA TORRE sat at his desk looking out over the city's red-tiled rooftops, half hoping the air-raid sirens would go off so that he'd have an excuse to leave the office tower. Zagreb was a city of low buildings, and this was one of the few to stand out, some forgotten committee's hopeful stab at modernity. Its height and central location made the building a landmark, and thus an appealing target for Yugoslav MiGs. So far, all the alerts had been false alarms. But the war was in full flower out east. It would come to them eventually.

He turned back to the stack of papers on his desk and lit a Lucky Strike. Maybe the nicotine would help him get through the drudgery. At the very least, the cigarette would distract him while he pretended to read. His masters had reduced him to whittling away at empty bureaucracy during this time of general paralysis. No, this was worse than that. The files crossing his desk had already been drained of any significance; these were documents the regime would be happy to pass on to those it no longer fully trusted but whose fate had yet to be decided on.

As it should be, he reflected. Because he was not trustworthy.

Della Torre had been an officer of the recently defunct UDBA. But now that Yugoslavia had broken apart, UDBA's people had drifted into different shadows. In a Croatia struggling for independence, della Torre had resurfaced as a senior member of military intelligence, recently seconded to a covert American government operation. The one that had left three of its team dead.

It dawned on him that his life could be measured by the whims of others. Half a decade ago, he had been co-opted by UDBA from his job as a young lawyer in the Zagreb prosecutor's office. He'd had no say when they handed him the intelligence job after UDBA's Croatian operations were quietly shut down. And then he'd been loaned to the Americans by a government minister, as a minor noble might solicit favour by proffering a useful family retainer to a powerful liege duke. The Americans had used him to plot a murder, with ruthless indifference to his wishes or his life. Somehow he'd survived when others had perished. And now he was left waiting to see where the forces beyond his control would drive him next.

The view of Zagreb's rooftops drew him away again. He was fond of the city, the pretty medieval centre, with its sagging wood-framed houses, surrounded by the well-ordered Hapsburg lower town with its ochre buildings and grand provincial architecture. The utilitarian tower blocks of the Communist-built new town, along with most of the other monstrosities of the new order, were thankfully out of sight.

There was a solitary socialist encroachment he didn't resent: the impossibly tall chimney of the Savica power plant. He felt a perverse pride in its narrow elegance, its tip banded red and white like layers of ash and ember on a cigarette. To him it was a gesture of defiance by a poor, backward eastern European city; it was as if Zagreb had looked to London with its Big Ben, Paris with its Eiffel Tower, and New York with its Chrysler Building and said, *Smoke this.*

He picked up the telephone and dialled. There was a dead tone. He waited a minute and then punched in the numbers again, and at last the phone rang. It was still ringing when he heard a knock at the door. He put down the receiver.

A young lieutenant poked his head into the room. "Captain — sorry, I mean Major." Della Torre's promotion was already two months old, but people still forgot. "There's a lady here. She insists on seeing you. I tried to deal with it, but she's pretty forceful."

The woman pushed past the lieutenant before della Torre could respond. She was as thin and as severe as a Roman matron, her hair piled up in tight curls and cut short at the sides. Her pale, almost lead-white complexion merely added to the effect.

"Major, is it? Well, Major della Torre, you are a difficult man to track down. No one is at the old UDBA offices, and when I went to police headquarters, the desk sergeant pretended he knew neither me nor you. I had to pull rank," she said, slightly out of breath.

There were spots of red in her cheeks from the eight-storey climb to the office. Two of the building's three elevators had broken down, their German manufacturer reluctant to send parts on credit to a government that no other country recognized. Clearly, she'd been too impatient to wait.

"That's fine, Lieutenant," della Torre said, standing. "Mrs. Strumbić is of course welcome."

The young officer made a half-hearted effort at a salute and then sidled out of the room, shutting the door behind him.

"Won't you sit, Mrs. Strumbić? Can I offer you a drink?" della Torre asked.

He felt ashamed for not having visited her, at least informally. Guilt had made it hard for him to face up to the man's wife. He'd sacrificed Strumbić to save three people from the Americans. And to save himself.

Officially, he had been told to steer clear of anything that had to do with the Šipan killings. Both he and Julius Strumbić were implicated in the events. But Strumbić had gone missing, and as a colleague, della Torre had a moral duty to the man's wife.

As the daughter of the fearsome and now dead chief of Zagreb's uniformed police, she knew the job could be dangerous. Her stoicism was undoubtedly fortified by the mutual antagonism between her and her husband. And she was used to Strumbić's long, silent absences.

Della Torre wondered if she knew just how corrupt her husband was — and how wealthy his corruption had made him. Strumbić had numerous foreign bank accounts and mistresses and secret apartments and houses — even one in London, one of the most expensive cities in the world. His wife was an intelligent woman, so she must have had an inkling. But then, being the daughter of Zagreb's police chief, maybe she knew it was all part of the game, the great socialist con in which the only sin was to be caught, exposed, shamed, and exiled to Goli Otok, Yugoslavia's infamous political prison.

No one played the system better than Strumbić, but in these past weeks della Torre had wondered whether Strumbić's luck had finally run out. The consensus view was that he'd skipped the country, maybe to one of his secret boltholes. Della Torre's conscience was assuaged by his knowledge of Strumbić's resourcefulness. More than any other man, Strumbić could weave gold out of a noose wrapped around his neck and buy not just his freedom but the thoroughbred to carry him as well. Della Torre was sure of it. He prayed it was true. Because he was fond of the man, as fond as he might have been of a brother.

"Nothing for me," Mrs. Strumbić said abruptly.

"I'm sorry, I have nothing to report on Julius. We still don't know where he is. I would have called, but —"

"I'm not here to find out where Julius is. I'm here to pass on a message from him."

"Julius sent you a message?"

"Well, what are you waiting for?" she snapped. "Get a pen, you'll need to write this down."

Under a stack of files on top of his desk, della Torre found a notepad and one of the fine-point mechanical pencils he favoured. "Please, carry on, Mrs. Strumbić," he said, sitting. "Are you sure you wouldn't like a seat?

She continued to stand, her oversized Italian leather handbag hanging off the crook of her arm. Her mouth was stern, her lips pleated, her cloying rose scent mixing unpleasantly with the room's cigarette-ash smell. "He said this would mean something to you, though only heaven knows what. He told me to tell you he's with colleagues near the staircase you so liked, and is using his pub name."

Della Torre looked at her blankly. "Could you repeat that, please?"

"He's with colleagues near the staircase you so liked, and is using his pub name. Don't tell me you don't know what he's talking about, because if military intelligence doesn't know its own codes, then we might as well be pissing on paper when it comes time to fight this war."

"No, of course. Yes, code, of course," della Torre said, looking at the words he'd written down in his tiny, neat handwriting.

"So now that I've told you, maybe you can tell your people to stop bothering me. I don't mind that you've got my phone tapped — don't deny it — but there's no point in having people telephoning asking for Julius. I'll unplug it if this carries on. As for the idiots you've posted to keep a watch on the building — well, at least they keep the vandals away. Little bastards. The vandals, I mean. Though the surveillance people probably are too. Stupid bastards at that. You can hear their brains rattle when they move. So it's just as well they don't move much. They'd give themselves a concussion otherwise," she muttered.

"I'm sorry, Mrs. Strumbić . . ." Della Torre reeled from the torrent of words. She talked faster than he could think.

"No point in being sorry. If I wanted an apology, you'd have known about it. Julius is enough of a pain in my backside without having to deal with everything else."

"I'm sure it's not intentional. Bureaucracy. You know how it is."

"Julius? Bureaucracy? What are you talking about, Major?"

"I mean keeping a watch . . . it's, you know, we like to keep an eye on the families — I mean, to ensure the safety of the families of missing officers."

"I just told you, he's not missing. Though I haven't a clue where he is. Disappears for months on end. He's lucky I'm not the jealous type, though it'd take some fancy imagination to be jealous over Julius."

"I'm sure you haven't got —" Della Torre stopped himself from saying *imagination*. "— reason to be worried."

"If you can't make those irritating phone calls stop, I'll find somebody who can."

"My apologies," della Torre said again. "Did Julius say nothing more?"

"Of course he said more, but that's all he told me to tell you."

"Oh. It's just that, maybe if you could share a bit more of your conversation —"

"Share my conversation? You've got the whole thing taped somewhere. I'm not here to make your life easier, I'm just here to tell you what Julius told me to tell you. Understand, Major?"

Della Torre stood up. "Yes, of course. Thank you, Mrs. —"

"Good day to you, Major. And when you find Julius, tell him he'd better get home soon or he'll regret it."

3

HIS EYES AND nose were still prickling from Mrs. Strumbić's perfume when the door opened. A tall man stepped in.

Major Anzulović, twenty years della Torre's senior, had been one of the Zagreb police force's most successful detective inspectors before being put in charge of the secret police's internal affairs unit. He'd personally recruited della Torre to be a part of Department VI, hired him to investigate UDBA's history of external assassinations. Until della Torre's recent promotion, given to him as an enticement to help the Americans, Anzulović had been his boss. Even though they now officially held the same rank, della Torre knew his place. Anzulović carried the authority of wisdom and experience. And a tenacious ability to survive.

"Hear you've had a visitor, Gringo," Anzulović said, invoking the nickname that della Torre so hated. He'd grown up in the United States; as a teenager, after his mother's death, he'd come back to Zagreb. The local kids, all of whom fanatically read strip cartoons and watched films about cowboys and Indians, had rechristened him.

Anzulović was holding a big mug of coffee. It was one of his few affectations. He was a movie buff, in particular an enormous fan of Hollywood westerns and film noir. And that's the way Americans drank their coffee. Not long after he'd recruited della Torre, Anzulović had asked the younger man to make him a pot of "real" cowboy coffee. Della Torre had offered up a thin, dirty concoction of instant grounds in tepid water, and Anzulović had walked around with a mug of something like it ever since. Though, della Torre reflected, he'd never actually seen Anzulović drink any.

"You are uncannily well informed for an officer in military intelligence," della Torre said, taking in Anzulović's pot belly, the tufts of black and grey hair sprouting from his ears, and his long, bulbous nose — a face like an old saddle.

"Got a cigarette?" Anzulović asked, sliding into the faux leather office chair opposite della Torre's desk.

"Lucky Strike?"

"If I must," Anzulović said. He was too frugal to buy foreign cigarettes, and he'd never been one for corruption, claiming to be too lazy and too fond of a quiet life to expend his energy on covering his ass. So he lived in a modest apartment in the new town with his wife, two daughters, son-in-law, and a decrepit yellow poodle he loathed.

Della Torre lit Anzulović's cigarette and his own. "Let me guess, you're here to find out what Mrs. Strumbić wanted."

"Not really. I've got some news," Anzulović said. "But if you'd like, that can wait. What did our esteemed erstwhile colleague's wife want? Her husband?"

"Actually, no. She came to give me a message from Julius."

Anzulović sat up a little straighter. "From? What'd he say? Where is he? He must know that a few people have some questions for him."

"That's the thing, the message was in a kind of code."

"I'm waiting."

"Something about a staircase and staying with mutual friends, and he's naming a pub."

Anzulović sighed. "So he's back in London?"

"I guess so," della Torre said. Where else but in Britain were there pubs? The staircase reference meant nothing to della Torre, though his shattered elbow had bled up the stairs to Strumbić's London apartment earlier in the summer. As for mutual friends, well, they'd both known a woman there too. She was hard to forget.

So why did he have a hard time believing that's where Strumbić had run to? Maybe because the Americans would have looked for him there already.

"Think his old lady knows about the London place?" Anzulović asked.

"No," della Torre said, after giving the question some thought. "She would have her hands on it by now. She doesn't know a quarter of what he actually has."

"A tenth."

"A hundredth."

"I wonder if even he knows how much money he's salted away."

"He was organizing a scam when I last saw him in Dubrovnik," della Torre said. "Something about smuggling pirated heavy metal CDs knocked off in Turkey."

Anzulović shook his head. A slow, sad motion, at once showing disbelief and an absolute understanding of how the world worked. Corruption suited some people better than others. Strumbić was good at being on the take. He revelled in it, lived for it, even. But della Torre's one foray into shady dealings had left him with a bullet in his elbow and a price on his head, which he still hadn't been able to rub off. It was at the beginning of the year and he'd been short of funds. Like almost everyone. At the time, Strumbić was in the market for UDBA's secrets, so della Torre had passed on to him what he thought were a few inconsequential files, and Strumbić paid him enough to buy the occasional carton of Luckys. But one of the documents, the Pilgrim file, had come back to bite him. An ancient Communist had gotten wind of the leak and set a couple of Bosnian killers on della Torre. He owed his life to Strumbić.

"Everybody else in the whole fucking country is hiding behind the furniture, scared to death about what's coming, and what does Julius do? He sells them shitty stolen music," Anzulović said. "Well, good luck to him in London, and well done to him for getting out. I used to resent him. But now I know he's the only sane human being this country has ever produced. Except maybe Irena."

"No, she's gone mad too."

Irena was della Torre's ex-wife. A doctor, she had recently gone east to Vukovar because so many of the local medics had evacuated the çity when the Serbs were besieging it. Tito had kept Yugoslavia together with charm, hubris, and an iron fist. But he'd died ten years earlier. After the collapse of the Berlin Wall and the subsequent continent-wide upheaval, bitter nationalist rivalries between the country's ethnic groups, especially the Serbs and Croats, had created a violent rupture. And Vukovar was on the fault line. Della Torre had been adamant that Irena shouldn't go. She went anyway, with her British "friend" (was *paramour* still the right word?), a specialist in bullet wounds. It'd been a week since della Torre had last managed to speak to her. The phone lines were unreliable in these times of war, and anyway, she spent most of her days in the operating theatre.

Anzulović shrugged. "Still trying to convince her to leave? They need doctors in Vukovar. Is her Dr. Cohen there still?"

"They need to evacuate the city," della Torre said, ignoring the question. "Because when they finish flattening it, no one's going to be living there anyway." And then, after a pause: "Yes, as far as I know he's still there with her. But I haven't been able to get through for a while. Last I heard, he was only allowed to assist. I guess British imperialist doctors don't have the right sort of political training to heal the proletariat."

"New regime, Gringo. Remember, we're now capitalist revanchists. No longer socialists with an inhuman face."

"I find it so confusing. Aren't we supposed to be nationalist socialists these days?"

"Shhh," Anzulović said, suddenly alarmed. It was one thing to joke about how the newly independent Croatia was shedding the trappings of Yugoslav Communism, but to hint back at the country's Nazi sympathies during the Second World War was to become allied with the Serbs. The new masters of Croatia were as fanatical as any revolutionaries and as cynical as old Communists — which many were, having been part of the Yugoslav government for decades. "Some jokes don't seem so funny from inside a prison cell."

"*Plus ça change*," della Torre said, but he felt less brave than he sounded. "So, what did you want to tell me about?"

"The Americans want to talk to you."

"They have my reports."

"Deputy Minister Horvat has been persuaded to allow the Americans to interview you." Horvat ran military intelligence, and therefore he was their lord and master. He was a political operator of the highest order, so if he was allowing the Americans access to della Torre, they must be providing him something valuable in return.

"I won't ask how you know," della Torre said. "Have you got a role in the investigation?"

"No, notionally it's still in the hands of the Dubrovnik police."

"And I take it the police in Dubrovnik have got so much on their plate, the Americans aren't making any headway."

"Not much."

"And it's driving them nuts because they can't do anything about it."

"You could say," Anzulović agreed.

"Except they offered something to Horvat and now he's letting them have me?"

"To talk to. Maybe." Anzulović got up. "Listen, Gringo, why don't we go out for a coffee."

Years of working for UDBA, where phones and offices were commonly bugged, had conditioned them to be wary of speaking too openly.

Della Torre noticed that Anzulović had left his full mug on the desk. He made a mental note to pour it into his indestructible potted rubber tree when he got back.

It was a relief to leave the office, even if the streets were looking scruffy. Buildings were inflamed with an eczema of graffiti while litter flecked the pavements like dandruff. Shops were short of everything. And though there was plenty of food for sale in the markets — the autumn harvest had been good — few people were buying, and the day-end spoils of mouldy and bruised vegetables were picked over by refugees who'd swollen the city's population.

As they passed the cinema, della Torre saw Anzulović glance longingly at the posters advertising the latest Hollywood import. His former boss couldn't resist even a second-rate film already forgotten everywhere else in the world.

The pedestrianized street was guarded by a sculpture of a man standing in a slouch, wearing a long overcoat and a hat pulled down over his eyes. It was of a writer, though he looked more like a secret policeman. A monument to the unknown spook.

They sat at an outdoor café table under the statue's gaze, facing the Square of Flowers. Della Torre was about to make a wisecrack about the symbolism but thought better of it. There was something about Anzulović's mood.

People had long underestimated Anzulović. His lugubrious demeanour and hangdog face made him unprepossessing. In serious discussions, he preferred to listen rather than to talk. With politicians he kept his mouth shut so that he seemed part of the furniture. Another know-nothing career apparatchik. About five years after Tito's death, when the Yugoslav parliament finally made an effort to show it could rule responsibly rather than just exist as a dictatorship's marketing tool, one of its first major expressions of power had been to hold the UDBA to account.

To that end, the lawmakers grafted an internal investigative unit, Department VI, onto UDBA and gave it to Anzulović. The UDBA hierarchy took a brief, supercilious look at Anzulović and accepted the imposition. After all, what threat could this time-server possibly pose to them, especially if he was kept at arm's length in Zagreb, well away from the centre of power in Belgrade?

By the time they appreciated that there was substance to this man who'd worked his way up from a traffic beat, Anzulović had created a smart and solid team.

There was something deeply paternal about Anzulović. But della Torre reminded himself that his old boss had survived so long for a reason.

Anzulović rubbed his hand over his face, and della Torre inadvertently did the same. Even now the absence of his moustache, which he'd shaved off earlier in the year, caught him by surprise.

"Gringo, just a bit of advice: lay off the political jokes. Our masters are touchy. And they're keeping tabs."

"I'll bear it in mind," della Torre said. "But we didn't come out here just for you to tell me to shut my mouth."

"No, I want to ask you what happened in Dubrovnik."

"Why?"

"I'm curious about what you're going to tell the Americans."

"You read my reports," della Torre said, shifting slightly. Their coffees arrived. Della Torre spooned sugar into his double espresso and lit a cigarette.

"And if they were satisfied with what you gave them, why do you think they want to talk to you?" Anzulović pressed.

"I don't know."

"Don't you?"

"Are you about to tell me I need a lawyer?" della Torre said. He made it sound like a joke, but the levity fell flat.

Anzulović considered the question for a long moment. "I think it's fine for now. Shall we go over what happened?"

Della Torre dragged on his cigarette. He felt the urge to talk. Anxiety had slowly been consuming him over the weeks. "Are you asking as an interested friend or as a cop?"

"Gringo, when haven't I ever been both?" Anzulović sighed. "Look, I've been asked — informally, mind you — to supervise the case. From our end. Rubber-stamp whatever it is that comes my way, for want of anybody else fit and proper to do the job."

"Horvat gave you authority?" della Torre asked, incredulous. The deputy minister had a deep antipathy for Anzulović, resenting his lack of zeal for the nationalist cause.

"No, Horvat gave authority to Messar. But seeing as Messar is still out of sorts —" Major Messar, an efficient secret policeman with enough private wealth through relatives in Germany that he remained an incorruptible and committed Communist, had taken a bullet to the jaw in the same incident that injured della Torre's elbow. "— he passed it onto me."

"Does Horvat know?"

Anzulović's shrug at once said: *yes, no, maybe, I can't do anything about what he thinks anyway, I just do my job.*

"It's like this, Gringo. The Americans want to think of themselves as St. Nicholas. They want to know when you've been good, when you've been bad, and when you've lied, so they can reward and punish fairly. Who knows, maybe they are — St. Nicholas, I mean. They're certainly fat enough — at least the ones who come to our beaches. Maybe the thin ones stay at home. We don't know what they know, what they think they know, and what they know they don't know. So your best approach is to tell the truth and to be consistent to the point that you don't incriminate yourself."

"You make it sound like you think I've got something to hide."

THE HEART OF HELL   41

Anzulović ignored this. "So, two rules. Number one, don't lie. Number two, don't help them dig your grave. Understand?"

"Yes."

"Right, so let's start with the dead Americans."

"A couple of guys called Bill and Rob."

"And your friend Rebecca Vees . . ."

Della Torre momentarily lifted his hands and then sat back. "Where did they find her?"

"She washed up on an Italian beach and was formally identified by people from the American embassy in Rome. Though our guy from Dubrovnik had already had a look and was pretty sure it was her. I don't think the Americans ever seriously thought she'd be found alive, do you?"

"No."

Della Torre had written in his report that both he and Rebecca had been thrown off the Montenegrin's boat. He'd neglected to mention that his bindings had been cut off. Hers hadn't.

The Americans had come to eliminate the Montenegrin, another piece of the Pilgrim puzzle, but they'd underestimated the UDBA's lead assassin.

"When did they find her?"

Della Torre drank his coffee and lit another Lucky. The place still made a decent coffee — elsewhere, standards had started to slip as prices rose. He stared out in front of him. Even in a time of war the flower sellers were out, though some had little more on offer than bunches of rosehips, fat and luscious and red against the square's drab grey concrete.

"Brg, our detective from Dubrovnik, went over two days ago. The Americans notified us that it was her yesterday afternoon," Anzulović said.

"Nice of them. Saves us from having to keep looking."

"Had we been looking?" Anzulović asked.

"I suppose not."

"Interesting timing."

"What?"

"You getting Strumbić's message at around the same time they fished up the corpse."

"And I suppose that's when Horvat finally agreed to let the Americans interview me."

"Maybe it's a coincidence," Anzulović said.

"Horvat's quite the operator."

"Whether he is or isn't, he says you're to talk to the Americans. Could be soon. Or maybe not. But let's get your story straight. Remember, tell the truth. But only so long as it doesn't tie a rope around your neck."

4

ESS THAN A week later, an unmarked Zastava with a military
police chauffeur drove up the concrete driveway of a house
on the lower slope of Medvednica mountain, behind Zagreb's
medieval old town. It was an elegant 1930s villa with thick walls
and a steep-pitched red-tiled roof, set in spacious grounds. The
high iron gate, painted red with rustproofing, was closed behind
the car by a soldier in dress uniform.

"Officially one of UDBA's safe houses," Anzulović said.

"Not one I've ever known about," della Torre said, getting
out of the car.

Anzulović laughed. "Bit like your apartment. Requisitioned
by the UDBA for reasons of national security, and then somehow . . . well, you know how it goes . . ."

Della Torre knew how it went. In the bad old days, a senior
Communist could have a private property requisitioned from
someone with inadequate political pull, claim it on behalf of the
state, and then quietly move in. That's what an UDBA agent had
done with della Torre's apartment. When the agent had fallen
out of favour badly enough to end up in Goli Otok, his family
was evicted. An accident of timing and a certain nous meant
that della Torre got it.

"I thought the new regime promised to give these places back to their rightful owners," della Torre said. "Rightful owners" generally meant the families of people who'd lost possession immediately after the Second World War, when socialist self-justification was at its strongest.

Anzulović's right eyebrow arched like a furry caterpillar. "Once they've taken it through the courts. But the courts are stuffed full of old Communists. Most of the judges will be sympathetic to the old functionaries like them, and half are on the take, along with the lawyers and clerks and officers and recorders and stenographers and secretaries. How long do you think they'd be able to hold up a repossession? I'm banking on at least a decade."

They climbed the stone steps from the driveway to the upper terrace. The house managed to be both grand and understated.

A young woman ushered them in. Della Torre's heart leapt at the sight of her friendly, open face. But she disappeared immediately upon taking them through the hall and into the room beyond. The ceilings were more than three metres high and the floor was laid in a herringbone parquet. Autumn light filtered through thin gauze curtains draped like veils over three sets of tall French windows. The furniture was from the 1950s or '60s. At first della Torre thought they were admirable Yugoslav knock-offs of western European styles. But then he realized they were actual western European pieces. A long rosewood sideboard to one side. Scandinavian sofas and armchairs. A stylish coffee table. The broad rug covering the floor around the seating area was a blue Persian kilim, either an antique or a very good imitation. Della Torre recognized an Odilon Redon painting on the wall, depicting flowers in a vase. He wondered if it was an original.

But mostly his attention was on Zlatko Horvat. The deputy minister sat in an armchair reading a document almost as if he were playing a role on stage. They stood in silence until at long last he acknowledged them.

"Major," he said, not rising. "How nice to see you again. Please sit." He motioned across the room. Della Torre took a corner of a long, low sofa, Anzulović a wing chair. After a first fleeting look of displeasure, Horvat studiously ignored Anzulović.

"Deputy Minister," della Torre said.

Horvat's half-smile was more insincere than ever, turned up in one corner, the other side of his face frozen by an old stroke. He pulled on a cigarette in an ivory holder. His skin was papery, his fingers stained yellow. His eyes showed intelligence, an efficient malevolence.

"Our American friends would like to speak with you," Horvat began. "I am confident that you gave their colleagues every assistance on their mission in Dubrovnik. I have read your account of the matter. I find it conclusive. The Americans overreached, and they suffered the consequences of underestimating the Balkans. But I fear the Americans are concerned that they don't have the complete story. It is understandable. No one likes to admit to errors of judgement."

Horvat spoke with studied neutrality, but there was something about the way he said the last sentence that made della Torre wonder whether the deputy minister was also referring to his own error of placing his considerable faith in della Torre. Horvat was not very different from Strumbić, an opportunist whose agenda primarily involved enriching himself. Except — unlike Strumbić, whose cynicism ran deep — Horvat suffered from a streak of idealism. Nationalism was his cause. And it was the hope of leveraging advantage for himself and his country that had originally encouraged him to offer della Torre's services to the American team sent to kill the Montenegrin.

Horvat rose, and della Torre and Anzulović with him.

"You will wait here," he said. "I'm afraid I have pressing matters to attend to. There is no end to governing during a war. You will give our friends all the information they require." He left, shaking neither man's hand.

The same young woman who had shown them in now arrived with a coffee service, which she placed on the low table between a pair of heavy cut-glass ashtrays. She poured four rich Turkish coffees into thimble-sized cups and then went back out, not having spoken a word to them.

Della Torre sat back down on the sofa and lit a cigarette, feeling seedy in his cheap leather jacket and polycotton trousers. At least he had on nice shoes, sturdy but elegant handmade Grenson chukka boots he'd bought in London during his brief escape from the Bosnian killers earlier in the year. Paid for with money he'd stolen from Strumbić.

"The minister seemed pleased to see you," della Torre said, irony helping to lift his tension a little. He'd barely slept for the past week, his thoughts constantly flitting between Irena and the Americans, from his father to the war to the regimented emptiness of his days at work.

"Nice man. A fine one to have in government," Anzulović said. They both knew the place was bugged.

They'd waited only the length of two leisurely cigarettes before the door opened again.

It didn't surprise della Torre to see John Dawes, the American who'd assembled the failed team and now undoubtedly hoped to lay the cause of the catastrophe at somebody else's feet. The man with him was also American. He had short greying hair and looked military, even though he was wearing a civilian suit.

"Mr. Anzic and Mr. della Torre," Dawes said, lazily failing to pronounce Anzulović's name. The smile was professional. "This is my colleague Jack Grimston."

Grimston's hand was surprisingly elegant for a man who looked like a marine. His fingers were long and he had clean, well-trimmed nails. But the grip was strong, with considerable reserves of power.

The Americans sat in the remaining two armchairs, leaving della Torre on his own in the corner of the sofa. He felt as if he were facing a tribunal.

"I would like to thank you for your cooperation, Mr. della Torre," Dawes began. He took a folder out of his black briefcase and opened it on his lap. Grimston did the same. "Your written statement about the events in Dubrovink was appreciated, as were your answers to our follow-up questions. The United States government cannot formally discuss these matters with the current Croatian administration, since it does not recognize Croatia as an independent state. And because of Croatia's . . . ah . . . estrangement from Yugoslavia, this has put the United States government in a difficult position with respect to investigating the deaths of the three American citizens who were killed in or around Dubrovnik." He paused. "Our agreement with Deputy Defence Minister Horvat is that we are here to speak with you informally and merely as an exercise in clarifying some details."

Anzulović wore a troubled expression, concentrating hard on the American's words. He spoke some English, but far from enough to decipher legalistic hedging.

"How can I help you gentlemen?" della Torre said.

"As you know, two American men were killed in a house on the island of Šipan, north of Dubrovnik, approximately one month ago," Dawes said. "We have just confirmed that a third American, a woman, died probably the same night. Her body was discovered on the Italian coast, and over the past week or so her identity was confirmed by officers from the U.S. embassy in Rome. We wish to understand in detail the events leading up to their deaths."

"Everything I knew was in the statement."

"For which we thank you. But there are some gaps —"

"Mr. della Torre, we're here to find out who killed these three American citizens and the circumstances of their deaths," Grimston cut in. He had a light Southern accent and a gritty voice. "I'm sure you don't want us to waste your time, so why don't we just cover that ground."

Della Torre nodded. "Rebecca Vees, Bill, and Rob — I'm sorry, I don't know their surnames — were killed by the former UDBA senior operative they were sent to assassinate."

"Mr. D-jay-las . . ." Dawes interjected.

"It's spelled D-J-I-L-A-S and is pronounced *gee-las,* as in *giants.* He's commonly called 'the Montenegrin' because that's where he's from. The Republic of Montenegro touches Croatia at its southern extremity, just beyond Dubrovnik." Dawes would know all this, but della Torre didn't want to presume that Grimston had any knowledge of the former Yugoslavia. Grimston showed no reaction.

"You were saying," Dawes said. Grimston remained silent, sitting back and observing.

"They were killed by the Montenegrin. He came at night, in a boat, and shot the two men in the villa. The villa is very private, on an isolated island, and the locals generally steer clear, so nobody took too much notice. I assume Rebecca was wounded while being captured."

"Did you see how she sustained her wounds?"

"No, but I saw that there was blood on her side when we were in the boat."

"What did you and Rebecca discuss on the boat?"

"Nothing. She was gagged."

"And you weren't?"

"I had been unconscious. It took me a while to regain my senses. The Montenegrin took us for a boat ride. Then he threw me into the sea late at night just off Orebić. I had to swim to land."

"And Rebecca?"

"He threw us both off," della Torre said.

"But you survived."

"I . . . I wasn't . . . my bindings came undone. So I could swim."

"And Rebecca's didn't."

"No."

"Did you make any effort to save her?"

"I . . . I couldn't."

"But you knew she was still bound?"

"Yes."

"How?"

"Because he threw her in first."

"And then you?"

"Yes."

"He must have known she would drown."

"Yes."

"Did you say anything? Did you do anything to save her?"

"No." No, he'd watched with horror, but he'd done nothing, said nothing.

"So it was likely his intention — the Montenegrin's intention — that Rebecca should die."

"Yes."

"Why do you think that, Mr. della Torre?"

"Because Rebecca and her team were sent there to kill him."

"This is your speculation."

"This is my absolute knowledge."

"It seems to me you're making a leap of judgement, coloured perhaps by extenuating circumstances. Did you disagree with this supposed mission to assassinate Mr. Djil . . . the Montenegrin?"

"It is contrary to law."

"You're a lawyer, aren't you, Mr. della Torre?"

"Yes."

"Specialized in international law. I understand you studied for a master's degree in London. From, let's see, '77 to '78, I believe."

"That's correct."

"And what was Mr. . . . . the Montenegrin's past?"

"He had been a senior member of the UDBA."

"With a responsibility for liquidations on foreign territory."

"He headed the wetworks, yes."

"Was that legal?"

"He always operated within the framework of Yugoslav law."

"This is something you know about, is it? This is within your expertise?"

"Yes, I was a member of UDBA's Department VI. We were in effect the UDBA's internal affairs. My responsibility was to investigate past killings UDBA had been involved in on foreign territory, to ensure that they had been —" Della Torre was about to say *executed* but thought better of it. "That they had been undertaken within the letter of Yugoslav law."

He was limiting himself to telling the Americans only what he already knew they knew, though he suspected they knew a lot more.

"And did these murders comply with international law?"

"How so?" della Torre said.

Grimston cut in: "Were the Montenegrin's actions permissible within the context of international law?"

"It was not my role to adjudicate on whether actions by officers of the Yugoslav state were in breach of international law, merely whether they had acted within the scope of domestic legislation. In my experience — and I investigated a number of past cases he had been involved in — he had always acted lawfully."

"Yet you're a specialist in international law."

"Yes."

"Setting aside international considerations and purely within the context of Yugoslav law, did you feel that it was your responsibility to prevent the assassination of . . . the Montenegrin?"

"It was my responsibility not to aid the operation directly."

"So, insofar as you thought Ms. Vees was out to kill this gentleman, you would have interfered."

"I would not have aided the project."

"But you wouldn't have actively intervened to prevent it?"

Della Torre paused, took out a cigarette, and lit it. How many had he already had that morning? He coughed. "I wouldn't have gotten in the way."

"Would you have encouraged someone else to do so? That is to say, encouraged someone else to interfere with such an operation, had it existed?"

"I don't see how your question is materially different from what you've asked already."

"Would you please answer my question."

"I refer you to my previous answer."

Anzulović looked from della Torre to the interviewers. Della Torre took a final drag of his Lucky and rubbed it out in the ashtray.

"Whether at your instigation or not," Grimston continued, "did someone else interfere directly with this operation?"

"Perhaps."

"Who else knew about what was going on?"

"No one."

"Your colleague Julius Strumbić?"

"I don't know what he knew. I don't know what Rebecca told him. They had . . . intimate conversations."

Grimston nodded. Another, shorter silence.

"If the Montenegrin thought you were involved in planning his liquidation, why did he let you swim to shore?"

"Maybe he thought I'd drown."

"He could have guaranteed it."

"Maybe he's a good sport."

"Did you collude with the Montenegrin in the murder of any of the three United States citizens?"

"No."

"It seems strange to me that he should have let you swim to shore but that he threw Rebecca overboard with her hands tied. She had no chance of surviving. Was that the sign of a good sport? Drowning a defenceless woman?"

"She was a professional assassin and she had tried to kill him. I was just a go-between," della Torre said.

There was a long pause. Dawes glanced over at Grimston,

but Grimston had leaned slightly forward in his seat, keeping his eyes on della Torre.

John Dawes broke the silence. "Mr. della Torre, since this is an informal conversation, I won't challenge your assumption other than to say it is incorrect, and that Rebecca's only intention was to persuade the target of our investigation to surrender himself to American justice so he could be made to answer for the murders he committed on American soil."

"Mr. Dawes, you may continue with that fiction for the purposes of any record being made, but you and I know you are being disingenuous."

Dawes smiled in an exaggerated show of patience. "We're not here to throw around accusations. Shall we continue?" he said, after a moment's silence. "Your contention is that the Montenegrin was punishing Rebecca for what he thought her intentions were. Surely, since you helped her, he'd have wanted you dead too."

"Is that a question or an assertion?"

"I am asking why he should have sought to save you and to kill Rebecca."

"You seem disappointed that I survived. Like I said, I don't think he particularly cared one way or the other with me. He was inclined to give me a chance."

"Why?"

"Because, I suppose, he knew my role was merely to offer an introduction."

"Yet you were instrumental in . . . ah . . . arranging the contact between Rebecca and the Montenegrin."

"Yes."

"He forgave you for that?"

"I suppose he must have."

"Mr. della Torre, your good fortune is a little hard to believe."

"Isn't that the nature of luck? Then again, maybe he wanted me to live so that I could tell you what happened. As a warning against trying it again."

There was another long pause. Della Torre stared longingly at the coffees on the table. He and Anzulović had drunk theirs but the other two remained untouched. He wondered whether the Americans would notice if he helped himself.

"What was Mr. Strumbić's role in these events?" Grimston said.

"He offered use of his house on Šipan."

"The house the two men were murdered in?"

"Yes."

"Did he provide any other services?"

"He was useful in getting us down to Dubrovnik, and there he did some background investigation into the Montenegrin for Rebecca."

"He left early to go back to Zagreb, at Rebecca's request."

"Yes. I believe Mr. Dawes travelled with him on the flight."

"But he returned to Dubrovnik immediately after," Grimston said.

"I think so."

"Why?"

"Because he . . . he had some business."

"What sort of business?"

"I don't know."

"Could it have been business with the Montenegrin?"

Yes, della Torre thought, *but not in the way you suppose.*

"I don't know."

"Did Mr. Strumbić set up Rebecca?" Grimston asked, catching della Torre's eyes, holding them, refusing to look away.

"I . . . I don't know." Della Torre broke eye contact, focusing on his cigarette, trying not to look as though he was lying.

"Yet you made an indication to her that he'd interfered with her plans, did you not?"

"I could have been wrong."

"Weren't you directed by your own defence minister to give Rebecca the utmost help?"

"Yes."

"Did you?"

"Within the limits of law." Della Torre crushed the cigarette and lit another one straight away, breathing the smoke in deep. As he exhaled, it curled blue towards the high ceiling.

"Law that permitted this man to organize murders around the world."

"Extrajudicial killing is as illegal in this country — in Yugoslavia — as it is in any civilized place. But many countries perform executions within the restrictions of law."

"Please, Mr. della Torre. In Yugoslavia your organization, the UDBA, practised extrajudicial killings for decades, all over the world." Grimston hammered away in his polite but unyielding tone. "And the Montenegrin led those killings for at least three of those years, after having been involved directly for almost two decades."

"If I may correct your observations, my job these past five years was to investigate the UDBA's assassination program and to determine whether its killings were done within the scope of Yugoslav law or not. Most of the cases followed due process. *Our* due process. They were sanctioned by the presidency and the high court. You may not like it. I don't like it. But capital punishment was as legal in Yugoslavia as it is in the United States. And practised."

"In the United States, people are given their say in court before they're condemned to death," Grimston said. "But we're not here to debate American justice."

Della Torre shrugged. "Here, *in absentia* rulings are . . . *were* legal. I'm not sure about the current state of affairs in Croatia." But he would have bet on the continuity of those laws from the Yugoslav state: *in absentia* justice and subsequent execution of the sentence.

"Is Mr. Strumbić as morally fastidious as you are?"

All during the conversation, della Torre had been working

hard to keep his nerves in check. But that question almost made him laugh out loud.

"The question seems to amuse you, Mr. della Torre." Grimston's expression was set hard.

"The smoke tickled my lungs."

"Maybe you should think about quitting, then. But I'll take it from your reaction that Mr. Strumbić is less scrupulous than you are on matters of ethics." The American was needle-sharp.

"I didn't say that."

"No, no, you didn't," said Dawes. "But it doesn't matter; this isn't testimony. Just a little chinwag between old friends." He sat back in his chair. Della Torre wondered whether he saw the American's lips curl with the faintest trace of a smile. "Do you know where Mr. Strumbić is?"

"No," della Torre answered.

"Where do you think he is?"

"I don't know."

"Do you think the Montenegrin did to Mr. Strumbić what he did to Rebecca and the others?"

Della Torre shrugged.

"You don't, do you. Is that because he helped the Montenegrin in setting them up?"

Della Torre shrugged again.

"Maybe that's because you think Mr. Strumbić has fled the country? That maybe he's gone . . . oh, I don't know. To Britain?"

Della Torre shot a look at Anzulović. Anzulović looked back, his expression blank, his eyes drooping. Maybe he hadn't understood Dawes's question. Maybe he didn't know what they were talking about. Maybe.

"I don't know why you should think that," della Torre said.

Grimston watched della Torre closely. Della Torre held the man's eyes for a long while and then looked away.

"Mr. della Torre, we would appreciate it if you would testify to these and other facts in your statement to a United States medical examiner."

Della Torre was silent, wondering at the implications of the request. "This would necessitate your making a statement under oath within a United States–administered jurisdiction," Grimston said. "That could be the embassy in Belgrade, though we appreciate it might cause you difficulty. So Rome or Vienna would do equally well."

And once in the embassy, he would be extradited to the United States. Then he'd be locked up as an enemy of the state, without trial. It unsettled him to think that his safety, his temporary immunity from these Americans, was down to the fact that no country in the world recognized Croatia as an independent state.

"I'll give it some thought," della Torre said, and stood up to end the meeting.

None of the others followed suit. Della Torre tried not to be obviously self-conscious. He had a sudden inkling that if he tried the doors they wouldn't open. Dawes smirked. *Even here, the Americans exert their power,* della Torre thought as he stepped over to the French windows and lit another cigarette.

"Of course, we could type up the minutes of our conversation today. We've recorded it, by the way; I knew you wouldn't mind," Grimston said. "And you could sign the documents without leaving Zagreb. That ought to be sufficient for the examiner."

"What's the catch?" della Torre asked.

"Catch? There's no catch," Grimston said. "But we would like some help. To apprehend Mr. Strumbić."

Della Torre had put the blame on Strumbić for the failed American mission to kill the Montenegrin and thus had implicated him in the Americans' deaths. And these men now wanted him to compound the sin of bearing false witness with helping to arrange Strumbić's murder. Because that, he had little doubt, was what it would lead to, whether it was a bullet in the back down a filthy alley or a lethal injection in the sterile death chamber of a federal penitentiary.

Della Torre laughed. "What, so I take a flight to London on the promise that you'll leave me alone once you have your hands on Julius?" Once he was out of the country, their promises, he knew, would be worthless.

"No, not to London. You'd only have to go to Dubrovnik."

Della Torre turned to face the man, confusion etched into his expression.

"That's where we think he is, Mr. della Torre. In Dubrovnik."

Della Torre struggled to keep his jaw from dropping. Anzulović looked just as taken aback. He'd understood that much of the conversation. Dubrovnik? Was that what Mrs. Strumbić had been hinting at? It seemed absurd. And yet, what had she said? The staircase he'd admired. It came to him that there was a staircase he'd admired in Strumbić's island villa, until he learned it had been stolen from someone else's house.

"I'll have to think about it," della Torre said finally.

"Don't think too long, Mr. della Torre. You can let us know through Mr. Horvat's office. He knows how to get in touch with us."

The girl showed della Torre and Anzulović out. "Gentlemen," was all she said. The Americans stayed back, offering perfunctory goodbyes.

The front door closed behind them. Della Torre noticed that the terracotta tiles on the terrace were showing their age, cracked from years of frosts. The gardens had once been beautiful, as elegant as the interior of the house, but now the pergola of vines was overgrown, weeds broke through between the paving stones, and the lawn was stubbly and scarred by molehills. It seemed that whatever senior UDBA official had had tenancy of the house was no longer around. If he was a Serb, it was likely he had left in the exodus at the turn of the year. Della Torre wondered whether Horvat was easing his way into the property. Good luck to its real owners.

Their driver was standing by the Zastava.

"Why don't you take the car back. We'll walk," Anzulović said. He sniffed the air, damp with the threat of drizzle. "Or we'll take the tram."

"I take it you didn't find that rewarding," Anzulović said as they passed through the wrought-iron gate, held open by the soldier in dress uniform.

"Did you understand any of it?" della Torre asked.

"A little. Enough to know they want Strumbić and that they think he's in Dubrovnik. The rest, it doesn't matter. The translated transcript will pass across my desk on its way to Horvat," Anzulović said. "Any ideas why they think Strumbić is in Dubrovnik?"

"Because they have better intelligence than we do?"

"Then why the hell don't they just pick him up?"

"I don't know. Maybe because of the blockade." In the past few days Dubrovnik had been subject to a land assault by the Yugoslav forces, Serbs and Montenegrins mostly, cutting off the city and its littoral from the rest of Croatia. At the same time, the Yugoslav navy had raised a sea blockade.

"But they want you to help find him?"

"That's what they say."

"What do you think?"

"They want me and Strumbić dead. Or in some military jail. Both, probably. You can bet they tried to find him themselves, without any luck. I'm the bait to lure him out of whatever velvet-lined hole he's curled up in. And then they'll have us both."

"You'd think they'd have learned by now," Anzulović said. "I mean, you fucked it royally for them with the Montenegrin. Why are they putting themselves in a position for you to screw them again?"

"I don't know."

They walked through the autumn leaves, down the hill, back towards the centre of the city. Rich, earthy smells filled the air, mushrooms and the compost from the forest floor. Zagreb was a green city, pocket-sized and close to wilderness.

"So, are you going to help?"

Della Torre was silent for a long time, long enough for Anzulović to suspect he might not have heard him. Something deep inside della Torre rebelled. A visceral reflex, like the urge to vomit. He was tired of running, tired of being set in clockwork motion at the whim of others. And he was tired of evading his responsibilities to Irena, to his father, to Strumbić. To himself.

They were back in the old town, gloomy under grey skies, when della Torre said, "No. No, I don't think I'll help."

5

THEY CAME FOR him three days later.

Della Torre was on his way to the office, called in earlier than usual by Anzulović. Around the corner from his apartment, a young couple was horsing around on the sidewalk. The boy had taken her scarf and was making her jump for it. *University students*, della Torre thought. Wealthy ones, in their foreign jeans and Benetton sweaters. Maybe a pair of Yugo-Germans visiting family. No, the clothes weren't quite German. It made him smile that there could be lightheartedness at a time of such general despair.

He stepped to one side in an effort to avoid them, and from the corner of his eye he saw a man step towards him from a building's shadowy doorway. Before he could react, the man had put a hand on della Torre's shoulder with a firm grip and slurred a greeting. He was unkempt, unshaven, his hair askew, his clothes rough and patched.

The man's thick accent was impenetrable. Della Torre wondered if he was speaking Slovene.

"Wish I could help, but you might just want to sleep it off," della Torre said.

The man continued to hold on to him, one hand gripping

his shoulder, the other his arm. He was leaning against him, almost pushing him.

"Mister, I won't say it again. Let go of me and find somewhere to get a bit of rest and tidy yourself up."

The tramp ignored him.

"I'm from the UDBA," della Torre said.

Those four letters could chill the blood of a Yugoslav and sober a drunk. People might shrug off the ordinary cops, dim flatfeet who shuffled away after being palmed a couple of folded banknotes. But everyone down to a primary school child knew the UDBA were another matter. They could make people disappear into the vortex of state security, only to emerge years later. If ever.

Della Torre began to register that this tramp was somehow different from the usual drunk peasant. He didn't smell. His teeth were straight and fine.

And then della Torre saw the young couple approach. Maybe they were coming to offer help, to mediate. By the time he realized they weren't, the rear door of a parked Mercedes saloon had opened directly in front of him and the young couple were pushing him into the rear seat.

A man sat by the far door. The young man edged della Torre over and shoved in beside him. The woman got into the front seat. The tramp remained on the pavement, looking both ways, speaking into the lapel of his jacket.

The instant the doors shut, the driver pulled into the road.

"Please be calm and sit still, Mr. della Torre," the man to his left said in American-accented English.

Della Torre leaned back and looked up at the car's fabric-lined roof. He didn't need to ask who they were or what they wanted. All he wondered was how they would get him out of the country.

They could be in Austria in little more than two hours. In Slovenia in less than one. Or at the airport and on a private plane in twenty minutes.

Would he be subject to a military tribunal? A secret trial? Would there be any formal legal process at all? It didn't matter.

It made him sick to his stomach how for more than six months, ever since the Pilgrim affair had emerged into his life, he'd been blown from one place to another like a leaf in autumn. He'd achieved nothing out of his own volition. He'd been little more than an automaton.

How did Strumbić manage to dance through the clockwork mechanism, riding a wheel and then jumping off an escapement, choosing which direction to take, which part of the machine to explore? Irena too. She was in Vukovar by choice, fighting the fates.

Della Torre knew that from this moment his life would be determined by the American authorities, from breakfast to lights out. Where he would walk when he took exercise. How long he'd have to brush his teeth. Every word he read would be scrutinized, subversion excised. He would be living a wakeful coma for the rest of his life.

They drove through the imperial Hapsburg lower town, passing the pale mustard-coloured buildings with their crumbling art deco detailing and the rows of horse chestnuts along elegant boulevards reminiscent of Vienna.

They paused at the intersection under the railway line separating the old city from post war, socialist New Zagreb to the south. From there, they passed tower blocks separated by weed-filled lawns that some functionary had once imagined would become parks for the proletariat, but now merely served to isolate residents in concrete islands. They drove through settlements of bare concrete and red cinder-block houses that were finished only just enough to be habitable but would never be beautiful.

The white-on-blue road sign pointed them towards the airport. Perhaps the Americans had a private airplane. Even so, surely they would need to go through passport control. Della Torre didn't doubt that they had black diplomatic passports, rendering their holders immune to any civil authority in Croatia. But how would they get him through? Had they bribed people already?

Could this operation have been carried out without Horvat's blessing? The new republic needed friends, and it needed to be recognized. How much American goodwill would be bought by sacrificing della Torre?

The car slowed into congestion, though it wasn't rush hour. It wasn't unusual to find a farmer driving his horse and hay wagon along the highway, but as traffic came to a standstill, della Torre wondered if there had been an accident farther ahead. Yugoslav roads and Yugoslav drivers were a lethal mix.

They sat for a long time. No one spoke. The men on either side of him were young, athletic, clean-cut; they smelled of soap and deodorant. All they needed were suits and ties and they could be taken for Mormons or Wall Street bankers. The driver was older, his blond military crewcut easing into grey. The woman in the front shifted uneasily in her seat, looking out the side window.

The silence was broken by the sound of sirens. They could see police cars racing the wrong way along the other side of the road. And then after a while, traffic started moving again.

They came to a police roadblock. When they got to the front of the queue, the traffic cop ordered the driver of the Mercedes to pull over. Another pair of cops, armed with submachine guns, marched over. The driver got out of the car in a quick, smooth movement.

"Of course, you realize that since the U.S. doesn't recognize Croatia, your diplomatic status — if that's what you have — is with Yugoslavia, not the Republic of Croatia," della Torre said. "So the legal ground is slightly tricky. If you need a lawyer who knows a bit about this stuff, well, that'd be me, then."

"If you could just relax, sir, and keep quiet, sir, it'll all work out fine," said the man next to him.

They sat there for a long while until eventually the driver opened the rear doors and asked all the passengers to step out.

Della Torre was led away by one of the submachine-gun-toting policemen, across the wide grassy central median to a waiting unmarked Zastava facing back towards Zagreb. He got into the back. Next to Anzulović.

Della Torre was the first to speak. "Sorry I'm late for our meeting. I was held up."

"Never mind, Gringo, these things happen." Anzulović raised his fingers, making it clear that now wasn't the time for conversation.

They sat in silence as the driver switched on the sirens.

At Zagreb's main train station, Anzulović asked him to pull over. "We'll walk from here," he said.

They strolled through the trio of long green squares that made an elegant park running through the centre of the Hapsburg part of the city.

"How did you know?" della Torre asked.

Anzulović shrugged.

"Who was being taught a lesson? Me or the Americans?"

"Who do you think learned one?" Anzulović said.

"Both, I suppose."

Della Torre dug his hands in his pockets. It was all he could do to prevent himself from turning around to see if he was being followed. Anzulović walked as if he were taking his wife's piss-yellow poodle for a stroll.

"Well, thanks anyway," della Torre said. "Though maybe next time you can tell me when you're setting me up."

"Sure thing."

"Who organized it? Horvat?"

"Let's just say that right now we're both little cogs in facing wheels. The wheels turn and sometimes you shaft me and sometimes I shaft you."

"In other words, you don't know," della Torre said.

"It's a mystery. I just do as I'm told."

Della Torre's hand trembled slightly as he lit his cigarette. It had been a narrow miss. Had somebody set it up to be a narrow miss, to show him what would happen if he didn't help the Americans get Strumbić? He couldn't be sure.

The two men were about to step into their new offices, the modern building housing military intelligence, when della Torre felt a tap on the shoulder. He turned to look into the eyes of Jack Grimston, who had appeared from nowhere.

"Major della Torre," he said in that soft, slow way of his, "I was starting to think that maybe you'd decided to take the day off."

Della Torre smiled uneasily while Anzulović watched them both.

"Could you spare a moment for a private word? We can grab a coffee or something," Grimston said. "Unless caffeine makes you too jittery."

6

THEY WENT TO the café he'd gone to with Anzulović, near the flower square and by the statue of the unknown secret policeman.

"I have to apologize for that little production we put you through this morning," Grimston said.

"And you're here to tell me that next time you won't fail, so I'd better cooperate."

Grimston smiled and shook his head. "Oh, no, Major, that was not for your benefit. I'm sorry we gave you that misapprehension."

Della Torre eyed him skeptically. "Who was it for, then?"

"I'm afraid we had to find some way of letting your deputy minister know he has less control over affairs in this country than he chooses to believe."

"So you kidnapped me? But you failed. The police stopped you and released me."

"Only after we dropped a few heavy hints. You see, Major, your colleagues were meant to find you. That was the best way we could make it clear to them you'd gone missing."

Della Torre let the words sink in. The coffees arrived, an Americano for Grimston and a sweetened double espresso for della Torre, who downed it in one go, hardly tasting the rich black liquid. He lit a cigarette, neglecting to offer one to the other man.

"I think I see," he said. "You called Horvat and said, 'Why don't you put a roadblock on the way to the airport and have a look at big, expensive cars, because you might find a present in one of them.'"

"Something like that."

"And it took a while to get the message across, which is why your people gave me a tour of the suburbs."

Grimston laughed. "These things don't always go according to plan down to the second."

"But you haven't brought me here to apologize for wasting my morning." Della Torre inhaled deeply from the cigarette.

"No, sir. I've come to ask that you help us locate Mr. Strumbić."

"Your people asked me to help before. And it worked out badly. I'd have thought you might have learned by now."

"Are you saying you sabotaged the mission, Major?"

"No. Just that I brought bad luck."

"I don't believe it's a question of luck, sir. My unfortunate colleagues weren't really operating within their field of expertise. I am."

"Why are you so intent on Julius?"

"Major, I want justice for our people. I think Mr. Strumbić could put us on the right road."

"And if I'm disinclined?"

"Well, sir, a little birdie told us that you might be."

"Your little birdie was right. My recent experiences have put me off. But you're here to persuade me by telling me that you could snatch me and have me out of the country anytime you like."

"We assumed you'd be aware of that anyway. Mr. della Torre, I am here to appeal to your better sensibilities."

Della Torre shifted in his seat. He let his cigarette rest on the ashtray and ran his hands along his trouser legs. He knew that, whether he helped these people get to Strumbić or not, his fate was ordained. He too would be implicated in the deaths of the three American agents.

"I can enumerate a number of reasons why you might decide to change your mind. But I'll keep them to two. One, your father is growing older. And lonelier. To lose his wife at such a young age must have been a bitter blow. But I'm not sure any parent recovers from outliving his or her child."

Della Torre and his father had been left alone after his mother's death. When della Torre married Irena, his father was full of grandfatherly plans: to install a swimming pool in the big courtyard behind the Istrian farmhouse, to renovate the house so they could all live there year-round — Irena could work at the university at Rijeka and della Torre could set up a small legal practice. But over time those hopes had faded until they were forgotten. And all his father had left was Marko, a few old friends, and Libero, his retainer from when he'd been a boy.

"And then there's your wife and child."

Della Torre turned sharply to face the man. "You're mistaken."

"Oh, I see. You mean you and your wife are estranged."

"We have no children."

"Sorry, you're right. That's imprecision on my part. When's your wife due? In April, I believe, isn't it?"

"Due?" Della Torre struggled with the word.

"You seem surprised, Major," Grimston said. "You did know your wife was pregnant, didn't you?"

"How do you . . . What makes you think she's pregnant?"

"It's in her medical records. She had an ultrasound at the hospital where she works. I believe everything checked out fine. No need for an amniocentesis, and she's still young enough for Down's not to be a risk. She is slightly underweight, mostly from overwork, but, well, I guess the doctors are busy. Very difficult conditions in Vukovar."

Each fact reeled off by the American hammered at della Torre. It was impossible. Was it his child? Why had Irena told him nothing? He didn't know whether to feel joy or despair, loathing or gratitude. Were these people capable of gaining access to medical records at a hospital in a city under siege? It was a lie, designed to manipulate him; he was sure of it. And it was a lie that they knew he'd have difficulty checking. He'd been trying to call the hospital for weeks, with no luck. The most news he'd gotten was second-hand, as a favour from military intelligence's man in Vukovar, to say that Irena and the British doctor were fine, if exhausted, like everyone else there. He'd heard about plans for the hospital to be evacuated at long last.

"Of course, it would be imperative for your wife to leave the war zone," Grimston continued. "Shelling isn't particularly recommended for pregnant women. But it's hard to get in and out of Vukovar safely. Just as well there's a European Community medical convoy being negotiated. They're taking all the patients and medical staff out of the city. You'll be pleased to have her back . . . and her British doctor friend."

Grimston smiled. Della Torre lit another cigarette while the one he'd been smoking still burned in the ashtray, forgotten.

Grimston wanted della Torre to know that Irena was in play. And if Irena wasn't sufficient, then this putative child would be enough to sway him. Della Torre had worked as a secret policeman long enough to know how threads of emotion could be plucked until they resonated.

"Now, shall we discuss Mr. Strumbić?" Grimston asked quietly, almost gently, steering della Torre back to the present.

Della Torre nodded, using all his willpower, his training as a lawyer and as a commando all those years ago, to force his attention back to this man.

"We need your help to find Mr. Strumbić."

"Why?"

"Because Mr. Strumbić is very, very good at hiding."

"So how do you know he's in Dubrovnik?" della Torre asked.

Grimston unzipped a leather document case he'd been carrying and pulled out some photocopied pages. "A feature article on Dubrovnik was published in the British press." He passed the papers to della Torre.

But even in these difficult circumstances, life goes on. Indeed, for some, like Mr. Caesar, as he wishes to be referred to, the siege is proving a boon.

Mr. Caesar, who asked not to be identified, could be taken for an average middle-aged east European bureaucrat, which is what he had been in Zagreb under the Yugoslav government. Medium height, stocky, he usually has a lit cigarette in hand and likes a drink and a joke.

And as with many former Yugoslav civil servants, Mr. Caesar has a keen entrepreneurial streak — as long as it helps his personal situation. Where once he might have been amenable to inducements to help people get through administrative quagmires, he now supplies those in the besieged city with some of life's little luxuries — cigarettes, fuel, tinned anchovies, Scotch whisky, even tinned Iranian caviar or French foie gras — as well as necessities like toilet paper, toothpaste, baby food, and fresh water.

But, as he admits, he's no humanitarian. In exchange, he exacts a high price. He accepts payment in Deutschmarks and American dollars. Those paying in British pounds, Italian lira, or French francs are charged ten percent extra. "For exchange rate," he says.

"Maybe soon I take American Express," he says in heavily accented English.

He buys assayed gold and platinum at a stiff discount on global prices — he keeps up with the daily London gold fix. He accepts gemstones.

"I would not sell diamond ring to me, is not good price. But I not expert, maybe you sell me glass. So is for my protection too."

He relies on a local jeweller for advice, paying for it in cigarettes, which are becoming a common currency. But he's one of the few ready buyers for heirlooms, so he gets a steady supply.

It's not just goods he provides. There are rumours he's taken the deeds to a grand private house in the old town in exchange for getting the whole family out of Dubrovnik, but he laughs this off.

"Is not true," he says. "No one gives me Dubrovnik palace."

But when asked whether he could get somebody safely out of the city, he shrugs.

"Everything is possible. Everything," he says with a smile as he lights a Marlboro cigarette.

Della Torre looked at the byline. The story had been written by Steve Higgins, a Canadian journalist he and Strumbić had met over the summer and grown to like. Higgins was one of the few Westerners covering the war from inside Dubrovnik. Della Torre looked back through the description. *Asked not to be identified?* Had Higgins been Dürer, he couldn't have etched a more precise portrait.

Della Torre looked up at Grimston, who smiled back at him.

"Could be anyone," della Torre said.

Grimston laughed. "This article about Mr. Caesar gave us the initial tipoff that Mr. Strumbić — Julius — is in Dubrovnik."

Della Torre looked at the date at the top of the page. The article had been published three days before his meeting with the Americans at the UDBA safe house.

"We've had several confirmations since then," Grimston said.

"So if you know where he is, why do you need me?"

"Major della Torre, Dubrovnik's population is fairly

substantial, especially with all the refugees in town. Mr. Strumbić might be busy, but he's stayed low-key. We don't know where he's living or how to get in touch with him. And with the city under siege, it's hard to get in enough people to do a proper search, never mind getting them out again. You might appreciate that we can't be seen to be involved in another country's civil conflict. Which also restricts the amount of manpower we'd be able to apply to the situation. The local police, meanwhile, have their hands full with other matters so they can't devote the time to our search." Grimston spoke methodically, as if running through the main points of a lecture. "We know Mr. Strumbić made an effort to contact you not long ago. So it isn't far-fetched to think he would be willing to see you if you appeared in Dubrovnik." He paused, allowing the information to sink in.

"We find ourselves needing help," Grimston continued. "Frankly, Major, our official position is that Croatia ought to stay part of Yugoslavia. But we do want to see justice served. If you were to aid us, the American government would show you considerable gratitude. You and your family. And your country. That is not an empty promise. We are not vulnerable or incapable. But we are looking for a friend. By the same token, Major, if our request falls on deaf ears, we will take note of that. And you would also do well to remember, sir, that our god — because we are a godly people — is an Old Testament god."

"If your god can't get you people into Dubrovnik, how do you expect me to get there?"

"A humanitarian mission called Libertas is being assembled in Rijeka. We're not sure quite when the fleet of ships is expected to sail to Dubrovnik. Negotiations with the Yugoslav navy are underway. But when it does set off, we'll have a few people on board. And we'd like you to join them."

Della Torre nodded.

"I am certain you'll do the right thing, Major, that you'll afford us your help," Grimston said. "Only don't take too long to think about it."

Whether it was the constant stress he'd been suffering; the anxiety of uncertainty; having been shot at, wounded, tortured; or just Grimston's smug, supercilious certainty — whatever the cause, something primitive rose through della Torre, took over his thoughts. He'd paid and paid again for stealing the Pilgrim file: something that had been worth no more than a couple of cartons of cigarettes had cost him a bullet in the elbow, had left him flinching from shadows, had brought him to the point of death at the hands of the Americans, who'd been desperately seeking from him the name of their betrayer before they themselves were killed. And now this man, thinking of himself as an avenging angel, had come, full of certainty, into a country where agnosticism and ambiguity were the only truths. Della Torre's expression tightened into one of ugly fury. It was all he could do to control his voice.

"Mr. Grimston, your people tried to make me an accomplice in an execution. I won't do that again. And not just because they failed miserably — and yes, Mr. Grimston, that's what happened. They failed. In all the years UDBA ran its wetworks program, there never was a disaster like yours. Sometimes agents didn't meet their objective and sometimes they made a bloody mess of it, but we never had an entire team wiped out during an operation." He paused for a second, realizing he'd never before spoken of UDBA as *we.* "At most an operative was arrested. But we never experienced this sort of catastrophe. What bothers me, though, is that you seem to think that because you're in a barbaric country, you can do what you like. That the rule of law, ours or yours, doesn't apply here. You decide what's convenient for you, for whatever reason, and you pursue it however you want. I'm not going to be party to this, Mr. Grimston."

Grimston watched him. Then he said, "Major, I think you suffer from a misapprehension. I belong to a different organization from the people you dealt with before — Mr. Dawes, Rebecca, and her team. You are right to believe they overestimated their abilities. Their work tends to be intelligence, generally with low-level active participation. Easy jobs. I think they had an incorrect impression of the situation here, and of you in particular. Please be assured, Major, that you are now dealing with people who know what they're doing. Whether you help or not, we will get to Mr. Strumbić. It might take a little longer — and, for reasons I'm not going to share with you, we'd rather accomplish our mission sooner. But a delay wouldn't be a disaster. It might be worth your while to see your father sometime soon, Major. You don't have much family left, and sometimes memories are worth preserving. And then maybe we can have this discussion again."

Grimston looked at the bill clipped to a small aluminum plate and replaced it with a substantial note. It was enough to pay for both coffees three times over. He left without looking back.

Della Torre sat back and smoked another cigarette as the waitress collected the money.

"Anything else?" she asked.

"Another coffee," he said. "And then keep the change."

THE LONGER DELLA Torre thought about his conversation with Grimston, the more convinced he was that the only right thing to do was ensure that Strumbić stayed hidden and beyond the reach of Grimston's brand of self-certain American justice. The irony didn't escape him. He was committing to protecting the most corrupt, venal, duplicitous person he'd ever known. But Strumbić was also innocent.

The knowledge that Irena would soon be leaving Vukovar, would be safe from that particular hell, helped with his resolve. He'd find a means of getting to Dubrovnik and find Strumbić and do the one thing he knew was right. He'd come back to her with his conscience less tarnished, his ability to face the future less equivocal. He knew Grimston had lied about the pregnancy, but there would be time for that too — to have the family he'd too long refused her.

When he returned to the office, della Torre gave Anzulović a brief summary of his conversation with the American and told him what he'd decided to do.

"The only way in is to run the blockade," Anzulović said at long last.

"If I can find someone to take me," della Torre said. "I've got a cousin. He was both regular and merchant navy. He's mostly retired."

"How old?"

"Bit over fifty. Those sailors retire young. Feather their nests with some unofficial importing and then they settle down to a life of fishing. Or, in the case of my cousin, making wine."

"So not too old to get you to Dubrovnik."

Della Torre shook his head. "I wasn't thinking he'd get me there. He's not going to risk his neck for me. But he might know someone who will."

They were in della Torre's office. He knew he was being indiscreet, telling Anzulović these things, but fatalism had descended on him. One way or another the Americans would find out about his plan.

"Fuck," della Torre shouted, jumping out of his chair a moment before Anzulović. "Fuck."

Everything they'd been discussing evaporated at the sound of screaming jet engines. Three, four, a dozen, maybe more. The air raid sirens sounded, but it was too late. Windows flexed under the impact of shockwaves as explosions rocked the old town on the hill a couple of hundred metres to the north.

"Get the fuck out of here!" Anzulović shouted.

The building's evacuation plans were widely ignored. A small crowd had formed around the elevators, pounding on the buttons, even though only one of the three worked. Della Torre and Anzulović took the stairs, joining the flow of people out of the building. A few tried to push their way down, triggering arguments, slowing the progress even further.

They spilled out of the building into the street, stumbling over each other, the ululations of the air raid alarms feeding their terror. Everyone was in a state of shock. Some were subdued; others were crying. A chemical smell of burning and of dust was in the air. Smoke was rising from the city's medieval heart and from the suburban slopes beyond.

Vapour trails scarred the late afternoon sky, and the sudden sight of a pair of jets sent everyone fleeing for the shelter of doorways and carriage arches in the Hapsburg apartment blocks, and then streaming into the bomb shelters.

As the screaming of machines overhead faded into a long, low mewling of police and ambulance sirens, it was hard to believe the attack had lasted no more than twenty minutes. Della Torre and Anzulović had been separated in the panic; by the time they finally made their way back to the office and found each other, it was early evening.

After calling his wife to assure her he wasn't hurt, Anzulović went back to della Torre's place. It was closer to the office than his own apartment was; he lived in the modern suburbs to the south. They ate fried eggs and cured ham, the only things in della Torre's fridge that were still fit for consumption.

"She took it stoically," Anzulović said, holding a nightcap of slivovitz.

"The attack?"

"That I survived. Dog'll be disappointed, though."

"I thought the dog's great pleasure in life was pissing on your leg."

"It would probably prefer my gravestone," Anzulović said. He knocked back the slivovitz and poured himself another. "Not bad. Your dad's?"

"Yes."

"American government has told all its citizens to evacuate." Anzulović lit a cigarette. His eyes were bloodshot and his skin yellow in the light of the naked bulb high overhead.

Della Torre yawned. "It'll take a lot more than a couple of bombs to scare away Mr. Grimston."

The attack had involved at least two dozen Yugoslav fighters, but most of the damage was confined to the old town palace, occupied by the Croatian leadership. Only one death was reported, not far from the UDBA safe house in the northern suburbs. Horvat had come to the office to rage at his intelligence department for its failure to give the government an early warning. The raid had hit the palace right at the end of a session of cabinet. It was a miracle none of the administration had been killed or seriously injured.

"No, but the general confusion won't make their lives any easier," Anzulović said. "Which should make it a good time for you to make yourself scarce."

"Horvat's going to go berserk. I doubt he'll be too happy if I disappear just now."

"How much real work have you been given over the past month? Do you think that's going to change?" Weariness slowed Anzulović's speech to the cadence of a rumbling freight train. "He doesn't know what to do with you. He still wants the Americans on his side. He knows they want your cooperation. We'll tell him that's what they're getting. By the time he's disabused of that notion, well, we'll figure something out."

After della Torre got Anzulović settled in the spare room, he sat with the bottle of slivovitz, exhausted but unable to sleep. He picked up the phone and dialled the number he'd been trying for the past few weeks. It rang without answer. He put the receiver back onto its cradle. And then, as an afterthought, he rang his father, knowing it was far too late, but also knowing that the old man had slipped into a stage of life in which time had become elastic. But there was no answer from him either.

They woke early, Anzulović looking no better for his short sleep, while della Torre felt worse.

"We'll need a car," Anzulović said, lighting a cigarette to accompany his breakfast of sweet black coffee.

"We?"

"Thought you might like some company."

"Horvat will love that."

Anzulović sighed. "Horvat is in so much shit with the leadership, we can ignore him for now," he said. As deputy defence minister in charge of military intelligence, Horvat would take the blame for the department's failure to anticipate the previous morning's attack. "The rumour is there's a good chance he'll be replaced by the time we get back. But I'm on special projects anyway, and will be until the order's rescinded. So, within reason, I can come and go as I please."

"Special projects?" This was the first della Torre had heard of it.

"Don't get too excited. It's just rubbish they can't fob off on anyone else," Anzulović said, with a finality della Torre knew would be useless to challenge.

They walked to the central pound that held cars confiscated by the Zagreb authorities; access to it was bickered over by the various branches of government. But they needed a car — Della Torre's was sitting dead in his father's barn and Anzulović's Zastava reliably broke down on hairpin bends, next to precipices, on narrow streets, and wherever else it was most inconvenient. He mostly left it to his wife.

"Let's see what sort of shit they serve us up with," Anzulović said. "The guys doing the admin somehow end up with BMWs and Mercedes, while their clunkers are left to us."

Della Torre shrugged. "At least it'll be something with wheels and an engine. If we're lucky it might even run."

The pound was on derelict fenced-in ground to the south of the railway line, not far from the central bus station. Anzulović was right: most of the cars they could see were Zastavas or Yugos, with a few Renault 4s. But one in a far corner of the lot caught della Torre's eye. "I think I might like that Citroën."

"Ah, the DS. The gentleman is discerning," Anzulović said. "That car always makes me think of Catherine Deneuve. She's almost as beautiful as Grace Kelly, especially in *Mississippi Mermaid*. Wonderful film . . ."

As they approached, della Torre could see the car was a beauty. It was at least twenty-five years old, burgundy with leather seats. Della Torre walked into the office while Anzulović loitered outside.

"I'd like to sign for the Citroën," della Torre said.

"Oh, I'm sorry, sir, but that car is spoken for," said the non-commissioned officer at the desk.

"By whom?"

"Well, you know how it is. I haven't got the paperwork. I'm sure it'll turn up. But I remember it was a big cheese. A colonel, high up in government, specifically set aside that car. He was due to collect it yesterday, but I guess in all the excitement . . ." The man shrugged indolently.

Anzulović made an ostentatious entrance.

"Sorry, Minister," della Torre said, turning to him. "Fellow here says the French car isn't available."

"Minister?" The man sat up.

"Yes, General Horvat. Minister of state security. Department names change all the time. Internally we just refer it as UDBA," della Torre said. "We really would like to see the paperwork. There's so much corruption about these days, sometimes we like to do spot checks. Impromptu investigations, if you like, to keep people on their toes. I find if you give them too much notice, they sort of tidy things up too much to find anything."

The man turned a shade paler. "I'm sorry, sir, I — I'd have to speak to my superior. I don't know . . . I mean, the paperwork is around somewhere, I'm sure," the man said nervously, glancing from della Torre to Anzulović and back. Both were in business suits. He was afraid of being conned but didn't want to run the risk that they were telling the truth. Even the lowest bureaucrat could dig in his heels out of stubbornness, but not against the UDBA. And in the army things were different still.

"Sorry, sir, since you — I mean, you mention doing things in the proper . . . I'd need to see your identification. Just as a formality," the man said.

Della Torre pulled out his military ID card.

"Major, ah, yes. Major della Torre," the man said. "Military intelligence." The rank was certainly high enough to be a minister general's aide-de-camp. And "military intelligence" sounded like it might well be UDBA's replacement. He looked at Anzulović as if building up the nerve to ask for his documents as well.

But his uncertainty showed, and Anzulović went on the attack. "Now, are you going to give us the car or am I going to have to call your superiors?" he said, impatient and irritated. The previous long night, lack of sleep, and incipient hangover meant he didn't have much acting to do.

"Yes, sir, Minister General. I mean, beg pardon. Only . . . I'll have to explain it to the colonel. I'm sure he'll understand, if you wouldn't mind signing the paperwork. I'll get the keys."

Della Torre smiled and signed the forms.

"We'll be sure to let your officers know how cooperative you've been," he said as the man passed over the keys and temporary registration forms.

"Your driver. I mean, he'll want to have the, umm, you know, the manuals and forms. They're in the glove compartment. Lovely car," the man said forlornly. "Lovely car."

Della Torre and Anzulović stepped out of the office and tried not to laugh as they made their way to the Citroën.

"Think there was a colonel?" della Torre said.

"Why not?" Anzulović replied.

Della Torre drove the car out of the yard. The man at the gate took a long minute looking over the documentation before letting them go.

"Well done, General Minister," della Torre said once they were on the road.

The Citroën was low-slung. The seats were leather, faded from the sun but otherwise in good, supple condition. Della Torre tested the hydraulics, raising and lowering the car. It felt like a small, luxurious boat, taking ruts and tram tracks with an easy sway.

Anzulović grinned. For a second his tiredness lifted.

But beyond the car's confines there was confusion. The roads heading out to the highway were busy while the ones coming into Zagreb were sparsely travelled, a sort of inverted rush hour for that time of morning. Pedestrians walked briskly, keeping their eyes to the sky.

Della Torre turned on the radio to catch a news bulletin. There was plenty about the air raids, but nothing more than he and Anzulović already knew. Afterwards came a short broadcast from the Croatian reporter Siniša Glavašević, who was posted in Vukovar, offering sympathy to Zagreb. His impassioned report on the conditions in Vukovar filled della Torre with dread. And now that Zagreb had had a small taste of the war, it overwhelmed him to think of the conditions that Irena and the British doctor had been enduring. "The last time the world saw something like what Vukovar is suffering was during the siege of Stalingrad," Glavašević said. "Please don't forget us."

8

DELLA TORRE TOOK Anzulović home to his "proletarian paradise," as he called it, before heading back to his own apartment to pack. He drove along the road under the spreading chestnut trees that lined the Hapsburg block and made his way into the building's terrazzo lobby, his footsteps echoing up the hallway.

The apartment was gloomy. He seldom bothered to open the external blinds, except the ones that shut off the kitchen from the small terrace. Irena had refused to live there. To her, it was filled with the ghosts of the dispossessed. Its high, narrow rooms, furnished in a heavy Mitteleuropean style, were filled with shadows.

He dug his official Beretta from the dirty-clothes hamper. He checked the chamber to make sure it was empty, slid out the magazine, and popped a box of bullets into his bag. Just in case.

He tried the hospital in Vukovar again, failed again. No one was at his father's place either. Finally he left a message with the nautical cousin.

He stepped back into the stairwell and locked the door behind him. He wondered whether he'd miss the place if he never came back.

He drove south to the stark tower blocks of the city's modern suburb.

Anzulović must have been sitting at a window waiting for him, because he got down to the front of the dirty concrete building before della Torre had parked the car.

"First time ever I haven't had to wait for the lift. Seems everyone's fucked off to the country," Anzulović said.

"What about your family?"

"Wife, one of my daughters, and the dog are going to the cottage, for as long as they can bear being more than a couple of tram stops from the shops. But they're waiting for tonight. By then the traffic will have dispersed a bit. Give them a chance to break down in the dark."

"Exodus."

"Well, let's go, Moses. At least in Istria the air's good and the wine's better," Anzulović said. "If nothing else, we'll chalk it up to a holiday."

The Citroën was a pleasure to drive, a dash of French elegance. Traffic heading out of town crawled, even though it was just after midday. Zastava roofs were stacked with mattresses and cupboards. Buses and taxis were full to capacity. But once they made it out of the city, the slow pace didn't seem to matter so much. Beech leaves had turned colour and the skies were overcast; fine drizzles came and went, but that only softened the scenery.

They made slightly better progress on the highway through the Sava plain down to Karlovac, where there were a number of military checkpoints. Breakaway Serbs supported by the Yugoslav National Army, the JNA, had taken vast swathes of Croat territory, moving to within a few kilometres of the main road that joined Zagreb and the hinterland to the coast.

Della Torre skirted the area, taking small roads through the hills to the Slovene border, but he didn't cross to the other side.

The roads wound through narrow valleys, and it didn't take

much to slow them to a crawl. Della Torre and Anzulović encountered a tractor-pulled wagon piled high with logs for the winter. Elsewhere, two cars had stopped side by side, blocking traffic in both directions while their drivers chatted. Farther still, where the roads fed back towards the highway, more police roadblocks were set up.

As they drew towards the pass in the chain of mountains that separated inland Croatia from the coast, broadleaf trees gave way to achingly tall pines with moss and lichen strung between their branches. Rolling hills collapsed into steep valleys. The drizzle had stopped, and wisps of fog bent and folded slowly in the air.

They had been on the road for the better part of three hours. It was afternoon now, and della Torre was hungry. They stopped for lunch at the roadside restaurant where della Torre's father had always broken the drive from Zagreb to Istria.

The restaurant was almost empty — no one was spending money, the proprietor said. Della Torre and Anzulović sat on benches at a rough table covered in stained oilcloth and drank watered-down wine. The food was good — pork kebabs grilled over an open fire, with fluffy flatbread soaked in the meat juices, chopped raw onions, and a homemade roasted red pepper and eggplant relish.

They didn't linger. Back on the road, they were held back by trucks grinding their way through the gears as other drivers passed on blind corners and through patches of fog.

"I sometimes wonder if Yugoslavs drive like that to make Italians look cautious," della Torre said.

"Italians are amateurs," Anzulović replied. "Our cars don't have brakes, and the passenger compartments are designed to crumple. Saves on hospital costs."

The landscape became more scrubby, white rocks showing through the earth like the fallen teeth of ancient giants. They crossed the watershed dividing the broad Danube basin from the narrow coastal strip. There the skies opened to a broad vista, and in the distance they saw a glint of the blue Adriatic Sea.

They skirted the port town of Rijeka, a narrow stretch of dock and tower blocks clinging to the hillside. Eighty years before, the city had been the subject of a dramatic nationalist gesture by a mad poet. Outraged by the fact that this once-Italian city had been handed over to the new Kingdom of Yugoslavia in a post-war redrawing of boundaries, Gabriele d'Annunzio had invaded Rijeka in 1919 with a modest band of idealists called the Fascisti, among whom was a great-uncle of della Torre's. D'Annunzio held the city for four years, in the face of international outrage. The Free State of Fiume, he called it. Now only a few historians remembered that this was the birthplace of fascism. Twenty years after the seizure of Rijeka, Tito's Partizans fought the German and Italian fascists from the mountains that della Torre and Anzulović had just passed through. The Partizans brought their own inflexible ideology: Communism. Now the region was again in the throes of nationalism. It was like a pendulum swinging from one extreme to another, cleaving innocent heads with each pass.

Rijeka was at the northern end of a deep bay; the southeastern shore became the Dalmatian littoral, while the southwestern coastline, the one they followed, formed one edge of the Istrian peninsula, once one of Venice's wealthiest provinces.

They drove past the imperial Austro-Hungarian resort town of Opatija, where, as a small boy and scion of a soon-to-be-obliterated nobility, Vladimir Nabokov had bathed. The road rose high along the cliffs past the fortress village of Mošćenice, from which they could see the stony white and green islands Cres and Krk fading into the distance.

Della Torre turned inland and drove through the verdant plains of central Istria. They passed row upon row of vines, leaves falling onto earth so rich with iron oxides that it looked like living flesh, skinned, scored, and damp with blood. White oxen with great wide horns, high-backed and as pale as the stone that broke through this earth, stood melancholy, their Slavic eyes watching them pass.

Stands of tall bamboo stood as windbreaks at the edges of hamlets, while every hill seemed to be crowned with a village marked with the virginal campanile of a church, an accusing finger pointing towards God, built by people terrorized by pirates five centuries earlier and bled by the Venetians for even longer before.

It was early evening when they finally arrived.

Della Torre followed a gently curving road, recently asphalted and without markings, through yet more vineyards, peach orchards, and copses until they saw on a small rise a white stone house with a red-tiled roof, its lower storeys obscured by a series of outbuildings that formed a broad courtyard.

"Home," della Torre said.

He stopped at a tall iron gate. It wasn't locked, so he swung it open and then drove into the grounds, pulling into an open-sided garage next to his Yugo, which had broken down during his last trip here and was apparently still unrepaired.

Anzulović got out and stretched, taking in the faint smell of sour wine, of engine oil from an old tractor, of a distant wood fire and the rich earth. The courtyard was broad and paved with smooth white Istrian stone. The house was built from the same white blocks. A vast pair of arched doors led to the massive ground-floor wine cellar, while the living quarters started at the top of a flight of steps, worn smooth like soap, that ended at a broad terrace overhung with a canopy of vines supported by stone columns and wrought-iron bars.

Della Torre climbed the stairs and knocked on the door.

"Dad?" he called in English. He usually spoke to the old man in English, an artifact of his American youth, though of late it was increasingly interspersed with Serbo-Croat. Sometimes they reverted to Italian for a change, his father reciting the great poets to him in all three languages, translating as he went.

The old man wasn't in. Della Torre unlocked the door with his key. Anzulović followed him in. The house was shuttered. His father really only lived in three rooms: his bedroom, his study, and the kitchen. The rest of the big house had been given over to memories and ghosts.

Della Torre opened shutters as he passed, showing Anzulović to a slightly dusty guest room farther down the hall.

"It's like this to keep asthmatics at bay," della Torre said by way of apology.

"As long as there isn't a piss-yellow dog crapping in my shoes, I'll be all right," Anzulović said.

After he'd organized their rooms, della Torre went into the cellar and tapped a barrel to fill a tall metal pitcher with his father's wine. He set it on the table on the terrace under the vines, together with cured ham he'd found hanging in the cellar's back room, cheese from the pantry, and what bread he could find.

The house had been built by a branch of the della Torre family two centuries before, on land owned by the della Torres since around the fifteenth century. His father had bought the house from the estate of a spinster cousin who'd let it slowly crumble around her. No one in the family had wanted the ruin. Della Torre and his father had restored it themselves, though once again it was settling gently into dilapidation.

He was telling Anzulović about the history of the house when a small new Mercedes saloon pulled in.

Della Torre went down to the car and brought back a good-looking middle-aged man with a broad smile and a military haircut.

"My cousin Angelo Brnobić," he said, introducing the two men.

Brnobić was equipped with a square briefcase of worn black patent leather. His hand was broad, a farmer's hand.

"Had you arrived earlier, you could have gone to the funeral," Brnobić said as he accepted a glass of wine.

"Funeral? Who died?"

"Haven't you heard?" Brnobić said. "Libero. Your father's with old Piero at the wake."

Piero Brnobić was Angelo's uncle, a retired priest who shared not only his Christian name with della Torre's father but also the occasional glass of wine, or six, as they philosophized and argued late into the lonely evenings.

"I only made an appearance at the service. Just enough to be civil. If you wanted to, you could spend three-quarters of your life toasting the dead around here. It's all old people these days."

"What happened?" della Torre said, shocked at the news.

"He went to bed and didn't wake up in the morning. You wouldn't believe it, but he was over eighty. Fit and working one day — he was here helping your father prune the vines — next morning, well, looks like he was pruned himself. Doctor said old age, but . . ." He paused.

"But what?"

"It just seemed strange." Brnobić shrugged. "Ask your father when he gets back. He'll tell you. I just got it second-hand from him, and I'll probably muddle what he told me."

Brnobić wasn't to be drawn out, so della Torre left it, though an uneasiness accompanied his sadness. Libero had long been more than just his father's workman. He'd been a welcome, if taciturn, daily companion.

"You know, I never realized how old he was," della Torre said.

"Funnily enough, everyone's been saying how young he died," Angelo said, and then, turning to Anzulović: "We're long-lived, us Istrians. People say it's because we don't like to give up anything easily, our land or our money or our lives."

"I guess you got my message," della Torre said. "Did you mention to Dad I was coming up? I couldn't get through to him."

"I didn't. The church was crowded and afterwards I slipped away. I didn't feel like going to the graveyard and then getting dragged off. I'm trying to lay off the booze. My liver's acting up."

"I'm sorry," Anzulović said to della Torre. "Do you want to go to the wake? I'd be happy to stay here."

"No," della Torre said, shaking his head. "It would be awkward. Too many people I only half-remember, reminiscing about someone who I hardly really knew. When Libero and I talked, it was about vines or making wine or tractor engines. Mostly he liked to keep his counsel. Libero wasn't what you would call a garrulous man. Though I remember one time, we'd been working late, and he said, 'They tell me people have been up there, walked on the moon.' When I confirmed it, explaining all about rockets and how long it took and basic physics, he just stood there shaking his head, as if I'd gone mad along with the rest of them."

"That was Libero, through and through," Brnobić said. "Had a hell of a war, though, not that you'd ever hear it from him. Italians tried to kill him, Germans tried to kill him, and then at the end the Communists gave it a go too. Still not sure how he survived, though he was as tough as they came. Speaking of war, it seems the Yugoslav air force finally took an interest in Zagreb."

Anzulović gave him a rundown of the modest physical damage but deep psychological wound the capital had suffered from the bombing.

"Right. If I were a proper Balkan we would sit here and chat into the evening before we got around to business. But for Istrians, time is money. Even when it's not," Brnobić said. "You wanted to know how to get through the blockade to Dubrovnik."

Della Torre poured him some of the strong yellow wine his father made.

Brnobić held up his hand. "I have brought with me charts and my brain. If I drink any more, the charts will still be here, but not the brain."

Della Torre cleared the table and Brnobić spread a water-proof chart of Dubrovnik and the islands on it. And then, using a grease pencil, he traced a circle around the city on the landward side.

"After you telephoned yesterday, I took the liberty of calling some friends down in Pula," he said. "The situation at the navy base there is confused, to say the least. It's still held by the Yugoslav forces. Plenty of Croat officers are waiting to step over to our side, but even the ones who aren't are being marginalized by the command structure. That's not to say they don't know what's going on, though their responsibilities are being stripped away. But they still hear things." He pointed on the map to the area south of Dubrovnik. "Here we have the JNA land forces. They have taken the territory up to Cavtat, and I think that'll also go before long. A week, maximum. In the north they've cut off the Dubrovnik littoral from the rest of Dalmatia here, just below the Pelješac peninsula, though they haven't taken the peninsula yet. Inland they've taken Mount Srđ, so they're effectively right on top of the city. They've mostly been shelling the suburbs and villages farther north and south. There's not a lot our people can do to defend against artillery that close and on such favourable ground. But it means there's no way of getting into the city from the landward side. There have always been smugglers' routes — goat tracks and stuff— through the mountains, but the Serbs are pretty densely packed on the other side, so it'll be hard to sneak through, not to mention the risk of being shot by somebody on our side once you've managed to get through all that enemy territory. Not that I believe their numbers, but our press is full of stories that the Serbs have got thirty or forty thousand men back there, just like theirs says we've got thirty thousand mercenaries in Dubrovnik."

Anzulović shook his head, disbelieving. "The propagandists have been busy. We've got between five and eight hundred defenders, depending on whether you think they need to be armed to count. Mostly police and volunteers. Best guess is that the Serbs have somewhere around ten thousand, three-quarters of them regular troops and the rest militia and Chetniks."

The conflict had started with the Croats' desire to break the Yugoslav yoke. But the desire for self-determination soon gave way to a virulent nationalism. Croats had resurrected the red and white checkerboard shield that had been the most dearly held symbol of their fascist predecessors, who'd allied with the Nazis and ruled in those dark years with a thirst for Serb and Jewish blood. And for their part, the Serb nationalists had renamed themselves after the Chetniks, who'd started the war fighting against the Nazis and finished up fighting for them against the Partizans, perpetrating their own atrocities along the way. Tito had bound them all into one happy family by being equally ruthless in wiping out Chetniks and Croat nationalists.

Brnobić nodded. "I figured it must be something like that."

"The numbers don't matter as much as the fact that the JNA and the Chetniks got plenty of heavy artillery, as well as wire-guided rockets, not to mention jets and naval guns," Anzulović continued. "They don't seem to be coordinating terribly well between the various branches. The navy takes the occasional potshot, and so far there hasn't been much bombing. Mostly it's field guns from high ground doing the damage. But that's not to say the navy is dozing. They've raised a very effective cordon."

Brnobić now drew some circles on the blue parts of the map. "This is where the Yugoslav navy is concentrating its ships to make sure no one gets in or out. You get a few very fast pleasure boats, including a couple of Italian smuggling boats, running the blockade. They go all out at fifty knots, in groups of two and three. Twenty to twenty-five boats in all, taking supplies back to Dubrovnik. Water, food, medicine. A few arms. They were pretty successful until recently. But then the Yugoslav navy figured out our tactics and started sinking the fast boats with infrared-guided fire. So now our heroic blockade breakers are having to do some rethinking."

"What does that mean?"

Brnobić shrugged. "The blockade running is being put on hold. There's talk the navy's got submarines in the area — the big pens aren't far away — and are laying mines. They've sent out Wasp-class missile boats and guided-missile boats. Even the most foolhardy of our people have been scared off. One or two smuggling boats still operate, but they go south into enemy territory. We figure they've rigged up some deal with the naval commanders, who turn a blind eye to backhanders as long as military supplies and people aren't being transported. One or two speculators with connections to the Montenegrin smugglers are said to be making a killing in Dubrovnik. If you'll pardon the expression."

Della Torre thought about the newspaper article Grimston had shown him. "So the best way into Dubrovnik is to go down to Montenegro and hire one of the smugglers," he said.

Brnobić shook his head. "I wouldn't want to be caught wandering dockside in Herceg Novi, asking around for somebody who could sneak me into Dubrovnik, unless I wanted an abbreviated life expectancy. The only half-possible way is the convoy that's being put together in Rijeka. European Union humanitarians, film crews, and some of our own worthies. You could take that, though I don't know how long it'll take them to put it together."

The convoy Grimston had mentioned. The Americans would be on it.

"That's it?"

Brnobić shrugged. "You could try your luck and see if you could find a fast boat with a good skipper who's got brass balls. The run from Dubrovnik usually takes them to Korčula, the nearest big port with access to the wider world." He pointed to an island a little more than a hundred kilometres northwest of Dubrovnik. "You can still get there, though even that trip is becoming more difficult. The ferries have been targeted, so their skippers are pretty nervous. If nothing else turns up, the humanitarian convoy will pass through. You should be able to hitch a ride." He gave an apologetic shrug and rolled up his charts.

"Guess we'll have to make our way down to Korčula and try our luck from there," Anzulović said.

"The coast road in that area is pretty uncomfortable these days as well," Brnobić said. "Serbs have been shelling the route around Zadar, virtually cutting the Croatian coast in two. Meanwhile the Yugoslav navy is harassing the ferries that are keeping out of field-gun range. No one is flying. The Yugoslav air force has taken to downing anything in Croat airspace —"

Brnobić was cut off by the sound of a car pulling into the courtyard.

PIERO DELLA TORRE was slightly unsteady on his feet. His eyes were bloodshot, and he was a little more stooped and aged than his son remembered. Della Torre thanked the stars his father never drove faster than thirty kilometres an hour, and that the service and wake had been only a quarter of an hour's drive away on quiet country roads.

It was unfair catching the old man off guard like that, but Piero composed himself, didn't slur his words, and was gracious about the intrusion after his son gave him an arm to steady his walk up the stairs to the vine-covered terrace where the others sat.

The sun had dropped below the treeline. Della Torre had switched on the outdoor lights, drawing the early evening moths. Where Zagreb had already tilted towards winter, here, just inland from the Adriatic, the evening air was a nostalgic memory of summer.

Among the pleasantries, the elder della Torre told them a little about the day, about the funeral and the wake, but his narrative was dishevelled, his thoughts tired, unsteady. Della Torre could see Anzulović's professional, clinical appraisal of his father under the veneer of sympathy. He was always the detective, always weighing the evidence and its source, and wondering about the uneasiness with which the old man glanced at his son.

Della Torre knew better than to ask too many questions about Libero's death. That would need to wait for breakfast. Piero excused himself after taking a small glass of white wine, and Marko accompanied his father up to his bedroom, where the older man said he was going for a little solitary contemplation and apologized for leaving his guests to fend for themselves.

When della Torre came back down, Brnobić also said he needed to be off. Della Torre left Anzulović on his own and walked his cousin back to the Mercedes.

"Thanks for coming," della Torre said.

"I'm sorry I couldn't be of more help. It's a good thing you came. Your father could probably use your company for a day or two. Libero's death came as a shock. It leaves him rather alone. It'll be hard to find anyone to replace Libero. He was a friend to your father, in his own odd way. I guess it's also a reminder of our own mortality."

"Yes," della Torre said. "What was it that my father said to you about Libero's death?"

"Nothing," Brnobić said, wary. "Or something that didn't make much sense. Ask him tomorrow. Get it out of him gently. He's a little confused, and the . . . well, I'd just muddy things if I tried to tell you what I thought he was trying to say."

Della Torre cloaked his disappointment but again decided not to press the issue.

Brnobić, in turn, seemed uncomfortable at withholding whatever it was he didn't want to say. "Listen, I had a little thought about one way of breaking the blockade," he said.

"Oh." Della Torre was suddenly all attention.

"Don't get your hopes up." Brnobić laughed. "It's a fantastically impractical solution. I wouldn't do it myself or recommend it, but it is possible."

"What's that?"

"You can sail to Dubrovnik."

"Sail?" Della Torre laughed, incredulous. "What, in a yacht?"

"No, not a yacht. A little boat — a dinghy, up to around five or six metres; more than that and it becomes risky if you've got a still night with a full moon. And only for the last few kilometres. You'd have to do it at night, which makes the sailing particularly tricky, dangerous even. You might even have to swim the last hundred metres or so."

"You don't think the Yugoslav navy would notice?"

"No, not at night. It would be incredibly hard for them to discover a dinghy unless you sailed right into them."

"What about radar and sonar and all those things?"

"Even the best radar can't distinguish a small sailboat from a wave. A dinghy's radar profile is tiny, all but invisible. Even fishing boats don't show that well if the seas are up. But anyway, the navy mostly relies on infrared surveillance cameras and sound for nighttime tracking of surface traffic. The acoustic tracking is particularly sensitive to engine noise. That's what it's tuned to. It's so good that even the quietest engine being run very slowly will provide enough of a signal for the weapons systems to target. That's how they've been sinking the fast blockade breakers. The infrared cameras pick up engine heat and exhaust. A couple of well-covered bodies in a sailing boat look no bigger than a pair of gulls.

"You're pulling my leg."

"Like I said, I wouldn't try it myself. But it's the only possibility I can think of. Sometimes low tech outperforms high tech in the most surprising ways. A mechanical pencil and a sheet of paper are still more useful to me when I want to do a quick engineering drawing than the best computer I've ever used. Though that's probably because I'm old."

"Why stop at a dinghy? What's wrong with a pedal boat?" della Torre said.

Brnobić laughed. "The reason I mention it is because there's a rumour someone's been breaking the blockade just that way. Not that I believe it. But it is possible."

Della Torre saw his cousin off and then turned back to the house. The light of his father's second-storey room filtered through the slats of his closed wooden shutters. Della Torre knew the old man had fallen asleep without undressing. It happened when he'd had a few drinks too many.

Anzulović was waiting for him on the terrace, helping himself to the remaining ham and cheese that della Torre had carved. There was plenty more of both in the pantry.

"Seems a nice guy," Anzulović said.

"He is. Smart too."

"Shame he didn't have any good ideas on how to get to Dubrovnik. I guess we'll just have to sit and bide our time at Korčula until something comes up."

"Yes," della Torre said. He was too tired to mention the sailing boat idea. He'd dismissed the notion almost as soon as he'd heard it.

They'd both had enough to eat and maybe a little too much of the strong wine, so they retired to their bedrooms. Della Torre first went to put a blanket over his father, who only half-woke at the intrusion. When Piero was tucked under the covers, della Torre switched off the old man's light.

Both della Torre and Anzulović had had breakfast by the time Piero appeared on the terrace the following morning. He bore the hangover with dignity and nursed himself with a large, sweet Turkish coffee and a glass of his own wine, mixed liberally with sparkling water.

"Ah, Libero," Piero said. "I think I've known him all my life. *Knew* him all my life. As far as anyone can ever say they knew him."

"Angelo told me some things about him last night that I'd never heard before."

"You mean about his family?"

"Yes."

"Well, we Istrians aren't very demonstrative people. We don't like to talk about ourselves much. Emotionally hard as stone, your mother used to say, and as warm." And then to Anzulović: "She was Istrian too, but Istrian Italian."

Istria had been part of Venice for centuries and was heavily Italian until after the war, when the Slavs forced many to leave the country under duress. Plenty were killed along the way for having Italian names or accents. Della Torre's branch of the family had been assimilated over the centuries. They were Slav and Italian and wholly Istrian, speaking the local dialect among themselves and equally fluent in Italian and Serbo-Croat.

His mother's family considered themselves Italian. Her parents had spoken only that language, never bothering with Serbo-Croat. They'd all left in the decade following the war. Their village was now entirely abandoned, a cluster of ruined stone houses on a small hill farther north.

"Ah, well, maybe you soften a little the older you get," Piero said. "All my life, I only ever shook hands with my father and always used formal language with him. But when you were small, Marko, your grandfather would perch you on his knee and wouldn't correct you when you addressed him informally. And I suppose I would have been even more sentimental with any grandchildren."

Della Torre smiled softly at his father, remembering how, when he was a child, Piero would put his arm over his shoulders, ruffle his hair, and kiss his forehead when they watched movies together. And how the old man must miss not having grandchildren.

"Angelo mentioned something yesterday," della Torre began, finding the gentlest introduction.

Piero looked quizzically at his son, waiting for him to complete the thought. And then an expression of alarm crossed his face, as if he realized where the subject was headed.

"Oh, that. Nothing. There was nothing. Just the ramblings of an emotionally addled old man," Piero said. "Libero's sudden death got me so confused, I just . . . Well . . ."

Anzulović was a silent observer. It had been his greatest skill as a detective, allowing people to talk. And when they were finished, he would wait in silence for so long that they'd finally come out with what they'd been hiding all along. It didn't escape his attention that Piero had given Anzulović furtive glances as he steered the conversation away from where he thought della Torre might be leading. Piero knew Anzulović had been della Torre's boss in the UDBA. They'd met before. The UDBA was not a topic of conversation in old Yugoslavia, even between father and son. The subject was still taboo, especially among Istrians, who in all their history had never trusted a government of any political stripe or ethnicity.

There was something immeasurably forlorn about the old man. His soft, deep voice seemed to come out of an Arvo Pärt composition. *Spiegel im Spiegel.* Mirror in mirror.

"It is sad about Libero, but we all come to an age. He lived the life given to him," Piero said. "He lived simply, never involved himself in politics or much with other people. Just with the land. He drank moderately. Less than moderately. Didn't smoke. He worked for my father and then came to me when Marko and I returned and bought this place. My father sent him and he stayed. He never said whether he was happy to have come or not. I paid him better, I suppose. Not that he ever cared about money. The Italians killed his brother, the Germans his mother and wife. I'd known him all my life and only learned after his death about his wife. They'd been married for a month. We Istrians don't talk much, and if someone doesn't want to talk, we don't pry. After the war the Communists took his father. They looked for Libero for a while, but after the break with Stalin they didn't look anymore. I don't know why. His sister-in-law remarried. He saw her once a year. She died a few years back. Was he my friend? I don't know. I know everything he thought about engines and how to cultivate vines. I've been to his little house, the one he lived in with his parents and brother and brother's wife and his own wife when they were all still alive. On his own, he said two rooms were enough. I offered to renovate a cottage behind the house here so he wouldn't have to walk three kilometres each way every day, but he wouldn't have it. 'Better the ghosts you know,' he said. One Sunday every month he'd walk six kilometres to the graveyard. Never to church, just the graveyard. All my life I knew him. We ate lunch together here, six days a week. When I gave him a week off, he'd spend it in the vineyard or in the sheds working on things. If he was around, I'd give him lunch. That was his life. I think he was content."

Now that Libero was gone, his father was, in a way, della Torre thought, twice a widower.

So they reminisced about Libero and talked about the practicalities now that he would no longer be around to help. Piero figured that if he wanted to keep up his small vineyards, orchard, and vegetable garden, he'd need a man at least two days a week in the winter months, and most days from spring to late autumn. It would be expensive and eat heavily into Piero's pension. Just as well he had foreign-currency income — abjectly small for anyone in the West but decent in Yugoslav terms — from the articles he wrote about Yugoslav politics.

Anzulović found an excuse to drive the Citroën into Poreč, a beautiful Venetian city on the coast, fifteen kilometres away. Father and son stayed back to walk around the fields, among the strips of earth that bled between the rows of vines.

"What happened, Dad?" della Torre said.

Piero shrugged, sunlight glistening along the fine edge of his lower eyelids. They brushed past vine leaves autumnal in their colouring. Libero had helped to plant them, thinned the branches in the winter, sprayed them in the summer, harvested them only a few weeks before. They were his memorial.

"I don't know. I was having breakfast when the telephone rang. The person spoke English, which made me think that he was from one of the publications I write for. Sometimes the editors call me to clarify a point. But they're almost all in the U.S., and morning here is the middle of the night for them. I've done some writing for a couple of English journals, except the man sounded American. But Americans work for English periodicals. I haven't anything outstanding with an English journal so I thought maybe this was a commission. All these things were occupying my mind when I spoke to him, so I missed most of what he said. And then he hung up, very soon after. But I did remember he'd mentioned Libero, who hadn't arrived yet. Sometimes he comes a little later, when he's tending his own garden or has to go to town." Piero spoke of his old companion in the present tense as he struggled to splice his thoughts into coherence. "He tells me in advance, but I never remember. I know he'll be here when he's needed."

"The American mentioned Libero?" Della Torre tried to hide his alarm.

"Yes, though I couldn't remember what he said. He didn't repeat himself, just spoke briefly. I got into the car and drove to Libero's cottage, but even as I was driving I wondered if I had really been telephoned or imagined it. My . . . sometimes things like that happen to me. Not often. But I've noticed . . ."

"And when you arrived . . ." Della Torre encouraged the older man, trying not to betray his urgency.

"His door was unlocked. I have a key to the cottage, so I let myself in. And there he was in his bed. I knew then that he . . . Libero doesn't have a telephone, so I drove back and called the doctor. He came with an ambulance, but they just confirmed what I knew."

"Was there an autopsy?"

"No, the doctor said age had finally gotten to Libero. It happens that way sometimes, he said. The heart switches off. Maybe because of a nightmare or because it's just run its course. There was absolutely no reason to believe otherwise."

"Did you tell him about the telephone call? Or the police?"

"No, I . . . it had lost significance after what happened. I told Angelo today, this morning. Or was it yesterday?"

Della Torre's breathing shallowed. He bent his head to compose himself. He needed a cigarette but didn't dare light one. "I should have guessed . . ." he said, more to himself than to his father.

"Guessed what?"

Della Torre paused and then whispered, "Libero."

"You knew something about this?"

For what seemed like a long time, but couldn't have been more than the span of three breaths, della Torre was silent.

"No," he answered, trying to remember what Grimston had said to him at the café in Zagreb. Just like his father, he was unsure of his own recollection.

"Do you know something about Libero's death?"

"I don't know." Could they arrange an autopsy? Yes, certainly on della Torre's suspicion. If he suspected. Anzulović would know the procedure. But that wouldn't be necessary. Had his father really been telephoned or had he imagined it after the fact?

An autopsy might or might not confirm murder. If that's what it was. If they wanted to, the Americans could make death seem natural, traceless, especially in such an old man. But maybe they didn't care, as long as it stood as a warning to della Torre.

"Why? What does Libero have to do with you?"

"Nothing," della Torre said, shaking the suspicion from his mind. It seemed too far-fetched. The threat, if that's what it was, was too obscure. And his father was too unreliable a messenger. "Are you sure you didn't imagine the phone call? You've been drinking lately, and —"

The blow had the effect of an explosion that struck every nerve and yet somehow failed to crush della Torre into dust.

The old man's open palm was heavy — big and flat, and coarse with age and manual work. When it struck Marko's cheek, the force almost caused him to lose his balance.

His father stood there, struck dumb, rooted like an ancient vine, staring at della Torre with horror.

Neither man said anything. For a long time they didn't move, and then della Torre's father turned back towards the house. The son lit a cigarette and then followed.

THEY LEFT THAT afternoon. The parting was strained. There was no mention of what had happened in the vineyard between della Torre and his father. The two men shook hands. Anzulović took the wheel.

As della Torre shut his door, his father passed a package to him through the open window. It was small but heavy. Della Torre didn't know what was in it. It could have been a piece of his father's cured ham, or the collection of baseball cards Marko had brought with him from America as a teenager. So he said an uncertain "thanks" and they drove off.

They headed south, down through Istria along the coast road. It was a long time before della Torre spoke.

"Dad always wanted me and Irena to come live with him. To leave Zagreb. Have lots of kids. Irena could work at the teaching hospital in Rijeka; I could stay at home, raising children and wheat, making wine. He said he'd build us a swimming pool and a tennis court and give it all to us."

"It's funny, we get to an age and we think only of how to get rid of the things we've spent our lives accumulating," Anzulović said. "For instance, I spend all my time thinking of how to get rid of my wife's dog and my daughters so that I can have just a little peace before I'm too old to enjoy it."

Della Torre laughed despite himself. More than the joke warranted.

He finally opened the package when they'd got past Rijeka. In it was a neat stack of six one-ounce Krugerrands and a thousand Deutschmarks.

Between the wars, Piero's father, della Torre's grandfather, had saved up gold and silver coins. Whenever he had a little spare money, he'd buy gold and put it aside. When the war came, he didn't touch the gold until he needed it to pay the Italians to get his brother-in-law out of jail. And then, after the war, when the Communists were shooting people with Italian surnames, he paid for the della Torres to be left alone so that he could keep at least some of their property. He'd been smart about how he paid bribes, because there was always a risk they'd take the money and shoot his family anyway. Smart and brave.

Della Torre's father had done what his own father had done and set aside gold, Deutschmarks, and dollars. Because one never knew . . .

South of Rijeka, traffic thinned. They drove past Senj, which centuries ago had been home to the ferocious Uskok pirates, who'd terrorized both Venice and the Ottomans. Now it was a modest port town at the base of rocky white mountains. Beyond Senj, notices were posted on the sides of the road warning of mines.

"If you need a piss, don't pull over," Anzulović said to della Torre, who was now driving.

A police roadblock told them JNA artillery had targeted the coastal road towards Zadar. Effectively, Croatia had been chopped up. One part consisted of Zagreb and the main inland region that stretched from the Slovene border to the Vukovar war zone. It was connected to Zagreb only by the thread of small roads through hilly country as the JNA pressed against Karlovac. The main part of Dalmatia was cut off from the northern Adriatic by JNA artillery in the hills behind Zadar. And farther south, Dubrovnik was surrounded.

The only way to Zadar was a little ferry across the narrow strait to Pag Island, a long ridge of white rock in the turquoise sea. But the ferry had recently been attacked by Yugoslav jets, making for a nervous crossing, crew and passengers watching the sky for enemy fighters.

They drove along the island's harsh stone-and-scrub landscape and then across a bridge back to the mainland, its checkpoint manned by three policemen keeping out of the wind in a parked Zastava.

They didn't stop in Zadar but carried on south, worried about becoming targets for the Serb artillerymen who'd carved out an independent territory in the mountains behind the ancient walled city. They passed occasional signs of war: a burnt-out building, a marked minefield, the empty road.

As the countryside flattened to sandy soil and pine trees, vineyards and olive groves, and the mountains receded, della Torre and Anzulović relaxed. The coastal cities on the way were under threat of naval bombardment and more limited blockades, so they skirted Šibenik and Split and instead stopped in small hamlets for food and fuel. Sometimes the going was slow, though most of the traffic was heading in the opposite direction, refugees travelling north from the battles around Dubrovnik.

Della Torre and Anzulović stayed on the road after nightfall, using their military IDs to get around the militia roadblocks. The militiamen were nervous about letting them through, for fear the Serb gunners would pick out the car's headlights and target them. But della Torre wanted to press on, and Anzulović offered no resistance.

They arrived at the small port town of Ploče in the early hours of morning. It was as far south as they could get by car. Beyond it, the JNA had broken through to the coast in their encirclement of Dubrovnik.

The previous day, Ploče had been bombed by the Yugoslav air force. Della Torre could smell the crushed concrete, melted plastic, burnt wood. The fear.

The town was in complete darkness. As they approached the town's harbourside square, a trio of local policemen flagged them down at pistol point. "What the fuck do you think you're doing?" one swore at della Torre, pointing his flashlight into the car.

"Looking for a hotel."

"I've seen some stupid tourists in my time, but I think you take the cake. There's Serb artillery not fifteen kilometres away. Might sound far to you, but they can drop a shell into your lap from there. Which I wouldn't mind at all, except if you're in my town when they do it. *Verstehen?*"

Della Torre showed him his credentials, which he'd kept in easy reach.

"It says 'major' here. Major what? Fuckwit?" The cop was insensible with outrage and didn't care who he was talking to.

"Your point's taken, officer," della Torre said, tired and growing irritated himself. "Show us to somewhere we might stay for the night and we'll switch off the headlights."

"You'll switch them off now or I'll shove this flashlight up your ass."

Della Torre recognized that he wasn't going to get anywhere with this man by pulling rank, and not just because the cops had their guns in hand while his was still in his bag. He switched off the lights.

"Now, officer, maybe you can tell us where we can park the car and find a bed. You do that nicely and I won't bother finding out your name." Della Torre left the rest of the threat unsaid.

The cop, for his part, was pulled back by a colleague, who took over.

"Here's fine. This is the main square. I'll take you to a place that has rooms."

Della Torre more or less left the car where it was, and then he and Anzulović followed the cop, leaving his belligerent partner behind.

The owner of the little hotel was reluctant to open up. Still addled with sleep, dressed in an undershirt and a loose pair of trousers, he finally directed the men to a room with two single metal-framed beds and a tiled floor that was designed to be cool in the summer but right now felt icy under sock feet.

Della Torre tried to find out what the charge would be, but the owner just said: "You'll pay what I ask."

"Friendly sort of place," Anzulović said five minutes later, as he pulled the sheets up to his chin.

"Guess getting bombed makes a person a bit tense."

Anzulović grunted agreement, eyes shut.

The owner of the hotel was no more welcoming in the morning, telling the men they'd have to get their breakfast at a café on the square. But the price for the room was modest, and the beds had been comfortable enough.

Ploče was a lovely harbour town surrounded by high hills; ornamental palm trees were planted along the waterfront. A handful of buildings had been damaged in the raid; according to the man at the tobacco kiosk, all the destruction was readily visible from the square. Della Torre didn't think it was too terrible, certainly nothing compared to the pictures coming out of Vukovar. But it had clearly shocked the locals.

Ferries still ran to Korčula, but the normal schedule had been abandoned. Now they went when their captains thought the navy would leave them alone and the skies did not seem conducive to raids by Yugoslav fighter bombers.

Starting early in the day, more and more people gathered at the dockside, most of them from the surrounding countryside, fleeing the war. But they all wanted to go north. The only craft they saw leaving Ploče's harbour that morning was a small, colourful sailing boat, which they watched in a desultory way, a modest relief from the boredom of waiting. Towards midday, a ferry loaded up with most of those waiting on the dock and headed gingerly towards Split, hoping the Yugoslav naval ship visible offshore would leave them in peace. Those waters weren't blockaded yet.

It was late afternoon before della Torre and Anzulović, along with a dozen other passengers who'd spent the day waiting, were collected by an ancient car ferry. It felt like boarding a ship in Southampton after the sinking of the *Titanic*.

They gave their tickets to a crew member, who handed them each a stub of a receipt badly printed on rough grey paper and drove the Citroën up the ramp. Before they knew it, the boat trembled and moved off.

"It looks like they're serving drinks," della Torre said, surprised to see the ship's bar open.

"Coffee?"

"More like wine. Want a glass?"

"Bit early, isn't it?" Anzulović replied.

"To be drinking?" della Torre said in surprise. This was a country where, as often as not, people woke to a shot of slivovitz.

"No, for stupid questions," Anzulović said.

"That's almost funny."

"It's from an American sitcom. You know how I know it's funny? Because every time they repeat it on TV, you can hear people laughing on the soundtrack," Anzulović said, deadpan. Maybe everything was equally funny to him. Or equally serious.

They drank watered-down white wine alongside a trucker and a heavyset middle-aged woman wearing a dark blue sweatshirt that said *Hot Babe* in English.

Hot Babe and other absurd sweatshirts meant something more than misappropriated language. They spoke of family abroad, of money to buy imported goods, of something different and exotic, if only a change from patterned polyester. It had been a long time since della Torre had found the slogans worth noticing.

The long, stony Pelješac peninsula slid past, a narrow band of white shoreline separating the green-blue waters from the brown-green brush. It was a line of limestone where sun, short tides, and storm waves gnawed away at even the hardiest flora. Higher up, scrub dominated, including thorn bushes, rosemary, lavender, stunted pines, and olive trees, wild and in groves.

The ferry's leisurely passage belied the constant uncertainty. Would they be attacked from the sky, or by one of the big grey ships etched on the horizon?

They rounded the end of the peninsula, and there was the narrow Korčula channel. The stone citadel jutted from its island promontory. Beyond, the high, massive mainland range was unflinching, like Odysseus standing before blind Polyphemus: a white bastion at the harbour entrance, white stone walls and palms, red-tiled roofs stacked in layers towards the central hill. Venetian, not Ragusan — Ragusa was Dubrovnik's ancient name — but for all intents and purposes Dubrovnik's twin, in miniature and in spirit. As they approached, the evening light turned the city pink, as if the red had run from the rooftops to stain the walls below.

There was a little water traffic. A couple of open-decked fishing boats, looking more like whalers, motored from somewhere along the coast.

The dockside was full of people, as busy as a city-centre train station at rush hour. All wanting to escape the war. How often had they heard rumours of a boat and stood there waiting, only to be disappointed?

The ferry's diesel smoke billowed as its engine revved hard into the moorings. Iodine shore smells mixed with salt and rotting fish. Warps were cast over to a shoreman, who tied the ferry to the iron bollards. Hopeful passengers moved slowly out of the way, but there was little pushing or shoving. There'd be enough space to take them all, though not their vehicles too.

A supply truck moved off first, reversing down the open

ramp as people dockside made way to let it through. The captain strode aft, expressionless in his short, dark coat, a white and blue peaked cap covering most of his black hair.

They drove off the ferry, squeezing past old women and young women and children and some men among them too. Most looked tired, their possessions packed in boxy suitcases and big woven polyester bags. The refugees stood patiently but were already staking out their places on the boat.

And then della Torre and Anzulović found themselves standing next to the Citroën at the edge of the old town. They left the car in a quayside parking space and went to find somewhere to stay. It surprised them that so many places were full. Refugees.

They were directed to the local police station, which doubled as the militia headquarters. After considerable deliberation among the militiamen, they were given the address of a *pension* in the heart of the old town. It was a simple townhouse, with worn tile floors and ceramic stoves fuelled by scraps of wood. But the rooms were clean, the sheets crisp, and each bed covered by an eiderdown in a lace-fringed cotton counterpane. The place was run by an old lady in a black head scarf and black dress, eyes lost in the depths of a round, wrinkled face like a shrivelled apple. She said they could call her Nonna, "grandmother" in Italian.

Once they'd negotiated a price, she cooked a simple supper, which they ate at the kitchen table. They sat at a corner table covered in checkered oilcloth, with a built-in bench that ran along two sides, helping themselves to slices of bread and cheese while the old woman stood beside a shallow soapstone sink, preparing food on a wood-burning steel and enamel stove. She served a soup with fine homemade vermicelli noodles, and fillets of indeterminate fish with a lukewarm potato salad dressed in oil and vinegar, raw onions, and a cabbage salad.

"Don't eat in the restaurants," Nonna said. "You never know what they will feed you. I will cook for you."

Although it had largely been a day of waiting, della Torre and Anzulović were exhausted and retired soon after eating.

The next morning della Torre went to find out what he could about blockade runners. The sergeant manning the desk at the police station shrugged and told him there'd been no boats that day or the day before, and he wasn't sure when to expect one. He said one or two speedboats based in Dubrovnik had ventured out to fetch water — the city had been relying on its ancient cisterns since the JNA had cut off the watermains, as well as the electricity. But none had come as far as Korčula.

"Could anyone be persuaded to take me?"

"Take you?" The captain looked at him, distrusting, wondering what sort of idiot or madman had been foisted on him. "Why?"

"Because I need to go to Dubrovnik."

"Mister — I mean Major — they're negotiating passage for a humanitarian convoy. Who knows, maybe in a week you'll be able to go and not get shot at on the way. Though I'm not sure the folks in Dubrovnik need outsiders giving them advice as much as they need water and ammunition. And I'm pretty sure they don't want tourists."

The convoy of ships Grimston had spoken about still hadn't set sail. Everyone was waiting for it, but no one knew when the negotiations with the Yugoslav forces would be resolved.

"What I'm going there for isn't particularly your business, if you don't mind my saying," he replied. "And I haven't got time to wait for this mythical convoy."

"Suit yourself. You can go and ask the fishermen. They might know."

He walked back into town along the quayside. People were about, either loitering or hopeful for another ferry to the mainland. He spotted a fisherman working on the inboard engine of his open boat.

"How hard would it be to hire a fishing boat?" della Torre asked.

"Depends how much you're willing to pay," the man said, casually looking up. "And where you might want to go. Orebić" — he pointed to the small town on the peninsula across the channel — "would cost you thirty Deutschmarks. Might be able to get you to Ploče, but that'll be expensive. Depends how many people, but if there's four or more I could do it for a hundred and fifty."

That didn't sound too unreasonable to della Torre, given this was a time of war, until the man added: "Each."

"That's a lot of money."

"It is. Most of us don't like to leave the inshore waters. Too many patrol boats keen on target practice."

"What about Dubrovnik?" della Torre asked.

"Dubrovnik?" The man looked up again, incredulous. "What is this? That hidden-camera show where they make you look stupid?"

"Honest question," della Torre said.

"Honest answer? Not if you promised to make me as rich as Rockefeller. Hard to spend it when you're dead. Try some of the other guys. You might catch one who's been drinking."

"Anyone else making the trip? I hear there are blockade runners."

"People who want to be fish food." And then, softening his stance, he said: "There's one or two who might give it a try. You get people desperate for money. But nobody I could point you to."

"If you change your mind . . ."

"Sure, I'll come looking for you," he said, shaking his head and going back to his engine.

Della Torre had as much luck with the two other fishermen he spoke to. The last one shook his head and added, "What is this, a lunatic convention? Or are you mates with the other guy?"

"Other guy?"

"Yes, other guy. Foreigner. German or something. Speaks crap Italian. Well, I'll tell you what I told him. A few of us go to Orebić," he said, "but unless you've got a speedboat and God on your side, you're not getting to Dubrovnik. Though I suppose you could ask the Serbs to stick you in one of their cannons and blast you over." He paused, holding his hand up for della Torre to be quiet. "Hear that? The guns."

"Who's the other guy?" della Torre squatted down so that he was on the man's level. The muscles in his thighs were tense, and he supported himself with three fingers against the damp, cool stone of the dockside.

"Some other guy. Didn't leave his business card. But it's not a big place. Not many foreigners about. Come to think of it, I think he said he was a journalist."

Della Torre strolled back into the town's narrow alleys. Most of the windows were shuttered, the louvred panels painted white rather than the green favoured in Istria. Ornate niches were carved into many of the stone walls; skeins of wires hung above, and sometimes a profusion of vines, still green, spilled over the tops of walls from hidden gardens. Each alley ended at either a building or a seascape narrowed to a vertical slice, as if seen through a castle's crenellations.

The sun had come out, so he stopped for a coffee on a terrace. The wind had turned, and the distant rumble of guns disappeared. For a moment he watched a small sailboat cross the channel. The blue hull, in combination with the red and white forward sail and the white main, made it look like the country's flag, without its checkerboard crest.

Della Torre thought about Libero with a shudder. He tried to convince himself that the man had died of a heart attack or just old age. Marko's and his father's suspicions were absurd. And yet . . .

Della Torre's thoughts drifted to Irena. He hadn't been able to get through to her from his father's house. Today, Anzulović had gone to commandeer an office at the police headquarters. Della Torre would try again from there.

He idly watched the little boat round the end of the port town. He made a mental note to track down the journalist looking to get to Dubrovnik. If this one was half as good as Higgins, he'd find a way. But something still bothered della Torre.

It wasn't until he'd strolled most of the way back to the *pension* that the thought snapped into a recognizable shape. Triangles. Sailboats. He remembered what his cousin Brnobić had said about breaking the blockade in a small sailboat, like the one he'd watched crossing from Orebić and then rounding Korčula's promontory, out of sight.

Earlier he'd spotted a sheltered marina in the bay between Korčula and the main part of the island. Now he hurried there, but the little boat had disappeared. He cursed his obtuseness.

The dull middle-aged man guarding the marina didn't know much about anything. None of the docked yachts had been sailed for months, and most of them not since the previous year. Few owners had come to see their boats, and the man had not noticed a small sailboat passing earlier. He was just there to keep an eye on his marina. There was another marina farther along the coast. He pointed vaguely away from Korčula.

Della Torre started walking the length of the waterfront, away from the town, in hopes of catching sight of the other marina or any other possible home for the boat. But it proved to be a fruitless morning's search, and he determined to drive around in the car later.

He found Anzulović back at the *pension*.

"Militia headquarters is a zoo," Anzulović said. "We might as well stick around here a while. Nonna's agreed to let us use her phone for a consideration, and we'll wait for the convoy, unless you've had some luck."

"Nothing. Fishermen all think I've gone insane. And apparently there's some foreign reporter looking to go to Dubrovnik too. Maybe we can share a ride."

Anzulović nodded. There was a time when journalists from abroad were closely tracked, but these days they came and went. Some bothered to get accreditation from the ministry in Zagreb; others just pretended to be foolhardy tourists.

Della Torre paused. For the past few days, something about Anzulović had been troubling him. He didn't know how to approach the question, so he did it bluntly.

"Why are you here?"

"Why?"

"Why are you still with me?"

"To keep you company," Anzulović said. "To keep you out of trouble. Because you're going to need help with Strumbić."

"Am I?"

"Aren't you?"

"What are we going to do with him when we find him? Warn him off? Or hand him over to the Americans?"

Anzulović paused. He lit a cigarette and slowly let the smoke seep through his nostrils. "He's an asset of the Croatian government. Let's leave those tricky decisions to others."

11

AFTER LUNCH, DELLA Torre left Anzulović at the *pension*, where he was stretched along the sofa in the parlour, drinking a glass of wine mixed with water and reading a novel.

"Detective work is hard, isn't it," della Torre said.

Anzulović grunted.

Della Torre drove the Citroën along the seafront, from village to village. None of the fishermen he spoke to showed any interest in taking him farther than Orebić or back to Ploče. They were making enough money on those routes that they didn't need to bother risking their lives for a single big payoff.

He kept his eyes peeled for the little sailing boat. Some of the locals he talked to had seen it sail to Orebić a couple of times a week, but no one seemed to know whose it was, though the consensus was that the boat was moored in a sheltered inlet.

Eventually he spotted it tied to a buoy some twenty metres off a pebbly shore. It couldn't have been more than six metres long. Its small tender lay upside down under a broad spread of long-needled pine in a quiet spot up from the stony beach. The track to and fro was little used, and from the road it appeared to belong to a neighbouring villa.

He knocked on the doors of the waterfront houses, but they

were all shuttered. Rich people's summer hideaways now closed for god knew how long. He wondered how many owners were Serbs praying for a quick victory so they could get back to their old lives.

On the way back to the car, he spotted a boy on a bicycle and flagged him down. The child kept a wary but polite distance.

"Are you from around here?" della Torre asked.

The boy waved inland, farther up the hill.

"Do you know who owns the boat that's moored in the water down there?"

The boy thought hard, then shook his head. "Some foreigner," he said.

"Do you know where the foreigner lives?"

"No."

"Has he got a car?"

"Yes," the boy nodded. "A yellow Cinquecento. A real Italian one, not a Zastava that looks like one. One of the doors is more orange. I think it was replaced."

"You sure about that?" della Torre asked, though it was a foolish question. Boys like this knew cars, all the makes and all their idiosyncrasies.

"Yup."

"Do you know where it goes?"

Once again, the boy waved vaguely inland. "Up the road and then right."

"Where does that road on the right go?"

"Up."

Up to the hamlets in the island's interior. It was a start at least.

It was too late in the afternoon to go wandering around the countryside. On the off chance, he drove back to the police station in Korčula, but no one was terribly sure about the owner of a yellow Cinquecento.

The day had been warm, and by the time he got back to the *pension*, della Torre was tired and irritated. He sat down to Nonna's supper of fried fish and boiled, oiled potatoes, not even bothering to mention the small sailboat to Anzulović, who seemingly hadn't stirred from the couch in the front room.

After supper, they played cards on the *pension*'s terrace late into the evening, by the light of a kerosene lamp. A blackout had blanketed the town in silent darkness.

Della Torre woke unaccountably early. The eiderdown smelled slightly of the seaside damp that seemed to infuse these old stone houses from mid-autumn until late spring. The tiled floor was cold underfoot. Nonna had given della Torre and Anzulović each a pair of her dead husband's slippers to wear around the house. She seemed to take comfort in the men's company. Was loneliness inherent in old age?

Anzulović hadn't risen yet, and Nonna was in her dressing gown, baking their bread for the day. She made della Torre a coffee from her dwindling supplies. It was becoming ever harder to find luxuries on Korčula, as the ferries and supply ships restricted themselves to essentials. Della Torre wondered what life might be like in Dubrovnik. Or Vukovar. Yet again he tried calling Irena, without success.

At a loss over what to do with himself, della Torre went out. On a whim he decided to drive inland, knowing he shouldn't waste gasoline but unable to resist.

Away from the coastal fringe, the settlements were sparsely populated. The red-tiled roofs of many houses had collapsed in on their empty shells. Weeds and wild shrubs overgrew ancient vineyards and orchards. Dry-stone walls were gap-toothed with neglect.

By midday he'd reached a hill with long views of the island, the sea, and the mainland beyond, the landscape scattered with cypresses like verdant columns from ancient ruins. He stopped to take in the view and smoke a cigarette by the side of the road. But his stomach rumbled with the distant memory of a modest breakfast, so he got in the car, aiming to get back to Korčula along an unpaved road that he suspected would cut a corner rather than retracing a long circuit. That's when he saw it.

The yellow Cinquecento with a slightly more orange passenger door was parked in the courtyard of a small, two-storey stone farmhouse. The house was old, the paint on its shutters peeling, its roof tiles mottled orange and bleached red. But there were roses climbing along one wall, and the garden was tidy and well tended.

He stopped and lifted the bar to the steel gate, which was painted with red rustproofing. But he didn't push it open just yet. Most farmers kept guard dogs that could be savage with strangers.

"Hello," he called.

There was no sound of barking.

"Hello," he called again, pushing the gate open and stepping onto the chipped stone driveway.

A figure came from around the corner of the house wearing a broad sun hat, loose shorts, and a coarse faded blue smock. From the legs he could tell it was a woman, though her face was in shadow and the clothes hid her figure.

"Good day," she said. "Can I help you? Are you lost?"

She was tall, and from her voice he guessed she sang alto. As she approached, she took off her straw hat and smiled. She had pale brown hair, tied back and falling behind her shoulders, and a long, thin face, high-boned, with a prominent nose. Her lips were thin and her pale green eyes sparkled with a wary intelligence. She didn't look Croat, though she spoke the language with only a slight hint of a foreign accent.

"Hello," he said again. "I was looking for the owner of a sailing boat that I saw crossing the channel from Orebić yesterday. I was led to believe that whoever drove this Fiat might know."

"Can I ask why you might be interested?"

"I have a proposition. Well, a possible proposition that might be of interest."

"What sort of proposition?"

"It has to do with the boat."

"You want to buy it?"

"No, nothing at all like that. I'd . . . I'd like to charter it."

"You want to be taken to Orebić, or Ploče?"

"I'd be happier speaking to the owner of the boat, if you don't mind."

She considered him for a long moment. "My name is Miranda Walker," she said. "I'm the owner of the boat."

"I'm Marko della Torre." He held out his hand. "Miranda Walker isn't a very Croat name."

"Neither is Marko della Torre."

"I'm Istrian."

"I guessed."

"Are you American?"

"English," she said, finally stepping forward to take his hand.

Her fingers were long but her palms were rough and told of physical work. Now that she was close to him, he saw the fine lines that creased the corners of her eyes; the tanned skin was no longer in its first youth. But there was no grey in her hair, and the freckles that ran along the bridge of her nose and under her eyes lent her a certain girlishness. He guessed she was a few years younger than him, in her mid-thirties.

"Would you like something to drink?" she asked. "I have some lemon cordial made with my own lemons, from the grove behind the house. Or there's some wine that my landlord gives me. It's quite strong, so you ought to add water to it, but I'm afraid it'll have to be from the tap. The fizzy kind is too expensive these days." Even before the war, a bottle of carbonated mineral water had cost more than a bottle of wine.

"The cordial would be nice. I've been driving around all morning looking for you."

"You must have been very eager to have wasted all that petrol," she said. "Come round the back. We can sit and you can tell me what you want."

He followed her around the side of the house to the rear terrace, which was shaded by a trellis of vines, the grapes long since harvested. They ripened sooner here than up north in Istria. She motioned to a chair with a plywood seat and back, by a rough wooden table, and went inside the house.

When she came out again with a tray of glasses, a bottle, and a jug, she'd taken off her smock and wore a simple white linen blouse.

She was only half a head shorter than della Torre, and he saw that she had a fine figure, deeply tanned arms and legs. Everything about her said that she was used to physical work but hadn't been born into it.

"So, Mr. della Torre, what can I do for you?" she asked.

"If you'd rather talk in English, I'm as happy to do that," he said.

Her eyebrows rose slightly but she didn't comment. Instead she said, "As you wish."

"It might be nice. I get out of practice."

"So you're American."

"In a manner of speaking."

"What is it that you want, Mr. della Torre?"

"Were you sailing to Orebić yesterday?"

Her smile was slightly strained. "What concern is it to you, Mr. della Torre?"

"Just curious."

"Then that's how you'll have to stay."

"Or were you coming back from Ploče? For some reason I remember seeing a small sailing boat like yours there the other day."

She continued to smile. "What is it that you'd like to discuss?"

"Do you take people off the island?"

"Mr. della Torre, I have a little boat and I sail places. It comfortably fits a few people, so if I'm making a trip I can usually squeeze in a passenger or two. The boat's sound and everyone gets to wear a life jacket," she said. "Would you like to be taken somewhere? I couldn't transport your car; you'd have to leave that behind. But if it's just you, or a couple of you, I'm sure we could negotiate a passage. But if you were in Ploče the other day, you'll probably know that the car ferry risks the journey every couple of days. It's cheaper than I am, though you can't always get a place on it. Plenty of people are trying to leave Korčula."

"How is it that an Englishwoman lives here, and speaks our language?"

"Is there a law against that?"

"Well, actually, it's quite difficult to get a residence permit. Or was, in Yugoslavia. I'm not sure what the latest laws are for Croatia."

"I have a residence permit for Yugoslavia, and I was told that it would be transferable to the Croat state."

"You've got a nice place here. Nice view. Must be expensive."

She laughed. "I think you know very well it isn't. This far inland, most of the houses are ruins. The farmer who owns the house is happy enough for me to maintain the property and pay the taxes and bills. Which is just as well, because that's about what I can afford. I'm sure if you were keen, you could come up with a similar arrangement for one of the other semi-derelict houses around here."

"It's delicious lemonade," he said.

"Lemonade is freshly made. This is cordial. Would you like some more?"

"Yes, please."

She poured him another glass, mixing it with cold water from the white enamelled jug.

"As nice as it is to have some company, and as nice as it is to be speaking English, I wish you would tell me what you want, Mr. della Torre. Otherwise I'll start to think you're a policeman on a fishing expedition."

The comment caught him off guard, but he tried not to show

it. "I came here on the very slight possibility of finding some-body to take me to Dubrovnik," he said.

She laughed out loud. It was a nice laugh, full of surprise and humour, not meant cruelly. But when she saw he wasn't laughing with her, she quieted, though she continued to smile. "You're not joking, are you, Mr. della Torre."

"No, I'm serious."

"You're probably aware of the fact that there's a blockade? And that the Yugoslav navy is shooting at ships that are breaking that blockade? Sinking them too."

"Yes, but none of the fishermen would take me, and the block-ade runners based in Dubrovnik don't seem to have moved from port in recent days."

"Very sensibly."

He stood to leave. "Well, thank you for the lemon cordial, Miss Walker."

"My pleasure."

She walked him to the car. "Out of curiosity," she said hesi-tantly, "what were you proposing to pay to get to Dubrovnik?"

"I don't know. Since nobody's willing to go, I have no idea what the price would be. What do you think it would cost?"

"Well," she said, "I'd be surprised if you could do it for less than five hundred Deutschmarks. More if there are other passengers."

He whistled. "Sounds steep." That amount could buy a return flight to Munich.

"It might sound steep to you, but I for one wouldn't do it for less than a thousand."

"That's funny. The fishermen said they wouldn't do it at any price."

"Maybe you just didn't mention the right number."

"You think for a thousand they'd take me?"

"Try them."

"But you'd do it?"

"For a thousand?" she asked.

"Yes."

"Sure." She smiled.

"Then, Miss Walker, it's a done deal," he said, surprising himself.

She laughed again, looking for the joke. When she couldn't see it, she stopped and contemplated him skeptically, quizzically. "I think, Mr. della Torre, we should do a little more talking," she said. "Would you like some lunch, seeing as it's about that time?"

"Yes, please. I'm famished."

TAKING SOME AUTUMN vegetables and herbs from her garden and frying them in olive oil, she made a simple pasta sauce while della Torre smoked at the table outside and nibbled at small brown brined olives and slices of hard cheese. The nicotine made him light-headed.

"I'm sorry there's no meat with lunch," she said. It was unusual for guests to be offered such simple fare in Croatia, where serving at least one meat dish was a sign of respect.

"That's all right. It makes for a nice change."

"That's what I think. I've almost become a vegetarian. Some fish now and again, mostly what I catch. But meat's become so expensive."

"Is that what you were doing on the water?" asked della Torre. "Fishing?"

"I run a line while I sail. It's a good way to catch mackerel. I caught a couple yesterday that I grilled. They were delicious."

"But that's not why you were on the water."

"No, you were right," she said. "I took a few people to Ploče."

"Because they couldn't get a ferry?"

"I didn't ask. But the ferry passengers are screened by the militia, so maybe they didn't want to be known."

"And you're cheaper than the fishermen."

"Substantially. Though I stay out of their way, they get enough business. Enough people want to get away, and transport is iffy."

"What else do you do? I mean, what were you doing before the war?"

"I taught English, did some translating. But I'm an artist. Painted ceramics mostly, though what sells is drawings and watercolours of Dubrovnik. I like the draftsmanship. I trained as an architect."

"Is that what brought you to Korčula?"

"No, I came for a holiday."

"And you stayed."

"No, I went back to London. But when I stopped being married, I thought it would be a nice place to live for a while."

"How did you get residency?"

"There's an Englishman, Sir Fitzroy Maclean. You might have heard of him," she said.

Della Torre had indeed heard of Maclean, an English adventurer, soldier, and hero who had befriended Tito during the Second World War. Maclean had been the British representative to the Partizans, with whom he'd fought against the Nazis and whose privations he'd suffered and victory he'd helped to achieve. After the war he had come back to Korčula with his wife for holidays. Tito's regard for the Englishman was so great that Sir Fitzroy was the only foreigner allowed to own property in Yugoslavia.

"What's your connection?" della Torre asked.

"There isn't one, really. My folks vaguely knew his wife. We visited once, when I was a teenager. But when I moved here, that connection was enough for the local authorities to turn a blind eye to the fact that I wasn't a run-of-the-mill tourist. It helped that I don't take work away from any locals, I pay taxes on whatever is due, and I don't use any of the social services. The farmer is happy to have me maintain this house and keep it from falling down — not that anyone else wants to live here. So everyone's happy. What about you, Mr. della Torre? How is it that you're American and Istrian? And why do you want to go to Dubrovnik?"

"I'm not really American," he said. "I lived there from when I was very small until I was a teenager, and then we came back."

"Did your parents come back to retire?"

"Oh, no. My father was still relatively young."

"It's unusual for people to come back to live in the old country unless they're retiring. Even then it's pretty rare," she said. "So your parents had had enough of the United States?"

"My father did, anyway. It was just him and me who came back."

"Your mother stayed?"

"Yes." He paused. "In a manner of speaking."

"And now you want to go to Dubrovnik to rescue somebody?" She'd surprised him again.

"Something like that."

"It's not unusual. There's a fair number of people in Korčula who are pulling their hair out trying to get family out of Dubrovnik."

"Something tells me you have some experience."

"Maybe."

"Isn't it a bit dangerous for an artist?"

"Why would it be more dangerous for an artist than for anyone else?"

"Sorry," della Torre said, bemused. "I meant it's not the sort of danger an artist usually takes on."

She shrugged.

"Have you done the trip before?" he asked.

"I've sailed to Dubrovnik many times," she said. "Once a month in the summers and then once or twice in the autumn or spring. Dubrovnik is a better market than Korčula for selling my pictures and pots."

"What about since the war started?"

"Yes, I've sailed since then too."

"And during the blockade?"

"Mr. della Torre, I feel that I should be the one asking questions if I'm expected to risk my boat for you. That thousand Deutschmarks is per round trip for a single passenger, by the way."

Della Torre was taken aback. "That's a steep increase."

"No, this is called hammering out the details. I'll take as many as four people there and back. Total fare would be four thousand. If it's just you going but three of your friends return with us, that's two and a half thousand. And a minimum of a thousand Deutschmarks even if it's you on your own and you decide to stay in Dubrovnik. I still have to come back." And then, almost hopefully, she said: "Are you having second thoughts?"

"Take it or leave it?" della Torre asked lightly.

"Mr. della Torre, I don't know why you'd want to go to Dubrovnik. Maybe you're a criminal escaping justice and the only safe haven you've got is a war zone. Or you're a romantic looking to join the fight. Or you're a bit crazy." She paused. "This isn't something I'll undertake lightly."

"But you'll do it because you need the money."

This time her smile was forced. "Whatever my reasons are, Mr. della Torre, I don't have a death wish."

"That's a relief," he said. "Neither do I."

He felt he was being read. She scrutinized him with an analytical intelligence he'd seen in the best lawyers and in a professor of medicine at the University of Zagreb — namely Irena. The Englishwoman's eyes narrowed slightly, so that the web of tiny lines radiating from their corners made it look almost like warmth. Almost.

"Would you like a coffee? I might be able to scrape some up."

"Yes, please," he said. "Semi-sweet."

She cooked up a thick Turkish coffee and poured it out into

two small cups. He let the grounds settle before tasting. It had cooled sufficiently not to burn his tongue. When he'd drained the cup, he turned it over in his saucer.

"You want your fortune told?" she said.

"Sorry, a matter of habit." Somewhere along the way, he'd come to assume that women who poured thick Turkish coffees would want to read the grounds. Sometimes, he realized, he was more Balkan than he cared to admit to himself.

"I'm afraid I'm not really one for reading the future in coffee grounds," she said. "I'm not very Yugoslav. Though I enjoy when other people do it."

"I never listen," he replied.

"You'll have your own reasons for wanting to go to Dubrovnik, Mr. della Torre. Maybe you don't want to tell me. But if we're to spend a few days together, it'd be nice to know a little bit about you."

"What do you want to know?"

"What do you do for a living?"

"Ah, you want to know if I'm good for the money." He grinned. "I'm a lawyer. Was a lawyer. I suppose I still am."

"For whom?"

"I work for the Croat government these days."

He spun her a story about where he'd worked and what he'd done, mentioning that he'd gone to London to study for a master's degree in international law after his mandatory military service. She listened politely, and they chatted a little about what he'd thought of Britain during his stay. But he knew most of her thoughts were elsewhere.

Eventually she said, "A one-way trip? Will it be just you?"

"Actually, there will be two of us going and three of us coming back — five one-way trips at five hundred each way. So two and a half thousand."

"I'd like to be paid up front," she said.

"What happens if you can't get us there?"

"Mr. della Torre, you know where I live. I'm good for a refund, less costs, if we have to turn around. The fare doesn't include incidentals, like staying somewhere along the way, food, or any necessary bribes. So you'll have to bring extra for that. And the turnaround time in Dubrovnik is two days. If you can't find the person you're looking for in that time, I'm afraid it'll be too bad."

"You're a tough negotiator," he said.

"I just want you to know I'm serious. And that I expect to be compensated for the risks I'll be running. Even small sailing boats can be expensive to repair."

I T WAS MID-AFTERNOON by the time he drove back down the steep hill to Korčula, having left with a promise to return in the next couple of days with money and the supplies that Miranda Walker had asked for.

By the time the track turned onto the main coastal road, he was laughing out loud at the thought of sailing through the blockade with this Englishwoman in her dinghy. Mostly he was laughing at himself, overcome with the feeling that his cousin had played a practical joke on him by planting the germ of the idea in his mind.

Nonna answered the door when he rang the bell. She'd given him the key, albeit with the understanding he was to use it only when she was out, or at night.

"Signor Anzulović went out with a Russian gentleman," she said. Her face belied a sly intelligence. She seemed to know the stranger would interest della Torre.

"Oh," della Torre said, stepping into the broad, dim hallway. "Did the gentleman leave his name?"

"No, he didn't introduce himself."

"What did he look like?"

"He looked like a military man. His hair was very short on

the sides and a little longer on top. He had very good teeth for a man with grey hair. He wasn't as tall as you, or as slim. I would have thought he was German, but he asked for Major Anzulović in our language and then spoke to the man in Russian."

"Did they say where they were going?"

"Ah, no. But Signor Anzulović said he would be here for dinner. Would a fish stew be good? There's not the choice we have normally. So the . . ."

Della Torre had already backed out of the *pension*, excusing himself, saying he had to buy cigarettes if he could find some.

He wandered around Korčula's little streets, vaguely looking for Anzulović. He was curious about the visitor. No doubt Anzulović would tell him later, over dinner. But the description of the man unsettled him. Russian? And then he remembered that Rebecca had spoken Russian, as did Anzulović — he was of the generation that had learned Russian and German at school; only now were children being taught English. Did the men speak Russian because Anzulović understood only the rudiments of English?

Della Torre then noticed a man standing five paces back. He would have bet every gold coin his father had given him that the man was American. A big guy with a short haircut, white chinos, blue polo shirt, and Ray-Bans. *Maybe it's a uniform*, della Torre thought.

After waiting for a long time at the tobacco kiosk, only to be told he'd be limited to one packet of Lords, della Torre finally turned to the man. "Who are you?" The man didn't answer. He just stood there with a drawn smile, perhaps pleased at how easy the tailing job he'd been given was proving to be.

Della Torre walked along the harbourfront — since it was pointless trying to lose his American shadow, he ought to stick to a public place. He didn't want to be detained again. Whenever he looked around, the silent, smiling American was still there. And then, not far behind, Anzulović and Jack Grimston appeared.

"Gringo," Anzulović said, poker-faced. "Our American friend came looking for you, so I left with him to help."

"You found me."

"Mr. della Torre," Grimston said, holding out his hand. Despite himself, della Torre took it. "I seem to have caught you by surprise."

"Yes, though I might have guessed it was you, given the tail you put on me. He's not very chatty, is he."

"Nope. My people do as they're told," Grimston said. "My understanding is that you don't speak much Russian, Major della Torre."

"Only what I had to learn at school. My English and Italian excused me from spending too much time on other languages."

"And your German?"

"Same."

"Shame. I haven't been around long enough to build up my Serbo-Croat. We'll just have to speak English." And then, to Anzulović, he said, "*Prostitye.*"

"Is no problem," Anzulović answered with a shrug.

"So it seems after our discussions that you decided to go to Dubrovnik after all. But you didn't want to come with us. I hope you weren't thinking of finding Mr. Strumbić on your own. Well, whatever your intentions, it seems you've had as much luck as we've had trying to organize transport to Dubrovnik." Grimston surveyed the channel and the high, rocky ridge of the Pelješac peninsula. "I must congratulate you on your perseverance. Though I think a little sailboat is going to extremes. You'll be looking to rent a canoe next." He laughed, shaking his head.

It dawned on della Torre that he'd been followed from the moment they'd landed in Korčula. Or since Istria.

"We thought we'd arranged for a fast boat the other day. We would of course have made room for you and Major Anzulović, but . . ." He shrugged. "No matter, the convoy to Dubrovnik should be leaving Rijeka in the next few days, so we'll just have to wait for it to collect us. In the meantime, if you do find a way to Dubrovnik you will let me know, won't you, Major."

Della Torre took a deep breath, "Yes, of course."

"You won't have to look hard to find me. I've invited you and Major Anzulović to stay with us at our hotel. It's right on the waterfront, with lovely views of the sea and the mountains. Major Anzulović was happy to accept on your behalf. Of course, in a time of war we can't really expect it to have all the usual comforts. But the hotel staff have found other accommodation for the refugees and have mostly tidied up the place. It's much nicer than that rather gloomy *pension* you've found for yourselves." Grimston was professional down to his smile. "And you can join me for dinner."

"I think Nonna is cooking for us," della Torre said.

"I'm sure that when you settle your account, she won't care much who eats the food."

Della Torre doubted it.

"Until later, gentlemen," Grimston said.

Della Torre turned to Anzulović after Grimston left.

Anzulović shrugged. "It was a generous offer," he said, glancing back at the silent American.

Nonna was in a fluster when Anzulović told her they were leaving and on the verge of tears when he added they wouldn't be having the fish *brodetto* she'd made. The aroma of cooked onion, garlic, and tomato seeping out of the kitchen filled della Torre with regret. Anzulović settled the bill, leaving a little extra for the old woman on the pillows of their beds so she wouldn't have a chance to refuse it. They packed in a few quick minutes and left.

The hotel was a handsome two-storey, built at the turn of the twentieth century, with rooftop eaves and rows of paired Norman arched windows. A quick count of the pigeonholes behind the front desk told della Torre that the hotel had around twenty rooms. That the Americans could clear a hotel that size in no time at all made Grimston's power brutally apparent. And there were so many Americans; della Torre saw more than a dozen guests or visitors who fit the bill. Grimston wasn't taking his mission lightly.

All this for Strumbić?

Della Torre and Anzulović were each given their own quarters under the eaves: light, airy rooms at the top of the building, with views of the channel and the mainland mountains framed by the ornamental palms fronting the building. Evidence of recent occupants could be found in the rooms, which had had only a cursory cleaning and smelled of meals cooked on single electric hot plates. What force could have cleared this hotel at such short notice? And then della Torre cursed his own simplicity. It was the same overwhelming might that Strumbić used so readily: the power of money.

They ate an indifferent meal of oily potatoes, boiled greens, and fried fish in the hotel's dining room, in Grimston's company. The American alternated easily between Russian, English, German, and a rudimentary Serbo-Croat.

Anzulović filled the silences by talking about the local hero, Sir Fitzroy Maclean, of whom Grimston was ignorant.

"Sir Fitzroy," Anzulović said, mauling the name as he struggled with his English-German hybrid. "He was model for James Bond. Was English officer, friend of Tito, helped the Partizans during war."

Grimston feigned interest.

All the while della Torre wanted to bring up Libero, but he didn't.

Back in his room, he lay on a dented mattress covered by a brown polyester blanket. Libero, Irena, and Strumbić nagged at him. There was nothing he could do about the old man now. Irena would be leaving Vukovar soon. But he could still intervene with Strumbić.

He dressed quickly and slipped his Beretta into one coat pocket and a box of shells into the other. He filled his shoulder bag with some changes of underwear and a couple of shirts and the money his father had given him.

He lay on the floor by the door and listened. For a long time, he heard nothing. He tried not to gag at the smell of cigarette smoke and cooking oil that had seeped into the carpet. Then he heard it. Footsteps. A shadow passed by his door.

He opened the window. The moon's soft light was enough for him to trace a path through the otherwise dark town. The streetlights were no longer on, for fear of drawing the interest of distant gunners and because there was no fuel to spare. He stepped onto the roof. The curved pantiles were slick with evening dew, but his sturdy British shoes gave him enough grip to scale the ridge. He made his way to the end of the building and realized there'd be no easy way down, no obvious handholds. The hotel had been built from smooth stone with microscopic joins. It'd be a long fall to a hard landing if he slipped.

If the Americans were guarding the hallway, they'd have some presence in front of the building as well, even assuming he could find some way of scaling the wall. But then another idea came to mind.

The rear slope of the roof was much shallower than the front; della Torre had little difficulty keeping his balance. The back of the building faced one of Korčula's narrow alleyways, no more than two metres wide. The building opposite was at roughly the same level, also with a nearly flat tiled roof.

Della Torre shoved his gun and box of bullets into the clothes in the shoulder bag and, whispering a small prayer, threw it over the gap to the opposite roof. The bag rolled and then slid back slightly but stopped well before the roof's edge. He reversed a couple of steps and, knowing the smallest slip would leave him a puddle of blood and bones on the street below, he made the short sprint and leap.

He cleared the distance easily, but his momentum caused him to tumble forward. The tiles complained, clattering with the force, though none broke or dislodged. But on landing his arm had hit the bag and sent it sliding sideways. For a moment he winced at the thought of losing the gun and the gold, but the bag stopped.

He rose to a crouch and, in slow steps, ever ready to fall to his hands and knees, he scooped up his haversack and slung it back over his shoulder. From here, the trick would be to find a way down. He could break open a roof hatch, but he didn't know what sort of reception he'd get. Too many police and militiamen with guns and raw nerves were billeted around the town.

But where he was going would be safe. If only he could get there without breaking his neck.

Like Dubrovnik, but on a smaller scale, Korčula was built around a central main street, with narrow alleys running off it like fishbones. All but a few were an easy jumping distance, needing little run-up. The heights of the buildings didn't vary greatly, and it wouldn't be difficult to trace a path across them. In theory it would be an easy passage.

But, from his time in the commandos, della Torre knew that theory and practice overlapped only at the narrowest margins.

The next roof nearly proved to be his undoing. It was steeper than the one he was on, and older. The tile he put his foot through upon landing might well have dated from the sixteenth century, when the house was built. The shards went crashing onto the paving stones below, while more tiles threatened to crumble under his weight. His foot was wedged under the battens supporting the tiles, one of which had broken and was now acting as a trap. He breathed hard, waiting for the alarm, but none came.

Pushing his boot up against the wooden fragments threatened to impale his foot. Somehow he couldn't twist around, either. The bag, which he'd slung over his back with its strap across his chest, had worked its way to the front and was now in the way. Della Torre sweated with the effort of trying to extract himself.

In the end, he managed by dislodging another couple of tiles and, doubled over, slowly working his foot free. He edged up to the ridge to catch his breath. By now the moonlight was fading. He had to hurry if he was to avoid being trapped on the rooftops in total darkness.

The next roof was slick, and he almost lost his footing, but his boot caught a metal support. He broke a few tiles on the landing. This time the noise set a dog barking, followed by a man's voice swearing at it to shut up and then cursing the cats that infested the town.

For a while della Torre feared he'd reached a dead end — the subsequent roof across the alley was too high to jump to and the adjoining one was also out of reach. But he found a series of attic vents in a wall and used them as footholds to climb the neighbouring building. And from there he made his final crossing.

He counted the houses. It was hard to be sure. He scrambled to the one he prayed was right, and after a long search by feeling in what had become almost complete darkness, he found the roof hatch.

It was bolted from below.

"Fuck," he muttered, wondering where he might find a lever to pry it open.

He got his fingers underneath the lip and heaved. The hatch groaned but didn't give. It was a modern replacement: he could feel the raw zinc edges bite into his flesh. He was cautious about the force he used, knowing that if it gave way suddenly, he'd likely pitch himself down the roof and over the edge.

But accidentally cracking a tile at the edge of the hatch gave him an idea. Once he'd worked that one loose, he eased the next one free, and then the one after that, until he'd made a big enough hole to get his arm underneath, between the wooden battens, and unbolt the hatch.

He slid into the roof space, careful to stay on the ceiling rafters. He flicked his cigarette lighter for a quick look around and found the hatch into the main part of the house. From there he slowly let himself down so that he was hanging above the floor below.

His arms weakening, he dropped as softly as he could, but he couldn't avoid making a thump. He stood dead still for a long time, hoping the noise had passed unnoticed, but he was out of luck. Torchlight shone from the floor below; footsteps followed. The beam blinded him after the darkness, and he smiled as fetchingly as he could.

"Signor della Torre?"

"Nonna, my apologies for dropping in at this late hour. I'd forgotten something, you see."

"But how did you get in?"

"You gave me the key, remember? I've left it downstairs. I forgot this little bag," he said, patting the holdall.

"But why are you up here? Your room is downstairs."

"It's the dark," he whispered soothingly. "I was disoriented."

"Ah, yes," she said. "I have that sometimes. Not knowing if I'm going down or up. It's a shame you missed the *brodetto*. It will be good tomorrow too."

"I will be sure to come back. The meal we had at the hotel was terrible."

"Oh, serves you right. Foreigners cook at those hotels. They don't know anything about food."

"But I think it's time I went, Nonna. It wasn't my intention to disturb you."

"Before you leave, I must give you back the money you and Signor Anzulović left. It is foolish to be throwing that kind of money at an old lady. You young need it more than I. I have my widow's pension, and that's sufficient."

"You hold on to it, Nonna. And tomorrow get a workman to look at your roof. I think there are some loose tiles. Spend the money on that."

"Oh, *mamma mia*, you got all the way up there?"

"Maybe you should guide me out."

"But won't you stay the night? It's so late."

"I really must leave. My apologies for waking you."

She led him to the front door, where he again whispered his apologies while she waved away his intrusion, as if such things happened all the time.

Della Torre had hardly stepped out of the house when he tripped over a cat making a dash across the alley. It yowled as he stumbled, falling heavily onto his knees. He swore and then laughed with relief that it hadn't happened up on the roof. He guided himself by running his hand along the walls and carefully toeing his way to avoid raised cobblestones and doorsteps.

He found the Citroën where he'd left it at the edge of town. For a while he wondered whether the Americans might be watching it. But this wasn't a big island. There wasn't really anywhere to run, and they couldn't have been expecting him to make an escape from the hotel.

He drove out of the town and along the coast road, and then found the rough track. He parked at the gate to the little farmhouse, and then for a long moment sat in car, wondering what exactly he was doing.

The iron gate creaked as he pushed it open just wide enough to slip into the courtyard. The gravel crunched underfoot. There was barely a ghost of light, only enough that he could make out the house in the darkness.

Far away, where the peninsula joined the mainland, he saw points of brightness, the small red twinkling of distant fires, and it struck him that the Serbs were burning houses.

He found the door and knocked on it. There was a window cut into it, the pane protected by a grille of wrought-iron foliage. A light shone on him almost immediately.

"I have your thousand Deutschmarks," della Torre said.

THE BEAM OF light was on him for a long time before she said anything.

"Are you alone?"

"Yes."

She unbolted the door and opened it, switching off the flashlight. A feeble kerosene lantern glowed in the stark hallway. "There's no power at night up here," she said. She wore a heavy linen dressing gown over her long linen nightshirt. Her hair was loose and untidy with sleep. "Come into the kitchen." The room made up much of the ground floor, with a tall ceiling, a fridge, an old-fashioned wood-burning stove, and a table covered with the blue-checked oilcloth found in almost every household in the country. Pots and pans hung from butcher's hooks along an iron rail fixed to the wall.

"I heard your car. Not many come along here at night."

"I'm sorry for showing up so late, but I want to take you up on your offer. Straight away," he said.

Her chin jerked up slightly with surprise. "We couldn't go now. We'd have to wait for daybreak."

"Can we get set up so we can leave at first light?" he asked.

"It depends on the wind. And I'd need to stock up with petrol and water. A few provisions, too. It's hard to know what we'll need."

"Petrol?"

"In case the wind dies or we get hit with a storm. It's useful to have access to the engine."

"We could siphon some out of the Citroën, if that's good enough. How much would you need?"

"Thirty or forty litres."

"Seems a lot."

"That's what I need."

"I'm sure I've got that much left in the tank. We filled up before Ploče and I haven't driven the car much."

There was something odd about the conversation. About how coolly she was accepting his sudden appearance.

"You don't seem particularly surprised that I've come back, or at how late I've shown up," he said.

"Since the war started, the unusual has started to become rather routine." She looked at him with detachment. "Not that long after you left yesterday, a couple of men came around. The one who talked spoke Serbo-Croat badly and with a strange accent. Russian, maybe. His English was better. He didn't introduce himself, just asked why you'd come."

"Did you tell him?"

"Yes. A few people know I'll sail them places for a price."

"Not in the militia or the police."

She shrugged. "No one would have suggested me if you asked to be taken to Dubrovnik. Everyone assumes it takes a fast boat."

"But it doesn't?"

"No, you just need darkness, silence, and a decent wind."

"Have you done it before?"

"I told you, Mr. della Torre, I've sailed that route many times."

"Since the blockade?"

She didn't answer him.

"So what did you tell my American friend?" he pressed.

"He didn't sound like much of a friend. More like a police-man," she said. "I told him that it was foolish and dangerous enough to try the trip in a speedboat. He seemed satisfied with the answer, but he asked me to let him know if I heard that you'd found somebody to take you. He said to call him at the hotel and that he'd make it worth my while. Tempting, except I haven't got a phone."

Della Torre pulled his pack of cigarettes out of his breast pocket. "Do you mind?"

"No."

"Would you like one?"

She hesitated and then pulled one out. He lit both. She went to the crockery shelf for a china saucer, which she placed between them as an ashtray.

"I'd offer you a cup of tea or coffee, but it'll take a while to get the stove going," she said.

"That's okay." He would have loved a hot cup of coffee. Or some sleep.

"I'll brew some up on board the boat. It has a little kerosene stove," she said. "Assuming you have the money."

From the inside pocket of the shoulder bag, he dug out the thousand Deutschmarks his father had given him, fanning them out across the table. She counted, checking the notes against the light, feeling them for the quality of the paper. "This will get you there and back, not including incidentals."

"I'll make sure you're paid the rest when we find our other passenger," he said. "And I'll cover whatever expenses we accrue on the way."

"You said there would be someone else coming with us from Korčula."

"I changed my mind. It's just me and the fellow we're pick-ing up in Dubrovnik."

She sat, smoking silently, apparently lost in thought.

He could see the outline of her breasts against the thin

material of her nightshirt. She noticed and gave him a critical look. He averted his eyes, but she made no move to pull the dressing gown more tightly around her. She seemed un-shy.

He got up as if to stretch and looked around the room. There was a shelf laden with pots, bowls, and jugs. The forms were rough and looked as if they were still part of the earth. The glazes had been allowed to run, mingling in earthy oranges and reds, deep greens, and the grey blue of winter skies.

On a table in the corner was a small stack of precise drawings of Dubrovnik and Korčula townscapes, finished in washes of watercolour. Propped up on the floor were a couple of paintings, landscapes in rich, deep colours, nearly abstract in their composition but still recognizable.

The two styles — the precise draftsmanship of the architectural drawings and the raw pottery and paintings — stood in sharp contrast.

"Yours?" he asked at last.

"The pen-and-watercolour drawings sell, the rest I just do. I have a kiln in the back, fire it with wood. The pottery studio's in a shed. When I say 'sell,' I mean used to," she added. "Lately my output has slowed to mostly pen-and-ink drawings on ordinary paper. Materials are hard to come by . . . and expensive."

"I guess the money you make from me will come in handy," he said.

"Mr. della Torre, the money will be the difference between my staying here and having to leave. For at least the next few months." She smiled back at him.

"Call me Marko. Maybe we should get started."

"I'll find you a couple of jerry cans and a hose. You can siphon petrol into them from your car while I get myself organized here."

"Is there somewhere I can hide the Citroën where it won't be obvious that I've come here?"

"There's a grove down the hill with an old barn. It has a roof and was reasonably clear the last time I looked. You can leave the car there."

By the time he got back to the house, his mouth tasted of gasoline fumes. He'd filled both twenty-litre metal jerry cans nearly to the top. He didn't have to wait long for her to get ready.

"I'm a little short of food. I'll bring some cookies, crackers, and salami, but that'll have to do until we can find a shop," she said. She added a couple of heavy ten-litre plastic jugs full of water to the bags that were by the door. "Right. We'll put these things in my car. Follow me down to the barn, and then you can ride with me after that."

The Citroën trundled slowly down the track behind Miranda's Fiat. She indicated at the turning, drove behind a clump of pines and cypresses, and pulled over.

"In there," she said, pointing to an old cinder-block barn in the path of her headlights. Its doors were missing, but the corrugated iron roof remained.

He squeezed the Citroën into the barn and was walking back up, alongside the Fiat's beams, when they suddenly went out. One had been flickering, so he assumed there'd been some electrical short. For a moment he was blinded, and his eyes tried desperately to adjust to the near complete darkness.

"What's going on?" he called, worried that she'd set him up somehow.

"Be quiet," she said. "Wait."

He heard her steps approach on the loose rocks.

"There's a car," she said.

"What?"

"A car. It's coming up the hill."

He listened hard. He heard the sound of an engine in low gear.

"It's coming up the track that runs to my farmhouse," she said. "You almost never get cars going up there at night. Not unless they're coming to see me, and nobody comes to see me this late."

"I did."

"I know."

They waited in the spot behind the trees. The car's engine grew louder and then they saw unsteady headlights breaking through the darkness, disappearing, and then breaking through again.

Suddenly the lights became sharp and bright as they swept past their little side road, and the car went farther up the hill.

"I'm starting to wonder whether a thousand marks is enough, Mr. della Torre."

He said nothing.

He squeezed into the front passenger seat of the Fiat, his knees pressed against the dashboard. The night smells — wild thyme and rosemary, pine resin and the faint fragrance of the sea — were overwhelmed by the fumes from the jerry cans in the back seat. Miranda started the engine again, turned on the small side parking lights, and drove slowly back to the junction and onto the track.

She turned the car down the track, in the direction from which the other car had come. She let gravity do much of the work, keeping her foot on the clutch so that the engine was near-silent as it idled. When they got down to the main road, she switched the headlights back on and put the Fiat into gear. One of the lights flickered like a strobe, distracting della Torre. He turned to look at the woman next to him. Her profile in the glow of the dashboard lights was severe, patrician.

"Don't go straight to the boat," della Torre said.

"Why?"

"Drive past. Just in case. Pull over around a hundred metres past the entrance and let me out."

"Mr. della Torre —"

"I've paid you the thousand marks already."

"That was for getting you to Dubrovnik. I should be charging you separately for getting you to my boat."

"We'll discuss it later."

He craved a cigarette but knew better than to light one with the fuel in the back of the car.

She drove past the turning to her boat, staying on the main road until she found a wide verge under some broad pines. Here there was some traffic; the occasional car still passed during the night. Without drawing attention to what he was doing, della Torre removed the Beretta from his shoulder bag and slipped it into his coat pocket. He took her big black Maglite flashlight from the footwell on his side of the car.

"I'll be back in fifteen minutes at the most," he said.

"And if you're not?"

"You go home a thousand marks richer."

He eased the car door shut and walked back along the road towards the turning. It was hard not to stumble, but he hurried. He was worried that the car that had gone up the hill would be returning soon, catching him in its headlights.

But he was in luck. More by feel than anything else, he found the little turning down to the cove where Miranda's boat was moored. He edged his way down the incline.

He moved at the speed of a stalking cat, careful not to make any noise, not to stumble or kick loose rocks. It was painfully slow going, and he realized he would be in plain sight to any- one with night-vision goggles. In his experience, this sort of American came well equipped.

His patience and his caution were rewarded.

He spotted a faint light, so fleeting that he wasn't sure he'd seen anything. But then there it was again, an almost imper- ceptible green glow. Della Torre guessed it was the luminous dial of a watch.

He crept closer. Small waves brushed against the rocky shore. Above, a faint breeze combed through the pines. From some- where came the distant sound of a car's gears shifting, and even farther away a dog barked. He thought he heard a low booming sound far away, but that could have been his senses filling in the emptiness of night.

He picked up a stone and tossed it in the general direction of the watch and heard the dull noise it made as it hit a tree or a branch. Whoever was attached to that phosphorescence moved sharply, breaking twigs underfoot.

One man, a single source of sound. Della Torre assumed the sentry didn't have any special night-vision equipment. If it was Grimston's people in the car, they might have dropped someone off to intercept him in case they flushed him down from the hill, which meant they'd be coming this way soon enough.

He took the Beretta out of his pocket, irritated that he hadn't put a bullet in the chamber earlier. But pulling back the slide would make an unmistakeable click, so he held off.

The man with the green watch froze again, listening. Della Torre knew he'd be wondering whether he'd heard a small animal dislodging a pine cone, or something more threatening.

Della Torre wondered how they'd known, how they'd figured it out so quickly. He was sure his flight from the hotel had been silent.

Grimston's professionalism and thoroughness were unsettling. Della Torre had an inkling that the freedom he'd been given since leaving Zagreb was illusory, that he'd always been on a short tether.

He could no longer wait to see what their next move would be. He had to act, knowing everything would move quickly from now on. This called for the sort of aggression he'd left behind him in the army, fifteen years ago. He'd been called up to the Yugoslav commandos because of his fluent American-accented English and had been trained to infiltrate behind the lines should there be an American invasion of the country. The irony didn't escape him.

He'd never been a particularly good soldier. And he'd probably been the worst Yugoslav commando junior officer in its history. But some of the training had stuck.

He threw another pebble, a little farther away from the man with the luminous watch. This time the man swung sharply and turned on his flashlight, pointing the beam away from della Torre and towards the water. Della Torre momentarily saw the tender to Miranda's little boat, upside down under the pine tree, as it had been earlier in the day.

The distance between him and the man was less than ten metres, too far to launch a surprise attack. But as the man swept the beam of his flashlight across the undergrowth, della Torre continued to creep forward. Each step he took sounded to him like a mountain cascade.

He was within five metres when the man turned abruptly, swinging the light towards della Torre.

In one motion della Torre flipped on his own torch and shone it straight into the man's eyes, simultaneously working the slide back on the Beretta.

"Don't move," he said in English. "I can't miss from here."

The man froze — the same man who'd followed him in Korčula the previous day, though looking less smug now.

"Switch off your flashlight," della Torre said.

The man did as he was told. "I just stopped to take a piss," he said, his tone assured but conciliatory. "On my way back to town."

"An American tourist out for a midnight walk?"

"That's right."

"Well, Mr. Tourist, drop the flashlight and get on your knees."

"You can have everything in my wallet," the man said. "It's just here." He reached towards his back pocket.

"Don't —"

The man pulled a gun from a holster in the small of his back. He fired in della Torre's general direction, but the bullet missed, slicing wildly into the trees. Della Torre threw himself sideways. As he did, he squeezed the trigger on the Beretta.

"Oh fuck," the man grunted, scrambling into the undergrowth.

Della Torre switched off the torch and crouched by the side of the path. He heard the other man move noisily away.

And then came the high whine of a car engine turning into the track with a quick downshift. The headlights swung down and della Torre shaded his eyes with his forearm.

Small stones scattered as the car braked sharply. The sentry's sprint was caught by the light, but then he disappeared into the darkness again.

"What —" Miranda started to say as della Torre stepped out of the beams.

"Ms. Walker, we need to get going. Right now," he said.

"Why have you got a gun, Mr. della Torre?"

"Because I thought I saw a pheasant."

"The season hasn't started yet."

"I was poaching."

"Mr. della Torre, if you expect my cooperation —"

"Ms. Walker, you have a thousand Deutschmarks to get me to Dubrovnik. You start now and get me there, I'll throw in another five hundred. Not including any passengers we take out."

"And if I don't like that deal, you've got a gun to make it sound more appealing."

"You know as well as I do that I can't force you to take me the whole way there by threatening you with a gun."

"Okay, Mr. della Torre, I suppose if I'm in for a penny, I'm in for a pound. Can you take the things out of the car and bring them down to the beach while I get the tender ready? The jerry cans and the water jugs and the various bags."

He did as he was told, wary lest the Americans return, while she launched the boat, all done under the illumination of the Fiat's headlights.

He was sure he'd wounded the other man, though not badly enough to fell him. The man didn't seem to present any immediate danger, but his colleagues would, once they came looking for him.

Laden, the little rowing boat sat low in the water, but Miranda assured della Torre that it wouldn't sink. He went back, switched off the car's lights, and locked it. Then he removed his boots, rolled up his trousers, and stepped gingerly through the cool, shallow water, rocks sharp underfoot, into the tender. It rocked wildly, and for a moment he thought it would overturn as he settled onto the bench in the stern. In the darkness, Miranda rowed with the ease of a practised sculler, making for the sailboat, which della Torre picked out with the flashlight.

They tied up the dinghy at the mooring buoy and got all their things aboard.

"There are some waterproofs hanging below that ought to fit you. They'll help keep the chill of the night air off," she said.

She'd lit a kerosene lamp down below and was pulling on plastic bib overalls and a rain slicker as he stepped down. The cabin berthed two and had a tiny galley that consisted of a gimballed stove and burner.

"It's a bigger boat than I thought," he said.

"Twenty feet at the waterline. She doesn't really have a keel, just a couple of fins to keep her stable, but it means she can travel in very shallow water. She draws only about a foot and a half unless she's laden, and I can take her out of the water when need be. She gets around, which is why she's called *Gypsy*."

"How soon can we get going?"

"Daybreak."

He climbed into the little cockpit at the back of the boat. "We'll need to move before then," he said, watching the beams of car headlights breaking through the trees that lined the main road, a modulated Morse code that took no deciphering.

The lights stopped for a time. Della Torre figured they were collecting the wounded man. Soon after that, he watched the car turn down the little path towards their cove.

"We need to get going," he said. "Now."

She didn't question him but instead flipped up a control panel behind the tiller, tinkered with the dials, and then started the engine. From there she went up front and undid the mooring rope.

She'd only just returned to the cockpit when *Gypsy* was lit up from the shore. Della Torre ducked low into the cockpit, turning to face the lights.

"Mrs. Walker. Mrs. Walker, we would like to speak to you." Grimston's voice carried over the water. "Please don't make the mistake of setting sail."

Miranda ignored him, throttling up and nudging the tiller so that *Gypsy* slipped past its mooring buoy.

"Mrs. Walker, as you sail away tonight, keep an eye on the hillside. Your house is up there, your car is down here. How much are you being paid for this trip? Will you make enough to cover what you lose?"

They heard the sound of glass breaking. And then there was a glow from among the trees, bright and orange-yellow at first, like a campfire, flickering, fading, and then suddenly billowing out in a fireball that silhouetted the big Mediterranean pine by the water in frozen agony.

"The trees will catch," Miranda said.

And then came bright rosettes from the side of the burning car, followed by the *crack, crack* of pistol shots. But *Gypsy* had moved steadily away from shore, and the torchlight on them weakened and faded. There were no sounds of the gunfire hitting its target.

"I'm sorry," della Torre said at long last.

"I've thought for a while that the war would come to me eventually," she said, her voice quiet, thoughtful. "It will touch everyone here. I don't know why I should be spared."

"But this isn't the war," della Torre said.

"Isn't it?"

He thought for a while and realized he didn't know. "Maybe it is."

"I don't know what's going on, Mr. della Torre . . ."

"Marko."

"Marko. Please call me Miranda."

"Miranda."

"I suppose I was getting too comfortable."

"Your art, your possessions . . ."

"My art was stale," she said. "I don't own anything else up there. Nothing that can't be replaced for a few hundred Deutschmarks."

Della Torre shook his head in the darkness. Small waves slapped the boat's bows. The engine muttered like an old man in the corner of a pub, unceasing but joyless and mortal.

"We'd better get as far as we can," she said. "I wouldn't be surprised if they found a fishing boat to follow us in the morning. They won't do it now without lights — anything with lights attracts the Yugoslav navy's attention. I won't be able to put up the sails until daybreak, though. There are too many islands around to risk sailing blind."

"Thank you," della Torre said. And then, after he'd listened for a while to the small waves tapping a rhythm against the wooden hull, the engine muttering: "You can't be doing this just for the money."

"I wonder."

15

THEY'D BEEN ON the water for an hour when della Torre saw the light on the Korčula hillside. It was a single point at first, and then two, three, four. The fire, at first an indistinct smudge, spread into a broad, flickering palette of citrus colours.

Miranda looked up and he heard her gasp: "Oh." Then, in the faint green light of the boat's binnacle compass, she turned away, facing the direction *Gypsy* was taking them, towards the mainland, towards the war. Della Torre turned to face the same way, and he saw other, similar glows in the distance, some solitary, others clustered in small groups. Fires were burning again that night, as they burned every night, like stars fallen to earth.

The chill in the air was made colder by the adrenaline seeping out of him.

"Can you sit here and hold the tiller while I brew us some coffee below," Miranda said. "Keep your eyes on the compass. The course we're on now will be safe until dawn." He took her place at the back of the boat while she descended the four steep steps into the dim cabin.

She brought up the hot, bitter drink in plastic mugs and sat next to della Torre. "People talk about Sir Fitzroy," she said. "He was heroic, but so was Lady Maclean. Her first husband died. He was a naval officer, killed in a cave in Crete during the war. She had two small children. After the war, Sir Fitzroy became a spy in Turkey, as he'd been in Russia before, though it's not commonly known. But she was there with him. By that time she had four children. Even so, she put her neck on the line."

"I didn't know."

"Well, now you do. Some of us don't scare easily, even if we spent our youth learning which way to pass the port or how to address a bishop."

"You sound like a Victorian adventurer," he said. "You were born a hundred years too late."

"Only if I were a man. But I'm not, so the present suits me just fine," she answered. "I learned to drive in an ancient Austin 7 built in 1928, top speed of thirty miles an hour. That was before I'd turned ten. It was my grandfather's car from when he was young. I used to drive it around the grounds. There was a narrow paved terrace between the house and its moat, no railing. It's tricky, double-declutching when you're barely tall enough to see the end of the car."

"They let you do that?" della Torre asked, incredulous.

"My grandfather encouraged me. My cousin once rode a motorcycle into the moat. They just fished him out. The Austin didn't have a roof, and I could swim. They figured they'd do the same with me if they needed to. Anyway, it wasn't nearly as dangerous as some of what Grandfather had us do. He used to send us climbing the beams of the barn, a good thirty feet up, to chase away the bats. The bats annoyed him but they're a protected species, and he couldn't shoot them or smoke them out. He used to say that if we were sensible, we wouldn't break our necks. And if we weren't, we deserved to. I suppose I'm trying to tell you I understand risk. I've taken risks all my life, one way or another. So don't feel too sorry for me, or that somehow you're the agent of my circumstances."

The coffee was hot and strong, and the night was still and deep. Now and again Miranda would alter their course as if steering by some other sense, like the smell or the feel of the breeze and damp air. Even with the caffeine, della Torre felt himself fading.

"I'm fine to stay at the helm until the morning. I always go to bed at dusk — saves on paraffin. So I had a decent sleep before you showed up," she said. "Why don't you go down and get a couple of hours' rest? I imagine you haven't slept at all night."

He was grateful, and did as she suggested. The sound of water flowing past, the odd syncopation of waves slapping the thin boards that separated him from the Adriatic, the boat's slight roll, the bow's dip in and up, his tiredness — all combined to create the odd sensation that he was floating inches above himself.

He woke with a start not long after daybreak, pale light spilling into the cabin. He climbed the four steps into the cockpit. The sails were up and the engine was off, and they were a couple of hundred metres off a rocky shore.

"Did you sleep well?" Miranda asked.

"Yes, thanks," della Torre said. "Where are we?"

"Off the Pelješac. The current was pushing us back towards Korčula last night, but I didn't want to run the engine any harder, so we haven't gone as far as you might expect. But we'll make four or five knots now that it's light. It's a decent breeze, southwesterly. Have you done any sailing?"

"Once."

"Do you know what a jib sheet is?"

"No."

"It's that red rope. It controls the front sail. Sit on the windward side of the boat and let out the jib sheet opposite you a little until I tell you to stop."

He did as he was told.

The little boat slipped neatly through the water, bouncing on the waves. They were moving at the pace of a leisurely bicycle ride, but for della Torre the speed was somehow exhilarating. Clouds scudded over the steep, high rocky ridge that crested the peninsula. The dinghy took the waves at a canter but the air felt deceptively still, as if there were no wind at all. In the anemic light, he could see warships — a corvette out to sea and a pair of gunboats in the waters towards Dubrovnik — but none seemed to pay them any attention.

They turned slightly towards the southeast. Miranda had him pull in the jib, and she did the same for the mainsail. It was hard to believe heavy guns were firing no more than fifty kilometres away. The wind now came over the starboard gunwales, and della Torre could feel it whipping through his hair, spray coming over the bows as the little boat bounced across the waves, making him glad of his waterproofs.

A couple of fishing boats were on the water. They were Orebić-based and didn't matter to them, Miranda said. She kept an eye out for any vessels appearing from the direction of Korčula. Skeins of smoke rose above the mainland mountains, washed out and drab, until they faded into the gloomy skies.

"We've got a head start on anybody following us," she said. "The fishing boats wouldn't have come out at night without lights. They'll have a couple of knots on us, but we've got around twenty kilometres on them. And they'll be reluctant to travel beyond Šipan Island. The mainland side is vulnerable to artillery fire; the Serb gunners in the hills have been getting better at hitting moving targets. On the seaward side the patrol boats have taken to running vessels up against cliffs. It seems to be a game for them. Anyway, that's the limit of the blockade."

"What are we going to do, then?"

"You'll see," she said. "We'll need some breakfast first, though."

They sailed until they reached a small fishing village, little more than a couple of rows of red-tiled white stone houses set behind a breakwater under the steep, raw white hills. Miranda took *Gypsy* in under sail. The wind, as long as it didn't swing, would guide them back out of the harbour.

There was a shuttered restaurant on the waterfront, set back from the road under the shade of bushy palms. But the village's little grocery store was open. The girl behind the counter made them sandwiches from local ham and freshly baked spongy white bread, and a couple of strong coffees that she served in heavy china cups that at one time must have belonged to a hotel. They ate sitting with their legs hanging over the edge of the harbour wall, della Torre feeling a vestigial rocking sensation from being in the boat.

He wondered whether he had been right to abandon Anzulović, knowing there was no way the older man could have made the rooftop crossing but feeling half guilty for having left without saying a word. Had he made an escape? Or was Grimston driving him? Was della Torre the rabbit chosen to flush out the ultimate game?

He felt the chill air slip down past the top of his shirt and over the back of his neck, reminding him it was late in the season. Not many people lived in the village year-round, and many of those who did had left when the Serbs got a foothold on the peninsula, less than thirty kilometres down the road. But a few came down to inspect these strange out-of-season tourists who seemed oblivious to the war. No one was forward enough to ask them what they were doing.

The wind blew steadily from the southwest.

"Looks like rain," Miranda said. "We're going to get wet."

They pushed the boat off the harbour wall. The onshore wind made *Gypsy* heel hard as they went out, both of them throwing their weight onto the seaward gunwale to keep the boat as flat as possible. Spray flicked at them, salty and cold. The clouds had boiled up, filling the sky, and della Torre saw that Miranda was right about the change of weather.

They sailed along a hostile shoreline. Small waves broke

against white rocks overhung by low, broad pines. The rain was a steady blowing drizzle that filled the air so that they breathed water.

The mountains' scalloped skirts at the water's fringes made a string of coves. For a margin of safety from shallow rocks, Miranda took *Gypsy* farther out.

Della Torre shivered. He'd pulled on his waterproof hat only after his hair had already been drenched, and now he felt the chill.

The wind became a squall, rain driven in bands across the water, while the waves picked up. Miranda strained at the tiller and sails, keeping the boat on course in conditions that had become difficult.

Della Torre worked the ropes controlling the forward sail, shifting his weight in the cockpit according to the orders Miranda called out. He saw a steeliness in her; she seemed practised at escaping, though maybe not under these circumstances.

"It's miserable sailing in these conditions," della Torre said.

"It keeps us out of sight."

They sailed like that, hour after hour, until della Torre saw in the distance the long green shadow of Mljet Island.

"All around the island there are these green forests and hills, and the lake is as blue as a crayon," Miranda said. "Then there are these tall stone walls and red roofs — a fairy-tale friary."

"Do you get friars in fairy tales?"

"I don't know. Castles and ogres, yes, but I don't know about friars."

When the wind gusted, rain swept into them, making *Gypsy* heel right over, leaving della Torre scrambling up the side and over the edge. His misery grew the colder he got, and he hungered for nicotine.

Miranda seemed immune to the weather, pressing on, holding firmly on the tiller and the main sheet, making small adjustments, and smiling against the wind and rain.

The morning drew into the afternoon and still they sailed.

"Šipan." She pointed ahead to the island's green-grey humps rising out of the water.

"How long will it take us to get there?"

"We'll get there," she said.

And then, over her shoulder in a break in the rain, he thought he saw something. At first he couldn't be sure, but over the next hour he saw it again, once, twice more. As time went on, it developed into a motor cruiser, a fast luxury boat.

"That's not a fishing boat," della Torre said.

"No, it's not. Go down into the cabin and get my binoculars. They'll be in the shelf opposite the galley."

When he brought them up, she had him take the tiller while she trained the binoculars on the boat.

"Hard to tell, but she looks like something called *Dim* — 'smoke' in Serbo-Croat, not 'stupid' in English," Miranda said. "If it is, Korčula's her home port. I don't know how they got hold of her. Maybe they bribed someone at the marina, because there's zero chance the owner would have let them have her. I know him. He's a bigwig in Belgrade. Most pompous man in the country, and it's not like there isn't plenty of competition."

"How long before they catch up with us?"

"She makes around thirty knots. But they won't want to travel that fast. Fishing boats go at twelve to fifteen knots. Anything moving much faster will have the patrol boats onto them in double-quick time, thinking they're blockade runners. We make six. The horizon's about two miles back. We're about half an hour away from where we want to be. It'll be close."

They crossed a narrow channel by a squat, square lighthouse. The small islands they passed looked uninhabited. There were no safe landing places, just rocky shores. It was early afternoon, but the light was difficult, the distant mainland disappearing into the general gloom as they slipped into a deep, long inlet between two hilly promontories.

Here the wind fluked, making the little boat dance, but it also blew less strongly. By the time they got to the harbour wall, della Torre could see the motor cruiser distinctly, towards the mouth of the bay.

Miranda moved with extraordinary speed, uncleating the main and jib halyards so that the sodden, heavy sails spilled into the boat as she went back to the tiller to steer into the landing in one deft move. She had della Torre grab the mooring line and guide it to a rust-worn ring on the harbour wall, where he tied it up.

"Wait here," she said. "They'll either come in slowly or launch a dinghy. *Dim* has a pretty deep draft, and the bay shallows quickly, but they can get in on sonar. If we're lucky they might just decide to blockade us until the weather clears. But we ought to hurry anyway."

A few people braved the drizzle, drawn to the harbour wall by curiosity. Miranda, still in her heavy raincoat but stripped of her sailing overalls and down to her shorts, disappeared into a building not far from where they'd tied up.

Della Torre watched the big motor cruiser slip in and out of the mist, waiting. An albino assassin with windows of smoked glass. He wondered if it went for anything less than a million marks. Or maybe dollars. Only people with the most serious pull in government could afford conspicuous wealth like that. How had Grimston gotten hold of it?

The American had them cornered in this deep bay. Šipan wasn't big. If he couldn't get off the island, they'd track him down soon enough. Only three hundred or so people, mostly old, lived here. Della Torre knew the island well enough to know there were few places where he could hide for more than a few days. Strumbić's secret villa, where the other Americans had died not even two months ago, was on the other side.

Miranda came back shortly and hopped into the boat. "We're going to give that motorboat the slip," she said.

"How? What?"

"Just do as I say."

With a practised hand, she rolled the mainsail around the boom and lowered it into the boat. Then for a few minutes she tinkered with a metal collar at the base of the mast.

"Hold this," she said. "Now, when I say so, help me walk the mast down the length of the boat."

It didn't take long to get the long aluminium spar down along the length of the vessel and beyond.

Della Torre wondered whether she might try to hide the boat but realized what a ridiculous notion that was. Then, from behind the shuttered hotel at the end of the bay, a Massey Ferguson tractor appeared, ancient but massive and still robust, towing a long trailer along the harbour wall. He watched it swing around to face the hill that led from the waterfront. And then it reversed down a stone ramp, slowly easing the trailer into the water until it was fully submerged.

"Here's our ride," Miranda said, starting up the boat's engine.

She steered *Gypsy* to the end of the trailer and then, with a burst of speed, drove it onto the middle of its now-submerged bed. The moment she cut the engine, she hopped off the boat onto the edge of the trailer. Working in the water, she fixed a big strap to the boat's bow and hooked it to a yoke attached to the back of the tractor. And then, hopping off to stand on the harbour wall with della Torre, she watched the tractor pull the boat out of the water.

It was a relatively slow business, but the operation went smoothly. And the moment the boat was out, she said, "Come on," and they sat on the big mudguards on either side of the driver as he towed the boat along the harbourfront and up the road.

They were partway up the hill when della Torre looked back to see that the motor cruiser had launched a Zodiac RIB. He couldn't see how many people were on board, but he knew they'd land before long.

"Can we go any faster?" were his first words to the tractor driver. He was a farmer, in blue coveralls and a blue rain slicker. His hair was grey and stubbly, and his thin face was heavily creased. He looked a bit like Libero and, like Libero, he smelled of the farmyard, straw and muck.

"This sort of job is lots of wear and tear on a tractor," the man said.

"I told him you'd pay a hundred dollars to get us to the other end of the island," Miranda said in English. "This counts as expenses."

Della Torre was about to protest at the cost. A hundred dollars to cross eight kilometres was outrageous. But it was their only way out. So instead he asked, "Would another ten dollars encourage you to go quicker?"

"Yup."

"Then for god's sake, speed up."

"Oh, I will," the farmer said. But he kept the tractor at its pace.

Della Torre could hear the RIB's engine echoing in the harbour below. How long before Grimston's men found a car and overtook them?

"I thought we had a deal to speed up."

"Oh, we do. When we get to the top of the hill. Then you'll be asking me to slow down," the farmer said.

"Don't worry," Miranda said, looking back at the town. "Nobody else on the island has any petrol. Your friends might be able to find some bicycles, but even that'll take them a while."

The farmer was right. Once they'd climbed over the crest of the low hill overlooking the fishing port, the tractor sped up, propelled in part by the weight of the boat behind.

The single-track road stretched along a shallow green valley that ran the length of the island. They didn't pass another vehicle on the way. Centuries before, Šipan had been a holiday island for Dubrovnik's nobility, but now the Renaissance palaces on their once-manicured grounds were ruins, their roofs long gone, their windows hollow-eyed, the stone columns that had held avenues of shading vines reduced to scattered bones protruding from the damp earth.

The trip took no more than half an hour, even at tractor speed. There was no further sign of their pursuers. The village at the other end of the island was smaller than the one they'd arrived in, and more tightly built around a narrow bay. Turning the trailer was tricky in those confined spaces, but the farmer seemed well practised, and in short order he was backing down a little sandy beach and from there into the water, where they refloated the boat. Della Torre paid the man, who shook his head at their madness.

Miranda found a woman at a guest house to feed them sandwiches made with her home-cured ham and a coarse loaf of mixed cornmeal and wheat she'd baked that morning.

Della Torre helped as much as he could to rig the boat again. While Miranda finished the preparations, he smoked a soggy cigarette and gazed at the walls of the harbour's small, dilapidated castle and their arabesque crenellations — another of Šipan's forgotten palaces.

"I suppose we should hurry," he said. "That farmer has probably gone back to collect the people who are after me."

"He's not collecting anyone else tonight. Your hundred dollars wasn't just to get us here. You hired the tractor and trailer for your exclusive use until the morning."

"You made that arrangement?"

"Yes."

"He'll keep to it?"

"He'll keep to it."

"How do you know? If the Americans can afford to make use of that big boat, they'll have enough money to persuade your farmer friend."

"Because they'll pay as much tomorrow morning to get their Zodiac across. But even if the farmer does break his promise, the Yugoslavs will shoot at the boat as soon as they hear it. Look around."

It was only then that he noticed there were no other boats in the harbour.

"This is where the blockade starts," she said. "Anyone with a boat has already taken it to the other harbour, or it's been sunk or stolen by the Yugoslav navy."

"So why won't they sink us?"

"They might, but we're not going to be on the water long." She pointed in the direction of the next island, which was lost in the drizzle. "It's getting late and we're not going far. I'd rather have gone in the dark, but we'll take a risk. We're not going to motor; they'd pick that up quickly. The rain cuts visibility. By the time anyone notices we'll be in Lopud . . . I hope."

As they set off, della Torre could make out a nineteenth-century sea captain's villa. It was a child's drawing of a house, a square structure of white stone, two storeys high, with a steep-pitched red-tile roof. The front was symmetrical, with the main entrance in the middle, three windows on each side, and seven above. The building was framed by mature cypresses on either side. Strumbić's villa now had the look of a tomb.

He could remember it vividly. The fig tree that overhung the rear courtyard. The white stone with its veiny rust-brown stain the colour of old blood. This was the place where his own blood had mingled with those of the dead men, where they'd tied him to the table and suffocated him until he talked. He felt again the thirst, the pain of being beaten while tied to a chair.

Snapshots of that night's turmoil flickered through his memory. Overturned chairs. Broken glass. The musty animal smell of dried piss. They'd concussed him and he'd wet himself. He had a brief atavistic urge to cross himself, as his grandmother might have done. Though he didn't believe. Or didn't think he believed.

Could he really be blamed for bearing false witness, for implicating Strumbić to save himself?

Yes, he thought. *Yes.*

He shook himself into the present. There would be new horrors ahead. There was no reason to dwell on old ones.

16

THE WIND HAD turned and was blowing from the east, not hard, not a bora, but cold nonetheless. Della Torre made sure his waterproofs were snug. Even so, he felt the chill in his feet, bare in the big rubber sailing boots.

He thought he heard thunder but realized it was the sound of big guns rolling across the water. A drawn-out beat of short bursts followed by long silences.

Behind him, Šipan faded into the mist and drizzle. He knew it was a short stretch of water between the islands, no more than a couple of kilometres, but to cross it still felt like madness. During breaks in the rain he could see three navy warships.

"Do you think they'll come after us? The Zodiac, I mean," he asked.

"They might. It's a big risk. The RIB's engine is very noisy. But even if they don't get blown out of the water, they won't find us."

"Why not?"

"You'll see."

It was a choppy crossing; the current running through the channel between the islands kicked up waves against the easterly wind. Despite his waterproofs, della Torre was soggy, bedraggled. Miranda was also wet, and once or twice he saw her shiver.

They slipped past a small, uninhabited island and were quickly in Lopud's broad bay. But rather than head into the sheltered harbour, Miranda steered the boat towards a distant stone pier. As she rounded the pier with a deft flick of the tiller, she jumped forward, dropped the sails, and hopped ashore.

She showed him how to stow the sails, and they went through the routine of dropping the mast again. And then she pulled the boat along the shore, where della Torre was surprised to see a narrow inlet sheltered by the canopy of a couple of big pine trees. *Gypsy* fitted snugly into that space, a couple of rubber fenders cushioning her from the rocks.

"Seems a clever place to park," della Torre said.

"You need to know the island well. None of the locals will tell you to keep your boat here. You don't have to pay mooring or harbour fees. It also means the Yugoslav navy won't see it."

"You seem to know a lot about evading the navy."

She shrugged. "The only downside to this parking place is that we stay up there." She pointed to the other side of the harbour, up towards a steep hill that towered over the village. "And it's a walk through the scrub to get to the road."

They trudged their way through the gloom and drizzle, carrying what they needed in their holdalls. The little port seemed shuttered, closed off from the wider world. They saw no one, though the smell of woodsmoke told them there was life.

The house was modern, crudely built and unfinished, with iron reinforcing rods poking out from between the first and second storeys, where someone might once have contemplated building a balcony.

The woman who opened the door for them was late-middle-aged, heavy though not fat, her apron-like dress patterned with small flowers.

She clucked at them. "Signora, I wasn't expecting you."

Miranda smiled. "I'm sorry, I should have warned you."

The woman crossed herself. "Come in, come in. You and the

gentleman will catch a terrible cold. Go to the back room and take off your wet clothes and I'll light the fire for the bath. It won't take long to heat the water. And then I'll try to find something for you to eat."

They entered, bedraggled and sodden. The woman led them to a concrete-floored back room, where they stripped down to their underwear, too tired and cold to be shy. They wrapped themselves in worn terry cloth bathrobes that were hanging on a peg, della Torre's not quite reaching his knees.

They waited for a quarter of an hour before the woman came back down.

"Oh, I didn't mean to leave you freezing here. I just wanted to make sure the water was warm enough," she said, horrified at how pale they looked. "Up, up." She pointed to the stairs.

"You go first," della Torre said miserably.

"Come, I think we can put aside chivalry and embarrassment in the name of thawing out, don't you, Mr. della Torre?" Miranda said.

"Marko."

"Marko."

He followed Miranda up the rough concrete staircase to the bathroom. The room was as basic as the one they'd left. The bathtub was the longest della Torre had ever seen. The hot water source was a tall white-enamelled cylinder tank in the corner of the room, fuelled by a wood fire in the stove built into its base. It was a primitive arrangement, but effective.

Miranda shut the door.

"It's big enough for two," she said. "I'm too tired, and I hope you are too, to get any ideas. You take one end, I'll take the other. Keep your feet to yourself, and we can both get the chill out of our bones."

Della Torre nodded, unable to think of anything other than soaking in some warmth. And sleep.

The water steamed as it filled the bath, condensation beading on the tile walls. When the water reached sufficient depth and was at a temperature just shy of scalding, Miranda stripped and slipped into the tub, her back to him, showing a modicum of modesty. When she leaned back, he could only just see the pink nipples on her pale white breasts. He followed suit, trying not to care how much the cold and tiredness had shrunk him.

They reclined there, each in their own end, mostly submerged, colour seeping into their cheeks, not touching except when their feet bumped against each other.

They were both too tired to talk. Della Torre lay in water to his chin, steam curling up in the yellow light of the smoking kerosene lantern. As with the other islands, the electricity supply from the mainland had been cut off; local generators provided power to only a few central buildings, and even then for only part of the day.

"We ought to get out before we fall asleep," della Torre said. But Miranda had already nodded off. The water cooled and he woke her.

They dried themselves with thin towels and dressed with their backs to each other. He regretted not bringing more clothes.

Their hostess had spread out a meal for them in the formal dining room, its heavy, dark Italianate furniture made gloomy by flickering candlelight. She'd prepared schnitzels — a neighbour had slaughtered a pig a few days earlier — and served them with thick ribbon pasta and boiled greens. It was just the sort of food their bodies craved after that long day, and was made more welcome still by the local wine, which was light enough to drink neat. The main course was served with hand-sliced home-cured ham and salami and a local cow's-milk cheese, which della Torre and Miranda picked at throughout their meal.

The woman sat with them, though she declined to eat. She was happy to have company, happy to have some new people to talk to. Her husband had died of cancer a few years before, and her son lived in Sweden with his Swedish wife. They drove down every summer, all that way, for just a week by the seaside. Now and again she'd interrupt her own monologue to ask, "How are we going to survive?" while dabbing at her eyes with a lace handkerchief that looked like a big doily.

After dinner, she brought them cups of tea made with dried chamomile flowers from her own garden, and a bar of milk chocolate, turned white with age, that both her guests politely refused.

Della Torre lit a cigarette. The warm smoke seeped into his lungs, soothing him. Miranda was visibly drooping over the table; the exhaustion of helming a small boat against a steady wind for most of the day and through the previous night was taking hold. As soon as it was polite, she said she'd like to turn in.

"Signora, I'm so sorry," the old woman said. "But I have only your room. The furniture I have taken from the upstairs rooms and stored away, in case they drop bombs."

"Never mind. The room still has a sofa as well as the bed?"

"But of course."

"Then if we could have some extra sheets and blankets, the room will be sufficient."

The room was warm. The woman had stoked the green-tiled stove in the corner when they'd arrived. Miranda stripped, pulled on a linen nightshirt, and slipped into the bed. The sofa was all right angles, lumpy, and a fraction too short for della Torre's frame, but it was as welcome as any he'd ever stretched out on.

"You're a puzzling person," he said as she blew out the kerosene lamp, leaving them in total darkness. "Is it really just the money?"

"Goodnight, Mr. della Torre," she said.

"Goodnight."

"And thank you for not taking advantage of the situation in the bath," she said in a tone that precluded any more conversation.

She woke him early the next morning. She was dressed and the blinds were partly drawn, the wooden shutters open slightly. The sun was bright, but there was a chill in the room. The faint smell of coffee pricked his attention.

"Your friends are here," she said. He sat up sharply and looked out the window in the direction she pointed. The water on the bay shimmered like fish scales. Beyond was a hilly ridge. It took him a while to spot the Zodiac in the harbour.

"How?"

"They must have crossed the channel after us."

"But I thought the farmer —"

"He must have gotten a good offer."

"Fuck," he said. "Have they found the boat?"

"Unlikely."

"It was unlikely they'd make the crossing in the Zodiac."

"True," she said.

"I don't suppose we could sneak out?"

"Tonight. We'll have to go in the dark," she said. "But we would have had to anyway, because of the navy ships."

"They'll be looking for us."

"I know, but there aren't too many people to ask. The town's mostly abandoned, and there are plenty of empty houses to search."

"What about the landlady here?"

"I've asked her to say nothing about us if strangers come calling."

"Will she?"

"She said she's spending the day up the hill digging her potatoes and harvesting the rest of her beans. She's got chickens and pigs that also need tending to. It'll be a long winter and the supplies are pretty uncertain. So it's us on our own. And if we don't answer the door, would they really break in?"

"Best we don't move around the house too much."

They shuttered the blinds and had a simple breakfast of bread

THE HEART OF HELL

with homemade plum jam and chamomile tea, then settled in
to wait out the day in their room.

"I thought I smelled coffee," della Torre said.

"It's not on offer."

Della Torre lay back on the sofa, Lucky in hand, watching
the smoke snake, blue in the dim light. Miranda sat patiently,
uncannily still, lost in thought.

Sometime in the mid-morning they heard a knock on the
door. Della Torre slipped onto the floor, out of sight of the window, and pulled the Beretta out of his bag, priming it with a
pull on the slide.

They heard whoever it was crunch across the gravel, trying
to look in. The shutter was latched from the inside; the man on
the other side made only a cursory effort to pull it open.

They heard him walk back down the path, no doubt to try the
house next door. Depending on how many people were searching, it would take most of the day to check all the houses on
the island.

Della Torre and Miranda stayed quiet for a long time. Even
their breath was inaudible.

Miranda broke the silence. "Would you have shot him?"

"Maybe," della Torre said.

"You're playing a dangerous game. For a while I thought you
were going to Dubrovnik to get somebody out. But now I'm
wondering whether you're going there to get away."

"Does it matter?"

"You mean, because I'm being paid?" Without waiting for the
answer, she said, "No, it doesn't matter."

He was silent for a while, scrutinizing her in the dimness of
the room. She wasn't what passed for beautiful to most people,
but she was striking, with her symmetrical, elegant features
and self-possession. And she had that hard-as-nails quality della
Torre had observed before.

"You've got me stumped, Ms. Walker. I keep wondering

whether you're really that broke, or if you're one of those suicidal types who don't care about themselves, or if you're just crazy. And I can't really believe you're any of those things."

"What about you?" she asked.

"I'm not sure."

"Except you've got to get to Dubrovnik."

"That's right."

"Well, why don't we keep it to that simple transaction, Mr. della Torre. And you don't need to worry about me."

He was glad they'd been exhausted in the bath, because he'd have been tempted. And he knew he would have been rebuffed in the most direct and unequivocal manner. No gentle letdown, no coquettishness, no half-flattery or suggestion that at another time, under different circumstances . . .

He put the gun down on the floor next to him, lit a cigarette, and waited for the day to tick by.

Their hostess came back for lunch. "A couple of men came asking if I'd seen you," she said. "They described you. I told them you don't see many strangers about these days. A neighbour told them I'd gone up to my vegetable garden."

"What language did they speak?" della Torre asked.

"Croatian, of course. What language did you think they would speak?"

"What did they look like?"

"The one who talked was tall, the other one wasn't so tall. Middle-aged. The quiet one dressed like a German." She shrugged. "Before this war you couldn't move for the tourists in the summer, all sorts. Even at this time of year. My house would be full all summer with foreigners and people from all over our country. An honest person could make a living. What will happen to us now? I'll have to go. The radio says boats are coming to rescue us. But where can I go? My daughter-in-law won't have me in Sweden. What's to happen to us?"

"Did you have a sense whether there were any more men?"

della Torre asked, trying to sound less abrupt and insistent than he felt.

"Ah." She held up her hands in supplication. "I saw two. If the ships don't come we'll starve before the end of the winter. It's just as well there are so few of us on the island. We have our hams and our gardens."

She cooked them a simple stew of potatoes, beans, cabbage, and tinned tomatoes, fortified by scraps of meat from their meal the night before. They ate in the kitchen, della Torre keeping a nervous eye on the window at the back of the house for any sign of the men.

He filled the long day in the house as best he could, but as late afternoon drew on, Miranda said it was time to move. He paid their hostess from his dwindling stock of Deutschmarks. She was still weeping into her handkerchief as they left.

They went out the back door and followed a path uphill through the scrub and trees, which were still damp from the previous day's rain. Della Torre guessed they were going to go around the village and approach the boat through the undergrowth. But the route Miranda took cut diagonally across the island. They passed another broad bay, opposite the village, this one sandy and beautiful, a magnet for day trippers from Dubrovnik during the good times. *Will they ever return?* he wondered.

Eventually they ascended the crest of a hill along a path that had sunk into the ground and was shaded by overhanging branches, to a promontory that made up the far end of the bay. There the land was wild, all scrub and trees — the air full of pine resin. They passed the ruins of a small chapel and then the overgrown foundations of another, larger building. Here the land had once been terraced, but slowly the stones were being reclaimed by the earth.

The colours of the light turned warm with the evening, and clouds had formed high above, the sinking sun making them an iridescent grey. Mackerel skies.

They came to a small clearing with what might once have been a hamlet, though only one tiny stone structure seemed in good repair. An old man sat on the doorstep, watching them come along the path.

"Good evening," Miranda said.

"Good evening," he said, his voice neutral.

"I've brought you some coffee," she said, pulling a kilo bag of whole beans out of her holdall.

The man wore an old blue beret and a week's worth of grey stubble. He rose slowly and nodded.

"Thank you. I'd run out. Cigarettes also getting low."

Della Torre offered him one from his nearly full pack and the old man took the lot, drawing one out before pocketing the rest. He went inside the little hut and came back out with the cigarette lit and the coffee put away.

"Not many of us left on the island. When they come, when they bomb us, we'll die in our houses. You can see them there." He led della Torre and Miranda to the edge of the clearing, where between the trees they could make out another small island and Dubrovnik's northern port and suburbs, now surprisingly close. But what caught della Torre's eye was the warships.

"Sweet Jesus," he muttered. "Any more boats and you'd have to step over them to get to Dubrovnik."

The old man shook his head. "We thought those times had passed. You see that island there, at the mouth of the harbour," he said, waving in the direction of the low, tree-covered emerald-green island. "That's Daksa. They say you can see ghosts there. I don't know; I'm so old my eyes are going. I can barely see the newspaper to read it. Doesn't matter, there might as well be ghosts. After the war the Partizans rounded people up in Dubrovnik. Collaborators, they called them. Maybe some were. In the same way we all collaborated with the Communists after the war. You do what you do to survive. But if the Partizans didn't like you, they'd call you a collaborator. Priests, schoolteachers, the mayor, who'd just been elected in a popular referendum. The Partizans rowed them out there in the night and killed them. No one goes to Daksa. Maybe Germans or Italians who don't know anything, but they have to go in their own boats. Nobody would take them there. We had a couple here, offered me forty Deutschmarks to take them across. I wouldn't. I have never set foot on that island and I've spent my whole life not seeing that island, but now they're making us remember."

They sat on a bench made from an old tree trunk split in half, sheltered from the breeze by a half-fallen dry-stone wall and lemon trees.

"After the war we just ignored Daksa. One of those bad memories. We tried to forget about it. But Daksa is always with us," the old man said. And then, raising his hand a little, listening to the wind: "Do you hear that? Guns. Down the coast now, the other side of Dubrovnik. But they're over here too. The shells can reach us from those mountains. Šipan has been hit, eh?"

Della Torre nodded.

"Or maybe the gunboats will use us for practice," the old man continued. "Well, let's taste some of that coffee of yours." He went into the house.

"So you brought me up here to show me why we can't make it to Dubrovnik," della Torre said to Miranda.

"No," she replied. "I brought you up here because this is the only way we'll get there."

The old man brought out three small unmatched china cups of strong black coffee. Della Torre's cup was chipped and the crack was stained dark.

"The rain wet a lot of the wood. Might take some time to catch," the old man said to Miranda. Something was happening here that della Torre didn't understand.

"We need to be away as soon as the sun sets," she replied.

The man shrugged. "God go with you."

They left as the sun was easing its way across the Adriatic, ducking beneath the building clouds. The northeasterly wind was coming off the backbone of white mountains that rose along the mainland.

They made their way along different tracks back to the hill-side where *Gypsy* lay hidden under its cover of pine trees. The harbour wall at the other side of the bay hid the Zodiac, but della Torre doubted his pursuers would have gone anywhere in the daylight. Not with the Yugoslav boats prowling.

A path led them down to the shore a little way from *Gypsy*, and della Torre had Miranda stay there in the half-light while he crept towards the boat. When he was sure it wasn't being watched, he brought her back to the boat. They launched it into the dusk. The other side of the bay, where the harbour lay, was brushed by the last of the twilight; this side was in deeper shadow.

The northeasterly made the lee shore dangerous, but Miranda was quick to hoist the sails and pull the little boat's nose towards the wind so that it heeled but slid along the promontory just beyond the rocks. And then they rounded the island and headed towards Dubrovnik, unseen.

On the seaward side of the island, the waves beat against the rocks. Here the cliffs offered nowhere to hide if a gunship approached. But it also made the boat impossible to spot in what-ever faint light was left. The sun dipped below the clouds, flat-tened itself orange across the water, and then disappeared. Water slapped against the hull, and the boat bucked along easily. Soon enough they had passed the length of the little island.

There was now a smear of moonlight, but not enough to navi-gate by. Della Torre knew there were island rocks to negotiate before they reached the peninsula where the Austro-Hungarians had built their villas, immediately to the north of the fortress city. He was uneasy, grateful for the bulk of his life jacket, braced against what he was sure would be an inevitable collision, will-ing himself to be calm but gripping the gunwales hard when-ever the boat skipped.

They moved in silence, the sea washing against the hull, the occasional flap of the sail as Miranda trimmed it by feel, unable to see how it shaped in the light breeze.

They saw some bright flickers on the mainland, like late-summer fireflies. Maybe a few people had their own generators. Most, though, would be using storm lanterns, candles. Higher up on the mountains were the Serb positions, pools of electric brightness. The warships had hung their navigation beacons, unworried about having to defend themselves.

Della Torre turned and caught a puzzling sight. Two fires burned on what he was sure was the hill rising above Lopud. And then he noticed that Miranda was frequently looking back to the same spot.

"Are those fires the reason we went to see the old man?"

"An old smuggler's trick," she replied, her voice low so that it was barely audible. "If I keep those two fires lined up, I'll avoid the next island and the rocks."

"For the price of a bag of coffee."

"And your cigarettes."

The wind was kind to them, blowing steadily. And visibility was clear, so there was no problem seeing the fires the old man kept burning.

And then, just perceptibly, della Torre sensed they'd come into the shadow of land again. The breeze shifted and Miranda had to adjust the sail trim. The air carried the smell of pines and garbage. Somewhere not far away, he could hear the slap of waves on rocks. He could swim to shore, he knew. It couldn't be more than a couple of hundred metres. There were no strong tides, so the currents would be manageable.

But as they sailed on, della Torre wondered how they'd find their way to the fortress city's harbour in the darkness. "How much farther, do you think?" he asked.

"Not far."

"How will you know where to come in?"

"Every few minutes you're going to shine a torch landward. Just for a second at a time," she said. "It's a risk, but there's no other way. The harbourmaster in Dubrovnik isn't keeping the navigation beacons lit; they present too nice a target for Serb gunners. But be careful, there's a Yugoslav ship not far off; those are her lights."

Della Torre ducked under the mainsail and swallowed hard at what he saw. The ship seemed to be almost on top of them.

He found a heavy torch in the cabin and switched it on, pointing the beam towards land. He wasn't sure where to aim and went too high at first, sketching the trees, but quickly lowered, only to find a rocky shore. He turned off the torch, and after ten minutes he switched it on again, sweeping the light forward, looking for the inlet.

"Turn it off," Miranda said with a catch in her voice. It was the first time he'd sensed that she might be frightened. Only then did he notice the low throb of an engine growing closer. But it was too late.

"Get ready to swim," she said as a searchlight swept the water until it caught them in its beam.

A single heavy-calibre shot fired, and a loud-hailer called for them to lower their sail. Miranda did as she was told, the folds of heavy canvas spilling over them in the cabin, the boat rocking gently on the waves.

"They'll pick us out if we jump. And shoot us," della Torre urged. Yet in that panic-filled moment a faint memory brushed through his mind, like a handful of notes from a familiar melody. He pointed his flashlight at the warship, desperate to remember how the Montenegrin had navigated these waters safely this past summer, the night Rebecca had died.

In Morse, he spelled out A-T-H-O-S.

"What are you doing?" she said. "Stop. Don't provoke them, please."

There was a moment when the ship's powerful beam stayed

on him, blinding him so that when he shut his eyes, dark colours painted themselves on the insides of his eyelids.

He tried again. A-T-H-O-S.

The searchlight swung off them and dimmed. A signal light batted out Morse at him. P-O-R-T-H-O-S.

It seemed beyond belief that it was working. He almost laughed with exhilaration. And in the same instant he was struck with desperation. What came next?

"What's the name of the musketeer?" he pleaded.

"What?" Miranda asked.

"Dumas. *The Three Musketeers*. The third one. Porthos, Athos, and . . . not d'Artagnan. The third one."

The warship flashed P-O-R-T-H-O-S at him again.

"Aramis," she said.

"Sweet god, that's right," he said, instantly signalling A-R-A-M-I-S.

The search beam switched off, and the ship turned back to its station.

Della Torre exhaled, giddy, overwhelmed. Without knowing it, he'd had a free pass into and out of Dubrovnik all along.

"What happened?" Miranda asked.

"It's the signal smugglers use. It's their password."

"But how did you know?"

"I didn't. Or I didn't really realize . . . It's a long story."

He turned the torch landward again. More rocks. And then the glow of flat white stone. He raised the beam higher and higher, and still the stone shone until it seemed there was no limit to the walls. A fortress from dreams and legends.

THE MAN AT the door was still bleary-eyed, even though it was mid-morning. He scratched his dirty-blond hair where it stood up on the side of his head. He was unshaven, with about five days' growth of stubble. He was dressed in a T-shirt and unbuttoned trousers. He was tall and slim and big-boned, and something about him reminded della Torre of a skinny horse. Or a cowboy.

He stood there for a moment, not saying anything, though a smile was slowly working its way across his face.

"Marko della Torre," the man said in a prairie accent that could have as easily been American or Canadian. He shook his head, clearing the fog of sleep.

"Morning. Hope I didn't wake you," della Torre said, standing in the hallway's unlit gloom.

"I'm not sure that you did, because this would make a lot more sense if I were dreaming. You raise so many questions, Mr. della Torre, that I don't even know where to begin. Come on in."

Della Torre was alone. He and Miranda had left the boat dockside in the old walled harbour. At first the militiamen guarding the dock thought they were invading Serbs, and then they refused to believe this little sailboat had broken through the blockade. When they couldn't think where else these two strangers had come from, they tried to arrest them for being spies. Or at the very least for breaking curfew. But when the local police sergeant was called down, bewildered and half-asleep, his initial officiousness was softened by Miranda's smile and della Torre's identification card, and he agreed that della Torre and Miranda could go to the Hotel Argentina under escort until their identity and story were verified.

The Argentina was south of the old town, on a low, terraced cliff above the Adriatic with a perfect view of the city walls. It was where all the foreigners stayed, and it was where della Torre knew he'd find Steve Higgins.

They saw little by the light of the militiaman's lantern on the kilometre-long walk to the hotel. A gutted house, a wrecked car. People had stacked sandbags in front of their doors and windows. The street smelled of sewage and the raw chemical reek of burnt plastic.

They could see dwindling fires farther down the coast, where, their escort said, the fire department dared not go, because it was too close to the front lines.

When they got to the Argentina, the night clerk found them an unoccupied room, with some encouragement from the militiaman. Even so, della Torre suspected that had he arrived alone, the room might have remained unavailable. But there was something about the Englishwoman.

The clerk arranged for a change of bed linen because he didn't know when the room had last been cleaned, and then apologized that water was at a premium and the hotel only ran the generator until nine in the evening.

The concierge, in turn, was sorry that the bar shut early, at which point the militiaman, who'd once or twice hinted at a sudden thirst, went back to his post, disappointed. There was also no room service, and guests were advised to draw their curtains at night, because the navy boats had fired on the hotel the previous week.

But the Argentina still had the feel of Dubrovnik's best hotels. And when the night porter took them to their room, the sheets were starched and clean, the bed large and comfortable.

There was one queen-sized bed and a pair of armchairs, no sofa. Della Torre offered to sleep on the floor, but Miranda shrugged and said if he kept to his side of the bed, there was plenty of space for them both.

Della Torre had strange dreams of sleeping in a rocking chair or an ancient train, the motion of the sailboat having imprinted itself on his mind.

Sometime in the night he woke pressed up against her. They were both in that half-world between dreaming and waking, and everything that followed was agreed upon without words, like the action of waves compressed into a narrow cove. And later, as they slipped back into unconsciousness, she said, "Thank you. It's been a while."

In the morning, they had a breakfast of coffee and fresh rolls. Afterward, Miranda left to have a swim in the Adriatic, which was warm enough, if only just, despite the time of year, while della Torre went to look for Higgins.

"Um, the maid service is a bit hit-and-miss these days," Higgins said vaguely, surveying the heaps of clothes on his floor and scattered notebooks, papers, camera equipment, and general detritus. "It looks like a nice morning. Why don't we sit on the balcony?"

They made themselves comfortable on the plastic chairs. The sea sparkled below, unperturbed by the brooding presence of the Yugoslav warships. "Sorry," he said, yawning. "It was a late night."

"Partying?" della Torre asked.

"One way of describing it. I went up to the fort on Mount Srđ," he said, referring to the white rock looming over Dubrovnik's old town. "The fort's held by a Croat platoon. Serbs and Montenegrin troops have been trying to capture it to take full control of the high ground overlooking the city. So far the defenders have been pretty hard to lever out. But you can really only get up or down at night. It's pretty exposed. I went up two days ago for a story and just came down last night."

"So business is good?"

"Business is great. There are only a couple of us here. Nobody can get in because of the siege and the blockade. And the American, British, Canadian, Australian, French — you name it, all the papers want stories about the attack on Dubrovnik."

"Seems pretty quiet," della Torre said.

"Well, there's been some shelling in the suburbs. But you're right, the old town hasn't suffered much damage. Still, everyone's horrified that such a culturally important city should be under attack."

"Shame they haven't had as much sympathy for Vukovar," della Torre said.

"No. Though I've only got the vaguest sense of what's happening there. We don't get much English news here. Just the radio. Most of what I hear is from the BBC World Service or what my translators tell me," Higgins said. "But enough about me. How the hell did you manage to pitch up here?"

"Sailed down last night."

"Sailed? As in a yacht?"

"Little sailing boat."

"You sailed in a dinghy?" Higgins grinned. "You know, sometimes it surprises me that anything about this country should surprise me."

Della Torre lit a Lucky and offered one to Higgins.

"Better not. I'll get used to them and then be sad when they run out."

"I'd like to thank you for what you did. Saving the girl. You put your life at risk," della Torre said, remembering when the Americans had tried to trap the Montenegrin by using his kidnapped daughter as bait. At clear risk to his life, Higgins had helped della Torre spirit the girl to safety, and in doing so saved not only her but her father as well. "I never got a chance to then. For a while, I thought I'd never get a chance to, ever."

"Think nothing of it. Part of the excitement of the job," Higgins said. "Besides, I've found it immensely rewarding getting to know Mr. Djilas."

"The Montenegrin? You keep in contact with him?"

"He's smuggled me out a couple of times so that I could get the story from the other side of the front line."

Della Torre shook his head and smiled. He looked down at the hotel's terraces, grass and ornamental palms at the higher levels, and below that a combination of concrete and bare rock surfaces descending step by step to the sea. "We used the Montenegrin's password to get past the navy. It was touch and go, though. I was probably a dot and a dash from getting us sunk."

"Us?"

Della Torre nodded with his chin down to the rocks. Higgins followed della Torre's line of sight to the woman in a blue bikini walking up from the water, her feet leaving wet imprints on the concrete.

For a while Higgins was silent, watching her as she stopped at the showers and sprayed the salt off herself, shivering at the cold water. "Mr. della Torre, I . . ." He trailed off as Miranda began to dry herself and looked up to see the men staring at her. She waved at della Torre.

"The captain of the sailboat that got me here. I'll introduce you later."

"Please do that," Higgins said. "That's twice you've surprised me in the space of ten minutes. I'm not sure my heart can stand any more."

Della Torre laughed. "I'm looking for Strumbić," he said.

Higgins smiled and looked back down to where Miranda had been, but she was gone. "Strumbić?" he asked.

"Julius. There was an article you wrote describing somebody uncannily like Strumbić."

"A lot of middle-aged men in this country look like Strumbić."

"Oh, I didn't mean his looks, though you described him to a T. I meant — how can I say this delicately? — someone who acted only as Strumbić could, taking advantage of the situation."

"Oh, you mean the article about the profiteer. The papers loved that one."

"Exactly what I mean. Caesar. Not a very good alias."

"His choice. Seemed rather proud of it." Higgins grinned.

"Where is he?"

"I'd love to help. But I have to protect my sources."

"Tell you what," della Torre said, lighting another cigarette. He was thirsty and in the mood for a coffee. He stood up and leaned against the balcony rail. "Why don't you tell Julius I'm here and looking for him. Tell him that I won't be the only person looking for him, and that the other people looking for him are neither as friendly nor as gentle as me."

"If Julius were around, which he isn't, he'd be sure to get that message," Higgins said. He yawned.

"I'm keeping you from your rest. You're tired."

Higgins demurred, but without much conviction, walking his guest to the door. "I'm not in much today, but if you and your friend are free, I'll be buying drinks tomorrow night," he said, showing della Torre out.

"On expenses?"

"Naturally."

"Then how could I say no?"

Della Torre walked the two flights up to his garret room, where he found Miranda dressing.

"Good swim?"

"Water's surprisingly warm, though it's cold getting out."

"I could see your goosebumps from the balcony. A pair of them, anyway."

"You're being vulgar."

They were interrupted by a knock at the door. It was a pair of Croat militiamen, rifles over their shoulders.

"Mr. della Torre, Mrs. . . . ."

"Walker," she said.

"We are under instruction to take you to the police headquarters. Please bring your documents."

They walked back along the coast road into Dubrovnik, a little nervously because of the crackle of distant rifle fire. The big guns had gone quiet again, having played their brief orchestral part. The whole of Dubrovnik seemed surreal to della Torre, as if the siege were a theatrical production put on for tourists.

They were led along the high walkway overlooking the harbour and then across the wooden drawbridge and through the narrow southern gate. They went across the barbican, an alley-like passage between steeply sloped white walls, over another high walkway, and finally through a gate carved into the fortress's huge stone bulk. And then they were guided along a winding alley with a high wall to one side, before they passed through another gate that opened out into the city's main square.

Della Torre looked up and wondered what sort of bombardment would be needed to break through this bastion. And then, if the Serbs tried an assault, how many soldiers would bloody these white stones before the citadel capitulated.

The old town was crowded with people, not the tourist throngs of summer, with their expensive cameras and expansive shorts, but ordinary people sheltering under the massive high white stone walls and filling the cobbled alleys, where open shops and cafés offered a semblance of normal life.

They were led to the town hall, which was in a grand building by the Rector's Palace, on a narrow square with a monastery at one end and a lovely baroque church at the other.

People were milling at the entrance, supplicants held back by fatigue-wearing militiamen. At the reception desk, della Torre showed his military ID and Miranda her British passport, and a policeman wrote down their details in a ledger.

The interior echoed with footsteps clattering against the terrazzo, voices pleading, admonishing, bewildered. The militiamen led the way up the grand staircase and along a tall, wide hallway. One of them knocked and opened the office door.

The secretary looked over the newcomers. She was thin, middle-aged, and della Torre guessed she must have plucked her eyebrows to achieve that particularly skeptical arch.

"Mr. della Torre and Mrs. Valker," said one of the militiamen, mispronouncing Miranda's name. "To see the chief. These are the people who broke the blockade last night."

The secretary gave a thin, pinched smile. "Do you have some identification?" Della Torre passed over his military ID. The secretary seemed puzzled. "You're Italian?"

"No, Istrian."

"Is the lady Italian?"

"No, she's British."

"Why isn't she Italian?"

"Why should she be Italian?"

"Well, the Italian name, for one thing."

"That's my name," della Torre said.

"But you're not Italian?"

"I'm not. The name is. I'm Istrian. Some of us have Italian names."

"We're always having to deal with Italians here. And other foreigners. And journalists constantly demanding to use the satellite phone. You're not going to want to use the phone, are you?"

"Not right now," della Torre said impatiently. "We came here because we were brought here by your officers."

"You want to see the captain, then. He's the director of security."

Della Torre nodded.

"He's not here right now," the secretary added as an afterthought.

"How long before he is?"

"A while. This afternoon."

"So you want us to wait here until then?"

"Oh, no," she said. "His deputy will see you. But he's engaged just now."

"He's in this office here?" della Torre said, reaching for a door handle.

"You can't go —"

The man inside looked up. He was solid, square, and wreathed in cigarette smoke.

"Are you the director of security or his deputy?" della Torre asked.

"I'm very sorry, but you can't barge in —" the secretary started to say.

"I'm his deputy in charge of policing. I'm afraid the director is in a meeting right now."

"You'll do. I've had a very nice chat with your secretary, but now I'd like to speak to a grown-up."

The man grinned and stood up. "The name's Brg. You're not the fellow who claims to have sailed a boat through the blockade, are you?"

"I didn't do the sailing. The lady did the sailing." Della Torre motioned towards Miranda, who followed him in. "I sat."

Brg scratched his head, bemused. "Well, let's have a look at your papers." He took Miranda's passport and della Torre's ID card.

"Mrs. Miranda Valker," he said. "You speak Italian maybe?"

"I speak Serbo-Croat," she replied, to Brg's surprise and relief.

"It says here you have a right of annual residence, and you have renewed this right for . . . four, no, five years. Is this correct?"

"Yes."

"And you live where?"

"In Korčula."

"And you presumably knew about the Yugoslav naval blockade but still came with this gentleman." And then, closely inspecting della Torre's card: "Major della Torre." Puzzlement creasing his brow, Brg looked up sharply at della Torre. "Major. You are in military intelligence."

"As the card says."

"In Zagreb?"

"Yes."

"I believe it is very unlikely that there are two Major della Torres in military intelligence," Brg said, sitting back in his chair and blowing out his cheeks.

"I can guarantee it."

"Then, Major, I know why you're here," Brg said, shaking his head as if he'd known this day would come.

It was della Torre's turn to be surprised, but he hid it by reaching into his jacket for his cigarettes, pulling one out, and passing the pack to Brg, who accepted it as the subject of a police interrogation might. Grateful and resigned.

"Maybe we should discuss this in private," Brg said, smiling uneasily at Miranda.

Della Torre turned to her. "Can you do me a favour and babysit the woman out there? I'm afraid she might do herself harm with a stapler."

"I'm sure we'll have plenty to chat about," Miranda replied, deadpan.

"Don't bother," della Torre said. "She'll just confuse you."

Miranda shut the door behind her.

"I apologize for our . . . secretary. She's the boss's . . . um . . . *friend*. Makes life interesting, because running a city under siege might otherwise be dull." Brg motioned for della Torre to sit. "Major, before we begin, can you tell me how you really arrived? Straight up."

"Sailed. In a little boat. From Korčula."

There was an embarrassed pause, as if Brg knew della Torre wasn't telling him everything but was afraid to insist.

"So, Captain," della Torre began.

"It's Detective," Brg said. "Who would I call in Zagreb to confirm that you're legit?"

"Well, I suppose Major Messar is around, though he's a little bit hard to understand these days. Got shot in the mouth a few months back. Normally it'd be Major Anzulović, but he's cooling his heels in Korčula right now."

"Are you all majors in Zagreb? No minors?" Brg smiled at his own weak joke. "That's okay. I won't need to make the call. Anzulović is in charge of the case, isn't he?"

Then della Torre remembered. Brg was the Dubrovnik cop who had been handling the dead Americans case.

"I'm afraid we've been too busy to do much detective work. We have had more pressing problems," Brg said, trying not to sound belligerent.

"I can see," della Torre said. He'd learned from Anzulović that the secret to successful interviews was to say as little as possible, let the subject fill the silences, and never be surprised by what came out. Act as if it was just a matter of confirming something already known.

Brg smoked down the Lucky before he finally spoke. "I'm afraid we haven't been able to track down Julius Strumbić again."

"Oh?"

"We think he's still here. There are various . . . signs. But we don't have the resources to conduct a proper search for him. Just keeping the situation stable is hard enough."

Della Torre fixed on the word *again*, wondering what it meant, trying to formulate a question without betraying his ignorance and silencing Brg. "What happened?" he asked quietly, like a priest gently drawing out a confession.

Brg turned up his hands in embarrassed apology. "I was exhausted. We didn't realize we'd had him the whole while. We thought the man we had in custody was some smuggler, and we kept him in a cell until we could devote some time to figuring out what he was doing. I got a call from the Italian police in Bari, asking me to come identify a corpse that washed up there. It was the American redhead. By the time I got back, it was morning and I hadn't slept, but the prosecutors said I had to interview this smuggler or let him go. If I'd seen him before, I might have put two and two together sooner. But I finally twigged, so we put him back in his cell. I went home for a few hours' shut-eye before getting in touch with Zagreb to tell them we had him. I figured a few hours wouldn't make any difference." He shrugged.

"But he got out."

"It seems he had a key. The keys. He must have picked somebody's pocket. Unlocked the cell and the door out of the jail wing and walked past the desk sergeant as cool as a night in November."

"And then?"

"And then he disappeared. We looked for him. I was going to make a full report. But circumstances . . ."

Della Torre smiled with some sympathy. He thought back to when they had found the body in Italy. It coincided closely with the timing of the coded message from Mrs. Strumbić. Why hadn't Strumbić tried to get in touch again? Maybe he had.

"And now you don't know where he is?"

"There are reports . . ." Brg said. "He's a smart guy. Smarter than any cop I've ever met."

"He is."

"I'll write a report as soon as this is over," Brg said. "When I get a couple of minutes. If I survive. I come in here to get my thoughts in order. We need to plan, and this is the only place I can get any quiet. Otherwise we're out there." He waved his arms towards the window. "It's only here that I can coordinate anything. We're so undermanned, we take the bodies we can get and try to do our best."

"I understand," della Torre said. "But before you write anything, get in touch with me or Major Anzulović. We'll help."

He passed the detective another cigarette.

"You took all those risks to find Strumbić," Brg said, shaking his head. "I still don't know how you managed to sail past the blockade. Few people do. Smugglers from Montenegro, mostly, who pay off the naval captains. There were rumours of one or two boats making the trip from Korčula, but I didn't believe them. I guess they're not just rumours."

Della Torre stood up to go.

"You know, Strumbić isn't all bad," Brg said. "They say he's a smuggler and a profiteer. But from some of the things I hear and see . . ."

"Like what?"

The detective shrugged. "I don't know. Nothing. Rumours."

Della Torre knew he wasn't going to get much more out of the man, but there wasn't much more he needed. Other than to find Strumbić.

THEY PLAYED TOURIST over the next couple of days. Though rain threatened often, there were long breaks of sunshine and warmth.

They swam in the mornings and got to know a few of the other journalists staying at the Argentina. The Serb artillery would bang on for a while in the suburbs after breakfast, and sometimes they'd hear gunfire up on the mountain overlooking the city. But apart from that and the ever-present warships and occasional low-flying jet, Dubrovnik seemed to be in a fugue state, without past or future, a purgatory of waiting.

But there were worse places to wait out a siege. The Argentina's linen was pressed. Lunch and dinner were served on the terrace; chicken and rice seemed to feature often.

Steve Higgins missed their drinks appointment and there was no sign of Strumbić, but the hotel was stocked with plenty of English-language paperbacks to keep them occupied, left behind by generations of British and American tourists.

Della Torre kept track of the news as best as he could. A fleet of ferries and other boats was being assembled to break the blockade. Every day it was to depart and every day it was delayed. The news from Vukovar was grim. The European medical convoy had finally entered the town but got caught in crossfire on its way out. People had been injured.

Though he and Miranda slept together, the sex had the quality of sport. She kept him at a distance, divulging very little about herself. Except once.

"You were married," he said.

"Yes."

"Any children?"

"No. I mean, yes, one. A boy."

"It seems strange for someone to forget they have a child," he said with gentle humour.

"I didn't forget. I had a boy. He died," she said.

"Oh, I'm sorry. I understand now. I guess that's what made you leave England."

"No, in fact you understand wrong."

She wouldn't be drawn any further. Instead she asked how much longer they were going to wait.

He didn't know what to say, so he turned his attention to the sliced ham and cheese they'd ordered with their cocktails. They were at a table on the hotel terrace, watching the sun set over the Adriatic and wash the old city in shades of pink and then deeper red, silhouetting the warships just offshore. *Et in arcadia ego.*

That night, della Torre fell asleep on his back and Miranda was lying on her side, facing away from him. He woke, struggling for breath.

Half-dreaming, he thought Miranda had leaned over to kiss him, but one of his nostrils was blocked and he wasn't getting enough air from the other one. Something was pressing hard on his face. He tried to sit up, to say something, but the hand pressed down on him. There was a nearly overpowering smell of nicotine.

A voice next to his head hissed, "Shut up, keep still, and listen."

Della Torre wanted to say he couldn't breathe. He reached up to push the hand away but the voice was insistent.

"For once in your life, do as you're told, okay?"

The hand lifted and della Torre took a deep breath. "Okay." He recognized the voice and knew it was sensible to keep still.

"She's a dish," Strumbić said. "You couldn't pull the sheet down a little more? Can't see much in the dark."

"Julius, what the fuck?"

"Shhh, I'd rather you didn't wake her. Get up and come out onto the balcony. We'll have a smoke."

Della Torre slid shut the balcony door as quietly as he could and sat on a plastic chair. The other man was only a vague form in the darkness until he lit a match. The guttering orange light momentarily carved Strumbić's likeness from twisting shadows, and then he disappeared again behind the amber-red ember glow of tobacco.

The night air was cold and damp, and della Torre shivered in his heightened state of waking. He'd pulled on some trousers; the wool of his jersey scratched against his bare skin as his bare feet grew numb on the smooth concrete.

"Long time no see, Gringo," Strumbić said in a hoarse smoker's whisper.

"Julius, you could have been less dramatic," della Torre said. "Not sure my heart could take that again."

"Then you better stay out of the Serb gunners' sights."

"Dubrovnik seems . . . pretty civilized for a war zone."

"Don't worry, it'll get worse. The Serbs are getting irritated at the resistance. Country boys don't like the rich cosmopolitan folks down here."

"Sounds like you've been discussing it with them."

"I have."

"Why do I believe you?" asked della Torre.

"Because it's true."

"So if you can get out and in, what are you doing here still? What's your scam?"

"You make it sound like a bad thing," Strumbić said. "People are worried. They're short of water and other necessities or they want to get out. I happen to know how to help them."

"You're profiting from their misery."

"Do you think they'd be better off with their pearl necklaces and diamond rings?"

"Julius, you haven't got an ethical bone in your body."

"Ethics? You're talking to me about ethics? What are the ethics of bearing false witness against a dear friend who's saved your life on at least one and possibly three occasions?"

"Look," della Torre started, and then ran out of steam.

"Gringo, I don't hold it against you, though you've complicated my life," Strumbić said. And then, after a long drag of his cigarette: "So you sailed here?"

"I did."

"Got past the patrol boats?"

"Eventually. You don't sound surprised."

"The woman's done it twice before. Never stayed, though. Turned right around and went back. Fetched up at the end of the promontory, where the navy boats don't dare get too close for fear of the offshore rocks. In and out. She works with a couple of old-time smugglers. They signal each other between the islands."

"You know this?"

"You think there's anything that happens in Dubrovnik that I don't know about? I've been trying to work out how to get in touch with her. So I guess I owe you some thanks for fixing up a meeting. This is even better. Normally when you do business you don't get to see the other side's tits. At least, not right away."

"You amaze me, Julius."

"Even after all these years?"

"I suppose not."

"That's better," Strumbić said. "So why are you here, other than to apologize?"

Della Torre fell silent.

"What did Brg say?" Strumbić pushed.

"You know I saw him?"

"Gringo, I know how many times you've taken a shit since you got here and how hard you wiped."

"Somebody on your payroll at the town hall?"

"You might say I still have a way with the ladies."

"No," della Torre said. "Not the secretary?"

"Why not?"

"Because she's an idiot."

"Gringo, why do you only ever see the worst in people? Did Brg tell you I was in his jail for a couple of weeks and he didn't realize it?"

"Yes," della Torre said.

"But you'd have known anyway, since I expect my wife passed on my message."

"Julius, I thought it meant you were safe in London. How the hell was I supposed to realize you were in Dubrovnik?"

Strumbić let out a long, exasperated sigh. "I always figured you weren't nearly as clever as you're made out to be. Nice to have that confirmed. Well, you found me anyway. Now what?"

"Now the Americans are coming to look for you."

"Let them come."

"They have some serious people, Julius, and some serious money to spend finding you. And they really want you."

"They going to sail too? Or take a submarine? Or maybe they'll buzz in on those little James Bond helicopters."

"They'll be in the flotilla that's coming to break the blockade."

"Well, when they get here, I'll start to think about leaving. But right now Dubrovnik suits me. Looks like you're not doing too badly either. Even in these hard times, the Argentina's not cheap."

"The company's paying for it," della Torre said.

Strumbić laughed and then coughed. "I know what that means. It means you sign a chit, the hotel presents it to the military, and the military says, fuck you. Bet the manager's pissing in your soup every night. Listen, Gringo, I'd love to chat all night but I'm a busy man."

"Where are you staying?"

"Do you seriously think I'd tell you that?"

"No."

"Then don't ask."

"Julius, we need to talk. Seriously. We need to think about some things. These Americans are going to keep chasing us until they've got us. They're going to hunt us to the ground."

"So why haven't they got you yet?" And then Strumbić answered his own question: "Because they're using you to find me. Well, it didn't work so well for them when they tried to use you to get the Montenegrin."

"These people aren't going to make the same mistakes."

"We'll see," Strumbić said, rising. "We'll continue this conversation later. But right now I have business to attend to."

"How am I going to get in touch with you?"

"You're not. I'll find you."

IF MIRANDA HAD noticed Strumbić ghosting through their hotel room at night, she said nothing the following morning. She and della Torre breakfasted and lounged as though on holiday. Apart from the occasional rumble of distant heavy guns and the few forlorn refugees who'd found accommodation at the hotel, they'd never have known they were in a city under siege. The JNA and Serb artillery men left the old city and its immediate suburbs alone in the daylight hours, and at night would lob shells only at pockets of illumination.

There was no sign of Strumbić the following day. In the evening, as della Torre and Miranda were finishing dinner on the terrace, Steve Higgins stopped at their table.

"I owe you a drink," he said. "Sorry I couldn't keep our date."

"Thought you might have had a better offer," della Torre said, looking up. "Miranda, meet Mr. Steve Higgins. A Canadian newspaperman and all-round cowboy. Steve, Miranda Walker."

"Won't you join us, Mr. Higgins?" she asked.

"It's Steve. And I'd love to, if you don't mind. Can I buy you some drinks?" He flagged the waiter.

"I'll have an amaro," della Torre said.

"They've got some old brandies, unless you'd rather a

cocktail," said Higgins to Miranda. "I know it's after dinner, but they make a decent Bellini here."

"Why don't you get me what you're having," she replied.

"I've developed a taste for the maitre d's slivovitz. It beats the usual embalming fluid," Higgins said.

"You're a connoisseur of embalming fluid?" Miranda asked.

"Best to get a head start. Just in case," Higgins replied with a smile.

"So where were you this time?" della Torre asked, offering Higgins a Lucky.

"Better not," Higgins said. Della Torre shrugged and lit his own. "I was wandering around."

"Discovering what?"

Higgins grinned. "Well, for one thing, the ships are coming. Down from Rijeka. The convoy should arrive in the next few days. Mesić is on one of the boats."

"Really?" della Torre asked, sitting back. Mesić was one of the rotating presidents of Yugoslavia, the one who had represented Croatia until Croatia declared independence. "I don't know if that makes it more or less likely that they'll be able to break the blockade."

"There are European Community observers on it too. And a bunch of journalists," Higgins added.

"You'll be getting some competition, then," Miranda said.

"Had to happen," said Higgins. "It's been a nice clear run so far. And the demand is picking up. People have holidayed in Dubrovnik. They find it hard to believe this beautiful place can be a war zone, so they're interested. And some of them are politicians."

"But nobody holidays in Vukovar," della Torre said.

"The pictures from Vukovar are shocking, but people think of it as far away — Cambodia or Ethiopia, except with white people. So they find it easier to shrug off."

The waiter brought their drinks. Miranda took a swig of the

slivovitz, grimacing slightly. "I could probably clean my brushes with this," she said. "In all my years here, I've never quite gotten used to it."

"Don't feel the need to finish it," Higgins said.

"Seems a shame not to see it through," she answered.

"You're British, but it seems you speak the language well."

"Passably. I've been here five years and used to come on holiday before that. But when you find yourself alone in a foreign country, it's very hard to survive without learning the language."

"Well, I'm managing somehow." Higgins laughed. "But only just. I have to say, the translators and fixers aren't all I could wish for. The ones I get always turn out to be spies, though I'm not sure who for. Or they're using me somehow. So how long have you known Gringo?"

"Gringo," she repeated, a half-smile on her lips as she looked at della Torre.

"That's Mr. della Torre's nickname," Higgins said. "Didn't you know?"

"Mr. Gringo hired me to get him to Dubrovnik and back. We're waiting for another passenger. That's about as long as I expect to know him."

"Oh, I thought . . ." Higgins began, then shrugged. "So you're at a loose end for now."

"Yes," she said.

"Well, maybe — if you're for hire while you're waiting — I could pay you to do some of my translating," he said, suddenly embarrassed as he looked at della Torre. "It'd be easier to interview refugees, women, and children, with a woman than with a supercilious waiter."

Della Torre shrugged as if it were of no concern to him.

"You can pay me whatever rate you pay your regulars," she said.

Higgins smiled at the deal he'd struck.

The evening grew chilly, but they sat on the terrace and drank as the sun sank slowly across the horizon, guttered, and disappeared. War seemed so far away, yet there it was, in the grey hulls on the water and hidden in the mountains. They drank and talked, unperturbed by the occasional sound of distant gunfire.

The next morning he was woken by a loud, long, unrelenting knock on his door. Della Torre couldn't remember having gone to bed. He opened the door to Strumbić, who was holding a near-full cappuccino and grinning at della Torre's miserable appearance.

"Don't you operate during civilized hours?" della Torre asked, his mouth dry and fuzzy. He pointed to the coffee. "That for me?"

"No."

Miranda sat up in bed, momentarily oblivious to the fact she was naked.

Strumbić grinned. "Hello, miss," he said in his heavily accented English, not trying very hard to suppress his leer.

Miranda sank back into bed, covering herself.

"Julius," della Torre said, "Miranda Walker."

"British?" Strumbić said, sticking with English. "Always new woman for Gringo, eh?"

Della Torre grimaced.

"You won't mind if I don't get up just now," she said, replying in the same language.

"It vould make me very happy, but I understand," Strumbić replied. And then, shaking his head sadly, all the while keeping his eyes on her: "Vat kind of man take his woman to war zone?" As if to say he would never do such a thing. And then, with a sigh: "I vait for you on terrace. I have coffee, you get dressed, then we go."

"Go?" della Torre said, his head heavy and painful.

"We have discussions," Strumbić said. "I vant also to talk bizniss with Miss Walker, but maybe another time."

"I speak Serbo-Croat," Miranda said.

"Ah, excellent. Well, it was nice to have met you. Gringo, I will meet you downstairs."

"Not worried about being seen?" della Torre asked.

"Not at this time of the morning. The people who watch like to stay up late and sleep in."

Della Torre stumbled into the bathroom and then remembered there was no water for a shower. He couldn't face going down to the pool to hose himself down. At least the hotel laundry was operating efficiently.

"There's something oddly . . . compelling about your friend," Miranda said.

Della Torre shook his head in wonder. "I should despise him, but all I can ever manage to do is admire him. He's like all of the wonders and exhilaration of life poured into the corrupt body of a fat, middle-aged bureaucrat."

She laughed and lay back in bed. "Well, don't keep him waiting."

When della Torre arrived Strumbić had drained his coffee and was lost in a cloud of smoke. His face was fleshy, the jowls heavy, the hair more grey than brown. His eyes were as washed out as the early morning sky, and he had the look of a man who spent his life drinking and smoking. But his skin was lightly tanned, and he looked as well as della Torre had ever seen him. Better, perhaps.

It felt odd to della Torre to be sitting down at the very table he'd risen from only a few hours before. Coffee and fresh rolls replaced the slivovitz and salty pretzels and slivers of cured ham, and Strumbić now stood in for Higgins. Though the Canadian was at least half a head taller, twenty kilograms lighter, better-looking, and younger, the men shared a similar vitality.

Strumbić hurried the waiter, who was bleary-eyed with the earliness of the hour, and then hurried della Torre too. When della Torre had finished his croissant, Strumbić led him out of the hotel to a double-parked Mercedes that had left barely enough room for other cars to pass.

"Why are we driving?" protested della Torre. "It's only a fifteen-minute walk."

Strumbić gave him a baleful look. "It's a Mercedes," he replied by way of explanation, opening the front passenger door, an awkwardly genteel gesture that made della Torre think of a taxi driver. With no traffic this early, the drive to the old town could be counted in seconds.

"Who'd you steal the car from?" della Torre asked.

"Steal?" Strumbić threw his hands up dramatically.

The narrow, twisting road was built into the hillside, with massive stone buildings landward and sharp descents towards the sea. Della Torre winced, clinging with one arm to the overhead strap. But just as it seemed the car was about to run into a metal bollard, Strumbić steered away, accelerating at the same time.

"I borrowed it."

"Borrowed?"

"Rented," Strumbić said, without elaborating.

"I'd hate to see the terms," della Torre muttered.

Strumbić parked by the old town's landward gate, a tall arch set into a sloped wall as big as a tilted field. The citadel was bound by two bastions and the sky, as permanent and unyielding as childhood dreams.

They walked through the side alleys off the Stradun, the broad central promenade that joined the harbour with the town's grand northern gate. They were under the huge east walls. The tall, narrow houses made a canyon that ended at a man-made cliff-face of neatly chiselled white stone.

Small children were up early while their parents slept. Laundry hung high above the narrow width of the alley, like row upon row of prayer flags.

Strumbić set a brisk pace, skipping down the frequent flights of steps, turning a corner and then heading up along another alley that was so narrow they could only just walk abreast. They went up a series of short flights of steps rising from the Stradun to the city walls. Strumbić already had the keys in hand when they arrived at the heavy riveted wooden door of a stone house, which had a massive ornate iron lock and a more modern one above it. Strumbić furtively opened up and quickly ushered della Torre in, switching on a flashlight the moment he'd shut the door behind them.

"Helps having a locksmith as a friend," he said. "There's no fear of the owner showing up, but there's no point in letting anyone else know the place is occupied."

"So this is where you've been hiding," della Torre said.

"Nope. This is just a house I found so that we'd have a bit of privacy. Haven't used it before."

"How many of these places do you have?"

"A few. I'm thinking of buying one or two permanently. They're going pretty cheap, though I think they'll get cheaper still. Downside is making sure the people selling it actually own the fucking place."

The entrance hall was narrow and Strumbić immediately climbed the stairs at the back. The alleyside windows were all shuttered, and the place smelled of ancient dust. They made their way to a top-floor sitting room with a rooftop terrace that extended the full length of the house and of the one behind it, giving the property a unique private outdoor space stretching from one alley to the next. Della Torre leaned against a wrought-iron rail, stunned by the view of Dubrovnik's rooftops, the pantiles a warm flame of burnt oranges, faded reds, and deep ochres, and beyond that the church towers, city walls, and sea. A modest jungle of potted citrus trees and palms lined the terrace.

"Not bad, eh? Not sure there's another rooftop terrace like this in the city. Nobody can destroy our architectural heritage for his own satisfaction like a Communist big shot. I can't offer

you coffee or anything, because I have no idea where anything
is or how it might work," Strumbić said.

He took out his pack of cigarettes as della Torre settled into a
white garden chair under the eaves of the neighbouring house.
Broken clouds were floating overhead and the air was fresh, but
Strumbić's attention was on della Torre.

"So talk, Gringo."

"I'm not sure where to start."

"Why don't you start with why the Americans are after me."

"They think you set up Rebecca and her crew with the
Montenegrin. That you told the Montenegrin about the trap
they'd set and that you helped him take his revenge."

"And why do they think that?"

Della Torre sat back and breathed deeply. He was tempted to
light another cigarette but knew it would make him retch at this
early hour. He felt miserable enough as it was.

"Because that's what I told them."

"You're honest at least," Strumbić said. "Is that because you
were squirming on the hook?"

"Yes, though it wouldn't have helped. They went to find you,
left me at your villa. I think their intention was to bring you back
to confirm what I'd told them. And then kill us both."

"So you knew you were a goner, but you dropped me in it
anyway, eh? Some friend."

"It was Higgins they really wanted. I figured you could take
care of yourself. I'm not sure Higgins would have come out of
it the same way."

"Keep talking. This is getting interesting."

"It was Higgins who helped save the Montenegrin's daughter.
He's the reason the Montenegrin survived."

"And the Montenegrin then took his revenge on the Americans
but let you live?"

"Yes."

"Well, that explains a lot," Strumbić said, lost in thought.

"Oh?"

"It explains why the Montenegrin has been so keen to do Higgins favours. I've come along for the ride. Their friendship has been . . . rewarding to me."

"I'm glad to hear it."

"So the next question is, why are the Americans so hot to kill the Montenegrin? And us, by extension. I mean, I know what they told us: that it's because the Montenegrin ran wetworks operations in America. I guess they don't much like foreign assassins doing business on their patch, even if it only ever concerned Yugoslavs."

"Some of those Yugoslavs had American citizenship."

"You know that's neither here nor there," Strumbić said. "So they want to kill the foreign assassin or bring him to justice or something."

"But you don't believe it."

"You know me. I'm a natural skeptic."

Della Torre reached for the pack of cigarettes and lit one. The hinges of a shutter squeaked open on the opposite side of the alley, and Strumbić held his hand up for silence. A woman moved across the window, talking to someone else, barely audible.

"Refugees in there," he said. "Places are either empty or stacked six to a room. Albanians as far as I can tell, but keep it down. I don't want anyone listening."

"Do you remember that Pilgrim file I sold you?" asked della Torre.

"How could I forget? Those fucking Bosnians made my life misery over it," Strumbić replied.

"Well, there's a reason they did. The file was about an assassination. By the Montenegrin."

"In America?"

"No, in Sweden. The Olof Palme killing."

"The Swedish prime minister Olof Palme?" Strumbić said, sitting forward, eyes wide.

"The same."

Strumbić whistled.

"Do you remember Dragomanov, Tito's translator?" della Torre asked.

"Of course. Right hand of God, only nobody was supposed to know."

"Well, Dragomanov assigned the liquidation of Olof Palme to the Montenegrin. It was a solo job. No one else was to know about it. The Montenegrin did it."

"And his reward was to take over the UDBA wetworks program?"

"That's right. He did it professionally, but it was outside the UDBA's purview. At least as far as the official files went. There were hints here and there about something called Pilgrim, but only random pieces of the puzzle."

"So why did Dragomanov want Palme dead?"

"I don't know. I just know that it had something to do with nuclear centrifuges the Swedes were making — they made some of the parts and brought in other parts from the Netherlands and Germany and then assembled the whole thing — and exporting to Yugoslavia. Those centrifuges were meant to be part of our nuclear power program. They're used to refine uranium. But we got many more than were needed for just nuclear power. To get enough of the right grade of uranium to generate electricity, you need only a few hundred centrifuges to do the refining. But we were getting thousands."

"And you need thousands to build a bomb, correct?"

"Yes."

"So Yugoslavia has the bomb? But I thought we abandoned the project in the 1970s because Tito said it cost too much. Me, I think the Americans bribed us to give it up."

"That's the thing," della Torre said. "We don't have the bomb. I'm pretty sure we don't. Those centrifuges didn't stay in this country. They came in and then went straight back out. I don't know where. I think Palme found out and was going to raise a stink, and that's why he was liquidated."

Strumbić put his hands behind his head, leaned back, and exhaled through pursed lips. "So where do the Americans fit into all this?" he said.

"I don't know. I wish I did. But I'm certain the Pilgrim file is why the Americans are after the Montenegrin. And us."

"And will keep after us until we're all fixed."

"Yes, there's something to the Pilgrim file that they want to keep buried," della Torre said.

"And the Americans are coming on that humanitarian flotilla making its way down from Rijeka right now."

"They'll get on board in Korčula, where I left them."

"Fuck, Gringo. You do know how to ruin a perfectly sweet siege."

They were silent for a long time.

"I did a bit of discreet research on Dragomanov when I got back to Zagreb," della Torre said. "There's not a huge amount of information. Most of the UDBA files were taken back to Belgrade, but some were duplicated, and the police had a bit on record too."

"So what do you know?"

Della Torre took out the little black notebook he always carried in his jacket pocket. He didn't know how many dozens, if not hundreds, he'd been through in his career, passing a few loose sheets of essential information from one to the next.

He opened the soft leatherette cover. His script was tiny and compulsively neat, usually written with a mechanical pencil. It didn't take him long to find the right page.

"I have his address. The building is a retirement home for old Communist big shots. High security. There's a permanent guard post at the main entrance as well as another one at the carriage entrance to the parking lot, in the middle of the block. And there are patrols around it at all times."

"I know it," said Strumbić. "Who needs capitalism when you can have hot-and-cold-running Communism on tap?"

"He has another place in Belgrade, where his wife lives, not far away."

"They get on?"

"Not really. He'd always been known for womanizing, but she put up with him for the fringe benefits. He's ill, and she visits now and again, once or twice a week. A nurse comes round every day. And he has a daily cleaner as well. The file said he used to screw her when she was younger. Now she brings his groceries, cleans and cooks for him."

"Wasn't there a rumour that he fucked all the Politburo's wives and daughters? The good-looking ones, anyway."

"None of the men dared complain, because he was Tito's favourite. And the women queued up for it."

"I guess looking like a movie star has its uses. Something you should know about, eh, Gringo?" Strumbić grinned.

Della Torre ignored the comment. "He had a falling-out with his sister, but a nephew visits once a week or so. Or used to, anyway."

"Kid making sure he gets his inheritance. So why'd he stop?"

"Because he lives in Vukovar."

"No shit."

"Dragomanov owns the house the nephew lives in. Name's Zidar, and the deal is like some sort of house arrest. In fact, it's the only property he has that he does own directly. The rest is 'rented' from the state."

"For the cost of a packet of cigarettes a month."

"Yes, well," della Torre said, shrugging. He lived in his apartment under the same generous conditions. "Nothing's too good for the proletariat."

Strumbić chuckled. "You make some prole, Gringo."

"Anyway, for whatever reason, Dragomanov owns the place in Vukovar," continued della Torre. "I dug up a little about his sister and her son, the nephew, because it seemed the best way to get something, anything, on the old man. Dragomanov doesn't have kids, and the nephew Zidar was a favourite until he fucked up. Dragomanov had set it up so the nephew had a cushy foreign ministry job. Took a posting in Berlin but was sent home in disgrace. Must have been serious. I've seen how some of those so-called diplomats behave. It'd be enough to shame the Whore of Babylon."

"Is she the one in our Iraq embassy?" Strumbić asked.

Della Torre laughed. "Anyway, he was sent back. It seemed he wanted to live in Belgrade, but the uncle shoved him off to Vukovar. He used to make the trip once a week to visit the old man, but the war intervened."

"So he's still in Vukovar, then?"

"Who knows? Or dead. I have an address, but there's no getting information about anybody in Vukovar these days," della Torre said, his voice inflected with misery.

Strumbić didn't comment. He knew Irena a little and, like everyone else, admired her.

"The fact is, he used to visit regularly and hasn't for a while. Which might be one way of getting to the old man," Strumbić said.

"I guess that's what I've been leading to," della Torre said. "Learning everything there is to know about Pilgrim — that might be the only way to protect ourselves."

"Or a faster way of getting ourselves killed."

20

THE CONVOY OF ships transporting the humanitarian mission arrived two days later, full of journalists, Croat politicians, United Nations observers, and European functionaries. They docked not long after the big guns in the hills stopped pounding Dubrovnik's northern harbour and suburbs.

Strumbić had spent much of the intervening time settling his affairs in Dubrovnik. All along, della Torre had been assuming Strumbić would want to leave Dubrovnik with him and Miranda, ahead of the convoy. But Strumbić remained noncommittal, smiling and saying he needed to do a few things before he could think of abandoning his "bizniss," as he called it.

Miranda seemed content to wait, to do as her clients commanded. She and Higgins disappeared for long stretches while the Canadian journalist squeezed out as many exclusive stories as he could before the competition landed.

Della Torre had also waited, though less patiently, reading, smoking the cigarettes Strumbić supplied after the ones he'd brought ran out, drinking, trying to shake off the stress of what would happen if Grimston and his people caught them.

And then Higgins had passed along information from his sources: a deal had suddenly been reached with the Yugoslav navy, and the convoy would be arriving the following morning.

So della Torre rose in the dark of the unheated hotel room, woken by Higgins and Strumbić. The men left Miranda sleeping in bed and made their way to a rare open café on the hillside above Dubrovnik's modern port. Morning light sparkled on the distant sea where the mountains' shadows no longer reached. The warships remained a glowering presence, but they let the convoy dock.

Della Torre was tired, thick-headed, as was inevitable after a late night with Strumbić. Strumbić had made it clear he'd worked out "something" for when the Americans arrived — something to remind them how high the stakes were. If the Americans thought their colleagues had been killed merely because they were bad at their jobs, Strumbić's plan was going to disabuse them of that notion.

The ships had arrived with first light, a parade of them slouching into Dubrovnik's modern port between twin lines of Yugoslav warships and the Serb gunners in the hills. A handful of people gathered on the harbourfront, curious, many still up from the night's shelling, which had left the freshly charred wreckage of a truck at the far end of the docks. At first only a few sailors disembarked. It seemed the politicians were waiting for word to get around and the crowds to build before descending to earth. Meanwhile, supplies were unloaded. To della Torre's eyes, the ships had come pitifully empty.

It was easy to distinguish the European observers, the humanitarians, and the journalists from the Croats on board. Della Torre saw Grimston in chinos and a blue baseball hat, and with him, two of the men who'd tried to kidnap della Torre in Zagreb — the tramp and the young lover. Them, he'd expected.

But not Anzulović.

His heart sank. But he should have known his old boss would diligently stick to his job. Whatever that was. Della Torre watched Anzulović descend the gangway, stooped, hands in pockets. He stopped on the dockside, looking around and then upwards in their direction. For a moment della Torre wondered if Anzulović had seen them. But then the older man looked away. He seemed forlorn, as if he'd expected to be welcomed, only to discover he was alone.

Grimston walked over to him. They spoke briefly and then separated. Anzulović took his bag and headed in the direction of the old town. Grimston and his men had already eased their way through the dockside crowd that finally started to gather.

Della Torre found it hard to tell how many Americans were among the arrivals, but he knew they weren't making just a token effort. He had no doubt about their seriousness, whatever their reasons. Vengeance. Finishing a job done badly. Atonement for sending colleagues to their deaths. Or just doing what they were paid to do.

But still he marvelled at their hubris. That they could come to a city under siege to conduct their own private war. As the Americans scattered, della Torre and Strumbić also saw the sense in withdrawing from their lookout.

"You can do?" Strumbić said. "If you don't vant, say now."

"I'll manage," della Torre said.

"You?" Strumbić asked Higgins.

"You promised me a good story. I believe you."

"Good. Is very good story," Strumbić said. "Is time to go."

They got into the Mercedes. Strumbić dropped off della Torre and Higgins at the hotel but didn't get out. He had things to do elsewhere, he said.

Della Torre went up to his room. His bag was already packed, and Miranda was waiting for him.

They went down and checked out ostentatiously, saying good-bye to the staff. Della Torre signed the hotel chit, backed by his military ID. The day manager wasn't happy about this proof of payment but accepted the arrangement. Della Torre, after all, had the backing of Dubrovnik's authorities. And Strumbić had given the manager a generous bribe.

Della Torre and Miranda walked back along the coast road to the old town, through the gate, and into the wide, elegant Stradun. From there they made their way up the alleys to the house where Strumbić had taken della Torre the previous day.

Strumbić had given him the keys, a heavy iron one with an ornate trefoil as well as two smaller ones for the modern locks. The door opened with a sepulchral groan. They walked through the house in the gloom, Miranda trailing behind, looking curiously through the rooms, and finally reached the terrace at the top.

"And now we wait for them to find us?" Miranda said, taking a seat on one of the wrought-iron chairs.

"Yes."

"And then?"

"Then Julius will tell us what we need to know."

The Americans came within the hour. There was a knock on the door. Della Torre looked over the railing of the terrace and saw two of them. As he did, he was spotted by a third man farther up the alley, towards the city walls, and a fourth at the Stradun end of the alley.

The game was on, much sooner than he'd expected.

The knocking stopped. Della Torre chanced another look down and saw the men disappearing into the house. Strumbić had promised to get him and Miranda out before the Americans could get hold of them. Della Torre felt abandoned.

He looked around for something with which to bar the terrace door. The best he could do was a couple of heavy ceramic pots. He shifted them, scraping the terracotta tiles, but he knew it was no more than a token effort. Miranda watched, uneasy. They were cornered.

Della Torre cursed Strumbić under his breath. There was no other way off the terrace. To one side, the roof of the neighbouring house was a full storey lower; the one on the other side was too high to climb. The alleys were narrow, but unlike those in Korčula, they were too broad to jump.

He heard the shutters of the house opposite swing open. For a moment his hopes rose that the refugees living there might intervene. He was about to shout for help when surprise silenced him. A plank started sliding out from the open window. A thick, solid scaffolding board, like a mottled brown tongue. It wobbled dangerously as it drew close to the terrace railings.

A familiar face appeared in the window, puce with effort.

"Lend a hand. Grab the other end before it drops," Strumbić grunted at him. Della Torre finally reacted, reaching across to grab the end of the plank and guide it until it was resting on the balcony rail.

Miranda looked at della Torre with shock, her expression asking what the hell was going on, what risk she was being asked to take. Although there was only a three-metre distance between the buildings, they were four storeys up from a hard stone pavement.

"Come on," Strumbić called out from the open window. "Don't fuck around now. The woman first."

Della Torre heard the men coming up through the house and knew he had no choice but to move fast. The board was wide and solid and extended deep into the house opposite. If it had been laid across the ground he could have danced a waltz on it without worrying about falling off. But at that vertiginous height, with Dubrovnik spread below them, della Torre became dizzy even contemplating the crossing. But he did what he had to. He lifted Miranda onto the board and urged her across.

She went, crouching, clearly nervous, holding her bag out in front of her as a tightrope walker might hold a balancing pole.

Della Torre followed, stepping onto the plank from one of the flimsy wrought-iron chairs. He pitched forward, the deep defile opening directly below. The chair hit the terrace's terracotta tiles with a clatter, and for a moment he thought he'd lost his footing. He stared down past the plank's rough wood, expecting to see the alley's stone steps come rocketing towards him. But his other foot swung forward and he found himself firmly planted on the board, though he could feel it strain and bow slightly under his weight. He paused, his eyes fixed on the specks of red paint that had once upon a time dribbled along the board, telling himself to follow those drips like a trail of blood. *Don't think*, he told himself. *Just move your feet, one after the other.* He was a step or two away from the opposite side when he heard the sound of the terrace door breaking open. Arms grabbed at him, pulling him into the house.

"Come on, Gringo, help me pull this board through." Strumbić was straining in the half-light, manhandling the ancient plank back into the house. In all, it must have been the best part of five metres long. It filled the length of the room, a bedroom with cots and mattresses stacked along the side to give them passage.

Two men stared back at them from the terrace. They were clean-shaven, their hair neat, their eyes hidden by Ray-Ban aviator glasses. Their checked cotton shirts and tan chinos told della Torre they were Americans. One pulled a radio out of a belt holster and spoke into it.

"Let's go, Gringo," Strumbić said, shoving him and Miranda down the winding wooden staircase through the tenement, curious faces peering out from each room.

When they reached the bottom of the stairs, Strumbić pulled out a roll of creased and worn banknotes and distributed some to the children who'd assembled there.

"There's more if you go around the corner," he told them. "There are some Americans making a movie. You can't miss them. If you annoy them enough, they'll give you money to piss off."

They emerged in a side alley with a dozen or so children, who immediately ran off. They hurried down its steps, wary, watchful, quick when crossing the narrow intersections. When they reached the Stradun, Strumbić made them run across, his grip on Miranda's wrist the whole while, pulling her along. Now and again she half tried to pull her arm away, but Strumbić was both stronger and more determined. Pigeons exploded into the air like pheasants at a shoot. Strumbić led the way into a warren of medieval canyons, some so narrow that two people could barely pass each other, and along one of the seaward alleys towards the northern walls.

Here della Torre could smell the sharp salt tang of sea, the smell of shellfish that lived and died along the rocks at the base of the citadel's massive walls.

They came to a decrepit house that looked long abandoned or left in the care of elderly, infirm tenants. Strumbić paused and looked around, and when he was satisfied they were alone, he let go of Miranda's wrist and unlocked the door. He ushered them in, bolting the door behind them, and only then relaxed, bent against the wall, holding his thighs and sucking in air.

"Fuck," he said, panting, gasping his words. "They were supposed to take a couple of hours at least to track you down. They must have had somebody right on your heels. Did you see anyone?"

"No," said della Torre, exhaling painfully with each word. "We were in such a hurry to get to the house that we didn't think to look. But I thought the whole object was to be found."

"Yes, but only after I'd had time to finish setting everything up. Sweet fucking Jesus. Did you chain the door when you went in?"

Della Torre shook his head.

"Well, never mind, if they had somebody who knew how to pick locks, they'd also have found somebody to break the chain," Strumbić said.

"I told you they were serious. And good. The guy running the show, Grimston, isn't playing around."

"I take it this isn't part of the plan," Miranda said. She was less winded than the men, though there were fine beads of sweat on her brow and top lip.

"Yes, I organized things so I'd have to spit up a lung along the way," Strumbić said, dripping irony with each exhaled breath.

"What now?" della Torre asked, trying to defuse Strumbić's obvious anger.

"We'll be fine here for a little while. We should be able to hold out for most of the day. They can't get lucky twice, can they? How big a crew could they possibly have? I didn't see anyone on our heels," Strumbić said. "A dozen local cops would take at least a couple of hours to find this place. A bunch of foreigners who don't know the town — well, let's just say we can relax for now while I figure some things out."

He led them to a gloomy little kitchen at the back of the house, barely illuminated by a narrow light well. Strumbić pulled out a chair for Miranda and with a firm hand sat her down. He pulled down three dusty glasses, filled them two-thirds full with yellow liquid from a plastic jerry can, and then topped them up with water from a second can.

"*Gemischt*," he said, referring to the wine-and-water mix. "Nothing quenches the thirst better."

They drank it down, then he poured them each another and then lit a cigarette.

"Fuck me," Strumbić said.

"How did you get that massive plank up that house?" asked della Torre. "I can't believe it fit the staircase."

"It didn't. I got one of the Albanians to hoist it up onto my terrace and then fed it across from there so that it was in the room waiting for you. Don't worry. I tested it out before inflicting it on you."

"You mean you walked across yourself?" Della Torre was impressed. Strumbić wasn't one to take unnecessary risks.

"Of course not. What do you think I am, a fucking idiot? Got one of the Albanian kids to give it a try. They'll do anything for money. Figured if he didn't splat neither would you. Silly little bastard decided to watch his piss fall four storeys when he got halfway across. Just as well it was too early for people to be wandering around." Strumbić wiped his hand across his face and shook his head. "Whatever happens, we've got to hold the fuckers off until tonight."

"I thought the whole intention was for them to find us."

"It was, Gringo. You were there to tease them along, make them think you're running. But it was supposed to be a show, not a fucking edition of *Jeux sans Frontières*," Strumbić said, referring to the absurd pan-European game show everyone watched. He smoked the cigarette down, lost in thought.

"Excuse me for a moment," Strumbić said, stepping out of the room.

"Being chased around Dubrovnik wasn't part of the deal," Miranda said after he'd gone. She spoke mildly, but there was steel in her words.

"I know. Charge him more. He'll be good for it," della Torre said.

"He seems intent on getting us killed."

They heard the sound of a flush from down the hall. Della Torre expected Strumbić to come back quickly, but he didn't. Instead, his footsteps climbed the stairs and moved about in the room above. And then, with alacrity, he charged back down.

"They're here," he said.

"What?" Della Torre stood up, horrified.

"Up. We're going."

Miranda rose. Della Torre saw the anxiety briefly etched into her expression.

"How do you know?" della Torre asked.

"Because I know. Because the mirror in the bathroom is angled so you can see a crack between the shutters, and I could see enough to get me curious," he said, in no mood to elaborate. "Up. You first, Gringo. Lady, you next. I'm at the back."

The stairs were wooden and ancient; they complained under the unaccustomed weight of bodies. Plaster, which had fallen

off in broad patches to reveal bare stone wall, crunched underfoot. The higher floors of the house had clearly long remained
uninhabited.

"Back bedroom," Strumbić said. He shut the door behind
them — a flimsy defence, della Torre thought, but then he saw
that it had hidden a ladder. Now that he was listening, he could
hear sounds coming from outside. Somebody was working away
at the shutters on the ground floor.

The back bedroom had a low ceiling built into the sloped
roof. A skylight let in dirty daylight. Strumbić pushed it open
and leaned the ladder against it.

"Up," he said.

Della Torre climbed up onto the roof. The rear pitch rose
from the city wall, forming a narrow gulley, which meant they
were out of sight of anyone in the street or the houses opposite.
Moss and grass grew in patches between the roof tiles.

Miranda followed him up, and then Strumbić, who pulled the
ladder up after himself. He shut the skylight with a kick and then
braced the ladder between the roof and the city wall.

The sound of splintering wood echoed up from the alleyway
and through the house, an odd stereo effect that della Torre
didn't waste time contemplating.

"Go, Gringo. Just get the fuck up there."

Della Torre climbed, uncertainly. The ladder creaked. He
wondered if its rungs would hold. When he got to the wall, he
swung his bag over the parapet, took a grip on the stone, and
with a heave dragged himself up, his arms straining, feeling the
cold, weathered stone against his face. A young couple, there to
enjoy the small measure of peace afforded by the heights in the
increasingly crowded city, stopped to watch. Della Torre ignored
them, turning to grab Miranda's bag and help her up as well.

When it was Strumbić's turn, della Torre pulled until he felt
the full agony of lifting the other man's weight, fearing he'd
herniate himself, that his weak elbow would give.

"Jesus, you need to go on a diet."

"Shut the fuck up and pull."

As he finally hauled Strumbić over, he realized he'd been lifting the ladder as well. Strumbić had hooked his foot under the top rung and now pulled it up after himself.

"God fuck their mothers, but these guys are starting to bother me," Strumbić said, shaking the strain from his arms. Without bothering to look where it might land, he heaved the ladder over the other side of the city wall onto the rocks below.

Strumbić led the way again with a firm hold of Miranda's wrist, half-dragging her and ignoring her complaints.

The walls rose to ever more exhilarating heights, as if they were on the edge of a chalk cliff. They pushed past people out for a morning's stroll or there to see where the Serb gunners were now aiming their shells. At a bastion as big as the keep of a castle, Strumbić stopped at the top of a spiral staircase.

Della Torre looked around. Men running towards them from both directions along the high walk. Leaning over the parapet, he could see people running towards the base of their tower. They were being bottled up.

"Julius, they'll be at the bottom by the time we get down the stairs," della Torre said.

"Just do as you're told, Gringo. Follow me. You too, miss — wouldn't want to leave you behind." He still had his hand on her wrist.

They wound their way down the stairs. Midway, Strumbić stopped by an iron gate covering a niche in the wall, half-hidden in the landing's deep shadows. He let go of Miranda, took hold of the bars, and with a mighty heave dragged the gate open and stepped aside.

"You first, Gringo. Just keep going until I tell you to stop."

The space was narrow and completely dark, smelling of salt and piss. It led deep into the city walls, back in the direction from which they'd come, descending shallowly all the while. Della

Torre stooped but still banged his head with every other step, muttering imprecations the whole way. There were no hand grips, but the passage was narrow and he could steady himself by flattening his hands against the walls.

"Faster," Strumbić said. Some shaded light reached him.

"Give me the flashlight up here," della Torre called back over his shoulder.

"You don't need it. You just keep going."

Della Torre could feel they'd stopped descending. He remained in a crouch, his back aching under the strain. The sides of the passage brushed his shoulders. His bag bounced against his back as he made his jagged progression; it felt like a hand shoving him along, pushing him deeper into the unfathomable darkness. He could hear voices far behind them and knew it was their pursuers.

"Stop, Gringo," Strumbić called. Della Torre turned with difficulty in that confined space. He could hear Miranda's breathing, feel the warmth of her body in the dark cold of the passage.

Strumbić was on his knees next to an arched opening, shining the torch along the floor towards another, similar opening ten metres back in the direction they'd come from, trying to decide between the two. He reached into his pocket, took something out, and rolled it into the opening directly beside him. They heard the faint ring of metal hitting stone.

"Must be this one," he muttered. "Okay, Gringo, down you go."

"What?"

"Down, Gringo. You heard me."

"Where?"

"Here. Go. It'll be hands and knees. But move. Now."

Strumbić backed off, shining the torch at the same spot. Della Torre was about to go headfirst when Strumbić stopped him.

"Backwards."

Della Torre took a deep breath and did as he was told. He could only just crawl in the space. Any narrower and he'd have had to slither on his belly. He moved centimetre by centimetre into the darkness. The passage was smooth and smelled of damp and sea. At first there was just a gentle slope, but it quickly steepened so that he slid as much as he crawled. Sweat poured off him, stinging his eyes, making the cold clamminess of that narrow sewer bite into his bones. Fear gripped him. Had the city's medieval rulers created these chambers in the fortress walls so that enemies could be lost forever, to starve in the darkness, to be entombed alive?

And then the passage turned suddenly vertical, and he plummeted along glass-smooth stone. He clawed at it with his fingernails, desperately searching for purchase, but there was none to be had. He was falling into the deep.

21

HE HIT THE hard ground with the force of a falling brick. But somehow he avoided doing himself obvious damage. Before he'd had a chance to register what had happened, Miranda's bag hit him, followed immediately by Miranda, who landed with a cry of surprise. An instinct of self-preservation made them roll away just in time to avoid taking the full force of Strumbić's weight.

"That comes straight out of the fairground in hell," Strumbić said, coughing and raising himself slowly, obviously sore.

They were on a stone ledge about five metres wide and of indeterminate length, in a half-built cave-like room suffused in a faint blue light. Della Torre crawled to the edge of the floor and saw that the light was coming up through water three metres below.

"Careful you don't fall in. Once you're in the water, it's impossible to climb back out," Strumbić said.

"Where are we?"

"Shh. We'll talk later. Just sit back and leave it for a little while," Strumbić whispered. He took della Torre's and Miranda's holdalls and positioned them on the floor directly below the hole.

They sat in complete silence, hearing only the echoes of their own pulses, the rhythm of their breathing, the smooth wash of water rising and falling against rock. And voices from far above.

After a while they heard another clink of metal on stone, and then a faint thwack as something hit Miranda's bag. Strumbić held his hand up, commanding absolute quiet from the others. Della Torre fought not to breathe normally. They waited. Every few minutes Strumbić checked his watch, and then, after they heard no further sounds from above, he reached over and picked up the coin, shining his torch on it.

"Abraham Lincoln," he said.

"Where are we, Julius?" della Torre asked.

"The water dungeon. It's not widely advertised in the tourist brochures, seeing as it's dangerous. Which is how it was intended to be. People got shoved down here. Eventually they'd get desperate enough to swim for it and drowned. Used to be an iron grille down there. The Italians yanked it out during the war. You get divers exploring sometimes. ."

"How do you know . . ." della Torre began and then stopped himself. "How do we get out?"

"We say 'open sesame.' Oops. Didn't work. I guess we're stuck," Strumbić said. "The Italians knocked a hole in the wall. There's a door not many people know about, just over there. Only we're not going to use it just yet."

"Mr. Strumbić, I get a little nervous in spaces like this," Miranda said. "I'm not enjoying the games you've been playing. However much you're willing to pay, I'm losing interest in the commission. Can we please leave?"

"Nope," Strumbić said. "No one's going to bother us here. It might not be as comfortable as one of the houses, but hey, this was only ever the third-choice backup to a backup. It'll give me a little time to think about what we're going to do."

Della Torre lay back on the smooth, flat stone, contemplating the hole from which they'd dropped. It wasn't much more than two metres above the floor, though the ceiling rose in an arch until it melded into the rough crags of the cave. He reached for a cigarette, but Strumbić stopped him.

"They'll smell it up there. The acoustics are tricky, but the smoke goes right up. Or so this very nice archaeologist who gave me a private tour told me."

Strumbić sat against the wall with his chin on his knees. "What troubles me," he said, "is how quickly your American friends keep finding us. They were meant to take most of the day tracking you down to the first house. The second place, I was sure no one had followed. They were completely lost in the alleys on the land side of the city. Even if they had watchers on every corner of the Stradun, they'd have had their work cut out."

"I told you they were good."

"I have no doubt, Gringo. I think they're very good. Probably better than you realize." Strumbić turned to Miranda. "Lady, show us your bag."

Della Torre sat up in surprise. "Why?"

"You keep your chivalrous instinct in check just now, Gringo. Lady, your bag, please."

She looked from one man to the other and then shrugged, passing it over.

Strumbić opened it up and pulled out each item of clothing, one after the other, patting each down and neatly folding it onto the floor. When he'd gone through the contents, he checked the bag itself, digging his hands into the corners. When he found nothing, he replaced everything he'd removed.

Miranda gave him a drawn, irritated smile, as she might have done with a stupid shop assistant. Strumbić ignored it.

"And now, please," he said, "all of your clothes. Off."

She looked at him, shocked.

"Listen, Julius —" della Torre began, standing up.

Strumbić pulled out his service automatic from a holster in the small of his back.

"Gringo, in a past life, you were a lawyer. And it's right for a lawyer to take a keen interest in the law and the rights of a defendant and all that. But I was a cop. And my interest was in making sure I wasn't wrong before nailing somebody. My intention right now is to nail Mrs. Walker here. So please, off with your clothes or I'll help you take them off."

Strumbić sounded dangerous, and Miranda could tell that he was. She stripped. He checked everything she took off, feeling the seams. He stood up and made her kneel with her back to him so that he could run a hand through her hair. Then he made her lie back and spread her arms and legs and then pull her knees towards her chest, clinically shining a torch over her. Apart from running his hand through her hair, he didn't touch her. When he was done, he allowed her to dress again.

She barely concealed her fury. She burned with anger and humiliation and moved away from the men. "Mr. della Torre, I'm afraid you and your friend are going to have to make your own way out of Dubrovnik," she said, only just controlling the tremor in her voice.

"Oh, don't worry, Mrs. Walker," Strumbić said. "We weren't going to take you up on your offer anyway."

Della Torre felt embarrassed for her, shocked at Strumbić, and ashamed for having allowed him to put her through the ordeal.

But Strumbić merely shifted his attention to della Torre. "Your turn, Gringo," he said.

"You going to look up my ass too?" he said defiantly.

"If I have to. But I want a look in your bag first."

Strumbić pulled out all the items in the bag, checking each with the same attention he had given Miranda's belongings. Then he found it, stuck with electrical tape to the inside corner of the holdall: a small black hard plastic box, half the size of a pack of cigarettes.

"Had this with you long?" Strumbić asked, holding it up between his thumb and forefinger.

"What is it?"

"It's the thing that's been telling our American friends where we are. Though I don't think the signal travels very well through a couple of hundred tons of rock and masonry. I imagine they're very irritated, having set us up so nicely." Strumbić inspected the transmitter. With his thumbnail he slid the recessed switch to Off. And then, just in case, he also removed the batteries, four AAAs, dropping them into one pocket and the transmitter into the other.

"Now there are two possibilities for how it might have come to be in your bag. One is that you're screwing me, Gringo, to save your own neck. But I don't think that's likely, seeing as what happens to me happens to you, and you know it, whatever promises those people might have made to you. The other alternative is that somebody else is setting us both up. So to find out, let's play a little game called 'airport security.' Did you pack your bag yourself?"

"Yes."

"When?"

"Last night. And I threw a couple of things in this morning."

"And has it been in your sight the whole while?"

"Yes. I mean, no. I was asleep, and then I didn't bring it with me when we went to watch the convoy come in."

"Was there anyone else with access to it during those times?"

"Julius, this isn't necessary," della Torre said.

"Was it Mrs. Walker here?"

Della Torre shook his head, not to deny the question but rather to admit his own foolishness.

"Would you care to admit to putting this in Gringo's bag, Mrs. Walker, or do I have to threaten to throw you over the side instead? Of course, that's a threat I can really only use once. Once you're in the water, there's no getting you out without the help of a good solid rope. Which I don't have. I think our friend Mr. della Torre here will vouch for my sincerity. Right, Gringo?"

"Yes," della Torre said, subdued.

"So, we accept that you planted this in Gringo's bag. And the assumption has to be that you're working for the Americans. Can we assume you've been working for the Americans all along?"

She remained quiet.

"Can we also assume that's because you work for either American or British intelligence?"

Still no answer.

"Your silences are revealing, Mrs. Walker," Strumbić said. "Were you sent to find me? Is that why you sailed through the blockade twice before, at great risk to yourself — because you knew Julius Strumbić would want to meet anyone who had figured out how to slip past the Yugoslav navy? Who knows, you might have enticed me to work with you."

Silence. Then della Torre spoke to Miranda, low, lost. "How much of that story you told me is true? About coming to live here on your own after splitting up with your husband. Nothing? Something? How long have you lived in Korčula? Not five years, is it. Five weeks?"

Still she didn't reply. She sat, legs drawn up, holding them, chin on her knees, her eyes glistening in the kaleidoscopic blue half-light.

"Gringo, you keep finding them. I'm not saying they're not good-looking, but fuck me, they've got venom in their fangs."

"How did you manage to set me up so well? I guess if you were based in Korčula it was a bonus for them that I stumbled onto you." Della Torre was talking mostly to himself. "And then when I did, you played it by ear. Why did they follow us to Šipan, though? To make sure I didn't chicken out?"

She shrugged.

"I guess that's why nobody in Korčula knew about you," continued della Torre. "You were too new. But you've sailed around here before, haven't you? Lots. With Sir Fitzroy Maclean? He was a spy, wasn't he? And I suppose it'd be natural for him to help out his side even if he was retired. Did he give you tips? Open doors? Were you always based on the coast? Or did you flit between Zagreb and here? Or maybe it was Belgrade."

"Gringo, you're not going to get anything out of this one. She knows we're not going to kill her. There's no point. But we'll figure out how to put her to good use," Strumbić said. "Anyway, there's a lesson for you in this: hookers are cheaper in the long run."

22

THERE WAS A modern steel door at one end of the cavern ledge that opened into a small concrete platform built onto the rocks at the base of Dubrovnik's walls. They left Miranda in the cave, telling her they'd be back later, or at the very least they'd tell Higgins where to find her. She said nothing.

Strumbić barred the door from the outside with a metal rail, though he left the padlock undone. After a quick glance around, they stepped out onto a narrow path that followed the base of the city walls. The rocks looked like raw, crumpled butcher's paper below a vertical sheet of parchment.

The late afternoon light was smudged by grey clouds, but even so della Torre blinked hard as he stepped out of the gloom.

"My guess is that they're going to be relying on technology to find us. The little box. They'll figure we have to surface sometime or other," Strumbić said. "They might have people on the walls, but I bet they're looking into the city, not out here. Just in case, let's not be fat German tourists about making ourselves scarce."

Once they moved away from the entrance to the dungeon cave, the path quickly became precipitous, in places barely a goat track. It rose, becoming almost sheer where the city walls turned inland. They had to hug the chiselled stone to avoid smashing themselves on the rocks below and then falling into the sea with cracked skulls and broken limbs. It was slow and painful going, sometimes an upward scramble in which the stone and scrub tore their hands, at other times a dangerous slide. They moved centimetre by centimetre, but eventually they reached the beach under the fortress's main northern drawbridge.

Without attracting attention to themselves, they headed away from the old city towards the peninsula, in the northern suburbs, Strumbić leading the way. Careful lest they be spotted, Strumbić ducked from one private garden to another, climbed a low wall or pushed through shrubbery, steadily moving farther from the ancient walls.

They passed a smouldering, newly gutted car. The Serb gunners, bored with reducing outlying villages to dust and cinder, had shifted their sights to Dubrovnik's suburbs. There was no method, no system to their shelling, nor any great urgency; it was a desultory effort, like boys taking potshots with their air rifles at random targets. But on the ground, the sense of panic was growing, sending ever more people to huddle within the sanctuary of the city fortress.

Della Torre knew war would come to the old town eventually. Higgins had said the Serb Chetnik militias were taking over the campaign, edging out the regular Yugoslav forces. Theirs was an atavistic hatred for Dubrovnik and what it stood for: bourgeois wealth, golden youth, gilded lives, foreigners and their condescension to the primitive people beyond the hills. The Chetniks grew frustrated at Dubrovnik's refusal to capitulate, even as its citizens grew dirtier, more frightened, more hopeless; irritated at Dubrovnik's pride in its long history of independence.

Della Torre feared for all those now seeking shelter within Dubrovnik's walls. Because ancient stones wouldn't stop the mortar bombs, the rockets, the high, arching shells.

After crossing a dozen gardens, they came upon a wooden door set into a wall. With a last look around, Strumbić unlocked it.

The house behind the wall was from the first decade of the century — Hapsburg art nouveau with a dash of Italianate influences. The windows were sealed with metal rolling shutters, but even so, it was a handsome two-storey building.

"Home," Strumbić said, unlocking the front door. "Swimming pool outside, views of the Adriatic and sunsets, an emergency generator I keep running so the ice doesn't melt — you can't hear it, because it's in a separate building. The only real downside is that I can't open the shutters. The Serbs would flatten the place if I lit it up."

"Yours?" della Torre asked, looking around in amazement at the wide hall with its big terracotta floor tiles and high ceilings.

"Borrowed," Strumbić said. "Look around. It's been decorated by an Italian pimp, all white plush and gold trim. Do you really think that's my taste?"

"Let me guess. Some big shot in Belgrade owns it."

"Actually, it's owned by a Herzegovinian mafioso who we banged up in the spring. The house isn't conventionally documented, if you know what I mean. I'm the only person who knows who it ultimately belongs to."

"Julius, you are remarkable."

"No, it's just that everyone else you know lacks imagination and gumption," Strumbić said. "We've got a couple of hours. Why don't you go up and have a bath."

"There's a water shortage in the city, but you've got enough to run baths?"

"I've got enough to fill a swimming pool. Which I've done. Bath is upstairs, room to the right. It's in the master bedroom. By the way, you might have a rummage in the dressing room. You're more the Herzegovinian's build than I am." Strumbić walked into the kitchen and opened the fridge door. "I'm afraid it's only imports. Do you want a Heineken or a Budvar?"

"Budvar," della Torre said, flabbergasted, as Strumbić produced a bottle.

"Whatever else you might say about them, the Czechs make decent beer," Strumbić said.

"What else would you say about them?"

"Nothing, except they got their asses handed to them by both the Nazis and the Russians and spent the whole time saying, 'Thank you very much.' And when they come here, they're cheap fucking tourists." Strumbić opened the beer. "Take this, have a shower or a bath or whatever, and then we'll eat when you come back down."

Della Torre was too nervous to soak, so he had a quick shower in an opulent marble-covered bathroom with gold taps and a floor mosaic that depicted either two women having sex or possibly a Christmas wreath.

The Herzegovinian's taste in wardrobe ran to too-tight bleached jeans and tank tops. But in among that, della Torre found a pair of blue cotton trousers and a shirt with buttons that went all the way up to his clavicle. The trousers were a size too generous around the waist and broke a little farther down his shoes than he liked, but he wasn't complaining.

When he made his way back down to the kitchen, he found Strumbić frying a couple of steaks. Pasta was cooking in another pot. Suddenly della Torre was ravenously hungry.

"Help yourself to another beer," Strumbić said.

Della Torre opened the fridge and pulled out another Budvar. "I'm worried about Miranda,"

"I just got off the phone to Higgins."

"Phone?"

"Yes, a thing with a handle you can speak into that's not a shovel."

"I didn't realize they worked."

"Oh, you can still make calls inside Dubrovnik. You just can't get a line out, unless you have a satellite phone. And, until the Americans came, there were only three of those in town."

"I was told there were only two," della Torre said. And then, when Strumbić gave him a long look, he again understood his stupidity.

When the steaks were cooked rare, Strumbić threw fresh cep mushrooms into the pan and then added cream and chopped parsley and chives and poured the sauce over the spaghetti. It reminded della Torre that the extent of his own cooking skills was limited to frying eggs.

"You were saying about phoning Higgins," della Torre said as they sat at the glass-topped dining table under a gold and crystal chandelier.

"I was saying that I called Higgins, who knows a boy who knows the way down to the dungeon door. Excellent storage space, by the way. Though cigarettes get a bit damp. The boy's to let your friend out as soon as the fireworks start."

"Fireworks?"

"A surprise, Gringo. Enjoy the food — it's going to be a long night."

They sat outside, smoking, drinking beers, and watching the sun set in an apocalypse of reds and oranges as the air filled with evening damp. When it was completely dark, they went back into the house.

"Right, Gringo, help me open the shutters upstairs."

In the dark, guided only by a flashlight, they went from room to room pulling open the roller blinds. They did the same on the ground floor.

Strumbić disappeared into what he called the utility room. He was in there for a quarter of an hour and then came out looking satisfied. At the front door, he punched a code into the burglar alarm and then played with the settings.

He put the batteries into the transmitter he'd found in della Torre's bag and then switched the unit on, shoving it behind a sofa cushion in the sitting room.

"Time to go," he said.

They strolled out of the house, which Strumbić locked, and

walked through the door in the garden wall and back into the
street.

Strumbić led them in the darkness to the Mercedes, parked
nearby, which he started up as della Torre got into the passenger
seat. And then, switching on just his parking lights, he drove
off at speed, tearing through the suburbs and up the steeply rising road behind the fortress city, where he pulled over by the
side of the road.

"What's up?" della Torre asked.

"Hop out and have a cigarette. We've got a show to watch."

They leaned against the rock face in the dark, the Merc
between them and the road. A few cars passed. In the distance,
past the citadel, della Torre could see the almost festive lights
of the Yugoslav navy ships, such a stark contrast to the city's
fearful darkness.

He wasn't sure what he was meant to look for, or where. The
amber glow of Strumbić's cigarette butt flew cartwheels in the
air, ending in a spray of sparks.

And then it happened. A brightness lit up in the middle distance. White-yellow incandescent lights. Floodlights. A solitary
house picked out clearly in the darkness. And then the shrill
sound of a distant alarm.

The brightness and noise lasted for a minute. Two minutes.
Three. And then he saw the flashes. Half a dozen in rapid suc-
cession like dry lightning. The shrieks of passing shells and
explosions followed almost simultaneously. And then bigger
guns from farther away started up, bellowing roars from up the
mountains. The house went up in red, green, orange streamers.
They could feel as much as hear the shock of the bombardment.

Strumbić laughed with a maniacal joy. "Holy fuck. Jesus, will
you look at that," he said over and over.

"Julius, what the hell?"

"If those Americans don't learn a lesson from this, well, I'm
sorry, but they're unteachable."

They got back in the Mercedes and drove. Strumbić parked it off the road just past the Argentina, leaving the keys in the ignition. "Hope somebody else gets as much pleasure out of it as I did," he said.

Like della Torre, he carried only a holdall, though his was bigger. And it was a leather Louis Vuitton.

They walked back to the hotel, but instead of going through the main entrance, Strumbić led della Torre to the service doors at the side of the old wing. He passed a folded note to the porter. Deutschmarks, della Torre saw in the brief flash of light as the door opened. Strumbić took the service stairs two at a time. On the third floor he stepped into the corridor and knocked at the third door. When he didn't hear anything, he slid in a key and turned the handle. Only then did della Torre notice that Strumbić had a gun in his hand.

Della Torre followed. The room was being used but was empty at the moment. Strumbić locked the door behind him and motioned della Torre to follow him to the balcony, where they took the two available seats. From the distance beyond the old city, they could see a glow and hear the sound of fire engines.

"You rigged it up so that when the Americans located the transmitter, they'd break into the house and set off the alarms," della Torre said. "How'd you know the Serbs would start bombing?"

"Why do you think there's a blackout? They see a pool of light on Croat territory at night, and they assume it's a target."

"Julius, had you put your mind to noble causes, you'd have discovered the cure for cancer by now."

"Or baldness," Strumbić said. "But you know, I don't think I'd like the attached celebrity. I'm sort of a low-key person."

"I'd be surprised if anybody survived that." Della Torre was suddenly worried about Anzulović.

"Funny thing is, bombardments like that are a lot more show than tell. It's surprising how often people survive. But it'll shake up the Americans, anyway."

"What now?"

"Now we wait for our ticket out of here." Strumbić looked at his watch. "Boat leaves in two hours and forty minutes. The Americans will be picking themselves up and trying to figure out what the fuck happened to them, while we'll be slipping out of a city under siege more easily than stepping on a number nine tram."

They smoked and sat back in the chill of the evening, listening to the voices of people talking on the terraces below as if an evening bombardment not five kilometres away was the usual sort of light entertainment. And then the voices faded, and all that was left was the sound of a Cole Porter tune from the bar piano and waiters tidying up glasses and cutlery. And then only the sounds of sleep and whimpering children.

The door opened and Strumbić stood up, gun in his hand. "Steve, my friend, how is?" he said in English, sitting back down.

Higgins joined them on the balcony, perching on a footstool. "Julius," he said, and then turning to della Torre: "Marko, nice to see you."

"Did you get story?" Strumbić asked.

"I got it. You didn't need me to tell them about the house in the end?"

"No, I had different idea," Strumbić said. "Same *rezultat*."

"Well, thanks for the tip, anyway. It appears that a handful of American observers and journalists were caught in a Yugoslav bombardment at a house they were visiting in the Dubrovnik suburbs," Higgins said. "I'll file it first thing."

"Anyone killed?" della Torre asked.

"Hard to tell," Higgins said. "House was totally destroyed. Someone seemed to think there might have been two or three people in it or around the grounds at the time."

"Only two or three?" Strumbić seemed surprised. As was della Torre. He'd been trying to work out the size of the American team and figured on at least six and most probably eight or nine, not including Grimston and Anzulović. And Miranda.

"Did you tell boy to open doors of sea dungeon?"

"Yeah, he went all right. Came back pretty quickly too. Said all he found was a woman's suitcase."

Della Torre sensed Strumbić stiffen in the dark. His silence was louder than rifle fire.

"How well did the British woman swim?" Strumbić asked della Torre in Serbo-Croat.

"Very well. She swam every day she was here."

"Proper swimming? Not lady-with-her-head-above-the-water swimming?"

"Proper swimming, like lady-who-swims-in-the-Olympics swimming."

"Fuck," Strumbić said. And then, once more in English: "Sank you, Steve, is interesting information."

"No problem, Julius," Higgins said. And then, quietly: "I'll miss you when you go."

They lapsed into silence. Both della Torre and Higgins sensed that Strumbić needed a moment to think.

"How'd the boy manage to do it so quickly?" della Torre asked eventually, remembering the painful and arduous trip he and Strumbić had taken earlier in the daylight. He couldn't imagine having to pass along those rocky cliffs at night.

"Oh, he drops a rope ladder over the walls. It's a pretty short climb down. From there, the rock rises and there's only around five metres of wall to scale. He went down, had a look, and came back up straight away."

"You owe me ten Deutschmarks for that, by the way," Higgins added. "Short notice and all. Had to pry him off his girl."

Strumbić pulled out a roll of notes and handed two to Higgins. "Is two hundred here," he said. "It may be little while we don't see each other."

"Mighty generous, Julius."

"So no woman? Not in water?"

"Not a hair, Julius."

For the next twenty minutes, the three men waited without speaking, Strumbić looking frequently at his watch. And then, finally, they saw something. The flicker of a light on the water, followed soon after by the low throb of an engine.

"Okay, Gringo. There's our ride." But there was a grimness to Strumbić's voice that della Torre guessed wasn't just nervousness about breaking through the blockade.

They heard shooting somewhere in the distance. The front line was encroaching. A Serb sniper farther along the bay fired at lights, a crack followed by breaking glass. Sometimes bullets struck hard things so that they made a sound like clackers, those hard orbs suspended on strings that children played with. Or worse still, nothing, so that it was impossible to know where the bullet had stopped.

Strumbić rose and went into the room. Della Torre started to follow, like an eager child worried about being left behind, but Strumbić waved him back. He picked up the phone and spoke briefly. Della Torre stood, anxiously watching. After four minutes the phone rang. Strumbić snatched up the handset before the second ring, listened for a moment, and then walked back onto the balcony.

"Gringo, you know it's just so bourgeois to use the stairs. Tonight we do things the proletarian way," he whispered. But there was no humour to his joking.

"Good luck," Higgins said, briefly shaking their hands.

Strumbić climbed over the balcony rail, motioning della Torre to do the same. He crept along the outside edge to the side of the building, against which a long ladder was leaning. They made their precarious way down, della Torre feeling unbalanced by his bag, worried that his weak left arm would give way.

He stumbled after Strumbić onto the terrace and down the stairs until they reached the swimming pool. In the faint light of Strumbić's hooded torch, he saw a boat.

A voice in the darkness issued soft, quick commands. Della Torre knew it well — an unmistakeable voice that had spooled out a thread of orders, woven into a leash by which della Torre had led an old man to his death. All those years ago, in his sleep, the memory of that voice had given him nightmares. And yet he'd come to respect, even like, the man behind it. The man who'd once headed the UDBA's wetworks, the man who'd assassinated Swedish Prime Minister Olof Palme, the man who'd killed the Americans: The Montenegrin.

23

THE GENTLE SPLASH and creak of oars swept in and out of the water as the long, open fishing boat was guided through the rocky shallows. Della Torre heard its fender bump and scrape against the side of the terrace. A man hopped ashore, crouching at the boat's bow. And then someone else stepped onto land.

"Hello, Gringo. Julius."

"Mr. Djilas," della Torre said, feeling the man's hand on his shoulder. He was a tall man, in his mid-fifties but more youthful than his age, and della Torre felt the force of his strength in that grip. "It's sooner than I expected to see you."

"Maybe we can save the reminiscences for the trip," Strumbić said. "Let's get a move —"

Two strong beams of light hit them from different points up on the terraces.

"Down. On the ground. Now." Someone on a megaphone. A woman, speaking Croat. Miranda.

Just then, an equally powerful beam flashed up from the boat, illuminating some of their ambushers. A heavy-calibre machine gun barked upwards, the impact of its bullets shattering concrete as its empty shells cascaded against wood and stone.

Gunfire opened up on them, smaller-calibre weapons but no less deadly. Della Torre and Strumbić threw themselves backwards, the boat rocking under their weight. Strumbić opened up with his pistol. Della Torre slunk down in the boat's wooden belly, scrabbling around in his bag for his Beretta.

Someone had started the engine, gunning it so that the boat leapt backwards. Della Torre lifted his gun and squeezed off a couple of shots, sightless. The fear of being wounded again grabbed hold of his gut, his elbow remembering the searing pain of a bullet gouging flesh, splintering bone.

Then from the sea behind them came a short series of loud coughs and violent eruptions of red and yellow and green as cannon shells burst against the Argentina's grounds. The boat's searchlight switched off, as did those of their attackers, all fearful of drawing further shots from the naval ship. The gunfire stopped as suddenly as it had started. It couldn't have lasted more than a minute or two.

Della Torre saw that a fire had started halfway between the sea and the hotel, catching hold in the chemical stores and pump room for the pool; they went up in an instant conflagration that lit the sea and shore like a Fourth of July bonfire. It cast a bloody red glow across the scene, and for a moment della Torre was sure he saw Grimston and Anzulović standing there, then watched them recede into the darkness.

He turned to tell Strumbić, but Strumbić and four of the boat's half-dozen crew where huddled in the bow. The former cop was pointing a flashlight downwards, and at first all della Torre could see was a red so deep it was black.

One of the boatmen recited a rosary, his voice automatic, panicked. Edging forward, della Torre saw the object of their interest. The Montenegrin.

"You and you, move," Strumbić said. "You, keep pressing on the wound. That's right, just press on it hard. You don't want your boss to bleed . . ." He thought better of adding "to death."

"How are you, chief?" he asked the Montenegrin. "Pretty sore, I imagine."

"Sore's not the word. It hurts like the devil," the Montenegrin said, panting.

"Course it does. Ask Gringo here. Getting shot is a painful experience. Actually, it's when you don't feel the pain that you start to worry."

"Where's he hit?" della Torre asked.

"Hip," the Montenegrin answered. "Caught me as I was jumping in the boat."

"You sure that's it? There's blood all over your chest."

"That's not mine, that's Tihan's," the Montenegrin said. "Tripped and broke his nose on the anchor and then bled all over me."

"I was trying to protect you from getting shot more, boss," said the man at the Montenegrin's feet.

"Never mind, Tihan, the shirt's had it anyway," the Montenegrin said. And then, to no one in particular: "See if you can get me some water and a mouthful of brandy. You think there's some morphine on the boat?"

One of his men had already rummaged through the first aid box, pulling out big square blocks of gauze, which they packed onto the wound, binding it as best they could. But the only painkillers the green box contained were aspirins.

"I'll survive," the Montenegrin said with gallows humour, though he looked pale yellow-green in the glow of the electric lantern. "Good thing the navy knows we're passing. I don't feel like getting shot at anymore."

He went silent for a while, and della Torre and Strumbić said nothing either.

"Shit," Strumbić said at long last. "Why do you always pick the crazy ones?"

"What?"

"The Englishwoman we left in the cave. Why didn't you tell me she was fucking insane enough to swim for it?"

"Because I didn't realize she was."

The Montenegrin growled. "Fuck, it hurts," he said. "So it was another woman, eh, Gringo? You're intent on having a woman kill me off. Well, I suppose it's just as well. The alternative is slivovitz."

"I'm sorry," della Torre said. "I didn't know. I was foolish."

"I hear you got through the blockade in a small sailboat. Gringo, you never cease to astonish me. You were lucky the torpedo boat's signal officer was drunk and the subaltern was easily confused. That password sequence you used is more than a month out of date. Well remembered, though. If the crew had any sense, they'd have pulled you in and you'd be in a naval brig in Kotor while they worked out whether you'd be hanged for being a spy or merely shot for being inconvenient."

Strumbić chuckled in the darkness. Della Torre shifted uncomfortably, feeling raw wood under the flecked varnish. That could still be where he was headed.

"Some more of that brandy," the Montenegrin called towards the man behind della Torre. "And tell them to quit bouncing the boat so much."

The bow beat against the waves as the man in the wheelhouse gunned the engine, desperate to get his wounded chief home.

"This will be a long war. It's careless of me to be wounded so early," the Montenegrin said. The skin on his face looked like a Noh mask in the dim light, the pain painted on. "Even without the Americans there are so many enemies. On my side and yours. Maybe it's foolish of me to believe I'll survive it. We understood the old bandits, knew how to appease them. The new ones, they are unpredictable. Allied to the most vicious killers." The Montenegrin spoke quietly, taking comfort from the sound of his voice but knowing he needed to conserve his strength. "But Snezhana will be well cared for, whatever the case. Don't worry, Gringo. She's writing a book about your adventures. You're the hero."

Della Torre smiled at the idea of starring in a ten-year-old's novel. But what a formidable ten-year-old the Montenegrin's daughter was.

For a long time after that, the Montenegrin said nothing. Were it not for the occasional groan, della Torre would have thought he was asleep. But each time the wounded man took a swallow of his homemade brandy, he seemed to revive a little.

"Oh, Gringo, it would be nice to sit and talk to you of a summer evening, drinking wine until after the sun sets and the cold drives us back indoors. I always enjoyed our discussions. It's a shame they won't happen anymore."

"Perhaps."

"Oh, you're right. Perhaps."

"How is Snezhana?"

"She is well. She mentions you often. It filled her with life, that adventure of yours over the summer. I would have thought a child would suffer nightmares. But she has a thirst for excitement. For once she could experience what she'd long conjured in her mind."

"It was hardly a fairy tale."

"And yet it resolved itself like one. The wicked witch was killed and the little girl rescued by a prince."

Della Torre said nothing.

"This wound makes me think of her. The woman. I'm sorry, Gringo. She was a professional. Like me. It was the normal course of an abnormal life. She understood. There is no time for sentiment in our business. The Americans know that. They are not pursuing Strumbić or me or you for reasons of chivalry or nobility or revenge for your Rebecca or her colleagues. There is something about Palme that they are afraid somebody will find out, and we are stepping stones to that discovery. They will eliminate everyone they need to, for whatever reason."

"Yes."

"It is distasteful. But it is the way of our life, Gringo. Yours too, however much you are justified in thinking that your hands are clean."

The Montenegrin looked tired. Not just tiredness brought on by a deep and painful wound, but the immense exhaustion of a retired executioner. Who more than hangmen know how to weigh mortality?

They passed the rest of the trip in silence, della Torre shivering as the cool sea air blew against him. The warships offshore ignored them. Landward they could see the almost festive glow of Yugoslav army emplacements, the Chetnik camps in the hills, the occasional white burst of rifle fire like a photographer's flash. Della Torre held tight as the open boat bounced against the small waves, the spittle of sea spray wetting him.

After an hour, the boatmen switched on the red and green port and starboard indicators and a powerful white beam. Strumbić dozed with his chin against his chest, like a habitual commuter on the last train home. Maybe the Montenegrin slept too. His men had covered him in blankets, tended to him tenderly.

It was a long ride south along the coast. Della Torre nodded off more than once, jerked awake by an inbuilt fear of falling or by the boat's judder against the water. The luminous dial on his watch told him they'd been at sea for more than three hours when he saw the beaded lights of a port town, which a boatman whispered was home, Herceg Novi, in Montenegro. They rounded the long peninsula guarding the mouth of Kotor Bay, a fjord twisting into the darkness of the mountains.

For a long time they seemed to make no headway, and then suddenly they were at the harbour wall. One of the Montenegrin's sailors leapt up and deftly secured the boat, and then della Torre saw the ambulance. A doctor ran towards them, followed by two navy orderlies pushing a wheeled gurney. The Montenegrin's men had radioed ahead.

The Montenegrin was unconscious and waxen, the bandages

on his thigh soaked black with blood. His men gingerly lifted him up on a stretcher and he was spirited away. Four policemen congregated at the boat.

"Shit," Strumbić said to della Torre. "Now we're fucked. The welcoming party is usually just one customs man who for some reason prefers lira to Deutschmarks. I have no relationship with these guys."

"Let me talk to them," della Torre said, enervated and exhausted but willing himself into authority. He hoisted himself onto the stone quayside and stepped into the middle of the group of Serb officials.

"Gentlemen," he said. His voice was hoarse with tiredness and the long trip in the cold boat. He pulled his wallet out and prayed that the card was still in there. With relief he passed around his old UDBA identification. In the old days of Yugoslavia it had acted like a universal key, unlocking any situation. Now it was more risky. People had become more openly skeptical about the UDBA. Increasingly, Croats were realizing that the unit had been disbanded and no longer applied to their territory. But here it carried the same force as ever. Montenegro was still part of the old Yugoslavia, with the old Yugoslav taboos and fears, including crossing the secret police.

The policemen's officiousness faded and they melted away in round-shouldered apology from the narrow circles of light cast by a row of lamps on ornamental posts.

Strumbić looked more disreputable than usual under the sodium glare. "Think he'll survive?" della Torre asked him.

"He'd better, at least until we get out of town. Because if he dies, those Serb cops and those boatmen, who'd kill their own grandmothers if the Montenegrin told them to, will be very unhappy with us," Strumbić said. "Our problem is getting out of town quickly. Not easy here, where you need a pass to fart. Not everybody's going to kowtow to you for being UDBA."

Della Torre and Strumbić made their silent way to a small

waterfront hotel. The handful of uniformed sailors and soldiers on the street paid them no notice.

Strumbić pounded on the door to wake the man who ran the hotel. He was groggy and wore a vest and pyjama bottoms and a growth of stubble.

"Be nice if you showed up at a civilized time for once," he said to Strumbić.

"I'll take my business elsewhere next time. I need a second bedroom too."

The man shrugged and led them to the first floor, opening a door for della Torre. Strumbić seemed to know where he was going. "Don't bother getting up too early," he said to della Torre. "If you want room service —"

"We don't do room service," the man said.

Strumbić ignored the man, focusing his attention on della Torre. "I was about to say, if you want room service you're out of luck."

The man who ran the *pension* scowled. "I'm not opening the door to all comers the whole night."

"That's okay," della Torre said. "I think I might just like some sleep."

Della Torre stepped into a room lit by a weak, barely shaded bulb. It was filled with the sort of heavy, dark furniture and crocheted doilies beloved of Italian grandmothers. But the bed was soft enough, and the eiderdown warm. He'd have been content to sleep upright on a wooden chair.

They stayed at the *pension* for three days. Strumbić said he had things to organize, and they had to be careful to keep their heads down. They were the only guests, and the laconic, irritable manager didn't go out of his way for them. He did lend della Torre a small transistor radio and supplied both men with newspapers and the comic strip novels, mostly westerns, that were as widely consumed by Yugoslav men as by boys.

Sometimes della Torre sat in the small, gloomy dining

room, or in the room that served as a bar, where the proprietor watched television for much of the day. In the evenings della Torre caught the news, which reported the Serbs' version of Vukovar's impending fall. The town was surrounded and all but crushed. He prayed Irena had gotten out. In those empty hours he imagined himself as a father. The thought made him at once happy and anxious.

The few times della Torre ventured out, the only other people he saw on the harbourfront wore camouflage and fatigues. The regular army and navy personnel didn't worry him; what did worry him was the fact that they were outnumbered by the paramilitaries, especially the ones with wolf insignia patches. They were Chetnik men, thugs, and their uniforms and equipment were newer. They strutted with self-assurance, while the JNA conscripts looked like what they were, boys just out of school.

The Chetniks' leader, the warlord Gorki, featured in the Belgrade papers every day, usually photographed with his pet wolf on a chain. He might have been a paramilitary, but he also governed regular troops. He had pull with the politicians, charisma, money, and the support of a private army.

He and most of his men were currently torturing Vukovar with their relentless explosive barrages. Della Torre shuddered to think what would happen to the town's defenders when it capitulated. And with Vukovar subjugated, he supposed, Gorki would come to Dubrovnik and do the same there, like a spreading pathogen, his forward guard making sure his presence was felt at a distance. The Montenegrin had better recover soon, because Gorki was a mortal enemy.

For the first two days the prognosis was good, according to what Strumbić heard. The Montenegrin had been stabilized and was being given the best treatment available. But then his condition deteriorated. It seemed the doctors had missed a fragment of metal or bone that had splintered from the hip to the gut. Sepsis had set in, and the latest worry was that his kidneys were starting to pack up under the onslaught of infection.

"It's time to go, Gringo," Strumbić said. "We don't want to be here if the Montenegrin kicks it. His men will remember us, and so will the police. I finally managed to organize some bus tickets and, more importantly, passes for us. Harder than it seems when you're in the middle of the fucking enemy's military zone. Would have been cheaper to fly the Concorde, if Herceg Novi had an airport instead of just a shitty bus station." He looked harassed. But for della Torre it would be a relief to leave this place, even though it would be to a new set of dangers.

They were going to the heart of the Pilgrim mystery: Belgrade, the capital of what had once been Yugoslavia. Some of its power might have been shorn with the secession of two republics — Slovenia and Croatia — but it was still the capital of the rump state as well as of Serbia, an industrial powerhouse and the military centre. Della Torre had never much liked the city — it had been heavily damaged during the war and then rebuilt in a spiritless socialist aesthetic. As the home of UDBA and of all the major branches of government, it represented to him an oppressive bureaucracy. But it shocked him to think of the city as hostile territory and himself as an enemy of the state that he'd so recently served.

After an early breakfast on the morning of the fourth day, they left. At the bus station, the transport manager handed them two passes printed on cheap grey paper and covered in the requisite stamps. He then drew aside the military policeman responsible for checking documents, for an impromptu cigarette break.

Strumbić found the slow coach to Sarajevo, where he had a word with the driver, handing him the passes along with a few dinar notes in addition to the fare.

The bus set off, making its way through the coastal valleys of striated white stone broken like old men's teeth, and then crawling behind columns of military vehicles. It was frequently stopped at roadblocks. But the soldiers manning the posts never gave Strumbić's and della Torre's passes more than a cursory glance. If they were looking for deserters, a couple of middle-aged men weren't going to interest them much.

The bus trundled deeper into Bosnia. Telephone poles marked the route like the crucifixes that once lined the Via Appia. The landscape slowly changed from hard stone and scrub to verdant mountains covered in larch, beech, and oak. Here were deep gorges and wilderness, a vast estate of lynx, bear, and wolf. In the old days, the men who lived there — hunters and, on the high pastureland, goat herders — had been just as untamed.

It was here more than anywhere that the Partizans and the Germans had fought without mercy, that Fitzroy Maclean and Tito only just escaped the Wehrmacht paratroopers sent in their hundreds to capture them, that Tito was finally forced to abandon his sick and wounded men, and that those men were slaughtered. But then, the Partizans had had no use for prisoners either. It was said their ghosts wandered those valleys with the morning mist.

It was a strange country, claimed by Bosnian Serbs and by Croats and Muslims, including those who had converted from Christianity and those who had come from Albania. Serbs had been transplanted there by the Austro-Hungarians to preserve a buffer against the Turks, and the Croats rightly or wrongly claimed precedence.

Every grudge, every debt was hidden deep in the chasms of history but secretly nurtured over generations. Who knew where they would spring up again or when. Bosnia's tribes were like the raw limestone landscape, into which streams of resentments would disappear only to rise somewhere distant, even under the sea.

Della Torre smoked Strumbić's endless supply of imported Winstons. "You must be the luckiest gambler who ever existed. You could park yourself in a casino and never need to leave," he said, tiring of their silence.

"Depends on what you mean by 'gamble.'"

"Oh, you know, taking these huge risks and always coming out of them with a bigger fortune. If London was a setback, you made twice as much in Dubrovnik."

Strumbić laughed. "If only, Gringo, if only."

"But even if you haven't made it all back, surely you've got enough. You don't need any more. What is it now? Why keep taking the risks? Or is it an addiction?"

"You've got me all wrong, Gringo. No amount of money can get you far enough from the memory of growing up poor. And I mean so poor that you don't own your own pair of shoes until you're old enough to earn the money to buy them yourself, when the house you grew up in is two rooms and the floor is boards on dirt, and when the only heat you've ever had comes from the wood you've chopped. Not something you Americans can understand. Over there, even the peasants are rich."

It was della Torre's turn to laugh. "My father would laugh to hear I grew up rich."

"Gringo, when you grow up using chestnut leaves to wipe your ass, the man with an indoor toilet is rich. You're right, though, I've got enough. The money is neither here nor there. But I'm not a gambler. For one thing, real gambling is putting something on the line you can't afford to lose, and the odds aren't particularly good. Think about things that way and you realize you're the gambler, Gringo. For me, mostly it's an intellectual challenge. Like Dubrovnik. How many cigarettes do you stock up on? How many should you sell? Or do you wait for the price to go higher? Do you dump your holdings when people find out the armada's coming to save them? Or do you pay some docker in Split to unload all the cigarettes and then sell into the panic when the boats arrive with only half the expected supplies? These are all hypotheticals, mind."

Strumbić grinned at della Torre's shock. "A lot of the money that comes in goes out. Who was the guy who said, 'I spent ninety percent of my money on women and booze, and the rest

I wasted?' Eh?" Strumbić laughed, but only for a moment. "But seriously, Gringo, ultimately money matters because it gives you control. You don't need me to tell you this."

"Power?"

"Call it what you like. Power. Surplus. Influence. An ability to say fuck off to the world if you want. The Montenegrin has it. Or maybe had it. Me?" He shrugged. "Sometimes. But not with those Americans you got me tangled up with . . ."

"Julius, I've never seen a man more desperate to be entangled. You did everything you could to get me to hook you up with the Americans."

"We're not apportioning blame right now, Gringo. We'll sort ourselves out, eh? Get the Americans off our backs, maybe even make them learn to love us."

"Sure, Julius," della Torre said, without a trace of hope.

The bus was slow and full, pulling into every town along the way big enough to have a steeple or a minaret. At longer stops, they got off to buy beers and to piss. They smoked and watched the landscape pass by, wooden farmhouses and modern concrete and cinder-block buildings, split-rail fence posts and clearings of corn or pasture hemmed in by forests, until at long last they arrived in Sarajevo, deep in the folds of its mountains.

They waited until everyone else was off the bus, and then Strumbić finished paying off the driver, who smiled at them as if he was fixing their faces in his memory.

They stayed the night in an anonymous hotel, Strumbić's Deutschmarks supplanting the need for identity documents at the front desk.

Della Torre tried to get through to Irena, but still no answer at the flat, her office, or the hospital in Zagreb. She had to have left Vukovar. He was certain of it. Maybe she'd gone to London with her Dr. Cohen, he thought with a jealous twinge.

In the morning there were problems with the train link between Sarajevo and Belgrade, so it was back to the bus station.

But there were no seats to be had until Strumbić had a word with someone, who had a word with someone else. The passengers who thought they'd reserved seats were irate, but there was a certain fatalism to their protests. Neither della Torre nor Strumbić felt ashamed. It was the way things had always been.

The highway was single-lane and winding. Military traffic in both directions kept the roads congested. Della Torre wondered whether the rail network had been taken over for tank transport, because there were only troop carriers and army trucks and buses on the roads.

They didn't arrive in Belgrade until well after dark. This time Strumbić maintained their anonymity not by paying off a clerk at the front desk of a hotel, but by taking them to a brothel. He didn't know how long they'd be staying, and the longer they did, the more chance they'd be sold out to the state security.

"It's more expensive than a hotel, no question, and they only take foreign currency. Cash. But the accommodation is nice. Food's good. They're discreet, and there's room service." He gave della Torre a conspiratorial wink.

Belgrade always made della Torre uneasy: its strangeness, the fact that everything was in the Cyrillic alphabet. He could read it, but, having grown up in America, it represented to him foreignness, Russia, the Cold War enemy.

But there was something deeper too. The feeling that here he was on the edge of another world. Jason and his Argonauts had passed this way, in their desperate flight towards the Adriatic from those mysterious lands to the east, after stealing the Golden Fleece. Belgrade's fortress on the bluff, overlooking the confluence of the Sava with the Danube, was where the Orient began. Or ended.

The brothel consisted of three inconspicuous storeys above a corner grocery store in a small, nondescript postwar block, grey flaking concrete and metal roll-down shutters over the windows. Strumbić pressed a buzzer between the shop and what looked

like a traditional family restaurant that was shut and dark. He
whispered a name into the intercom and the door buzzed open.
They were in a hall with a terrazzo floor; a stairwell was in front
of them, and there was no sign of anyone or anything under the
stark fluorescent lighting.

Strumbić took the stairs two at a time, moving fast for a heavy
set middle-aged man. The door to the second-storey apartment
opened before he knocked, and a pleasant-looking woman of
indeterminate age, though probably not much younger than
della Torre, ushered them in.

"Two rooms for a few days. One full service." Strumbić looked
questioningly at della Torre, who shook his head. "One full service; the other hasn't yet decided."

"Do you mind staying in the top-floor suite?"

"Busy?"

"Not really, but if you're here for a few days, it gives you a
little extra privacy." Her eyes explained that privacy had a price.

"Discount?"

The woman was at once friendly and coy and ironic. "But you
always get a discount, sir. And so do your friends."

Strumbić shook his head and grinned. "Discounts like yours
will send a man to the poorhouse." He pulled a fat roll of German
currency out of his coat pocket and lay down some notes. "Three
days," he said, looking over to della Torre and then putting down
a few more notes. "Four. One full service. Any add-ons, stick on
the bill. Any chance of sending something up for us tonight? A
man develops a hunger."

"Whatever you desire."

"Then a couple of American steak sandwiches with fried potatoes. You want cheese, Gringo?"

Della Torre nodded with as much *savoir faire* as he could
muster.

"Make it with cheese on both, and a couple of blonde beers.
And a couple of blondes to deliver it."

24

DRAGOMANOV'S APARTMENT WAS less than a twenty-minute walk from the brothel. Winter was already settling on the city. Cleaners swept the fallen leaves off the streets, but more accumulated behind them. Della Torre could see his breath in the air and feel the cold through his light autumn coat.

They set out in the morning and found the building without trouble. It had been built between the wars, somehow retaining its reserved art deco detailing, which lifted the mood of its grey pebble-dash. It was five storeys high and took up the whole of a big city block. The main entrance was guarded by two uniformed sentries in what looked like adapted phone booths on either side. They sat, bored and watchful, on high stools, rifles on the floor next to them. Formerly UDBA, now Serb secret service, della Torre figured. Through the double glass doors he could see a reception desk manned by another uniformed guard.

He and Strumbić took a turn around the building. A large gated archway led to a central courtyard, where they could see about a dozen top-end German and Italian cars and a couple of Zastavas that looked like beggars at a banquet. In the centre of the block, a great spreading chestnut tree officiated. Della

Torre wondered whether its conkers dented the cars when they dropped in the autumn. All along his road in Zagreb, they fell with a sound like hail on shantytown tin roofs.

The carriageway was also guarded, though the sentry boxes here were under the shelter of the entrance arch, behind the wrought-iron gates. Two foot patrols, each with a pair of uniformed police, made the rounds. And there was a patrol car at each of the building's long ends.

"Well, nice to see our masters take their security seriously," Strumbić said.

"I think maybe today we'll go to that place across the road, have a coffee, and watch for their shifts to end," della Torre said.

"Well, we shouldn't make it too obvious. I'd be surprised if the staff weren't bosom buddies with the sentries."

There weren't many pedestrians, and della Torre knew that if he and Strumbić loitered, they'd be clocked by the police and quite possibly asked to present documents. His UDBA ID definitely wouldn't pass muster here, and when they found his Croatian military document, his circumstances would almost certainly become very unpleasant.

"Maybe somewhere else," Strumbić said as they were about to cross the road to the café. He stooped suddenly and pulled della Torre by the sleeve.

"Why, what's the matter?"

"Just keep your head down and walk fast. Remember that American who escorted me on the flight to Zagreb because Rebecca found me inconvenient in Dubrovnik? You know the guy, seemed to be running their whole show."

"John Dawes?"

"That's the man."

"Are you sure?"

"No, but I don't want to go back and ask."

They found another café with a worse line of sight but no other customers.

"He's probably just there for the coffee. The American embassy's not too far away."

"Or an early morning beer," della Torre said, lighting a cigarette and passing the packet to Strumbić.

"Maybe he's here for the weather."

"There are plenty of other leading ex-Communists who live in the building. He could be visiting any one of them."

"All of them."

Neither found the joke funny just then.

They stared out the plate-glass window, straining to see the apartment building's front door.

"They've beaten us to him," della Torre said.

They both had the same thoughts. The Americans had tried to kill the Montenegrin. They were hunting for them both. After that, only Dragomanov would be left.

"Or they're keeping an eye on him. Or waiting for us to show up."

"Maybe we shouldn't delay our visit," della Torre said. "Though it won't be fun trying to figure out how to get in."

"You've got the apartment number, right?"

"Yes."

"So we can work out approximately where he is."

"Third floor."

"The building's a lot like mine," Strumbić said. He lived in one of the best Hapsburg blocks in Zagreb. Most of the apartment buildings from that era were more like a collection of very large townhouses, separate buildings each with a front door leading to a staircase with two large or four small apartments on each floor. But Strumbić's was an integrated block, big enough to have central corridors with larger apartments facing the street and smaller ones looking into the courtyard. The biggest apartments were at the ends of the corridors and faced both the street and the courtyard. Strumbić had one of those, and they were betting Dragomanov did too.

"You know what?" said Strumbić. "Normally I'd have said let's spend some time scouting the place, do some planning. But fuck it, Gringo, we haven't got time. What we've got instead is money. You got your gun?"

"No."

"Well, we have to settle our bill with the ladies," Strumbić said. "Might as well get ourselves sorted there now. If things go tits up, we won't want to hang around."

It was early and only two people were at the brothel, a middle-aged receptionist and a girl barely out of her teens, sitting on the sofa and smoking a cigarette with her morning coffee. Strumbić drew the receptionist aside.

"Janica, what do you know about that hairdressing salon . . ." he was saying as della Torre disappeared upstairs to their suite. He packed his few things and popped the Beretta into his jacket pocket, and then waited for Strumbić to sort himself out. They left their bags with the receptionist.

"You know where to send them in case we can't get back," Strumbić said, passing the woman a fifty-Deutschmark bill.

"You'll be back," she said with a wink and a smile. Their footsteps echoed down the stairwell as they left.

Strumbić led them to a hair salon della Torre hadn't noticed. It was one of the various shops set into the ground floor of Dragomanov's building, around the corner from the main entrance to the apartments. The place was marked by a narrow, tall window in which an unlit neon Frizerka sign hung, along with a poster of a woman whose hairstyle was a 1970s Yugoslav imitation of 1960s British chic.

Strumbić pushed the door to the left of the window and walked up the steps into the long, narrow salon. A woman sitting under a large dryer hood flicked her eyes towards them, and the youngest of the three hairdressers got out of her chair and gave them a bland, bored look. She, like the others, was wearing a baby-blue uniform dress with white piping. Her hair was cut straight in a bob that looked like a wig.

"This is a ladies-only salon," she said, the vowels rounded in what might have been mock elegance if they hadn't sounded so earnest.

"Is Mrs. Gavrilović here?"

One of the older women stood up and approached him. "That's me."

"Janica said you might be able to do me a favour."

She stared at him and then nodded. "We can have a cigarette outside," she said.

Della Torre stood, embarrassed, while Strumbić and the woman stepped out onto the pavement, out of sight of the main window. "Getting cold," he said to the women there, who looked at him appraisingly, as an auctioneer might consider a prize steer.

"Winter," said the youngest of the three. "Every year it's the same."

The other two laughed, and the girl said, "What?" Blushing, she turned her back to della Torre.

He sat down on a red leatherette seat, but not for long. The woman Strumbić had been talking to came back in. "Your friend's waiting for you," she said.

"What's up?" della Torre asked, stepping back onto the pavement.

"Now we wait for lunchtime. We'd better wait in that friendly café. I don't feel like being stopped by a cop and having to explain why I've got a gun in my pocket."

So they sauntered over, behaving like any pair of Belgrade bureaucrats armed with newspapers and cigarettes.

"So what do you tell Mrs. Strumbić?" della Torre asked, once they'd ordered sandwiches.

"About what?"

"About how much time you spend away. About how you've got more money than a pasha. About anything."

"I tell her whatever she's willing to believe."

"And you think that's enough."

"You ever hear the one about the guy whose wife tells him she'll divorce him if he ever comes home drunk again? Well, he goes out and drinks most of the night and throws up on himself. His friend says, 'Not to worry. Put a twenty-Deutschmark note in your pocket, and when you get home, you tell your wife that some stupid German tourist vomited on you but gave you a twenty-Deutschmark note for the cleaning bill.' So he goes home. Wife opens the door and is immediately outraged. But he holds up his hands and says how somebody threw up on him and gave him the money for the dry cleaning bill. 'But you've got two twenty-Deutschmark notes,' she says. 'Ah,' he replies, 'the other one's from the guy who shat in my trousers.'"

Strumbić roared with laughter until the tears trickled out of the corners of his eyes, and della Torre found it impossible to resist the humour.

At twelve thirty they left and went back to the hair salon. The older woman was waiting for them at the front door. Otherwise, it was empty.

She led them in, and then to a door at the back. "You steal anything or tell anyone about this, and I'll make sure Janica hears about it," she said.

The door opened into a stockroom that smelled of peroxide and perfume. Strumbić passed her two twenty-Deutschmark notes. His calling cards. Della Torre marvelled at how the cop hemorrhaged money without batting an eye.

She found a key for a door that led to a very steep set of wooden stairs, switching on the light for them. "We don't reopen until three. Make sure you're out by then."

Strumbić didn't reply.

The cellar was low and smelled of damp. It hadn't been used to store coal for at least a generation. Now it was filled with junk: a couple of old hairdresser's chairs, dusty drying hood, boxes, paint pots, and a child's bicycle. But the path to the little door at the back was clear. They walked through cobwebs.

The back door had swollen into its frame so that it budged only when Strumbić put his shoulder to it. Cautiously they stepped into the courtyard. A buttress of wall hid them from the guards at the carriage gate, but they had to surface soon enough when they crossed the car park, the open space under the chestnut tree, to the building's back door. Della Torre ducked between a Mercedes and a canvas-sided truck.

"Get up," Strumbić said.

"The guards will see us."

"So what? It's their business to keep people out, not to bother anybody who's already in. For all they know, we came in through the main entrance and had to come out here for a smoke or to fetch something for whoever owns this car. Just act normally and they'll mind their own business. But if you go scuttling around, they're going to start wondering."

So they walked between the car and truck and then across the courtyard, as if in conversation. Not hurried but not aimless either.

The back door was unlocked. It led down to the basement, and they stepped into a dimly lit low corridor bounded by storage rooms along both sides and ending at the bottom of the main stairwell. To climb up, they knew they'd be in sight of the guard at the desk just inside the main entrance. With hands in pockets, slightly stooped, they took the stairs looking as if they were talking about money. When they got to the first landing, they moved to the wall side, out of sight of the main doorway. It was all della Torre could do to stop himself from bolting. His heart pounded as though he was running it at a sprint.

When they got to the landing they wanted, they followed a long corridor off the staircase, lit mostly by daylight. At the end they saw a door with a black plastic rectangle with the name *Dragomanov* engraved in white. It had three locks needing three different keys, one ordinary, two special security.

"I guess we either knock on the door or break it down," della Torre said.

Strumbić knelt at the door. "Gringo, you stand facing the hallway, give me a bit of cover."

"What are you going to do, slip yourself through the keyhole?"

"Something like that."

Della Torre saw he had a ring of keys in his hand and then realized it was a set of lock picks.

"Eyes on the corridor," Strumbić said.

"That'll be fine for the simple lock, but those picks won't work for the security locks."

"They don't have to. Didn't you tell me that a nurse comes once a day, and so does the housekeeper or whatever she is?"

"Yes."

"What are the chances a nurse or housekeeper triple-locks behind them when visiting? What are the chances he gives them copies of the security keys? He'll make it secure at night. But if people are coming and going, it's just going to be this one."

Strumbić worked quickly while he spoke, manoeuvring the pins in the mechanism.

"Two one-point-five-millimetre hex keys do the trick, one straight and one curved. I keep them with a couple of bump keys. If I can't pick them I can bump them open, if they're standard types. Crowbar works best for security locks," he said. The lock clicked and he pulled down the handle, pushing the door silently.

"Old people are always being burgled because old people's places are usually easy to break into," Strumbić continued. "No matter how many locks they have on their doors."

They stepped into the apartment's long, high central corridor. Strumbić shut the front door behind him as quietly as he'd opened it. Rooms led off along both sides of the hall. The floor was a polished parquet with a long Persian runner, and on the walls were coat hooks and a shoe rack, followed by gilt-framed mirrors and a couple of dark paintings. One of a pair of double doors immediately to the right was open a fraction. Strumbić, gun in hand, pulled it wider and sidled in. He stepped back out, shaking his head. The door on the opposite side was to a store-room. They walked along the corridor slowly. The following door was open, showing a dated but well-furnished kitchen with a big window overlooking the internal courtyard, a row of pot-ted plants covering its sill.

The next room was connected to the first one Strumbić had looked into, and to the following one as well. A sitting room opening onto a formal dining room. They were both furnished with massive, overstuffed Biedermeier bookcases in bird's-eye maple, a matching table, and 1930s sofas and chairs. Both were also unoccupied.

They found Dragomanov in the room after that. The old man turned, startled, when della Torre opened the door.

25

"**Y**OU — BUT YOU'RE not to come until this afternoon. How did you get in?" the old man said.

It took some effort for della Torre to recognize Dragomanov, the man at Tito's side in photographs, in the background of Tito's meetings with foreign leaders, in the glossy centre pages of books about the war and about the foundation of the Yugoslav socialist paradise. Only a shadow of that once famous Dragomanov remained in the frail shell before them.

He rose, stooped, leaning back against his grand desk. His thinning hair was as white and wispy as spun sugar. The man was gaunt, his skin and eyes yellow, and his arms so thin that the bones of his wrists protruded awkwardly below the loose cuffs of his flannel shirt. Against that fragile skeleton, the round, distended belly looked absurd. His hold on life seemed as tenuous as a withered autumn leaf's. The wind wouldn't blow hard or long before it carried him away.

Yet his voice and manner still conveyed authority. "You've no right to be here so early," he said again as Strumbić followed della Torre into the room.

"Please sit down, Mr. Dragomanov," della Torre said.

The old man looked confused. "They said an American was coming."

"That's me."

"But I was led to believe you didn't speak Serbo-Croat."

"Well, I do," della Torre said. "This is Mr. Smirnoff."

"Russian? Bulgarian?"

"Neither."

"And your name is?"

"We'd like to ask you a few questions, Mr. Dragomanov."

"I would like to see some identification," Dragomanov said, frail but unyielding. Slowly, glacially, he retreated behind his desk, putting the massive piece of furniture between himself and the men.

"Mr. Dragomanov, we don't have time —" Della Torre stopped short as Strumbić moved to intercept the old man.

"Will this do?" Strumbić asked, halting Dragomanov's progress with his Beretta. "Do you mind moving out from behind the desk? Wouldn't want you accidentally treading on an alarm button or just happening to find a gun in a drawer. Too many temptations."

"You've come to threaten me?"

"Only a little," della Torre said. "We've also come to warn you. There are men who we suspect would like you dead."

"Mr. . . . whoever you are, there have always been men who want me dead. And as far as I can tell, you do too. Who are you?"

"My name is della Torre. Does that ring any bells?"

Dragomanov went momentarily rigid and then settled heavily in the nearest armchair. His breath caught in his throat.

"So you know who I am," della Torre said, taking an over-stuffed club chair opposite the old man. Strumbić continued to make a slow circuit of the room, taking an interest in objects on the shelves and papers on the broad desk, like a curious child in the presence of a dull adult conversation.

Dragomanov said nothing. His jaundiced, hollow eyes were wide, expressing something between fear and wonder.

"I've not come to kill you," della Torre said. "Only to ask you some questions."

"How did you get in here? Where did you get the key?"

"That's not relevant."

The old man's eyes narrowed. "Everyone's for sale these days, eh? Was it the nurse?"

"We don't have much time. Other people are coming. What is it about the Pilgrim file that the Americans don't want us to know?"

Dragomanov barked a short laugh and then coughed until his eyes were wet with tears.

"Would you like some water?" della Torre asked.

"I'll be fine," he said, his breathing settling into short, quick gasps. "I don't know which of my diseases will get me first." Slowly, he caught his breath. "Pilgrim, eh?"

"Pilgrim," della Torre started again. "It's the file that made you set those Bosnian killers on me. You know they were amateurs, don't you?"

"They were . . . available. The people I once knew are retired or dead."

"They were as expendable as I was. And after they'd killed me, who would you have hired to eliminate them in turn?"

The old man shrugged.

It both bemused and horrified della Torre to be discussing his own assassination attempt so dispassionately with the man who'd arranged it. His sore elbow twinged. His left arm would always be weak. For the rest of his life, he was told, he'd have problems fully extending it.

"Why?"

"Why?" Dragomanov shrugged silently.

"What is Pilgrim about?"

Dragomanov remained silent.

"I'll help you," della Torre said. "Pilgrim was your code name for Olof Palme. You sent the Montenegrin to kill him. His murder had something to do with nuclear centrifuges that were sold to Belgrade and then shipped on. That much I know. I can guess why you wouldn't want me to know about it; after all, the Palme murder is still a mystery. It's never been connected to UDBA or Yugoslavia. So you want to keep it secret. But why did you order the killing? And why do the Americans care so much about the Pilgrim file?"

Dragomanov watched della Torre with hooded eyes, his fingers nervously skittering over a belly pregnant with disease.

"Mr. Dragomanov, what I told you were facts. The Americans are going to come here this afternoon, for what you think is an interview or a conversation or maybe just to pay you off. But they're going to kill you. They sent a team to kill the Montenegrin during the summer, and when that failed they sent another, bigger, more professional team. They are hunting us all down. And when they've bagged those of us at the periphery, they'll set their sights on the only person who knows the whole story. Tell."

"Foolish boy," the old man said, his voice gathered from deep within him, carrying surprising strength. "You know nothing of my relationship with the Americans. Your suppositions about Pilgrim are meaningless."

Strumbić spoke up from a corner of the room. In his hand he had a large syringe and a needle in its sterile packaging.

"Cirrhosis?" he asked.

Dragomanov shrugged.

"This for the nurses who come?" Strumbić continued. "How often? Once or twice a day?"

"Mornings and evenings," Dragomanov said.

"I guess they must take good care of a high-ranking member of the Party. Even though the Party's dying. Bar's shut, everyone who's got a warm woman is already gone, and the only ones left are the sad fucks who are too drunk to find their way home and can't afford the hookers. It was a ball while it lasted, though. So long as you were invited and didn't have to be carried out prematurely, feet first. How many of your long-ago friends did you sacrifice for the good of the nation?"

Dragomanov gave Strumbić a supercilious smile.

"Sorry, one should never talk politics when one is threatening people. Waters down the message. I'll get back to my point." Strumbić made a show of removing the needle from its package. "Actually, the point is water. Do they use these to drain your belly? I bet those nurses of yours would never think to piss in a syringe. Terrible for a cirrhosis patient if he were accidentally injected with it. Piss, that is. Especially when he's already retaining so much water. And then of course making the already weak kidneys and liver work extra hard. Probably wouldn't be very comfortable. Agonizing, really. Wouldn't take much to trigger organ failure. They can keep you alive for a while on dialysis. Not so sure what they do when the liver finally packs it up."

The nature of Strumbić's threat dawned on both della Torre and Dragomanov at the same time.

"I'm sure much worse has been done in the name of the state. But I'm no hypocrite," Strumbić continued. "I won't pretend to have higher ideals when I torture an old man. I propose to do it not in the interest of creating a universal socialist utopia but for my own benefit." Strumbić looked at him coolly. "You will answer my colleague, and you will do so as efficiently and thoroughly as he demands, or you will die in great discomfort. But before you do, there'll be plenty of time for you to beg to tell us what we need to know."

Strumbić spoke almost jocularly, the way another man might tease a colleague over how badly his soccer team had done over the weekend. But Dragomanov knew the threat was real. And the horror on his face came from knowing he'd met someone exactly like himself.

He raised a handkerchief to his lips, coughing again. The crumpled, yellowed square of fine cotton trembled as he lowered it to his lap.

"You are correct about Pilgrim."

"Why was he killed?" della Torre said.

"Because he was about to put a stop to the centrifuge exports. The parts were built across Europe, in the Netherlands, Germany, and Sweden, and they were assembled by a Swedish firm. A German manufacturer found out where they were going; he'd been asked by the ultimate recipient to make some alterations. He met Palme at a dinner celebrating Swedish-German industrial cooperation and told him about what was happening to the centrifuges, and Palme got in touch with our embassy to demand an explanation."

"What was happening? What's important about the centrifuges?"

"They were nuclear centrifuges, shipped to Yugoslavia supposedly for our civilian nuclear program. To build our power plants and some for research. The Swedes had agreed to the deal under American pressure. The Americans said that it was important for us to develop our nuclear industry so as not to be dependent on Russian gas. We only needed a few hundred, but we were getting thousands. So the rest we shipped on for American goodwill and a bit of profit. Anyway, the Swedes should have known that they weren't just for nuclear power. We ordered far too many. But the money was good, their businesses were happy, and the Americans were encouraging. Yugoslavia, after all, was non-aligned. And even if we were building the bomb, it would be to protect us from the Soviets, so no one complained.

"But the German industrialist found out that the centrifuges were going to Pakistan. The stupid Pakistanis may have thought they could assemble their own centrifuges from components at a smaller cost, so they started asking the German manufacturer for specifications and tolerances and other details. But the German went to Palme and told him, and Palme came to us and threatened to end the supply agreement. We stalled until we could make the Palme problem go away. The industrialist was killed the same night as Palme, though no one noticed. The perennial problem of dying on the same day as someone more famous."

As he spoke, Dragomanov watched Strumbić prowl around the room, fingers flexing with agitation. Age had withered his self-control. In his prime he'd been famous for his sang-froid. In negotiations he'd faced down both the Nazis during the war and Stalin after it. But now, as death approached, even without Strumbić's help, he feared for every lost moment.

"So we were shipping centrifuges to Pakistan to help them build the bomb?" della Torre asked.

"Yes."

"But where do the Americans fit in?"

"The Americans? But that's why we were doing it. They requested our assistance in the matter. The Soviets had invaded Afghanistan. The Americans were encouraging the Pakistanis to help with the guerrilla warfare. The Pakistanis didn't want the Soviets on their border but led the Americans to believe that they would tilt in the Soviets' favour. India already had the bomb. Pakistan wanted one. But they needed vast amounts of technology they couldn't develop or build at home, and which international non-proliferation agreements prevented them from buying directly. So they negotiated. And the Americans thought, well, if they have the bomb, they can at least defend themselves from further Russian encroachment. The Americans bought the right to send equipment and advisors to the Afghani mujahideen across Pakistani territory by allowing the Pakistanis to build the bomb."

"And you helped the Americans."

"Yes."

"Why?"

"It is always good to have powerful friends," Dragomanov said. "That is perhaps something you have learned by now."

"There were rumours you'd been a spy for the Americans."

"A spy? Stupid stories. I didn't need to spy for anyone. I was Tito's conduit. How do you think Tito survived the break with Stalin? How do you think Yugoslavia was richer and better off than Hungary or Romania or Bulgaria? I won't even mention that benighted Albania. We made deals, we negotiated, we were . . . flexible with some of our ideals. For the greater good."

Della Torre inadvertently looked towards Strumbić. Yes, flexibility, adaptability, fluid morality, malleable ethics, pragmatism — those were the secrets of Yugoslavia's putative success. An evolutionary response that eventually became instilled in its people. It was funny to think of Strumbić as representing the pinnacle of Yugoslav humanity, but maybe that's what he was.

"I helped to arrange things for our American friends."

Della Torre digested the implications. Dragomanov had secured the purchase of highly restricted technology by Yugoslavia and had then arranged its secret transfer to Pakistan as a favour to the presidency's — or was it Dragomanov's own? — American friends. And when Palme had threatened to halt the shipment of centrifuges, Dragomanov had offered the Americans a solution.

"Including assassinating the Swedish prime minister," della Torre said.

"One man's death. Well, two. There was the German as well . . ." Dragomanov began. "Odd, isn't it. Kill a vicious dictator, and the revolution that follows will cause untold misery. Kill a Western politician, and all that results is a stack of Ph.D. theses and conspiracy theories. Tito died a natural death, and slowly the world he built crumbles. Palme is killed, and . . . nothing."

"Just another dead man," della Torre said.

"And what do you propose to do with the information now?" Dragomanov asked. He had recovered his composure. "It's worth less than you think."

Strumbić had been studying the room in a desultory way.

"Where's the key to the safe?" he asked.

Dragomanov paused, and then said, "In the top right drawer."

Strumbić contemplated the desk for a moment as if slow to understand. Then he opened the drawer. He removed the keys.

"Now, where's the safe?"

Dragomanov nodded to a cupboard at the base of the bookshelves behind della Torre. Strumbić stepped around the desk and then stopped. He continued walking, behind della Torre to a corner of the room opposite the window overlooking the spreading chestnut tree.

"Not there," Dragomanov said. "There."

Strumbić ignored him.

"What are you doing? I said there."

Strumbić stopped at the corner stove. It was like any other ceramic stove in the country, tall and broad and decorated with green tiles. The lack of gas pipes told that it hadn't been converted but was kept in the old style, fuelled by scraps of wood in its small, low firebox. Utilities weren't always reliable but wood could often be collected cheaply, and it burned, leaving barely a dusting of ash. The complex system of flues would dissipate all the fire's energy into its brick-and-mortar structure, so that the exhaust gases, when they finally climbed the chimney, would be no warmer than a man's breath. It was eminently practical, efficient. Another technological gift from the distant Swedes centuries before.

Strumbić put his hand on the stove and contemplated it.

Dragomanov rose from his seat, his face flushed, tiny rosettes of colour high on his yellow cheeks. "I said it was —"

"I heard you," Strumbić said. "Sit down and calm yourself. I just wanted to warm my hands first. The keys are small, and I've got problems with my circulation."

"Oh," Dragomanov said. "Well, you won't get any heat out of that. Hasn't worked in years."

"Room's not too cold."

"There's an electric radiator behind the desk. I'm surprised you didn't notice it."

"Expensive way of heating a big apartment."

"It's only this room. The stoves work elsewhere."

"Gas?"

"Of course," the old man said, sounding relieved.

"I suppose, if it doesn't work, you won't mind my taking the top off then?"

Dragomanov jerked upright.

"Sit down. If I have to say it again, I'll nail you to the fucking armchair," Strumbić said as he gripped the top of the stove with both hands, the gun back in his coat pocket.

Della Torre was transfixed. Normally stoves would have to be chiselled apart, tiles taken off first and then the mortar knocked off the bricks. It was, he well knew, an expensive and slow business cleaning these things. But the tiled top came off easily and Strumbić placed it on the floor.

And there was the safe he was looking for. He turned the key, pulled a lever, and opened it.

"So, what am I looking for? Or shall we take the whole lot?" Strumbić said, removing box after box of files. The stove seemed to be a bottomless well of secrets.

Dragomanov shook with rage. And fear.

"Wait, you don't need to tell us." Strumbić passed a box to della Torre, clearly labelled *Pilgrim* in Cyrillic.

The storm within the old man had passed and now he sat there, drained.

"Those won't do you any good," Dragomanov said, waving his hand with a show of indifference.

"Why?"

"They are incomplete. Worthless without their other half."

"There's more?" della Torre asked.

"What sort of fool do you take me for? Do you really think I'd keep everything in one place?"

"Where's the rest?"

"Ah, where no one — not you, not the Americans, no one — can reach it now. But later, when I need it . . ." He shrugged as if to say he wasn't finished yet, not by a long shot.

"Where?"

The old man laughed. "Where no one can go just now. Where they're safe from you, from the Americans, from everyone."

"We're not playing games," Strumbić hissed, looming over Dragomanov so that there was no mistaking his intentions.

Dragomanov shrank back, but his knowledge gave him the strength of defiance. "In Vukovar." He laughed with a sepulchral hollowness.

Della Torre and Strumbić looked at each other with a sense of defeat as the light rekindled in the old man's eyes. In the middle of a bitter siege, a war zone of total destruction, Dragomanov was right to feel victorious.

Della Torre rose, feeling as ancient as the man he faced. "Can I ask one more question?"

Dragomanov looked up from his lap, his face yellow with sickness and a lifetime of nicotine.

"Why Pilgrim?"

"I explained —"

"No, why the name?"

"Oh." Dragomanov's breathing was shallow and laboured. "English is my favourite language, even more than Latin. Difficult to learn, but infinite. You can never properly appreciate Shakespeare in any other language." He paused. "*Palmer* is an archaic word for pilgrim in English. Pilgrim, palmer, Palme."

The buzzer at the door sounded. Dragomanov revived. His eyes were alert, and a faint look of satisfaction creased his face.

26

STRUMBIĆ TURNED TO the old man. "When did you say you were expecting the Americans?"

"In the afternoon."

"Who else comes during the day?"

Dragomanov shrugged. "A neighbour, maybe."

"The nurse?"

"Not now."

"Someone to bring you lunch?"

"I fix my own lunch. There's a woman who brings my shopping, but that's not her."

"Who is it?"

"Ask," Dragomanov said, suddenly insouciant. In that moment, della Torre could see a flicker of the once powerful man inside the fading carapace. The light, the force of charisma, the luck. Women had thrown themselves at him all his life, film stars and wives of famous Communists. Tito had retained his services for all those years when the dictator had broken with so many other ancient allies, exiling some, having others murdered.

"Wait here," Strumbić said. He crossed the hall and went from room to room until he reached the apartment door.

The buzzer sounded again.

"Now that they know you're here, you won't get out," Dragomanov said.

"They know we're here?"

"I have no doubt. The guards downstairs are mostly for show, to keep the riff-raff out. But this building is under close observation. Because they're as afraid of us as we are of —"

"The apartment is bugged," della Torre said.

"Of course. And watched. They'll know who you are by now."

Why had he been so complacent? He picked up a pen and a yellow legal pad from the desk and wrote: *What's the other way out?*

Dragomanov shook his head.

The buzzer rang again.

Strumbić slipped back into the room beside the front door and then heaved a massive walnut rococo side table with a marble top against the tall twin doors. Men began pounding and pushing from the other side. The wood creaked under their weight, the blows accentuated by their bellowed command to open.

"Time to go, Gringo," Strumbić said, panting down the hall. "And bring all that Pilgrim stuff. If people are willing to kill for it, it must be worth something."

Della Torre grabbed the files and turned away from the main entrance. The back end of the hall was a good thirty metres from the front, but still too close. The door cracked, split, was only just held shut by the marble console.

"There's another staircase at the back, right? These rich places all have one. Mine has one," Strumbić said. Big 1930s apartments like Dragomanov's often had separate servants' entrances through the scullery or a storage room with a separate, narrow stairway, so that the bourgeois owners wouldn't need to pass each other's servants in the public areas.

The room at the end of the hall was full of tins with rusty rims, dusty cartons of juice, and stacked cardboard boxes. Della

Torre had only just stepped in when he heard the crack of a bullet hitting the wall somewhere near him. He caught sight of Dragomanov standing in the hall, holding a long-barrelled pistol.

"What the —?" Strumbić said, turning in surprise.

"I think it's a P38. Must have got it from some dead German officer . . ."

"The fuck I care where he got it. Shut that fucking door and bolt it, then come in here and help me move some of this shit so we can get to the back door before the old bastard blows our brains out. If the fucking Americans or whoever it is don't get to us first."

Della Torre did as he was told, securing the storage room door behind him.

Strumbić was already moving with whirlwind fury, shifting boxes full of papers and books, clearing a way to the back door and what he knew must be a servants' staircase. The space was too confined for della Torre to help. It was a one-man job, so he looked ineffectually on. A second shot rang out from the hall.

"Rather than being as useful as tits on a nun, why don't you have a pop back at him," Strumbić said.

Della Torre pulled the Beretta from his pocket and fired at the door. The noise in that small, hard-surfaced area left his ears ringing. It shut the old man up for the moment. Strumbić had reached the little back door, which was built to fit under the slope of a flight of stairs. He pounded at the rusty bolt with the fat spine of a law book he'd pulled from one of the boxes, until the book's cover shattered. But he'd loosened the bolt enough to wiggle it free.

Della Torre could hear more people on the other side of the door. If the Americans had Uzis, they'd make short work of them. Strumbić sweated, heaving at the little back door until it finally gave way under his weight.

"Come on," he said.

The stairwell was gloomy, lit by a tiny window. The stairs were steep and wooden, the space narrow, barely wide enough for Strumbić. It smelled of damp and ancient whitewash turned powdery on the walls. Strumbić negotiated the stairs with incredible speed while della Torre followed clumsily, tripping at the bottom step and almost ploughing into Strumbić's back.

"Fuck," Strumbić muttered, looking over his shoulder.

"What is it?"

"Somebody's shoved a fucking sofa down this stairwell and there's no fucking way we'll get past it unless you remembered to bring an axe."

They could hear the sound of splintering wood above them.

Strumbić levelled his handgun at another little servants' door, a twin of the one upstairs, and fired at the lock at an angle, to avoid any ricochet. Once, twice, three times, until the lock broke. And then, with a series of mighty kicks, he pounded at it until the frame gave way.

"Open fucking sesame," Strumbić said, his breathing laboured.

They were in another storage room, this one marginally less packed full of junk. They still had to squeeze over a dusty armchair and a chest of drawers to get in. The wallpaper was a faded floral pattern, peeling and water-stained, almost certainly pre-dating the war.

Della Torre dropped the box. The files spilled out into the narrow space between the chest and the wall. Overhead, he could hear the besiegers making progress. "Wait," he shouted.

"What now?"

"I dropped the files," della Torre said.

"Smart."

Somehow della Torre managed to gather all the papers and tapes and keep a hold of them as he righted himself. He burst out of the little room, shoving the papers back into their box, panic mounting as noise built in the small stairwell behind them.

An ancient couple stared in shock as della Torre and Strumbić raced down their hallway. The man belatedly gathered his voice — reedy, hollow, but so familiar.

Strumbić scrabbled at the various bolts and locks on the door, then threw it open. And then della Torre almost knocked him over as Julius reached back into the apartment to grab a lady's large white handbag the size of a small suitcase.

They tore down the main staircase until they were at the back door that opened to the courtyard. They could hear their pursuers' footsteps, sprinting now.

"Run like your life depends on it," Strumbić said. "Because it does."

They ran past the giant chestnut tree and reached the parked black Mercedes before the *pop pop* of a small-calibre handgun reached them. The door to the coal cellar was open. Strumbić ducked in, followed by della Torre.

"You know what, Julius?" he said, panting up the wooden stairs, "I've figured you for a lot of things, but never a purse snatcher."

The door to the hairdresser's stockroom remained unlocked.

Strumbić handed the bag to della Torre. "Stick the files in here so you don't lose them."

They passed through the salon and down to the front entrance, but it was locked from the outside.

"Jesus fucking Christ," Strumbić said, rattling the plate-glass door. "What did she think, that we were going to sit around and do our nails until she got back?"

He looked at the door and then went back up the stairs. He lifted a massive dryer hood, hauled it down the steps to ground level, and heaved it at the glass door. He stepped past the jagged shards that clung to the steel frame and over the machine's carcass onto the street.

Della Torre followed, carrying the handbag.

Strumbić jumped in front of a taxi with its light on.

"You got a problem? Want to get run over?" the driver said, but he was too slow to turn them down. Both Strumbić and della Torre had already squeezed into the back seat.

"Go, just go. Straight. We'll tell you where to turn in a minute."

"If you've just mugged an old lady —"

"We haven't mugged anybody," Strumbić said. "There's a hundred Deutschmarks that says so. But only if you're fast."

The driver put his foot on it.

Neither della Torre nor Strumbić dared to look back; they just slid low in their seats.

As they caught their breath, della Torre realized there would be nowhere safe for them to hide in Belgrade. They'd be found. Even the brothel, in some ways as safe and sacred as a confessional, wouldn't hide them for long. And there were the rest of Dragomanov's papers. Della Torre didn't know what was in the Pilgrim file they'd taken, but he knew enough to believe the old man when he'd said they were incomplete.

So he leaned forward and said to the driver, "Keep going west. Head towards Vukovar."

"**T**HE FUCK?" STRUMBIĆ said, staring at della Torre as if he'd lost his mind.

"In English," della Torre whispered.

"You crazy fucking?" Strumbić said in English.

"Three things. I believe him when he says that the rest of the papers are at his house in Vukovar. I believe him when he says what we have is worthless without the rest. And three, how long do you think it'll take for those people back there to find us if we try to get out of the country by any of the usual border crossings or by going through Bosnia?"

Strumbić thought about this for a while. "But is war in Vukovar. How we can cross front lines?"

"I know the only man who can help. He's there and I have something he wants, enough for him to be willing to help us."

Strumbić stared at della Torre for a long while. And then he leaned forward in his seat, tapping the driver on the shoulder. He passed him a hundred-Deutschmark note, promising him another if he got them as close to Vukovar as possible.

The man kissed the note, folded it, and then slid it into his shirt pocket.

There was traffic on the road, and the driver looked like he'd been at the wheel for days. His thinning black hair was greasy and uncombed, his shirt rumpled. Maybe he slept in the cab; some did. But he drove efficiently, without asking too many questions, and kept the radio on a Hungarian classical station.

As they crossed the Sava on the big bridge close to where it flowed into the Danube and passed into the sterile Communist suburbs of New Belgrade, della Torre recalled the story of Jason. With the Golden Fleece in his possession, Jason went up the Sava until he reached the limits of its navigable waters, beyond Zagreb. And then he and his men went up into the mountains and trudged through the dangerous forests patrolled by bear and wolf, until at last they crossed Dalmatia's bleached spine. Had Jason been with Medea then, or had he already abandoned her? It didn't matter; his flight had taken him to the Adriatic, joyous, victorious.

Della Torre wondered if he'd make it too. He watched the countryside pass. The radio played the prelude to *Parsifal*, and for a long time both Strumbić and della Torre were silent, the Zastava charging through the flatlands.

"How did you know about the stove?" della Torre asked after a long while. Strumbić passed him a Winston. The cigarette trembled in della Torre's hand as Strumbić lit it.

"Because I've got one just like it." Strumbić grinned, though it looked more a grimace. He too was feeling the after-effects of their escape.

"You've got a safe in a fake stove?"

"Real stove. Hollowed out and used as storage. Excellent hiding place. I keep my fake secrets in it."

"Your fake secrets?"

Strumbić inhaled and then blew the smoke out of his nose. The driver rolled down his window a hand's width, and della Torre did too.

"Sure, don't you have them too?" Strumbić asked. "You know, not terribly sensitive documents, false record books that might get you into a little trouble but not too much. A bit of money. Some deeds. A small illicit bank account."

"Why?"

"That's not really a question, is it?" Strumbić said. Sometimes della Torre's naivety shocked him. "Because people will keep digging until they can pin something on you. So you give it to them. Take Mrs. Strumbić. She's a pro, unlike the police department's bloody internal affairs department. That place is full of morons who can't be let loose on a public road. Anyway, think she trusts me? Course not. She's not stupid. She spends her life looking for the rope to hang me by. But as long as I give her enough thread to do a bit of embroidery, she's content."

"So where do you keep the real stuff?"

"Everywhere and nowhere, Gringo. But mostly in here." He tapped his head. "A safe nobody can get into."

"And if you forget?"

Strumbić shrugged. "What you don't remember, you can't regret."

The tension following their narrow escape from Dragomanov's apartment slowly faded. But soon enough it was replaced by the anxiety of the approach to Vukovar. The drab browns of the late autumn landscape and the greyness of the skies melded into the malevolence of the military camouflage they passed with increasing regularity: the canvas-sided transport trucks, the heavy guns facing backward on tractor-wheel trolleys, the soldiers — most in standard uniform, though in places there was a worrying number of irregulars.

They approached a roadblock, and as the driver slowed into traffic, he said, without turning back towards them, "The fare's just gone up. Two hundred. Paid in advance."

Strumbić grinned. He pulled out his wallet, and tore a hundred-Deutschmark note in half, and passed it to the driver.

"What the hell?" said the driver, looking at the bill.

In his other hand, della Torre saw, Strumbić now had his

service automatic. Keeping it down, out of sight of neighbouring cars, he chambered a bullet. The sliding click was unmistakable to anyone who'd heard it before.

"You know what that was?" he asked.

"Yes," the driver said, subdued. But there was a belligerence to his tone.

"Let me explain it to you another way. If you do something stupid at the roadblock, you will not only not get your hundred Deutschmarks, you will gain a hole in the back of your head. Not right away, mind, because we will show our UDBA identification and the soldiers will let us pass. But the next time we stop. Say, when you take a piss. I won't need to take back that half-bill because I've got the bigger half, and German banks will redeem a torn bank note if there's more than half of it. And because I'm not a thief, I'll leave the hundred you already earned for your next of kin. It will cover your funeral expenses, if anybody ever bothers to identify you. On the other hand, if you don't make a fuss, you will earn that larger half of the note. And maybe more. Plus your wife won't have to have your shirt dry-cleaned. Does this transaction sound agreeable to you?"

A long pause. "Yes."

"Why don't you show our driver your identification card, Gringo, just in case he doesn't believe us."

Della Torre held out the old UDBA card so that the driver could see it clearly by glancing down.

The taxi slowed and then pulled over onto a gravel verge. Soldiers, submachine guns hanging off their shoulders, walked from car to car. Sometimes the occupants were asked to step out and their vehicles were searched. But mostly they were either waved on or, occasionally, turned back towards Belgrade.

"Can't take rifles, machine guns, or anti-tank weapons past here. Got any?" the boy in the Yugoslav army cap said.

"Nope," Strumbić said.

"Where are you going?"

"To visit our auntie."

"Where's that?"

"How far's the road open?"

The boy shrugged. "Up to Tovarnik, I think."

"Well, then, that's where we're going."

The boy looked puzzled for a second and then waved them on.

"See how easy it is to be cooperative?" Strumbić said to the driver as they carried on along the suddenly emptier road. And then to della Torre, more quietly, he said, "Makes you wonder what sort of fuckers we'll run into in Vukovar if they've got the army screening for anti-tank weapons. Who the fuck goes around with anti-tank weapons?"

"Militia," della Torre said. "Chetniks."

They reverted to silence, subdued by the flat skies and the raw earth and the smudge of smoke on the horizon before them as the radio played a late Beethoven quartet.

Tovarnik was at the border of Croatia and Serbia. Once upon a time, the border had been an irrelevance, a red line on maps to keep functionaries busy. Now that line was being drawn in blood.

"Matoš was born here," the driver said.

A couple of the poet's lines threaded their way to the front of della Torre's memory: *I didn't weep. I didn't. Struck wordless, / I stood in the great hall full of the beautiful dead . . .*

Vehicles were being turned back at the Tovarnik checkpoint. Many stopped and parked on the opposite side of the road or on a gravel parking lot to the side of the roadblock, their occupants either walking into the small town or leaning against their cars, smoking.

Everyone seemed to be dressed in the olive drab of military uniform. Many wore Chetnik hats, and a few had outrageous beards and moustaches that echoed the Serb militiamen from half a century before. Tito had killed Chetniks as ruthlessly as he had Croatia's fascist-supporting Ustaša. But Tito was dead, and the Chetniks had risen again.

Once again a young regular soldier stopped them. "You can't go any farther. This is a military zone."

"So what's everyone waiting for?" Strumbić asked, jabbing his thumb at the Chetniks.

"There's a bus that takes them in."

"To Vukovar?"

"Where else?"

Della Torre got out of the car. The other members of the young soldier's squad took an immediate interest. They stood, rifles swung towards della Torre.

"There's no stopping here. Move the car," the young soldier said.

Della Torre had his UDBA card in his hand. "You know what this is?"

"Yes," the boy said uncertainly.

"I'll spell it out for you. U-D-B-A."

The boy nodded uncomfortably, looking over towards his buddies, who had in that moment found other things to occupy their attention.

"Gorki's Wolves are over there, aren't they?"

"Yes," the boy said. Gorki's Wolves, his paramilitaries, had haunted this borderland since before the siege. And, della Torre knew, they would stay late. If there was an authority beyond the military hierarchy these soldiers would yield to, it was Gorki. Because he was beloved by the Belgrade powers, a warlord who reminded them of the glories Serbia could aspire to. Glories, and riches — the Wolves were notorious for their rapacious looting.

"Well, I have an appointment with Mr. Gorki —" he started to say.

He hadn't noticed the man who now stepped into his field of vision — a man with the wolf's head flashing on his shoulders.

"Do you, now," the man said. "And who might you be?"

Della Torre faltered for a moment. He should have known Gorki would have his own people at the checkpoints.

"Major della Torre," he said, as coolly as he could.

"Of UDBA. Funny, I thought UDBA had been replaced by the State Security Service. But what do I know?"

Della Torre didn't answer.

The man had a radio set clipped to his hip, which he now put to his ear. Cars behind the taxi started honking, but the militiaman paid them no attention. The conversation the man had was brief, and then, still with his back to them, he had another one, turning briefly to have a look at della Torre.

"Ivo," the man called over his shoulder, "I'll take these people in. Seems Commander Gorki would like to see our friend here with the Italian name."

A second paramilitary touched his finger to his forehead but otherwise showed no interest.

Gorki's man sauntered to the taxi's passenger side and got in next to the driver. Even before the barrier was lifted, the militiaman retuned the car radio to a Belgrade station playing nationalist tunes.

"Proper music," he said, and then stabbed his hand forward to direct the taxi driver.

28

STALE SMOKE HUNG listless in the sky. Earth had been churned raw by tanks and heavy guns among amputated trees. Having seen the destruction in Dubrovnik, della Torre thought he was prepared for the ruins of Vukovar, but what he saw now could have only been conjured in hell.

"Mother of God," he said to himself.

No wall was unmarked; the smallpox scars of bullet holes defaced every façade, and many buildings had fallen in on themselves. The taxi slowed. A path had been cleared along the road, but the tires crunched as if on cinders.

Strumbić watched, stunned, swearing near silently, a thin stream of *fucks* becoming a prayer to ward off evil. Even the taciturn taxi driver sat up straight, gripping his steering wheel, his sallow complexion blanched. Only the militiaman in the front passenger seat observed what passed with indifference.

They drew towards the fringes of the town, a village just beyond Vukovar's southern suburbs. Della Torre marvelled that Vukovar's water tower, visible in the near distance, had managed not to collapse. It looked like an ancient Roman ruin, flayed of its concrete skin, its bloody brick exposed.

The taxi driver switched off the radio. The militiaman turned to him as if to protest, but then just said, "Left there. Pull in behind the trucks."

They stopped in the shade of a mostly collapsed office building. Opposite was a villa without a front wall. In what was once a large kitchen and dining room, a folding card table had been set up, surrounded by an assortment of chairs. Della Torre was wondering what had happened to the original furniture, but then he saw that a washing machine and a tall grandfather clock were being carried out of the neighbouring house into one of the army trucks. The looting was efficiently organized.

A massive, square-built man with a large, round head was sitting at the card table, speaking into a large hand-held radio set.

Della Torre got out of the cab with the militiaman, who told Strumbić and the driver to stay in the car. The half-dozen men with Kalashnikovs ensured that they wouldn't think of doing anything rash.

Della Torre and the militiaman walked through crushed concrete, glass, and shattered tiles. The man at the card table motioned for della Torre to sit and flicked his fingers at his soldier, who left the room.

Della Torre noticed what looked like a big dog lying to the side of the table. The creature looked up at him, half-curious, and then lay its head back down on its front legs.

"Wolves need an astonishing amount of exercise. I have my men run with him every day so that he covers, I don't know, thirty kilometres," Gorki said. His voice was pleasant. He was moderately good-looking, though the eyes were too wide-set and the mouth too small and thin-lipped. His uniform was pristine, his hair neat, and his face close-shaven. The faint scent of lavender surrounded him.

"So, Major, we keep encountering each other," Gorki said. "I think the documentation I saw the last time we met was out of date. It said 'Captain' and you didn't correct me to say you'd been promoted."

"I had other things on my mind."

"Of course you did. So who are you working for now? The Americans again? The Croats? The Europeans? They're itching for us to call a ceasefire, to make a truce, so that we can all shake hands and walk away and be friends," he said with a broad smile, sharing a joke. "Or are you working for yourself?"

"I need your help."

"Help? I'll help dig your grave." Gorki roared with laughter. "You must realize we're enemies. I have no obligation to you. So you will join the rest of the Ustaša prisoners, and then we will decide what to do with you when we have tidied up Vukovar."

Della Torre felt light-headed. His throat was dry and he held his hands against his body so they'd stop trembling. For Gorki, Vukovar's defenders were indistinguishable from fascist Croats of the Second World War. He would have no compunction about murdering them. "I have something to give you in exchange for your assistance," he said.

"What could you possibly have that I can't get for myself?"

The wolf kept its eyes on della Torre.

Della Torre swallowed, summoning up his courage. "The Montenegrin."

Gorki grinned, eyes raised as if he was waiting for the punch-line. "What makes you think he interests me?" he finally said.

"It's a gamble I'm taking," della Torre replied, willing himself to speak evenly and clearly. "I know there's history between you two. I think he was responsible for the death of someone you were . . . friends with. And you're not a man who forgets. Or forgives."

He knew very little about their history, only that there had been a boy at the fringes of the Yugoslav mafia in Sweden who'd helped the Montenegrin with Palme's assassination, at a time when Gorki was, coincidentally, in a Swedish prison.

"Even if it were true," Gorki said, waving away one of his soldiers, who'd drawn up to the house on a motorcycle, "why would you think that I won't just have my men beat the information out of you?"

"It's a gamble I'm taking," della Torre repeated.

Gorki laughed and shook his head. "People take extreme gambles when they run out of options," he said. "Okay, Major. Say I was interested. What would you want in return for this information?"

Della Torre knew that if he asked for too much, he'd be refused, and Gorki's men would extract the information from him. He'd seen the corpses of people that Gorki's Wolves had tortured. They'd killed for no reason other than to satisfy visceral, sadistic hatreds.

"I want for me and my colleague back there to be taken through the front lines into Vukovar."

Gorki's eyes narrowed. "I'm not giving away any military secrets if I tell you that we will completely take over the town in a day or two. Three at most. I won't be responsible for what happens to the fascist Ustaša who have been instrumental in destroying Vukovar. They are insects to be exterminated. If you are there, we will crush you too. Tell you what, Major, if you ask to be taken somewhere safe in Croatia instead, I will allow it."

"So you have Vukovar completely surrounded?"

"Essentially."

"But the reports say there's still a route through the cornfields."

"Major, there are ten thousand people in Vukovar. A few dozen get in or out by that route. Four times as many try and fail."

"I'll take my chances."

Gorki considered him. "Why, I'm wondering, are you so eager to make your way into a condemned city?"

Della Torre toyed with the thought of not responding, but he knew that an unsatisfactory answer would raise the man's suspicions and ensure a refusal. "My wife works in the Vukovar hospital," della Torre lied, supposing that a few doctors might remain after the evacuation. "I want to get her out."

Gorki thought for a long time. "Yes," he said. "Very well. I'll make sure we show you a way into the town. What happens to you after, I won't be responsible for. Now for your part of the bargain."

Della Torre stared into the man's hazel-green eyes. Gorki was an intelligent man who spoke half a dozen European languages well. And he had fooled many with his charm and seeming civility. He was ruthless and deceitful, yet also believed himself to be a man of his word. "He's in hospital. In Herzeg Novi. A private room. An unnamed patient."

"My men will give you and your colleague a drink. You can wait over there." Gorki pointed to some chairs laid out around a table under a restaurant umbrella, set up in the middle of the street. And then he picked up the telephone.

Della Torre and Strumbić waited. Strumbić was holding his old-lady handbag, which no one questioned. Gorki's men had let the taxi driver leave, though they made him take an unpaid fare back to Belgrade. He'd been only too relieved to go. And Strumbić had done as he'd promised and given the man the other half of the torn German note.

An hour later, Gorki made an impatient flicking motion with his fingers. "The boss wants you," a militiaman told della Torre.

He approached carefully. Gorki's expression betrayed nothing. Della Torre wondered whether the Montenegrin had been discharged, gone home, disappeared. Or maybe he'd died and della Torre's gamble had failed.

"You are correct," Gorki said. "Mr. Djilas is in the hospital. It's a poor bargain you've given me, though. He's said to be in a coma. His organs are failing and he's expected to die. But you knew that, eh?"

He waved over one of his men, who was working a combat radio set by an armoured personnel carrier.

"That boy who you brought in yesterday. The one you cornered in the sewer," Gorki said.

"Calls himself Plavi, and he's a little faggot," the soldier said, spitting on the ground.

"I didn't ask you to describe his habits. He was to remain unharmed."

"We haven't touched him."

"Bring him to these men and then take them to the sewers so the boy can guide them into Vukovar."

"You want the kid free? The little fucker's been a complete pain in our ass for a month now —"

"I'm not asking, I'm ordering. Do it now."

Gorki stood, and the wolf stood next to him. Both looked dangerous. Gorki leaned over the little table and stared at della Torre.

"Goodbye, Major," he said. "Pray you die before you see us again."

29

THEY CAME TO a group of farm sheds, the biggest a long, high
cinder-block barn with a run of small, high windows and a
roof of galvanized metal. Gorki's men were smoking outside.
They came to attention, saluting self-consciously, when the
officer commissioned with finding the boy for della Torre and
Strumbić stepped out of the armoured car. One tried to hide a
bottle of Bell's whisky.

An occasional cry rose from the barn, and then they heard the
sound of gunfire from the cornfield behind them. Farther away
was a near-continuous roar of field guns, followed by explosions.

A militiaman pulled open one of the barn's large sliding doors.
The interior was dimly lit.

Five Serb militiamen went in ahead of them. The scores of
people inside edged away from the soldiers. The straw spread
across the concrete floor was dark in patches. The room smelled
of barnyard and sour blood. A few voices called out, begging for
water, claiming their innocence. One of Gorki's men raised his
rifle butt and told them to be quiet. Della Torre saw women and
old men among the prisoners.

They found the boy called Plavi hiding at the back. The small,
skinny youth was dragged to his feet by one of the militiamen.

He had shoulder-length fair hair and a small, slight build, and he was wearing a sleeveless dark blue dress patterned with small blue flowers underneath a plaid shirt and a heavy canvas camouflage jacket. He also had on heavy woollen stockings and solid hiking boots. Plavi looked like a girl.

The soldier dragged him towards the armoured car. His mascara had run and he had a split lip and a crust of blood under his nose. "In." The soldier shoved the youth inside and directed della Torre and Strumbić to climb in as well. The boy looked fearfully up at them as the car moved off.

"Are you the one called Plavi?" della Torre asked.

He nodded.

"We're friends. You've been released so that you can help us get into Vukovar. I'm a friend of Lieutenant Boban's. Do you know who he is?" Boban had been the right-hand man to the police chief in nearby Osijek; the chief had been assassinated for trying to reconcile the Serb and Croat communities. Last summer, della Torre had met and warmed to both men.

Plavi nodded. "Yes, sir. Thank you, sir." It was a boy's voice, high but with a male resonance.

The armoured car took them along an asphalt road. Through a small porthole, della Torre could see a handful of collapsed suburban houses, each with a courtyard and front garden, the roses all gone to hips by now. There was no sign of life in any of them.

They saw a couple of militiamen squatting down on the narrow grass verge by the side of the road. Immediately beyond, lining both sides of the road, were the rich, green, and unfeasibly high cornfields. A fragment of a tune trickled through della Torre's brain: *as high as an elephant's eye.*

"That's as far as we go. Out," Gorki's officer said as they pulled up by a clutch of suburban ruins within sight of Vukovar's water tower. Della Torre nervously stepped out of the armoured car, followed by Plavi and Strumbić, who was still clutching the white handbag.

From somewhere they heard a shot and its whining whistle passing overhead. Della Torre's throat was dry. They stood in the shadow of a half-destroyed wall as the armoured car pulled away. Plavi looked as though he didn't believe what was happening.

"Can you get us into Vukovar?" della Torre asked.

The boy nodded.

Strumbić had been shocked into silence.

The boy guided them past houses whose roofs had collapsed and rafters were exposed, revealing home-cured hams hanging like strange fruit.

They made their way through overgrown back gardens with unpicked beans, their dried husks hanging from bamboo canes made into tripod frames. A glossy toy tractor sat neglected in the grass. Della Torre stumbled on an iron reinforcing rod, leaving him with a sore shin.

They heard a roar of engines not far away.

"Tanks," the boy said, sniffing the air.

Della Torre couldn't see the tanks, but he could hear them spitting angrily. He was hit by the pungent smells of cordite, powdered cement, burning plastic, rubber, and wood, and by the sharper odour of rotting flesh. Buildings exploded and crumbled, metal squealed, and then they heard a sudden cascade of tiles.

"Midway through life's journey," he spoke from memory, amended to his circumstances, *"I found myself in a dark ruin. How I got there I know not, nor did I know the way back. It was a harsh place, harsh to remember, wild, lacerating, so that even its memory fills me with fear. A place as bitter as death, and though among its debris and destruction there was good to be found, so too was there much else."*

They were lines his father had often recited over the years. Sometimes he said them as a joke, like when they were repairing the decrepit farmhouse. But sometimes he'd spoken them with great melancholy.

"Gringo," Strumbić said, "this may be cheering you up, but it isn't doing me a lot of good."

"Sorry."

Plavi motioned for them to halt. Looking both ways along a street full of rubble, he led them to a gaping hole to one side, into which he disappeared.

"Well, if you haven't got any better ideas," Strumbić said, "I guess we follow the kid with the fashion sense."

Like rats, they scrambled into the crater and discovered they were at the opening of a sewer. The concrete pipe was low and the central groove slick.

"There's no piped water, so people don't use their inside toilets anymore," Plavi explained almost apologetically. "The Serbs don't like coming into the sewers, so we're pretty safe."

"How did they catch you?" della Torre asked.

"Foraging," the boy said.

"Foraging?"

"The hospital needs medicines, so we go to pharmacies in no man's land."

Della Torre wanted to ask the boy about the hospital, about whether he'd met Irena. But this wasn't the right time; he focused on keeping his balance in the confined space. It was hard going. Strumbić grunted behind him.

"How far?" della Torre eventually asked, stopping under a sealed manhole to stretch his back.

Plavi, who had forged ahead as if he'd been born in the tunnel, turned to call them forward. "Don't stop. It's not long."

They reached a side passage and pulled themselves over a concrete wall.

It was good to be out in the air. Della Torre leaned against the channel's steep, rock-lined side, feeling his muscles complain. The sky was pewter and smelled of the autumn rains.

The boy scrambled down to the stream and hopped nimbly over some big concrete sections of a collapsed building to the other side. Della Torre followed, ungainly, feeling his age.

They reached a cluster of ruined buildings, where Plavi

stepped over a threshold of broken cinder blocks, through what was once a window, and into the building. "We might not want to make too much noise now," he said. "We've been following along the line of no man's land, but now we can go towards our side."

They moved through the dark interior until they reached the front door, which somehow had survived intact. Plavi poked his head out of the gaping hole in the wall next to the door and then motioned for della Torre and Strumbić to follow. They ran across the rubble-filled road, slipping on bits of brick and tile, and ducked into the house opposite.

The darkness of the ruined building was oppressive. They moved as quietly as they could along hallways, crunching shattered glass, feeling their way along the walls. From one building to the next, they walked in near silence. A big diesel engine revved up somewhere not far from them. They stopped; della Torre shrank into the damp wall he stood against. They continued after they heard the vehicle pull away until the sound was lost among the lacerating explosions wounding the very air.

They stopped at a shop with a shattered façade that emanated the vague smell of antiseptic. That's when della Torre realized they were not far from the centre of town. They were near the restaurant where he'd had a disquieting dinner with Deputy Minister Horvat only a couple of months before. Horvat had used the occasion to have a close look at della Torre, to gauge the potential reliability of this former UDBA man who'd lived in America. Somehow della Torre had passed. And from there his fate had been written in the stars, the line of which he was still following.

Della Torre remembered Vukovar as it had been, a sleepy town on the shores of the Danube. The river was wide and easy-flowing through the fertile land, and poplars stood sentry along its banks. Vukovar's citizens had always been well off, bourgeois even, under Communism. Much of the town was

Hapsburg. Elegant façades had been painted ochre or yellow or robin's-egg blue, evidence of wealth that had lasted more than a century. The farmland was productive and the factories, including the one founded before the war by the Czech shoemaker Bata, paid well.

Of course, the Communists had also made their mark. They always did. The Venetian towns along the coast had their brutalist hotel blocks, Zagreb its power-station chimney, and Vukovar its concrete water tower on a prime site on the Danube, near the centre of town. It was a monument to socialist ambition, to remind people that aesthetics were irrelevant in the face of proletarian progress.

When della Torre had been there last, the tension had been palpable. Back then, the smell in the air had mostly been of fear. Now it was the smell of destruction. And death. The pungent assault of burning plastic, rubber, of rotting meat, more penetrating than raw ammonia, dug its way into his sinuses and into the back of his throat.

He was shocked by the sight of the wounded trees, their branches severed. A dog loped towards them and then lost interest. Della Torre caught sight of the water tower, which was pockmarked with bullet holes. Farther along, the pretty church had lost a corner of its baroque copper steeple. He stood there for a long moment, his eyes watering involuntarily from the battering his senses were taking.

"Fuck," Strumbić said again, retching.

Then a voice called out from a ruined building: "Plavi? Where the fuck have you been?" Plavi raced towards it and disappeared inside, leaving della Torre and Strumbić exposed on the street.

"Don't shoot. We're friends," della Torre called.

"Come over here with your hands up. Slowly. You make any sudden moves and we'll shoot you Serbs."

"We're not Serbs. We're friends," della Torre called over.

"We'll be the judges of that."

They edged forward, hands up, frightened of being shot from behind or in front or of having a rocket land on them. The constant noise and violence was shattering.

When they reached the building, the Croat soldiers made them lie belly down on the rough concrete, then took their handguns and Strumbić's white handbag. Three of them marched della Torre and Strumbić through the rubble-strewn streets, deeper into Vukovar.

They arrived at the entrance to a cellar. One of the soldiers spoke into the opening: "Captain, we've detained these Serb spies. Would you like us to shoot them?"

"Spies?"

"They forced Plavi to guide them from the Serb lines."

"Plavi's back?" This was said with a shout of enthusiasm and relief. A man flung himself through the narrow opening of the cellar, both hands grasping the door frame. He was hugging Plavi when he looked up at della Torre and froze. "Captain —" he said.

Della Torre recognized him immediately, but it took a while for him to believe who he was seeing.

"Lieutenant Boban."

Boban's face was more gaunt and angular than it had been two months ago, when della Torre had last seen him. His hair was no longer closely cropped, and his clothes were covered in a film of dust.

Boban let go of Plavi and grasped della Torre with a two-armed handshake.

Della Torre could see their militia escorts looking puzzled and worried. They started to withdraw, but Strumbić stopped them. "My gun, my money, and my bag," he said with considerable authority.

"Lieutenant Boban — or is it Captain? — this is Captain Strumbić of military intelligence," della Torre said. "My colleague."

Strumbić made a cursory nod as he collected his possessions from the men with Kalashnikovs.

Boban led the way into his cellar headquarters. A dozen men were down there, some sitting, some half-asleep. One was on a telephone; another spoke into a military radio, going through a list in a children's notebook. The men immediately gathered around Plavi, ignoring Boban's two guests.

"We can't hold out much longer," Boban said. "It's coming to the last days. They prod and we push back, but we've run out of anti-tank rockets and we're low on supplies. As soon as they round themselves up, they'll overrun us. We can hear them planning the assault over the radios; they use normal frequencies and don't even bother coding their messages. It was fine when we were up against the regular army. The conscripts ran away or hung back during attacks, and we dealt with them. So they just sat back and bombed us. They say we've been shelled as much as Stalingrad . . ." Boban shook his head. "But gentlemen, I'm remiss. I haven't offered you anything to drink."

He turned to the nearest man. "Any slivovitz left, Damir?"

"Sorry, boss, they needed it at the hospital."

Boban shrugged apologetically. "They ran out of disinfectant." With a smile, he added, "Your Irena has been a blessing. I don't know how many lives she and her British friend have saved."

"It must be hard since the convoy evacuated the doctors. Are you managing to get the wounded out under truce?"

Boban looked surprised. "No," he said. "The hospital is still functioning. Most of the medical staff elected to stay."

"But I . . . I thought . . . the reports said they'd been evacuated." Della Torre slid into a chair, his knees weakening.

"The Serb press says all the medical staff left; that way, they can claim anyone remaining belongs to Ustaša. But I can assure you . . . Well, I don't need to assure you. I'll take you to see Irena."

30

DELLA TORRE FOUND himself on what had once been a lawn in front of the hospital. The modern square-block building was riddled with bullet holes, and the white paint was smeared black from where fire had licked out of the upper storeys. Most of the windows were bare of glass, their wooden roller blinds unspooled like the tongues of hanged men. The parking lot and the expanse of once-pleasant grassy space had been gouged by shells; the earth was turned over, raw with roots and iron reinforcing rods to which clung clots of concrete.

"The JNA have done a bit of redecorating," Boban said.

Della Torre flinched as the sound of a blast came from the other side of the building. He ran towards the hospital, followed by Boban and Strumbić, handbag over his arm.

The early evening light was fast fading. The corridor leading from the hospital entrance was crowded and dim: the building was on generator-powered emergency lighting. Della Torre felt lost amid the long row of people waiting to be seen. An orderly shooed him to the side to make way for a gurney carrying an unconscious young woman covered in a pink polyester blanket.

Boban spoke to a middle-aged nurse whose hair was hidden

under a stained wimple. Her eyes were tired and the skin on her face sagged.

"Is Dr. Irena free?"

"Ah, Captain. She either works or she sleeps. I'll see if I can find her for you."

The hospital was surprisingly clean and well ordered. Here, antiseptic slightly deadened the general Vukovar smell of rot and shit and burning.

They waited like the patients. Della Torre's breathing was shallow. He hated himself for assuming that Irena had long before escaped to the relative safety of Zagreb. And now he was afraid for himself and for her.

"You know what, Gringo," Strumbić said, looking around. "The world can be unconscionably shitty."

"Welcome to the heart of hell," said Boban.

Strumbić shook his head. "Vukovar could teach hell a few things."

Della Torre didn't see Irena arrive. She just appeared at his elbow. She had a boy's haircut, and she looked wan, drained, thin, her eyes drawn into their hollows.

"Oh, Marko," she said, smiling, a tear running down her cheek. He'd never known her to cry. She hugged him tight, and now he noticed her pregnancy. The swelling of her belly was still small, but noticeable against her thinness.

Her appearance made him want to weep. What sort of husband was he to have failed her so? Shame rocked him.

"Irena," he said, taking her into his arms, kissing the top of her head. How could he have forgotten how tiny she was? Barely bigger than a child. The force of her personality somehow stretched her in his memory. This moment too he felt he was experiencing as memory, even as it occurred.

She quickly gathered herself together. "Why did you come?"

"Irena, why did you stay?"

"Because we're needed. Don't worry. They might be targeting

the hospital with their bombs, but we're fine in the basement. We do the operations in the bunker. They'd have to drop an atom bomb to get us there, and that's where I am most of the time." She smiled fondly at him but held him at arm's length. "David has been good to me. We've been a very effective team. I didn't know you were here or I'd have woken him."

"No, please, let him rest. But you've got to get out. The Serbs will overrun you in the next day or two."

"We'll be safe here. What could they do to a hospital and patients? We'll be protected by the Europeans. They'll send observers. Besides, you forget I learned to shoot. What was the line? 'Optimists learn English, pessimists learn Russian, and realists learn how to use an AK-47.'"

A nurse came up and spoke a word into her ear.

"I'm sorry, Marko, I have to go back down. It's a tricky chest wound. David's sleeping, so I'm the only specialist. I'll be done soon and then we'll talk." She turned away from him.

"Wait, Irena," he said. "It doesn't matter, but is . . . is it mine? There was that night in the summer . . ."

He'd come to her apartment looking for painkillers for his shattered elbow after his supply had run out. She had just finished a two-day shift and was exhausted. They'd drunk some wine and fallen asleep in her bed. Neither was willing to think about or discuss what had happened in the night.

She put her hand on his forearm and smiled.

To look at her, to see her, made him ache in the small of his back and deep in his belly; it bound his chest so that it almost hurt to breathe. He realized again how deeply he loved this tiny woman, if he'd ever really forgotten.

"Irena . . ." He didn't know how to say what needed to be said. "I'm sorry for making such a disaster of our lives. But . . ."

"People are much more resilient than they think," she said. "I've discovered that here, in Vukovar. People are as strong as the ancient gods. Your father endured when your mother died.

And so did you. We're both still young, Marko. There's a lot of life beyond what our small imaginations allow us."

He shrugged, the pain obvious in his eyes. In a place so full of death, she seemed to him the very essence of life.

"Those aren't just platitudes, Marko. It's true. We'll talk about it when it's over. We'll talk, I promise," she said. And then she disappeared.

Della Torre turned to see Boban in conversation with one of the orderlies. He'd turned away, looking for an excuse to give della Torre and Irena a semblance of privacy.

But Strumbić had watched. Cool, thoughtful, but making no judgement. "Gringo," he said, "if we're to make an escape before the Chetniks come, we're going to have to find that place of Dragomanov's."

Strumbić had collected himself. He'd absorbed the shock of witnessing Vukovar's horrors; he flinched as the bombs exploded, but he'd controlled the naked fear.

Strumbić turned to Boban. "Captain, two things please. Do you have someone who can show us how to get to a house in Vukovar . . . Where is it, Gringo?"

"Fifty-two Dunavska."

"It's dangerous there, on the river, in sight of the Serb gunners and snipers on the other bank," Boban said. Della Torre suspected, from the way Boban spoke, that it would be suicidal trying to get there. "Plavi's the best person. If there's a way there without getting killed, he'll know. We'll ask him when we get back." He paused. "He's an odd fish, that one, but the bravest I've seen. He thinks dressing like a girl will save him. What else was it that you wanted?"

"Second, how do we get out of Vukovar?"

Boban laughed. "Alive?"

"Captain, not only alive, but with my teeth and all my limbs intact."

"We've been slipping our militiamen out. I hope the Serbs leave the civilians alone. I think they will. But they'll execute anyone who's holding a weapon at them. It's not easy slipping out. We take groups early in the morning. I'm making a trip tomorrow."

"You're leaving?"

Boban smiled, but his expression showed deep exhaustion, running near its limits. Like Irena.

"No, I'll come back. I won't leave just yet. We still need a few people around to keep the hoi polloi out."

They made their way back to Boban's command post, only a few blocks away. Shells rained down remorselessly. Sometimes they sounded like express trains rushing through a provincial station, at other times like lengths of fabric being torn. Della Torre watched rocket-propelled grenades crease the air so that it looked like a fold of gelatin. He no longer heard the individual explosions; instead he felt them as a constant tremor, one melding into another. He trotted, hunched over, his eyes stinging from the dust in the air.

Plavi was still being feted when they got back. Someone had found a bottle with a couple of fingers of slivovitz and it was being passed around. Plavi looked small in that rough company.

He agreed to what was asked of him. Boban said he always did. All he needed was a working flashlight.

He led them through the darkening streets to one of Vukovar's nineteenth-century apartment houses. The door had been blown open and the windows were all smashed, but the interior was surprisingly untouched. Its walls were at least a metre thick at ground level.

As they made their way through the building's hallways, a framed portrait of Tito caught della Torre's eye. He supposed it shouldn't be that surprising. It wasn't long ago that every public building had a portrait of the dictator. But this image was different. The photograph was taken during the Second World War, when he had been relatively young, spare, his features chiselled; he looked heroic in his simple uniform.

And in that moment, della Torre thought of the utopia Tito had intended: a nation cleansed of ethnic rivalry and animosity, dedicated to building a proletarian ideal. And now here he stood in the wreckage of his failed experiment, looking down at them from his perch high on a wall.

"Tito," della Torre said. And then he felt foolish for having said anything.

They hurried down the stairs to the building's central courtyard and passed what must once have been a big tree, now agonized in the strange light of flashing explosions and fire, its limbs splintered, still standing amongst fallen tiles and broken glass. They went through another doorway, where a long hall opened to an alley and from there into another townscape with simpler, wood-framed buildings. Gaunt, gutted carcasses of barns, dating back to when Vukovar was a smaller farming settlement, still smoked from fires set off by the previous night's rocket attack.

Plavi pointed to a battered blue sign with white lettering, fixed on the side of a ruined old building, that said *Dunavska 15*. The buildings all around had suffered heavy damage, and Plavi was careful to hurry della Torre past the gaps between them, through which the pewter-coloured Danube could be glimpsed.

"Snipers," Plavi said by way of explanation. Della Torre's heart pounded. He knew they were in danger not only from the Serb snipers and the JNA field guns but also from frightened Croat defenders.

They finally found the house. Someone had cleared the front of rubble, piled it neatly in the street. The windows were sealed with strong green shutters and the door was intact.

Della Torre knocked, instantly feeling ridiculous for doing so. He thought he'd heard the sound of voices from inside, and then another noise, something falling over or a sliding tile. He tried the door handle. It turned. He opened the door and then heard another sound, a heavy metal slam. It was the sort of noise a shell fragment made hitting a big railway tank car, but there wasn't the accompanying sound of an explosion or of more shrapnel.

"Hello," della Torre called. The house was empty and dark. Amid all the usual Vukovar smells was the strong odour of kerosene.

"Thank you, Plavi. If you can spare the flashlight, we can make our own way from here. You should go back to the bunker and get some rest," he said, taking the boy's flashlight. The boy shrugged and turned away.

Strumbić pulled out his plastic lighter and struck it with his thumb. Its flickering glow was wan in the gloom, but it was better than nothing.

"I think the garage is through there. Might be some stairs to a cellar or bomb shelter," Strumbić said. "I'll take a look. You see if there's anything in the rest of the house. Give a shout if you find Zidar."

Della Torre went farther inside. "Hello," he called again, uneasy.

He pushed open the nearest door. He could see the room had once been a living room but was now used for storage. The middle was filled with stacked furniture covered with sheets. One wall was completely taken up by a heavy wooden bookcase. On closer inspection, the books were double and triple stacked, and several shelves were filled with stamp albums. Another wall had industrial metal shelving piled with canned and boxed food and perishables in big plastic boxes. Della Torre stepped back into the hall.

He tried the door opposite. This room was warm and smelled of cigarette smoke and coffee. He swung the flashlight around and saw a table on top of which a tall church candle sat, slightly bent, in a holder. He lit it and left it on the table to shed its soft glow through the room.

In one corner of the room was a massive ceramic stove covered in green tiles. When he opened the small grate, he could see the dim glow of embers in its narrow firebox. To one side of the stove a big galvanized basin stood on a folding stand. On the other side was a small table, covered in a towel and obviously used for drying dishes.

The walls were covered in more shelves containing bottled and preserved food; dried salamis hung from a rail on the ceiling. A few potted plants enlivened the space, and in the corner was a lemon tree with a single plump green fruit clinging to one of its branches.

A dozen butts were in the square crystal ashtray on the kitchen table. Despite the smell of smoke in the room, the butts were cold.

Della Torre wandered out of the room to explore the rest of the house. Whoever was living there was fastidious and, judging by the size and location of the house and its furnishings, well-to-do.

"Hello," della Torre called out. "My name is Major Marko della Torre, and I'd like a word with Mr. Zidar if he lives here. I am not here to take you away from your house. I would just like a little information, and then I'll leave."

Silence.

He wandered farther along the hall to the real kitchen, which faced the back of the house and the river. The room next to it had a large window overlooking the Danube. The window had been reduced to jagged shards and a broken frame.

He climbed the stairs. The floor above followed a similar pattern: furniture had been moved from the back to the front two rooms and covered in white sheets. Once again, everything was neat and tidy. But here there was no warmth. Dust had been allowed to settle.

Della Torre pushed aside the planks and plastic sheeting that blocked access to a smaller wooden staircase and climbed it into the attic. The floor was a thick, solid layer of concrete. He saw piles of old suitcases and cardboard boxes. A few rafters were charred, but the fire hadn't taken hold.

And then something in a corner caught his eye. He edged over, ducking under a broken beam. A smell hit him with undiluted force, punching its way to the back of his throat, and he retched up a mouthful of saliva. He stepped closer, the cylinder illumination of the flashlight casting strange shadows over the atrocity. Bodies were stacked under a black, swarming mass of flies, breeding in open orifices, wounds, mouths, eyes.

A mortal terror ate into him. In that instant, he saw a flash across the river. And then another one. A tile near him smashed. Realizing he'd been in an exposed position, he ducked back down the stairs.

The flashlight dimmed, its battery already largely drained. As he reached the landing below the attic, a strong beam of light shone in his face, blinding him. He raised his forearm to cover his eyes. "Julius, lower that bloody light."

"Up. Back up the stairs," a hidden voice said. "Keep your hands raised."

Strumbić's voice came next: "Do what the man says."

Della Torre could vaguely make out Strumbić's form behind the blinding light. He wanted to ask what this was all about, but he knew.

He turned and climbed back up the raw concrete steps, with Strumbić following behind.

"Keep your hands up. Walk over there," the man said, flicking the beam of the flashlight towards the gap in the roof where the bodies had been stacked.

"He's not joking," Strumbić said. "He's got a fucking cannon."

"Shut up," the man said.

They shuffled in the direction they were bidden. Again the shooting started. Della Torre and Strumbić dropped to their knees at the sound of splintering tiles.

"Up," the man said. "Stand up."

Della Torre understood now. The man hadn't been killing trespassers. He'd left that for the snipers across the river. The attic was a shooting gallery. Maybe that's why the artillerymen had left this house intact. The man had fed them sacrificial victims, and they'd spared him the devastation his neighbours had suffered.

"Up, I said."

A stone kicked up from the concrete, cutting into the back of della Torre's hand. He flinched.

"I will count to three. If you don't stand up I will shoot you kneeling where you are. One . . . two . . ."

Della Torre and Strumbić rose slowly from their knees, knowing they were exposing themselves in the beam of light to the merciless snipers across the river.

And then the flashlight beam swung sharply. The heavy-calibre automatic rifle issued a brief explosive belch. Della Torre and Strumbić dropped back down on their knees. Della Torre dug a hand into his jacket pocket, finger on the trigger of the Beretta, and fired back towards the man standing at the stairs.

D ELLA TORRE HEARD a shriek of agony. The man rolled on the concrete floor, pounding his hands against his head, which was wrapped in flame.

Strumbić was onto the man first, beating out the fire and at the same time wrestling the rifle away.

"Let's get him down the stairs," Strumbić said as more and more broken tile and concrete kicked up around them.

They half-dragged, half-carried the screaming man down to the kitchen. Della Torre had salvaged the powerful torch, but the rifle they'd left behind.

The man's face was charred and blistered on one side. His hair was burnt off and he had a raw open wound on one hand.

"Find some salve or something so that bastard stops moaning," Strumbić said.

Della Torre took a jar of congealed cooking fat from one of the shelves and, with Strumbić, slathered what he could on the wounds. The man whimpered and motioned to a drawer in the dresser. Della Torre pulled it open to discover a pharmacopeia of pills and bottles.

"Codeine, codeine," the man said. Reading fast through the labels, della Torre broke open four blister packs and brought the pills over. The man downed them all, dry.

Della Torre found a bottle of water and glasses and poured some out for all of them.

And then, in the doorway, he saw another ghost. Plavi, pale in his vivid dress, which was as bright as the burn victim's opened flesh.

"I'm . . . I'm sorry."

"Plavi — goodness, you frightened me."

"I'm sorry," he said again. "Is he okay? Will he be okay?"

"Nothing more than he deserves, trying to kill us up there. What the fuck was that?" Strumbić said.

"A charnel house," della Torre said. "I counted at least a dozen bodies."

"Fuck."

"I'm sorry," Plavi said. "All I had was a lamp. I . . . I threw it at him. I didn't mean for it to burn him so badly."

The man continued to whimper.

"That was you?" della Torre asked.

"Yes. I saw him hit you and take your gun," Plavi said to Strumbić. "And I didn't know what to do. It was too far to go back to get someone."

"You did the right thing, boy," Strumbić said. Della Torre saw a long bruise along the side of Strumbić's face. A stinging sensation reminded him that the back of his own hand had been torn open.

The man moaned less now. His eyes blinked rapidly, rolling a little.

"Who are you?" della Torre asked. "Are you Zidar, Mr. Dragomanov's nephew?"

The man gave a vague nod.

"Have you been living here the whole while?"

Again he nodded.

"Why didn't you escape when you could?"

The man's head rolled back. Della Torre wondered how strong those codeine tablets were.

"Gringo, we don't want his life story. We just need to know one thing. Where are Dragomanov's papers?"

The man's head rolled again.

Strumbić leaned forward. His upper lip had risen, baring his crooked teeth. "Wakey, wakey, Mr. Zidar. I won't ask again. Where do you keep the papers?"

Zidar's head shook slightly.

Strumbić pressed a finger into the flesh of the man's arm that had been most severely burned by the lantern's sticky, napalm-like fuel, through the white translucent coat of fat and down into the wound.

The man bellowed and mewled as the instant, unendurable pain cut through the effects of the drug. Della Torre was transfixed by the man's electric reaction, horrified at himself for not looking away. For allowing it.

"Where are they?" Strumbić repeated.

The man's eyes were wide. His head turned towards the other side of the house.

"Of course. It's through the garage, isn't it. I wondered where you'd appeared from when you blindsided me." Strumbić dug into Zidar's pocket to retrieve his confiscated Beretta. "Boy, how old are you?" he asked Plavi.

"F-fourteen."

"You ever shoot a man?"

Plavi shook his head fast, afraid he might be asked to.

"It's not so hard. This thing is loaded. All you need to do is pull the trigger and it puts a hole in Mr. Ghost there. Just remember, anybody wandering around this part of town lately would have gotten a bullet, thanks to this fellow. You sit over there, and if he moves, you squeeze that trigger. We'll come running. But you make sure the barrel is pointed at him. Here, sit on this side of the room, away from him." And then, turning to della Torre, he said, "Let's go and have a little look."

They found a steel door leading to a set of concrete steps that stretched at least two full storeys underground.

"Fucking nuclear bunker," Strumbić said, leading the way.

"Could be why Dragomanov bought it. Far enough out of Belgrade and deep enough underground to survive a strike."

"And anonymous enough that the first wave of invading Russians would ignore it," Strumbić said. "Smart guy."

The door into the bunker itself was heavy but well balanced, a good thirty centimetres thick. The room was square, four metres by four metres, a raised bed at one side, the shelves underneath stacked full of tins of food. A little kitchen was to one side. The only sound they heard was coming from a fan overhead. Strumbić swung the flashlight around and found a switch. The fluorescent lights flickered on.

"Can you believe that? It has its own electricity supply," Strumbić said. "Must be a generator in a service room behind that door."

They looked around and saw a desk, a radio, and stacked boxes. A number of paintings hung on the walls.

"Would you look at that," della Torre said.

"What?"

Della Torre motioned to a painting in a dim corner. It was of a hellish scene: a burning city in the background, and in the fore were destroyed buildings, tiny figures in the throes of humiliation and agony, St. Anthony tempted by a satyr, by gold, and by the demons that were threatening to tear him apart.

Della Torre stepped towards the painting and then stood in front of it. He touched its frame, shocked not by its subject matter but by its provenance. "This isn't a copy."

"Of what?" Strumbić asked.

"Hieronymus Bosch," della Torre said. "The National Museum now lends out its paintings?"

"Gringo, if you're a big shot, everything's available."

"But it normally hangs in the National Museum. In Belgrade. Have they already started looting —"

On another wall was an abstract of geometric shapes on a white background. "Malevich?" he wondered. He pointed to another small painting with bold colours. "Matisse?"

"Well, maybe that explains why the nephew stayed behind. Somebody had to watch the stuff."

Della Torre was too shocked to comment.

Strumbić began rummaging around the two tall filing cabinets in the corner just behind the entrance door. "Fuck, he's got enough here to worry half the presidency. The Pilgrim file ought to be in a safe — but then again, that's what this place is: one giant safe." He stopped, picked up a small black silk bag and looked inside. "Oh, and look, a bag of little shiny stones." He laughed. "I'd bet my left nut they're diamonds."

"How much?"

"In value? I'm figuring this bag is around two hundred grams. My recent experience in Dubrovnik has taught me that this equates to a thousand carats. Most of these diamonds seem to be the two- or three-carat variety. Reasonably good quality, one carat runs around two thousand dollars wholesale."

"Two million dollars," della Torre said with a small gasp.

"A very good day's work. I had been wondering why I let you convince me to come to this hellhole," Strumbić said. It didn't escape della Torre's notice that he'd pocketed the bag of stones.

"Ah, and the other Pilgrim file," Strumbić said, slipping it and a few other files into the big white handbag. "I'd say help yourself to one of the paintings, but somebody might notice that it looks a lot like the one that used to be in the museum. That's the nice thing about diamonds —"

They heard the sound of a gunshot.

They raced up the steps and into the house. Plavi was still sitting where they'd left him. The burnt man lay on the floor, bleeding heavily.

"I . . . I didn't mean . . ." the boy started to say, holding the gun in his palm. Strumbić took it from him. "He got up and, I thought he was going to —"

"You were just protecting yourself, like Julius told you," della Torre said softly.

The boy nodded, wide-eyed from shock, horror, or maybe curiosity — della Torre couldn't be sure.

"Never mind, Plavi. They'd have shot him anyway," Strumbić said.

Della Torre knelt by the man. He was still alive.

"If we patch him up we might get him to the hospital," della Torre said.

"And what then, Gringo?" Strumbić said. "He was a dead man from the moment he failed to kill us."

"Would you have done it?"

"Nope. I'd have marched him up the stairs and made him take his place there. But Plavi here has saved my conscience. Not that it would have been very bothered."

"Let's get out of here," della Torre said.

32

P LAVI LED THEM back to headquarters, where they slept.
They were woken before first light. The first group of militiamen was retreating from Vukovar. Boban had organized the
withdrawal of the troops, though his own unit wouldn't leave
for a couple of hours. But the headquarters needed to be cleared,
so they staggered into the cold of the pre-dawn hours.

Della Torre was groggy, stumbling in the half-darkness, lit
by countless fires. He passed the yard of a family home where a
dead horse lay on the ground, its entrails being eaten by a pair
of golden retrievers whose ribs showed through their coats. As
the troops passed, the dogs looked up to watch with guarded
indifference, then returned to their bloody meal.

A fog had risen from the river. Della Torre could taste ash
in the cold, damp air. Somewhere in the distance he heard an
echo of gunfire. The shelling had started again. Far away the
great guns coughed, and above, the sky fizzed. The explosive
impacts made him jump.

He desperately wanted a cigarette but refused himself. He
didn't want a sniper shooting it out of his mouth.

As the sun rose, he could see the light twisting the fog into
vortices. The fog softened the edges of Vukovar's destruction

while sharpening his sense of its doom. Rattling gunfire punctu-
ated the muffled echoes of parents calling for their children. A
starburst shell flooded the sky with rippling illumination. Della
Torre's mind desperately sought connections to reality in all the
unreality that he saw and heard and smelled.

"Did you find what you were looking for?" Boban asked.

"Yes," della Torre said. Yes, they'd found what they'd come
looking for. He didn't know how they'd use it or what good it
would do them. If they survived Vukovar. They had the secrets
for which Dragomanov had killed and for which the Americans
were prepared to kill.

He thought of Irena.

He had a couple of hours before Boban's group was due to
make its dangerous foray out of Vukovar. He wanted to see
Irena again.

It was still the small hours but there'd be no chance of catching any more sleep. Fires lit the town in an orange-red glow.
Shells traced meteorite paths across the sky, though the JNA was
desultory in its destruction. Had the Yugoslav soldiers tired of
it? Had the unceasing bombardment also broken their sleep,
shattered their days, so that now they too wanted to see the
end of it?

Despite the rubble and the flickering light, della Torre realized he knew where they were. Even hell had its familiar roads.

"The hospital's not far, is it?" della Torre said.

"No, though it's probably the most dangerous place to get to,
outside of the front lines. The Serbs use it for target practice,"
Boban said. "I'm not sure the doctors will have time to look at
your hand tonight."

Della Torre looked down at his wound, blood dried on the skin
where it wasn't wet and open. "Oh, that's nothing. Stings a little
but it's just a graze. I thought I'd try to say goodbye to Irena."

"Oh," Boban said. "Of course. I'll send someone to collect you
when we leave. He'll find you."

Della Torre made his way to the hospital alone, scrambling through the rubble hurdles on the way, flinching at the sound of each explosion. When he got there, he found a seat in the long hall where visitors and the walking wounded waited to be admitted below ground. He sent messages to Irena and waited hour after hour for her to come. In the gloom, he thought of his father in his big farmhouse near the sea.

His father drank in solitude, and della Torre knew that if he survived Vukovar and whatever else this war brought, he'd take the old man's place at the lonely kitchen table with the worn oilcloth, pouring glass after glass of his own yellow wine until he too dissolved into those infinitesimal floating specks of dust.

After coming back from America, he and his father had rebuilt the house with frantic urgency. It was the only means for his father to survive his wife's death, and now it was decaying. The stones would outlast them. They'd survived seven generations and would stand, one on the other, for seven more. But the wood was slowly rotting under loose roof tiles. Plaster crumbled. The roots of a great vine dislodged mortar and lifted the packed dirt of the cellar floor.

Maybe, if he were lucky, della Torre could grow old in that house with his books and music, a solitary man with the taste of a nineteenth-century Sicilian aristocrat.

He came back to the present when the middle-aged woman sitting next to him in that dark hospital corridor spoke. "I remember my mother telling me how during the Second World War my eighteen-year-old sister died, my father died, my grandparents died, the baby in my mother's arms died," she said. "And I remember thinking to myself, *Dear God, I could never survive that*. And yet here I am. The same has come to pass for me and I'm still alive."

Della Torre looked at her lined, exhausted face and wondered what survived of the person she had been only a few months before.

This thought was interrupted by an outcry at the hospital's entrance: "Come, quick. We need hands." The urgency of the appeal galvanized della Torre and a handful of other waiting men.

Dawn had broken; the skies had cleared and it was a beautiful late autumn morning. They crossed an open patch of ground on the north side of the hospital and went up a wide road towards the Eltz Palace, keeping out of the line of fire. The grand baroque building was surrounded by lawns and set back from the road. Its plastered façade, still an imperial yellow where it survived, had largely been peeled back to rough red brick. The ancient chestnut trees on its grounds had been butchered by shellfire into sad, twisted stumps.

"This way." The soldier waved them over. Rocket-propelled grenades fizzed past them, sending up clots of earth when they hit parkland. From farther away they heard a howitzer's deep bellow, its shells thankfully dropping somewhere in the main part of town, behind them.

They found their way to the building's cellars. The early-morning light penetrated through the caved-in roof into a grotto not even Bosch could have depicted. The floor was awash, ankle-deep, in wine that had burst from giant barrels. The room looked like a cistern of blood. And then della Torre realized there really was blood mixed in with the wine. Deep scarlet was seeping from the torn bodies of women and children lying in that shallow, infernal pool. Their pale, pinched faces betrayed their final moments of pain.

Body of Christ. Blood of Christ.

The militiaman had been mistaken. There was no one left to save. Della Torre staggered out of the building into the shelter of a corner and sank into a crouch, disbelieving the horror of what he'd just seen. He left the others to deal with the carnage and the burials.

The hospital had swung into full gear when he got back. He made his way to the nurses' station in the basement, a Maginot

Line between the doctors and unsorted patients. On learning who della Torre was, a kind orderly took pity on him and led him to the small lounge set aside for the doctors to take their rare breaks. Both Irena and David Cohen were there, playing cards laid out on the cushion between them.

Della Torre smiled at Irena and then, uncertainly, at Cohen, who rose from the other end of the sofa, scattering the cards.

"Doctor," della Torre said, holding out his hand after bending to give Irena a half-kiss.

"Marko," Cohen replied. He was tall, slightly stooped. His hair was cut very short, showing a widow's peak. His nose was a beak in a thin face, his eyes deep-set behind a pair of small, round glasses. His Adam's apple protruded prominently from above the open collar of his shirt. He was close-shaven, exposing a reddish rash along his right jawline. He took della Torre's hand gently. "How's your elbow?"

"A bit stiff still, and my left arm's noticeably weaker than the right one, but it seems pretty healed up."

"The strength will come back as long as you exercise, but I'm afraid some of the flexibility may be gone permanently."

Della Torre shrugged. "Doesn't matter. I only ever used that arm to fill my shirtsleeve."

Cohen smiled politely.

"Sit down, Marko," Irena said, pointing him to a sofa on the opposite side. "We've caught up on some sleep. The cards are an excuse not to think for ten minutes, while the operating theatre is prepped."

She spoke in clear but accented English. Della Torre replied in the same language, out of politeness to Cohen. "When was the last time you got out?" he asked.

"We take turns touring the bomb shelters," Cohen said.

"I meant out of Vukovar."

"Shopping in Paris, lunching in Rome? We'll get around to it eventually," Irena said lightly.

"You'll get rickets, sitting around in your caves."

Irena laughed. "Rickets in here or shell splinters out there."

"Which is the main reason I'm here," della Torre said.

"You're our fix of vitamin D?" Irena said, her voice more arch than amused. "Marko, my little ray of sunshine."

"Irena, you need to leave Vukovar. And you too, Dr. Cohen. The town can't survive another couple of days. The militia are leaving."

"We know, Marko," Irena said quietly. "It's the end of the road. But we'll be safe in the hospital."

"They've been targeting the hospital with artillery from day one."

"The international observers will make sure we're safe. And we'll just have to stick up for ourselves against the soldiers."

"It's not the Yugoslav army that's coming, Irena. It's Gorki's Wolves, the Chetniks. I know what they're like —"

"Marko, we can't abandon our patients. And we encouraged the militia to leave. There'll be less fighting. It will make things easier, cleaner."

"Look, martyrdom is all good and fine in the history books, but . . ." Della Torre threw up his hands. But what?

"I have no intention of being a martyr, nor does David. And the decision to stay and work here is ours alone." She looked at David, who smiled, almost shyly, in return. He stood.

"Excuse me," he said, "I need to find some clean scrubs. It was good to see you, Marko. Take care of yourself. We'll do the same here."

The men shook hands, awkwardly but with real warmth.

"We'll see you in Zagreb," she said to della Torre when David Cohen had left. "In a few days or a week, but it won't be long."

"Irena —"

"I know, Marko. I promise, I'll take care of myself."

"I was going to say I love you."

"I know that too."

He hugged her, feeling her small bones against him. A bird trapped in a city's apocalyptic cage.

He prayed she was right.

He kissed Irena again. Then he left the hospital, led by the boy who would take him to Boban and the way out of Vukovar.

33

BOBAN WAS IN command of a group of about forty militiamen, joined by della Torre, Strumbić, and Plavi, who was now wearing a dress with a green geometric pattern over a checked shirt and blue jeans, the outfit completed with a blonde wig. "Camouflage for the cornfields," he explained.

"I'm sorry," he whispered to della Torre as they marched off through the ruins of Vukovar to the beat of thumping shells and rocket-propelled grenades. "I didn't mean to. It was an accident . . ."

Della Torre couldn't assuage the boy's guilt.

The ragged troupe varied in age; some were teenagers not much older than Plavi, while others were approaching middle age. Everyone was dirty; their clothes, odd assortments of military and civilian, were torn. Most, though, had managed to keep their rifles. Della Torre patted the Beretta in his pocket.

One big young fellow with pale eyebrows and lashes reminded della Torre of the oxen that were rapidly disappearing from Istrian farms, baggy white creatures, placid and calm as if always ready for the yoke or the slaughterhouse.

They reached the battered end of the town, which was marked by a cluster of farm buildings. Farther across the fields stood a concrete grain silo. Unmilked cows bellowed in their swollen agony from relatively undamaged sheds.

"Have to get someone in to deal with them after dark," Boban said. "The yard's in the line of sight of a sniper. He's been a pain in the ass for three days now, but we can't get to him. You can't see him. He's over in those trees about a kilometre away."

Della Torre was focused on what looked like a pair of fallen mannequins in the field just beyond the barns. Corpses. One was being nuzzled by a pig. A pair of chickens pecked warily at the other, scattering whenever the pig raised its head and grunted.

"What a death. What a way to finish life, being eaten by your livestock," Strumbić said.

"Have you got a cigarette?" della Torre asked. "I'm all out."

"Here, keep the pack." Strumbić passed della Torre a mostly empty packet of Lords. "I've got another one, though I tell you, it's been work to find them. Cost me twenty Deutschmarks."

"Not too bad for a packet of cigarettes, all things considered," della Torre said. They'd become a de facto currency and were in painfully short supply.

"A packet? Try each cigarette," Strumbić said, though he wasn't complaining, just stating a fact.

"Fuck. I've never tasted a twenty-Deutschmark cigarette before."

"You'll find that knowing how much they cost makes even shitty Lords taste like Havana cigars."

Boban turned to the men. "This is the most dangerous area. We go in two groups, in pairs, up the road to that cornfield over there. Once we're in, it's reasonably safe. Corn won't stop a bullet, but the snipers can't see you. It'll be different when they start using heavy machine guns. They'll figure it out one day, but for now we're all right."

Della Torre nodded. He and Plavi were in the second group. They stooped, running low and hard. Blood pumped in della Torre's ears, and his heaving breath deafened him to any other sounds. The high corn was a blessed sanctuary, and he slowed down, winded.

A soldier posted just inside the cornfield wouldn't let him stop. "Never know when they're going to start dropping shells. If the sniper had half a brain he'd have called in the artillery, but all he does is sit there and take potshots."

They met up with the others at the end of a wide path, deep in the crop.

"Only just sighted us when I was coming through," Boban said between gasped breaths. He'd been the last of the squad. "I swear I heard the bullet whistle past my ear."

They went deeper into the cornfield, single file along the rows. They waited in a crouch at the edge of a narrow wood and then moved through it quickly and silently.

"Serbs have been using the wood as a screen," Boban said.

After walking a while, they forded a long, zigzagging drainage ditch. Della Torre slipped on muddy grass and half-fell. His right leg was sodden to the crotch.

They heard bullets whistle through the corn nearby, like deadly insects, and overhead the screech of shells destined for the town and the thudding of the guns.

It was in the depths of another field that Plavi fell. When della Torre reached down to help him up, he saw the clot of blood, as thick and bright as strawberry jam, on the boy's face.

"Boban," he called, his voice high with fear. "We've got a casualty."

Boban rushed back while the whole troop stopped.

"Spread out. Stay down and low, and shut up," Boban ordered.

He and della Torre checked Plavi's vital signs. The boy was still breathing, but the side of his head was a bloody mess. Boban tore open his kit bag and pulled out a big block of gauze and a bandage, working fast to put on the compress.

"Shit," he said. He raised his head and looked around. "We have to keep going. He'll get better care in Vinkovci than in

Vukovar. If he makes it that far."

Boban called in a terse report on his radio. They improvised a stretcher with rifles and a pair of jackets. The boy was slight and easy for four men to carry, even in the makeshift litter.

"Poor kid," della Torre kept saying. And then, to Strumbić: "He was so traumatized by shooting Dragomanov's nephew."

"Probably," Strumbić said.

"He was clearly still in shock this morning," della Torre said. "It was a horrific accident for a fourteen-year-old."

"He might have been in shock, but it was no accident. The safety was on and there was no bullet in the chamber when I gave him the gun. I did it on purpose so he wouldn't accidentally shoot us when we came back into the room. He was understandably jumpy."

Della Torre fell back half a stride, taking in the revelation. "So he did it on purpose?"

"Unless he accidentally switched off the safety, accidentally chambered the bullet, accidentally aimed from around three feet away, and then accidentally pulled the trigger. There was a scorch mark at the entry wound. At first I thought it might have been from the kerosene lamp burn, but it didn't quite fit. And Dragomanov's nephew certainly didn't threaten him. He was out cold from a combination of shock and codeine."

"But why?"

"Why? Have you had a good look at this fucking place? It's a mystery why people don't rip chunks of flesh off each other with their teeth," Strumbić said. "How do you keep even a margin of civilization in these circumstances? The kid probably wondered what it was like to kill a man, and here was a golden opportunity."

"Jesus."

"Jesus is dead, Gringo. Don't you remember your Communist catechism?"

The jog through the cornfield was hard work. The ground was rough, tripping them up. Every five minutes the stretcher bearers rotated, though Boban took more than his share of the duty.

As they marched, two other men were hit. One was wounded slightly, while the other, the big, blond, bovine one whom della Torre had noticed earlier, was killed instantly. They carried his body too.

The sun rose and began to dip again, and della Torre started to wonder how much longer his shoulders would be able to bear his regular stints carrying the wounded and the dead.

Boban's men were uncomplaining. And of them all, Boban worked the hardest.

And then, when della Torre had grown convinced that the journey had no end, they reached a road guarded by a Croat defence force platoon. A couple of hundred metres beyond was a hamlet with a local command post. Medics loaded Plavi and the other injured man into an ambulance that was waiting for them. The dead man was zipped into a heavy black body bag, with his light haversack placed at his feet. A neat row of about twenty bodies was lined up on the verge, waiting for transport. The militia who had escaped earlier in the day had been slaughtered when a stray Yugoslav shell hit them less than a kilometre from the hamlet. A few were civilians.

Behind them, in Vukovar, the noise of the bombardment continued, but here they were safe among dozens of defence force soldiers and auxiliaries. Della Torre was just taking a long swallow of slivovitz when he heard a familiar voice.

"Nice to have you back in one piece, Gringo."

Anzulović smiled softly, smoking one of his usual Lords. But rather than offer one to della Torre, instead he produced an unopened packet of della Torre's own brand: Lucky Strikes. "I figured you would have had a hard time finding these in the past few days. We heard that you got to Vukovar and that Boban was getting you out."

"I shouldn't be surprised. Thanks," della Torre said as he took the packet.

Anzulović stared at the smoke rising over Vukovar, only fifteen kilometres away. "You wonder how anyone can survive that . . ." He turned back to della Torre. "We lost you after Dubrovnik. We didn't hear you'd been through Herzeg Novi until after you left." Anzulović took a drag of his cigarette. "I was told that the Montenegrin died yesterday."

Della Torre winced.

"The Americans finally got news that he was in hospital. They had people there . . . From what I understand, he was already on the way out. His organs had packed up. Septic shock."

Della Torre moved away from the collection of houses towards the cornfield, where there were fewer people about. He turned abruptly to Anzulović. "How long have you been helping the Americans?"

"I don't know myself. I get orders, and I mostly do as I'm told."

"So said all the concentration camp guards."

"Gringo, I like you. I always have. You won't thank me, but I figured if I was the guy doing the Americans' bidding, you'd at least have someone looking out for you." Anzulović turned around to face the hamlet. Della Torre followed his line of sight. Grimston and two other men stood apart from the clusters of Croatian militiamen. Casual, aloof. Observers. They stared at him without acknowledging him, though della Torre wondered whether there was a look of smug satisfaction on Grimston's face. "So, rather than let them shoot you or kidnap you where they could stick you in a military jail and leave you to rot forever, I pointed out that with your cooperation they'd be able to get Strumbić and the Montenegrin. And then maybe we'd discuss some terms to get you off the hook."

"I appreciate it."

"Speaking of Julius, where is he?"

Della Torre looked around. It struck him that he hadn't seen Strumbić since they'd emerged from the cornfield. He could see Anzulović growing uneasy at his puzzlement.

"Boban said Strumbić was coming out too," Anzulović said.

"He was with us," della Torre said, still trying to spot the man.

Somehow Grimston seemed to have sensed what was going on, because his look of self-satisfaction evaporated. He spoke to his men and they moved with alacrity. Then he picked up his radio.

"He can't run anywhere," Anzulović said. "He'll be picked up soon enough. The military police have checkpoints just beyond here. They know to stop him."

"And when they find him, what happens to us?" della Torre asked.

"We all go back to Zagreb, and both of you will have a chat with our friends. I'm afraid the minister has already signed an agreement for Strumbić's extradition. In your case, we're refusing."

"So, one morning on my way to work, a car hits me and runs, and that's the end of this particular problem for the Americans," della Torre said.

"We'll give you all the protection possible. You can go to your father's house, and we'll post a surveillance team to make sure you're left alone."

"Like they left Libero alone."

"He was an old man," Anzulović said. "I'm sorry, Gringo. I'll do what I can. But we'll all go the way of Vukovar if the Americans don't help. And we need to show them we're on their side."

Della Torre nodded. A wave of self-pity rolled over him.

They turned and began to make their way back towards Grimston. To his right, della Torre saw Boban and two of his men heading back towards the cornfield, their shoulders bent under the weight of emergency supplies for the hospital. Boban had hardly had a break and was now making the treacherous journey again. Della Torre admired the man for his stoicism, for his single-minded focus on doing what he knew was right.

"I'll join up with you in a second," della Torre said to

Anzulović. "I'm just going to say goodbye to Captain Boban. It's the least I can do. Especially since Irena is in his hands."

Anzulović made a little grunt of approval.

As della Torre hurried towards Boban, he passed the row of body bags, black, zipped up, neatly assembled along the flattened grass by the side of the pitted road. Two militiamen stood sentry. Della Torre nodded at them in sympathy and they smiled back at him, looking happier than they ought to under the circumstances. For a moment the incongruity of their expressions troubled him, and then he decided they'd just shared a joke. Gallows humour.

When he got to the end of the row of black-shrouded corpses, he saw a large white handbag. The sort a grandmother might own.

He stopped and opened it. It was empty. And then he understood what the two soldiers were smiling about. They'd hit the jackpot. And Strumbić had escaped. Strumbić would always be safe. He had the Deutschmarks and he had the diamonds. He had Dragomanov's papers, the file on Pilgrim that incriminated the Americans in Olof Palme's assassination, and he would know how to use them. There were no limits to his resourcefulness and ingenuity.

Della Torre was overcome by a powerful feeling of pride and inspiration because of Strumbić, and because of Boban, who had just reached the edge of the cornfield with his men, and because of Irena and her Dr. Cohen. There, among the tall stalks of corn, yellowing tops rippling like an oriflamme, was a bloody path that would lead della Torre from his past and into his future. For too long he'd tried to navigate the competing forces in his life using what few skills he possessed. Maybe he hadn't been bold enough. Or brave enough.

Now he knew what he needed to do.

As flies to wanton boys are we to the gods. They kill us for their sport. *Ora pro nobis peccatoribus . . .*

Maybe the poets were right; maybe constellations high above really did weep. Maybe comets blazed.

"Boban. Captain, wait," della Torre shouted, running to close the gap. "Here, let me lend you a hand."

EPILOGUE

ON NOVEMBER 18, 1991, the Yugoslav army, led by Serb paramilitaries, finally overran Vukovar after nearly three months of siege and bombardment. It is estimated that the city suffered the most massive and sustained barrage of fire in Europe since Stalingrad.

By then, most of the Croat defenders had escaped through the cornfields, leaving civilians and the wounded behind. Those people, they thought, would be protected by human rights and military conventions accepted across Europe since the fall of the Nazis.

They were wrong.

Women and men at the hospital — doctors, nurses, patients, and those who had gone seeking refuge — were separated. The women were bused out to an internment camp and were released back to Croatia after some days.

The men were taken to a farm south of Vukovar, where they were kept in a barn until it was their time to be taken out into a cornfield and executed. In all, some 260 were killed in this manner after the end of hostilities.

Years later, Croatia recovered the territory. Since then almost all the remains found in the mass graves have been identified. Among them were a number of foreigners, either mercenaries or adventurers or idealists just there to help, though the name of Dr. David Cohen does not appear in the memorials.

Nor does that of Captain Boban. Or Major Marko della Torre.

But not all the dead have been found. Nor are all those who perished remembered.

ACKNOWLEDGEMENTS

This is a work of fiction, albeit hung very loosely on a framework of history. The destruction and suffering caused by the Yugoslav civil war of the 1990s was enormous and left none of the country's ethnic populations unscathed. But this book covers only the beginning of the strife, the sieges of Dubrovnik and Vukovar, and only from a very narrow perspective.

The timing and circumstances of the events I describe aren't necessarily as they happened. I've used authorial licence to shape history to suit my plot. Needless to say, the characters are all products of my imagination. And it's purely coincidental if they resemble anyone living or dead.

Steve Higgins was a friend and a journalist, though never in the Balkans. On the other hand, the real Jack Grimston is a journalist who reported from the former Yugoslavia, albeit not during the war. While I can't think of a gentler or kinder person, he has the perfect name for a secret service hard man and I thank him for lending it to me.

I would encourage anyone interested in the history of Yugoslavia's violent end to read Misha Glenny's *The Fall of Yugoslavia* and Allan Little and Laura Silber's *The Death of Yugoslavia*. Both books are exceedingly well written and skilfully navigate the reader through an often complex subject.

I also found contemporary newspaper accounts and television and radio reports useful in developing a sense of place and time. Alec Russell's memoir of reporting from the Balkans during that period, *Prejudice and Plum Brandy*, includes a terrific first-person depiction of what it was like to be in Dubrovnik during the siege.

The Internet is full of stories of the war in Vukovar and Dubrovnik. Two I found particularly affecting were "A Girl in My Arms: A Story of a Paediatrician from Vukovar" by Branka Šipek, from the journal *Archives of Diseases in Childhood*, and a collection of witness statements from Vukovar, *The Town Was the Target*, by Anica Marić and Ante Nazor.

Though I visited the former Yugoslavia during the war, I was never anywhere near danger. But my sister, Nives Mattich, lived there throughout the 1990s. As an aid worker, she witnessed the attacks on Zagreb, the siege and destruction of Sarajevo, the NATO attacks on Belgrade, and much else besides. I am deeply indebted to her for giving me an inkling of what it must have been like and admire her stoicism and bravery to have voluntarily endured numerous discomforts and dangers.

Other accounts came from relatives and friends, many of whom lost those they loved during the war.

The book is dedicated to my parents, who left Yugoslavia at the height of Tito's powers. It is sobering to think that had they stayed, I would almost certainly have had to serve in the military, on one side or the other, during the conflict. I am grateful to them for their decision, however hard they sometimes found the life of immigrants: having to learn a new language, to adapt to new cultures, to struggle and persevere through what for a long time was outright poverty in order to give their children better lives and more hopeful futures.

I owe further thanks to my wife, Lucy, and my children, Pippa, Tilly, Kit, and Bee, for their support and forbearance as I sank into the corner of the sofa to write yet another book when there were so many other things I ought to have been doing.

I'd be remiss if I didn't mention others who gave me encouragement, moral support, or just a welcome night away from the computer, including, in no particular order, Andrew Steinmetz, Fred Biggar, Alistair MacDonald, Patrick Amory, Robert Kirkby, Beverley Mackenzie, Andrew Shutter, Bill and Elaine Vinten, and, not least, Luke Vinten.

The greatest thanks, though, have to go to my editor, Janie Yoon, to copyeditor Peter Norman, and to my agent, Hilary McMahon, all of whom made this book not only possible, but as good as it could possibly be.

ALEN MATTICH is the author of *Zagreb Cowboy* and *Killing Pilgrim*, the first two novels in the critically acclaimed Marko della Torre series. Born in Zagreb, Croatia, he grew up in Libya, Canada, and the United States. A financial journalist and columnist, he's now based in London, U.K., and writes for *Dow Jones* and the *Wall Street Journal*.